D1448291

DEATHLING OF DORN

JOHN TIMMIS

Copyright © 2016 John Timmis

The moral right of the author has been asserted.

Apart from any fair dealing for the purposes of research or private study,
or criticism or review, as permitted under the Copyright, Designs and Patents
Act 1988, this publication may only be reproduced, stored or transmitted, in
any form or by any means, with the prior permission in writing of the
publishers, or in the case of reprographic reproduction in accordance with
the terms of licences issued by the Copyright Licensing Agency. Enquiries
concerning reproduction outside those terms should be sent to the publishers.

This is a work of fiction. Names, characters, businesses, places, events
and incidents are either the products of the author's imagination
or used in a fictitious manner. Any resemblance to actual persons,
living or dead, or actual events is purely coincidental.

Matador
9 Priory Business Park,
Wistow Road, Kibworth Beauchamp,
Leicestershire. LE8 0RX
Tel: 0116 279 2299
Email: books@troubador.co.uk
Web: www.troubador.co.uk/matador
Twitter: @matadorbooks

ISBN 978 1785893 742

British Library Cataloguing in Publication Data.
A catalogue record for this book is available from the British Library.

Printed and bound in the UK by TJ International, Padstow, Cornwall
Typeset in 11pt Aldine401 BT by Troubador Publishing Ltd, Leicester, UK

Matador is an imprint of Troubador Publishing Ltd

To Mum.
Thanks.

INTRODUCTION

L ong has the Eternal Triangle been a bane of mankind. This
was no less true in ancient times when magic and sorcery
held sway. One mighty sorcerer – Eq – seeking immortality as
a god, forged the Equilstones. These stones were the ultimate
allegory of this bane but with the power to steal souls – souls that
returned youth to ageing frames.

For thousands of millennia these stones worked for the gods
that were then. Sacrifices were made to them and through this
harvest of souls they lived on... and on... And while the gods
lived, they laughed at mortals – controlling their greed – a greed
which threatened to ravage the balance of the world. Mankind
kept his place.

Separate, the Equil's components are themselves, one as
powerful in its way as the other. In a pair they work better, their
two powers increased; but together, in an Equil, they are reduced
to nothing, all the powers of each one forgotten, worthless,
meaningless, cancelled, and their ceaseless banter may be heard
through time in the Netherworld.

Such were the powers and the weaknesses of the gods' stones
– and so did they fall piecemeal into the hands of men...

From Virdil's notes: "The Fall of the Gods"

1

A WOODMAN OF DORN
IS SEIZED!

The Forest of Dorn was an 'old place' before time was reckoned, eons before even the thought of Gullen was there. From its bowels had been born the human denizens of Endworld and the balanced tide of life that had endured. Now the Woodmen of Dorn served and were served by the forest, though others had long forsaken its sanctuary and begun their histories in other places. Indeed, one such place was the city of Gullen, nestled deep and peaceful in the rolling green Southlands of Endworld.

The forest's vastness stretched from the mountains of the North Chain far into the Southlands and all the way to the Western Sea. In these lands, trees were shelter, warmth, a home and a great preserve of game. Cleared in small areas, the ground possessed a seemingly endless fertility – attributed to the ceaseless work of the mighty trees – and was famous for the taste and succulence of the vegetables and fruit grown there. Never did the icy north winds drive below the tree-tops; rarely did snow remain on the soft, cushioned floor. The lash of the western rains was tempered into a simpering drip by the tangled maze of ancient branches and evergreen leaves; the stark heat of the midday sun in the Sunseason reduced to a warm, green-tinged radiance. The forest floor, damp and leafy, was often vibrant with the nodding gleam and fragrance of Astellots, Dundells, Achemes – flowers of the Great Forest – as regular in their appearance as the sun and stars themselves. Often the woodmen called the seasons by the names of these flowers; Astellin, the time when the snows were gone from the tree-tops and the high icicles dripped and disappeared, when Sunseason is soon to come; Achemin, the height of the Sunseason when the sun's rays penetrated and danced yellow on its delicate flowers; Dundellin, the twilight of Sunseason when the north winds stirred the upper branches restlessly but the forest's warmth remained for many days below the cold.

It was during Dundellin, when the woodmen prepared for the Coldseason and the nights which drew into the days, that Lindarg had taken a wife. Now he toiled alone but with great enthusiasm to build a home. Already he had cleared a score of trees – each a day's work – and in the space at one end he had fashioned the rudiments of a log dwelling. Every vestige of every tree was put to good use and far away in a deserted glade he had planted a new seed for every tree he had felled – such demanded the Lore gleaned from the wisdom of time's lessons.

Six huge trunks formed its corners and door posts: thick, bark-stripped branches its walls; lighter branches were roof timbers and sinewy twigs the basis for the thatch of leaves – dense and resistant. The roots were used mainly for burning but some would form the curved back of a chair or gnarled axe haft. The stripped bark too was used for burning – but most was spread over the new glade to enrich the soil for the first crops which would be planted in the following Astellin. This too was according to the Lore of the woodmen.

Now Lindarg rested, bare arms gleaming ruddily with vitality and the rigours of his labours; a trace of steam curled upwards from the mess of brown hair which crowned and surrounded his facial features. The features of a strong, true woodman; humour, caring and trust were in those soft lines; wisdom and adamant determination behind the eyes. The short skins he wore while he worked showed the stark sinews behind his knees, muscles on his thighs and calves beneath the soft, red-brown skin. Under the brief tunic was a body that was trim, though broad and well-built. He was young by woodman standards to be starting his own life and family but he had learned fast and shown well in his early years.

Lindarg was fully ready to follow the paths of the woodmen, ready to forge that secure but hard-won life of the Woodmen of Dorn; ready to follow the Lore and wisdom that guided the people of the forest. He was no newcomer to hard work – few are those of the forest whose youth was not fraught with it and thus few were there who did not understand how much better was the leisure after it was done. Also, the Law clamoured against any who, in the rash impudence of youth sought other ways; ways which in small measures over the decades, would work to estrange the forest and its denizens, parting them finally. Woodmen and forest had come into Endworld together, together they had grown, comforted and nurtured each other; together they had formed the Lore. Any who pulled against the Lore – as the independent minds of men are ever wont to do – were dealt with swiftly. Theirs was the choice of being cast from the forest into the out lands where there was no life save for a constant battle with death, or to go willingly to endure publicly the pain of the woodmen's whip and afterwards to serve the forest for a Starseason. Most chose the latter, accepting and upholding the Lore, coming in that Starseason of service to appreciate the depths of its wisdom as their hurts were healed and comforted.

Lindarg was well-learned in the Lore of the forest. From his earliest days he had learned fast, almost instinctively holding all knowledge and wisdom in greater esteem than did most of his contemporaries. This wisdom had nurtured in him a deep understanding of the ways of the forest and unlike many other woodmen he saw and felt the need for the Lore, realising that without it, the life-span of the forest, and therefore that of the woodmen who depended upon it, would be finite. Small changes would become larger ones and the large ones would become irrevocable. He had seen it at the forest's north margins, far from the ways of the woodmen; Baeths had come to cut the trees.

They did so without feeling; to the forest they dealt death; no nursery trees to shelter the young where they had ravaged; left only tumbled spars and lifeless stumps and in their wake came the choking brush which enveloped the unproductive lands north of the forest. No new trees ever grew there again; deep nutrients were lost to the soil; the harsh Coldseason froze the ground and the seeds of trees that reached there were washed away by the rains and lost in a dusty tumble on the plains beneath the dark mountain peaks.

Standing there he recalled those earlier days, remembering a feast when he and other youths – particularly one called Tarron – had discussed the Lore and an old man had heard them. That old man was dead now – he had passed several Starseasons ago – but Lindarg well remembered that night in the Dome and what he had said of the Lore to Tarron.

"You would ask, Tarron, why the Lore should be served when the forest is in retreat. Is that what you would know?" The question was heavily laid on the young lad and he wavered, not wishing to seem against the Lore but the old man had continued. "It is true, Tarron, that there is change; it is true that despite our efforts, the forest perhaps will not endure forever, but in resisting these changes for as long as we can lies our best hope. That is what the Lore does now." The old man settled and sipped his drink. We had all known the story that would unfold and waited in silent eagerness – it never faded with the tellings. Around us, in other parts of the Great Dome, we were aware of laughter and singing but here, our hearts furtively fluttered in the silence.

"Long ago he came to Castle Hill in the west, before your father or your father's father, Tarron, and settled there within those crumbling walls…" The old man paused, catching each one of his listeners with an eye, the other closed as if remembering long back and struggling to recall. "A ruin since before the men of the forest remember and none has explored the depths beneath it – dark tombs, they say; in the rock itself, delved far below the hill. A legend with no beginning in this age, a shell

4

with no answers to its past. A wizard he is; come from the north it is supposed; one called Venain." The old man took another sip from his drink, both eyes closed now; the darkness of the name he had just uttered crept over the gathering. Tarron had shuddered. Suddenly the man looked up, enjoying the effect of his voice upon his audience, then went on. "Quietly at first he lived there in the ruins. He was seen but we did not reckon with him, thinking him perhaps an outcast from the Southlands or Gullen maybe. Our king then, old though he was – yet wise – decreed that he should be left, for then he offered no threat or trouble. For many Starseasons this remained so and even when the wizard brought strange men from other lands the king's word was held and Venain re-built the castle, stone-by-stone." He had paused in his tale to hold Tarron's eyes, then continued in a low tone.

"Now Tarron is your answer. He put forth his power from that strong place and it was felt throughout the forest, upsetting the balanced tide of life that had endured. Our new king challenged him with a following of his valiant council but was thrown down. The power in the castle was greater than they; they were too late. Many did not return from that first bleak encounter – kept as slaves to serve the wizard." The old man had spat the last word with contempt – but it was said quietly and with fear. "Our king did return but knowing then that there was a new king – a sorcerer – and one who cares little for us or the forest, taking from it what he wishes and returning nothing. He it is who has turned the balance and that is why we the more must serve the Lore, ruin would surely come the sooner should we not."

A horrified silence had transfixed the listening youths. Over their young lives had always hung the threat of the wizard. 'The wizard will get you' was an awful thing to say.

"Mainly he leaves us alone," the old man had continued, "but some have gone that way and never returned; he is too great for woodmen."

"Then we should fight him," Tarron had suggested excitedly.

5

"We cannot match sorcery – we who can only tend the hurts of the living things and the land, we would go to our deaths like so many others," another had said;

"We are doomed then, in time?" The old man had cocked an eye at the questioner.

"It could be so," was all he said in reply.

"Then," Tarron had said with a flourish, "so is the Lore at the end!"

For a long time, the old man had scowled at Tarron, then relaxed and finished his tale.

"Ah, but the story of the wizard is not finished here. There is another wizard in Endworld…"

"Tell us of him. Are they going to fight?"

"Will it be soon?"

"Who is the other wizard?"

"Where is he from?"

"How do you know?"

"Tell us!"

"Will we see the battle – the lights and the fires?"

"Is he a good wizard?"

"Does he like the forest?"

"Tell us!"

But he never did.

It had caused him, he remembered, a little sadness, for it portended the decline of their realm. But for now Lindarg's spirits were high, and banishing such thoughts his eyes turned to the newly-built home where his betrothed, Nayella, already busied herself in its shell, sewing Yanish skins for coverlets and rugs for the wooden floor. Desperately short of everything she thought was important, resin lamps, utensils to clean and cook with, serve with and eat from – a whole host of items she needed. But Lindarg saw to the trees, the land, food stocks and the home itself before raising a hand to her wants of the household. Nayella did not complain for a woodman knew his ways and it was not good to alter or interfere with them. She managed as all wood wives did, had and would do.

6

She knew also from her mother, and secretly too from her father, that for her patience and frustrations, Lindarg would grant her wishes far in excess of what she might coax from him now, since the Law had to be served first – then a man's wife – and how much better for the wait!

Then, when most of the tasks had been done in preparation for the Coldseason, came the feasts of Dundellin. This was when those who were newly-joined and had laboured to build a home enjoyed the hospitality of the forest and were treated by other woodmen and women to entertainment and jollity in the forest Dome, when all woodfolk laid down their tools and chores were forgotten. At these times too, the forest tracks were lamp-lit; folk came and went; lovers paraded; people visited neighbours, friends, relatives; and songs, dances, stories, tales and feasting went on through the night. But for Lindarg and Nayella, this Dundellin would be theirs to remember – they would be set with honour at the grand tables with the other newly-joined; presented with gifts; their ballad would be written and they would give the balladeer some of their gifts since they would have more than enough for themselves. So pervasive and benevolent was the spirit of Dundellin that it permeated the whole forest and seemed to remain long into the Coldseason.

At last Nayella was ready for their journey to the Dome and for the simple ceremony of their betrothal. Dark haired, tall and regal, yet exquisitely feminine, she stood in the doorway of their home; dark eyes glittering with love as Lindarg gazed upon her. She wore a short tunic of the thinnest hide – no Yanish skin this – which caressed provocatively the smooth, youthful curves it covered – leaving almost all of her satin-skinned limbs bare. Nayella was a dancer, her skill renowned in the forest and it showed in the lithe curves of her calves and thighs. Long hair reaching down her back had been lovingly brushed; its sleekness emphasising her stance, cascading over pale shoulders. All of this Lindarg drank in, but at least as much he loved her gentle nature and captivating smile.

She smiled for him now and later, at the feast, he knew she would dance for him.

Lindarg drew her into his arms. "Ah Nayella, flower of the glade, the memories of this night and the feasts to come, we shall treasure always."

"Yes, my love." They kissed warmly in the cool of the forest. "And you, Lindarg, I will cherish – hard though you were for my love to conquer – yet the greater will that love be. Our children will grow strong in its guidance; true and blessed as the people of the woods; secure in our forest realm."

"Come, Nayella, let us start for the Dome. The song of our betrothal will already be written. Are you not eager to hear the balladsmen sing it? And my mother has a gift for you which is beautiful…"

"And to you, Lindarg, my father is to give…" Nayella laughed at the fleeting frown on her lover's face and teased the Lore saying, "Oh, but I must not say – cannot tell you – but it is a great gift; a gift worthy of a fine man and my heart's desire."

Accepting the tease playfully, Lindarg slapped her thigh lovingly as they embraced on the edge of their home's clearing, sweet with the smell of newly dug soil.

"Ow!" she exclaimed quietly, smiling tantalisingly, coquettishly.

Lindarg responded, caressing her close up; lifting her he made as if to slap her again, but instead kissed her long, his hand stroking the warmth of her legs. Lovingly he chided her, smiling, "If it takes us this long to cover a short distance, we will never reach the Dome!"

Still she clung to him, teasing, enjoying his caresses, goading him to force her a little. Lindarg set her down and taking her hand led her from the glade onto the tiny path which, after meeting others, would take them to their bliss in the Dome. She hung behind, pretending to resist his urging, laughing, knowing his response.

8

"Come quickly, my love," said Lindarg.

But she hung back, her eyes sparkling a mock defiance.

"Now Nayella!"

"Yes, now." Her eyes were imploring, wide, expectant; she hesitated still.

Lindarg turned swiftly, whisking her off her feet with one massive arm and running down the path with her, bare legs dangling, rubbing with his own, he chastised her lovingly and her blissful laugh of submission echoed among the trees and was lost in the tangle of their branches above.

This was as the Lore decreed, for they were now full of desire for each other; a loving desire which filled their hearts with a joy which was like a fire that would not easily be quenched. That aura would remain with them until after the feasts; until after they had coupled with each other in their home. So it would be that the Dome was filled with a sublimity that transcended all other feelings for it applied equally to others at the feasts making them much more of a festivity than anything before or since that man has ever contrived; a time when the hearts of humankind were deeply melded with love and the spirit of the event was a flux of joy. And after the feasts many a child would be conceived, to be born in the Warmseason of plenty. Thus the Lore which served the forest worked also for its denizens and those who chose its designs gained succour from them.

They passed down their own path to join the first of the lamp-lit ways. Though the forest seemed silent, withdrawn, Lindarg and Nayella stepped lightly to the direction of the Dome, knowing that they would yet meet larger tracks and routes – and many woodfolk – journeying as them.

The Dome was set in the heart of the forest and served as a city in the realms of the woodmen. It was where those trees which perhaps had beget Dorn in the beginning had formed an arching cover so dense that beneath it the floor was dry and the air within could be heated with the smallest of fires. Giant trunks, crazily shaped by time, made natural divisions below the protecting canopy, forming places – almost rooms – large and small, where folk could gather in groups if desired, or just wander between, meeting, talking, sampling the gatherings here and there. Some places were for games, others for eating, yet more for quiet talk, singing, tales and the exchange of wisdom; places where gifts were bartered, small contests arranged and places too to be alone. At its centre was the largest place; held in great reverence by woodfolk and used only for the feasts of Dundellin in the honour of those who would be newly-joined. Never twice was the honour of the Dome-feast given, but to be received there that once was the right of all and any who could claim their birthright in Dorn.

They came upon the first track which angled from the left, joining theirs at a fork. They saw no-one and though they were far from the Dome, there should perhaps have been a few folk – even here.

Almost imperceptibly the silence deepened and they became uneasy. There was no explaining the feeling they both experienced; the suspicion that something had changed the forest – it no longer held that secure welcoming ambience. Without seeming actually hostile, there was a resentment; a withdrawal of shelter; of support. They began to feel exposed; watched; vulnerable. Nayella drew closer to Lindarg, whose muscles tightened slightly, unsure.

"Can you feel it?" Nayella's voice was a whisper with the unmistakable tremor of fear.

"Yes, keep close."

She gripped him tighter, knuckles whitening round his arm. They continued for a while then stopped; listened. But the listening worsened the silence – giving it depth. Nayella's paling face met Lindarg's.

"What is it? What is happening?" There was a desperateness in her voice.

"I do not know – cannot understand it…" Then Lindarg tried to reassure her but fear was beginning to shape itself within him too and would not be concealed. They proceeded warily with no answers; a building apprehension gripping them.

There was a rustle overhead. Nayella screamed; was silenced, and at the same moment a crushing weight fell across Lindarg's shoulders throwing him spinning to the ground. His stout muscles flew into action amid the turmoil of shouts and bodies but a head blow caught him, sending him tumbling into a whirling oblivion.

It seemed only seconds later when he was roughly jolted back to a jagged grey consciousness of pain and haze. His limbs were stretched taut, bound to thick branches, vaguely he heard a woman's screams; pleas which faded rapidly in the distance as his suspended, pain-wracked body jogged to the rhythmic trot of the woodmen who bore him. Woodmen! What kind of treatment was this from his own kind? He tried to call out but only a strangled moan escaped his lips and his bearers paid no heed. He struggled violently but it was useless against the biting cords and the extra pain brought blackness once more and none of the woodmen so much as cast him a glance.

2

A SOUL SO TAKEN

Venain now stood atop the ancient tower of his castle which commanded a view over the surrounding Forest of Dorn. Far in the distance to his left the hazy line of the Northern mountains halted the forest and beyond the horizon behind him lay the Western Sea. Often in his lonely life had Venain gazed over this vast forest valley before him which he considered to be his. With his mind he could see things far off and learn through his sorceries of events elsewhere. These days he did so less and less since he was fast ageing and losing the energy which his powers needed. Often in his younger days he had journeyed far beyond the Southlands and even beyond the realms of the Farfolk and the mountains to lands he could barely remember – save one. Ah! The Plain of the Great Stone – a body blow dealt to a declining god by his father's father – the memory of its sight he cherished and reflected upon often.

Enormous wisdom he had gained in his life and much malevolence had he spread through Endworld as he scoured it for treasures and mysteries. Few if any places remained where he was welcomed; his name uttered as a curse under the breath. And now, by the frailty of uncounted years he was chained to the castle of his own rebuilding and though still a powerful sorcerer, had ceased to be more than a thin legend in those distant lands.

Venain hated being old. To him it was a useless twilight of boredom and struggle with no rewards and few challenges – feared only by the peasant-like peoples of the Great Forest which he called his. This also angered him, for even here, so close, he had never quite achieved the control and power he had coveted; always he had striven yet somehow effective dominion over the forest and its peoples had eluded him. Soon, even those few who did fear him would forget and walk tall again; ransack his castle; butcher his servants – or worse, free them! They would steal his wealth too but worst of all they would, sooner or later, plunder his treasures and mysteries, dividing and diminishing their powers in ignorance. For now, though, they were safe in the vast caverns delved beneath the castle, deep in Castle Hill itself. Long ago those deep dark places had taken capacious powers to hew them out of the living rock: powers long forgotten and lost. To them Venain had added altars and places for rites; these days he spent most of his time down there while his spell-locked minions toiled to do his bidding – keeping his castle in perfect order – well-lit and warmed; well-stocked with food and drink.

But now, at last, after an age of searching and enquiry he had uncovered the secret: a crystal – stolen from the halls of a god in years gone by – and a book of cabalism had, at last, revealed it. So today he trembled with excitement – as a child with his first bow. This Dundellin he had chosen as the time.

Restlessly and anxiously he paced the ramparts, ears straining for the slightest sound from the forest below; eyes peering into the distant trees. He reflected with frustration how easily he could have espied and sorcerously lured that which he sought, however far away. But seasons ago, in accordance with the strictures of the ancient book he had vowed to abstain from all sorcerous deeds until this – his most diabolical undertaking, had been fulfilled. But oh! How limiting to rely on the weakness and slowness of ordinary men! How tedious! Yet he knew this was the only way – he must wait – and hope…

His heart skipped a beat when he heard the scream – very faint – a plea, a howl, drifting up to him from a forest track far below. Delirious with anticipation, Venain scuttled along passages, down the tower stairs, through archways and turns, down more stairs, across a stone-paved courtyard, through warm, bright-lit rooms, passing servants who went about their business heedless of their master's haste. Down further he went, through tunnels dimly-lit with torches which guttered and flared; angling down deep into the hill to his subterranean lair. From a balcony there he surveyed the cavern, rapidly going through all the preparations; mentally ticking off all the items which he had carefully assembled there.

"Rope, altar, book, stone, knife, robes, flints, candles," he thought out loud to himself. Of course there was nothing missing – but he had to be sure! Snatching a swift, last look he hurried back up long passages, checking torches to ensure they would not burn out during the rite. "Nothing must go wrong!"

Garbed now in a black cloak, he slipped beyond the maw of his castle and down the slope. The screaming and pleading was louder here and the shuffle of heavy feet was just audible between the moans on the still evening air. Determined, weary steps struggled out of the forest and started up the slope bearing a triangular frame of thick, rough-cut poles – three men to each side. In the centre of the frame – cruelly bound to it – was the figure of a youthful woodman whose lack of clothing displayed bronzed, well-muscled arms and legs straining at the unyielding bonds. So tight were the bonds which secured the man that his hands and feet were a garish purple in the fading light; their movement feeble. His body, glistening and steaming in the cool air, writhed and contorted uselessly.

Just as the sun's dying vermillion orb dropped below the horizon, the woodmen halted before Venain and the sorcerer felt a twinge of real fear. This near the forest – almost within it – the silence was awesome and it seemed to brood threateningly. The nine men were large and strong: he knew they hated him. They hated the way he had always used them, their produce, their labour; giving nothing in return. Venain knew too that without his sorcery he was as naked and helpless as their captive; his castle too lay vulnerable behind him. These men could tear him limb-

14

from-limb; no wizardry could he call to his aid – for seasons Venain had been just an ordinary man – weaker perhaps than most; abstaining from all sorcery. Ah, but they did not know, these woodmen – they still feared – and in that lay his power yet. He must bluff and succeed in it until the business was over – then… yes, then… the things he would do!

"Bring him, your reward of gold lies within the castle." Venain turned swiftly, beckoning them to follow.

"We will not enter your castle, Lord Venain. We fear it," said one.

Venain halted. "I will make your passage safe – and yet more gold will be your reward. None need fear who work for Venain."

Still the woodmen showed no sign of movement. The captive body moaned and stirred afresh.

"Come!" insisted the sorcerer, "for you there will be no danger inside my keep." He shivered a little, realising that for once he spoke the truth. Hesitantly, given no better alternative, the men at last followed, taking Lindarg their captive into the lair of the evil Wizard of Dorn.

The passages echoed to their many feet; the frightened men marched squarely; eyes ahead, fearing to cast about, following Venain.

"What is his name?" the wizard suddenly asked, turning and motioning to their captive.

"Lindarg," the man who had spoken before answered woodenly.

"And his age?"

"We… I do not know," stammered the same man.

"I must know his age – it is important to me!"

"Perhaps twenty Starseasons, Lord – maybe less." This time it was another who spoke – one who had been a friend of the man they held; too quickly had the lure of gold sundered the ties between them.

"That is good – one so young will please the forest god." Venain allowed himself a chuckle at the joke which the nine men could not yet comprehend.

15

At last they arrived in the altar cavern, the men shivering with fear, let their victim fall where Venain indicated below two rings hanging from thick ropes which disappeared into the smoky mirk of the chamber's roof. On the floor, set into the stone, was a similar ring. From behind the altar the sorcerer drew nine skin pouches which chinked with the gold coins they contained.

"Your payment, kind folk. May the forest gods guard you." Venain indicated the passage which led back to the gates. "None will bar your return to the forest – go!"

They needed no encouragement, within seconds their hurried footfalls were dying to a mere patter far up the long passage.

But up there they encountered the dark shadows of minions in the fitful torchlight and never did the sorcerer's gold leave his own castle.

Venain flew into action. Swiftly he turned a wheel at the rear of the chamber and the two rings were lowered slowly down until they touched the frame on which the captive was bound – now silent, ashen-faced, shaking with terror. Venain then secured each ring to an end of the top spar of the frame, returned to the wheel and hoisted it and the victim into a half-upright position. This done, he took more rope and passed it round the frame and Lindarg's arms until they were firmly bound right up to the shoulders. 'During the rite there must be no movement of the body'. The instructions from the book went through Venain's head. He further secured Lindarg's feet – just to make sure, then completed the hoisting until the man and frame were upright and in exactly the right position. Locking the wheel, Venain donned special robes and checked the positioning of the crystal stone on the second altar. Now the main altar, the victim and the stone on the second altar formed a perfect Equil of three corners. Between each, connecting them, a channel was hewn out of the stone floor. Everything was ready for the Equilflow.

Venain returned to the book 'Gems of Endworld' which lay open at the page entitled 'Royal Stones' – but was otherwise blank.

"Reveal to me the secrets of Eq!" Venain demanded of the book. Slowly the page changed to reveal a spidery legend. For the thousandth time he read through the rite; everything had been done as it commanded:

Practice ye no magic for one Starseason.
Let menfolk gather ye willingly a soul.
Set the stone upon the second altar
And the soul upon the third corner
Scar ye the breast of the soul – let nothing hinder the flow.
Take ye the first corner to complete the Equil.
Pronounce then "I claim thy soul."

Let no escape
Lest for

The ends of the last two lines had been torn from the page. It was a warning, Venain knew that, but a warning of what he had never been able to discover. He had tried and searched until age gave him no more time to dither in indecision. The missing piece, he conjectured, was in Gullen – the one place he had not been able to plunder. Finally, he had dismissed the warning – though not lightly – concluding that its import was probably petty and not in any way relevant to the new era which he was about to begin.

It was no more than a slight niggle and one which paled into insignificance in the shadow of the enormity and arrogance of what he was about to do. Eternal life was to be his and his alone – forever!

He pushed caution to the back of his mind – he must complete the work! Taking up the knife he traced a deep cut across Lindarg's chest. Lindarg gasped at the sudden new pain, feeling the warm drips of his own blood on his legs. He had ceased struggling and was resigned to death – wishing only that it would now be swift. Venain returned to the main altar and trembling, pronounced the words from the book.

Instantly the crystal stone glowed with an inner light and Venain felt himself captivated by a linking force. Lindarg moaned and struggled afresh – his feeble efforts to no avail – then uttered a loud anguished wail of misery. From the cut in his chest issued a hazy white vapour which, after collecting and hovering for a moment or two, fell slowly to the floor and into the channel which led to the crystal. Along the channel it flowed to the second altar, hesitated, then slid along the next channel to Venain. Transfixed, Venain watched it and as it drew near he knew that it was a soul and he knew its name; calling to it. The white vapour that was Lindarg's soul gathered around his feet; he felt an enormous surge of power from the stone and the soul entered him.

There was no pain – just a moment of black senselessness followed by a great elation of youth and vigour. The crystal's light faded and Venain stepped back from the first altar flush with success. He knew it had worked. He was young again! His body thrilled with energy and vitality. At last! Once more he would wield his power and travel; would take all the lands far and near for his own – for now he was eternal: nothing would escape him this time! He would make all the secrets and mysteries of Endworld reveal themselves to him; he would have all his own will and all his own way; he would be God of Endworld.

Himself: a god.

The god.

Lindarg's body was limp but still alive, stretched taut on the frame. Venain released it.

"Ha! You will be my first message. You whose soul has given me more time – the first of many I shall take as I force Endworld to its knees and mould it to my will. You will walk empty among its peoples; recognising none: nothing will be your life and your life will be nothing. You have no name, no soul, no being: a body, soul-less and useless. Ha! Perhaps they will guess what I have done and come to know real fear, paying homage – lest they be next. Deathling they will call you; Deathling of Dorn – and you will herald the age of a new god; the more so than if I were to emblazon it on every rock and tree in the realms."

Conscious now but unfeeling and uncomprehending; knowing no emotion; no hate for the one who chided him and who has so ill-used him, Lindarg barely stood, wavering in the dusky hall as Venain carefully concealed his possessions and changed back into his normal robes with a swiftness which he had never before shown – even in his youth. This done he turned to the body. Quickly he washed off some of the blood – which by now had stopped flowing from the chest cut and, chuckling, refastened the remnants of Yanish skin round the body's hips. Expressionless, it watched him like a brainless child and when Venain led it by the arm down a dark passage, followed stiffly without a murmur.

"Go," said the sorcerer. "Back to your people. Give them my message. Show them a hint of just one vestige of my might. Ha!" He gave the Deathling a guiding push and it shuffled off down the passage and out into the fading evening light on the slopes of Castle Hill.

Venain was already in his tower re-casting protective spells over his castle, sealing open ways, planning the things he would do with his new life of power; planning how to lure his final enemy Virdil, Wizard of Gullen and how to finish him once lured – how to lay that last puny yet obtrusive obstacle to his complete, unchallenged domination of Endworld. And after Endworld there were yet lands beyond the seas… But before his spells were complete, before the final word was uttered, there came noises from the forest at the foot of Castle Hill. The noises swelled into cries as scores of Southfolk broke the cover of the trees, charging defiantly up the hill sweeping in the wake of a mighty wizard. Swords and spears waved menacingly; death cries drifted up to the tower; challenging it. Venain rushed to the ramparts to gaze down upon those who would dare to challenge his might. He saw their leader – flowing dark hair beneath the cowl, riding a steed of Gullen; lean features aglow with red wrath; cloaked in shimmering blue – bright, though the evening was dim; determined; powerful – his enemy came to him so soon – yet too late!

"Hail Virdil of Gullen – Wizard of the Southlands! We meet at last!"

"Hold, Southmen!" cried Virdil casting a hand high into the air.

The Southfolk hordes fell still and a sudden silence descended. From above them Venain spoke again.

"So you learned, Virdil, of my vow and you sought to catch me unawares, unprotected – and destroy me." He laughed as he caught the look of fear which crossed Virdil's countenance. "Ha! See this good wizard," he sneered contemptuously. With a gesture to the castle gates, he created in the path of the attackers an armoured knight on a black beast which snorted restlessly as its fearsome rider impatiently swung a spiked flail of gleaming steel. Virdil's face whitened and those of his followers who glimpsed it saw the terror there.

"Flee, Southmen! We are too late! Back to the forest – this is sorcery and no place for mere swords. Go!" The last word was a screamed command not to be gainsaid.

Reluctantly, men fell back beneath the eaves of the forest but remained there where they could watch the fray.

Now alone on the slope before the great castle, the sound of Venain's evil laugh reached Virdil and that very sound sapped his spirit. He knew there was no escape. Retreat would mean certain death from the fell creature at the gate, attack was useless against a sorcerer within the fastness of his defences and Virdil was now sure that his bid was ill-timed to snare Venain unguarded. In a flush of anger and frustration Virdil sliced the air with a finger and the rider at the gate disappeared.

"Keep your illusions to amuse you, slaves! You play children's games!" he challenged the leering face atop the battlements.

Venain applauded. "Surely this is my lucky day – you wish to play? Then be at your moves dog!" His voice scornful; goading.

Once more the armoured rider appeared – this time but a short distance away and charging. Beast and rider rattled by; the spiked flail humming through the air grazing Virdil's side deeply as he tried to evade the deadly blow.

"How does my illusion feel, Lord Virdil? You provide good sport!"

Once more Virdil sliced the air and the rider dissolved – but more slowly; reluctantly. Realising his only possible chance lay in speed, Virdil spurred his steed up the hill toward the castle's open gate. Gloriously he charged; steely blue in fading light and like the wind. Venain waited, sure as a spider until Virdil was a few paces from the walls…

"Kyranneq!" In one word Venain sealed the sorcery for his castle's shield: Virdil was stopped short; immobilised – nearly upon the gate. In a flash he was surrounded by a ring of fire which closed around him like a noose and with a plaintive scream, was engulfed and finished.

No sooner had Virdil's wail of anguish died away than it was answered by a multitude of death cries as Southlanders swarmed from the forest to avenge their wizard. In their expressions was etched stark terror and blind fury as they raced up the slope. Venain laughed.

"Such sport!" he shouted exultantly from the battlements amid the din of the charging rabble.

Ten armoured warriors on black steeds; grey faces matching

the fell grey of their weapons; stinking of death; leering with dead faces turned away from the light, materialised between the Southfolk onslaught and the castle wall. Southlanders wavered.

"Finish them, Nethermen!" cried Venain from above, "and bring me one alive that I might be further entertained."

In answer, his Nethermen charged and skulls cracked; bodies were torn; the grass of the hillside turned from green to red as the fell riders butchered and crushed the small army of Southlanders in moments. A few turned back into the forest in a desperate bid for freedom but the grey knights rode them down and screaming, they were cut down and left to rot.

A dead quiet descended, broken only by the cries and pleas from the last living Southlander who was being dragged back to the castle from the forest by an armoured rider. From the battlements Venain applauded them and their dark, uplifted faces were contorted with satisfied smiles.

"You have excelled my warriors for it is long since you had such a task." He pointed to their captive. "Bind him and stow him – tonight we must feast and be entertained."

It wasn't until the heat of the battle had faded that Venain was assailed for the first time by a doubt. Of course there was no need for any he told himself, he had won, completely; decisively; there was nought to fear now. There could be no challenge – not from within Endworld – not now. And yet the doubt was there. It had been too easy, too convenient. Virdil had fought – yes – but like a child only. Perhaps, he considered, he had over-estimated his age-old enemy, perhaps he had always been so much more powerful than Virdil. That must be it, he decided, he was now invincible and probably always had been.

Vaguely, Lindarg – the Deathling – was aware of the cool twilight air on his face and body but there was no emotion, no thought, no direction. He was free – but what was that? It meant nothing; there seemed no point to existence. Behind him the cave

22

entrance was replaced by hillside and was gone; he was a lone, soul-less body at the edge of the Great Forest of Dorn. There was nothing for him but life and life promised nothing – for now he was no-one: a body which would react, feel hunger and thirst; move mechanically; perhaps feel pain – until mercifully it died. A Deathling! The first since before the history of man. He stood limply, seeing without comprehending with no plan or direction in his mind. To his right in front of the castle, men mounted and on foot, charged up the hill like marionettes with one mind. There were voices and they fell back into the forest. Then came fire and a scream; more men; sounds of butchery and spilled blood: then silence… as the long Dundellin twilight gave way to darkness.

Through glazed, staring eyes Lindarg saw a misty vapour – a white sinewy shadow – drifting through the trees; running along the ground; dispersing; thinning at its edges. Touched by a force unknown; unbidden; Lindarg called softly to it, knowing its name.

"Virdil… Virdil… Virdil!" The urgency of the whispered voice checked the tendrils – they wavered – then the thinning wisps drew back together. Shimmering, the white stream flowed toward Lindarg's body, slowly at first – then with greater urgency as it coalesced and touched him.

Lindarg felt the surge of presence; was aware of an intense sensation within him; then he knew panic; sensing danger all around: the presence of the magically sealed cave entrance and death; death in the air; death; death everywhere. He was overwhelmed by frustration and fear, failure and futility. His whole body thrilled with an entity: throbbed with it; his head reeled and he ran; ran far into the forest, ignoring paths and tracks: deeper and deeper; following only blind panic in the darkness. He remembered the soft, damp earth rushing up to meet him as later, his tortured frame succumbed to the strain of flight and he crashed into a restful oblivion on the forest floor. Everything was blackness, dark, deep and long.

The preparations for the feast of victory were well under way; Venain had bathed and the fragrance permeated the whole castle mingling with the sweet aromas of cooking and the tang of log fires in the air. The castle's main hall was alive with scurrying of minions; the long feasting table already well spread with fruits and produce of the forest. At one end of the table a crackling fire burned comfortingly adding dancing flashes of light to the flickering glows of torches and resin lamps. Music – quiet or loud to command – swelled and sullied round the pillars: thick Yanish skin rugs cushioned the noise of the bustle so that the weird, disharmonic notes held sway. Nethermen were already gathered there; silent, grey un-animated along the feasting table; a golden chair – immovable in its own weight, was empty at the table's head.

At last Venain entered and held all present in his stare, making them rise and look to him with respect.

"Ah Nethermen – my lieges, this day has been glorious beyond recall. You have fought well and truly earned your feast; never before have I seen so clean and cruel a triumph – nor so swift!" He raised his glass, "Blood and victory!" Then added, "To the God of Endworld! Drink to me!"

The call was demonic; irresistible; they worshipped, together, as one – and the wine they drank was Southland blood. By their master's command they laughed, gambolled, fought and feasted. Venain enjoyed their merriment; shared their mirth and glee – which was theirs because he had bestowed it upon them and the reflection of him in their faces gave him grace and pleasure which lasted long into the night – until the time he silenced them and rose to his feet again – mighty in his own halls.

"Stop! It is time, bring the captive. Tonight you will devour flesh." A roar of approval greeted Venain's announcement as two minions left the hall. The man was brought.

The captive, unscathed by battle, preserved as if precious among the carnage of the fight was now wild-eyed and struggling fiercely.

"Loose his bonds and strip him! He should be free to enjoy our hospitality." Peals of raucous laughter echoed through the vast room as the man was set free and disrobed.

"Run!" Venain shouted to him. The man ran for the door unable to believe that he might escape – but his way was barred by an invisible barrier. He tried to skirt it but instead its circle closed around him until he ran as if in a large jar. The laughter rang once more as the man was dragged by the invisible ring before Venain.

Scornfully, supremely, the sorcerer watched his panic, then said; "Hear this, knave. None escapes the mighty Venain. And none who dares to challenge me is shown mercy! On the wheels with him!"

Strong, calloused hands pulled the man's arms and legs between opposite wheels on a wide frame, binding him like an axle between them. Then the frame was dragged over the blazing open fire. Muscled whipped taut like bowstrings with the blistering pain of the flames but the screams of agony were drowned at Venain's unspoken command by a surging symphony of death and the long, guttural laughs of the Nethermen.

Later, when grey faces had feasted on roasted flesh and were dissolved by their master, minions came to clear sinews and blood from the stones of the floor.

With returning quiet, the sorcerer was once more assailed by the doubt. Leaving the hall, he made his way up to the keep's topmost tower. In the dark through an open window he sought outwards with his mind, seeing far off, whispering "Virdil, Virdil", finding nothing but the darkness of night. "Lindarg…" But blackness too was his answer and that was as it should have been for Lindarg only existed as part of himself. Then he clutched the Knavestone which glowed with an eerie light – dim but powerful – and uttered the same names into its glimmer. In its depths too was blackness, complete, unbroken; that was surely death; nothing in Endworld bore those names now; they were a memory – destroyed utterly.

For a further two days Venain searched for any trace of his enemy and found none. Satisfied at last and now fatigued, he called off his searchings and began to contemplate rather his commencing rule of Endworld as an immortal; a god. Soon he would journey to Gullen and take from there what was now his; the powers and treasures of he who had been Virdil...

3

FLIGHT NORTH

A whirling confusion surged through his head as Lindarg dizzily awoke. He knew it was morning and it was still warm even though, he realised, as he surveyed the withered Dundells, it would soon be Coldseason and above the forest canopy the north wind was beginning to stir. Leaning against a tree Lindarg tried to remember and link the scar so new and stark on his chest with strange thoughts and feelings; with an encounter; with Nayella... his thoughts stopped short. "Nayella, the Feast of Dundellin." Vaguely he had an urge to seek this Nayella... his betrothed! She would be worrying; missing him – or perhaps even given him up forever and already mourning his passing in the forest Dome. He had to find her. Lindarg's brain at last made a decision but his heart wasn't in it. He knew he should seek Nayella but had little wish to. There seemed to be other, more important things deep inside him – ideas and suggestions which were inherent and insidiously pushing other purposes. These he could not understand and swiftly he set off to seek Nayella.

Slowly and wearily he walked, keeping to the bushes; low, inconspicuous, until he encountered a forest path. Instinctively he could tell in which direction the centre of the forest lay and he struck out to his right, keeping to the edge of the path. The way, it seemed was safe and he met no-one. Further along, a forking path joined his track from the left and he knew by its angle that he was proceeding in the right direction. The track widened;

he was hungry and thirsty but still pressed on, sure now with the widening way that he was headed for the Dome and would reach it 'ere nightfall. With the easy going his mind wandered, fluttering from thoughts to thoughts, unable to concentrate on any one thing; a muddle of experiences; then a hint of hidden, aged depths; then of Nayella but nothing lasted.

Then the path forked, not joining, separating. Lindarg halted, dumbfounded. Occasionally there were cross tracks between those which radiated from the Dome but he should not come upon a fork like this unless he was travelling away from the Dome and that he certainly wasn't doing since he had not reached it yet and up to now he was sure he had been travelling toward it.

The ways seemed to have changed from what he remembered. Instinct told him to turn back the way he had come but instead he decided to take the left fork. Hunger again assailed him, sharper than before and he tarried to pick some nuts – full, juicy and wholesome at this time of the season. Slowly he continued, eating as he went. A forking path merged with his from the right, suggesting once more he was travelling toward the Dome. But the track he now followed didn't widen as it should have done. Almost imperceptibly at first the track narrowed; later dwindling to a winding path dodging in and out of the unmoving trunks of the forest trees. He felt almost certain now that he was moving away from the Dome but having come thus far he carried on. There were no more junctions, just the one narrowing path. Twilight came; then darkness crept over the trees. Exhausted, disheartened and confused, Lindarg eased himself up into a high dense tree and nestled down in its sheltering tangle of branches; yellowing leaves caressing his face he drifted into a weary sleep.

How long he had slept he had no idea but it was still dark. Fear had awakened him – his spine tingled with it – yet he could sense no reason. Part of him seemed tensed to breaking point, another still asleep, uncaring. Then below the tree he heard sniffing followed by a hoary bark.

"Yanish." He realised immediately, hissing the word to himself. From all around the base of the tree there came noises, then an ear-splitting howl followed closely by others nearby. The forest was alive with the fiercest of all the Endworld beasts. Lindarg had only seen one and that had been dead, for generally they shunned the haunts of the woodmen preferring the desolate far northern reaches of the forest where they could roam and kill unmolested. He recalled the long pointed snout of the one he had seen; the many rows of deadly teeth – acute and shiny, but most he remembered the hollow ones, six of them, through which the creature pumped a poison which killed a man agonisingly in moments. He had been told how men danced and cavorted in pain then suddenly fell dead whereupon the animal tore off limbs and crunched them up in its small but immensely powerful jaws. Mountain folk he had heard, hunted them for their skins which they traded but many of them died; Yanish were deadly, cunning and quick. Below him the pack closed in, thirsting for meat; scratching at the tree trunk. Lindarg wished for light so that he could see down there – then he did not want to see.

He did not know that Yanish could climb when pressed to do so but the rustle close by gripped him with a surge of terror; waking his whole body, alerting every sense. An evil snout thrust through the branches at his feet; jaws wide, poison teeth dripping. Lindarg recoiled but checked himself when he realised that to fall into the rest of the pack below was just as certain a death. Two burning yellow eyes regarded him and Lindarg was forced to look into their depths. At that moment the jaws closed; the animal simpered, swallowing hard; he could feel the animal's aggression slip away, then the face disappeared with a yelp. The whole pack fled, returning the forest to a profound silence. Lindarg breathed heavily, sweat beaded his brow but it was over, something had scared them and Lindarg felt he had played a part but could not guess how; it could not have been he who had set the beasts to flight, so what had? Hardly breathing, Lindarg listened long to every minute sound in the dark forest; torrid imaginings racking his mind but there was nothing to hear and after what seemed like an age of vigilance, he once more relaxed into sleep, undisturbed and deep.

For the whole of the next day he followed the path which wound doggedly on through the trees. It had obviously not been used – at least for several Starseasons since saplings grew on it and occasionally a few Astellot leaves. Fruits and nuts were becoming less frequent and the forest floor damper under foot. Again he spent the night – this time without incident – in a tree.

The following day saw changes. The Coldseason was beginning to make its presence felt and with only a small sliver of Yanish skin, Lindarg awoke shivering; hunger pains gnawing at his belly. Sliding quietly from the tree he picked up a stout branch and crept off the path in search of game. In no time he heard a rustle slightly ahead. Crouching, immobile he surveyed the clearing in front of him. A furry creature browsed over something in the grass, Lindarg inched nearer; the animal caught a sound and turned.

"A Yanish!" Realising the futility of fleeing before such a fleet creature, he remained still. Nonchalantly the animal returned its attention to its meal. "If only it was nearer and hadn't seen me," he thought weighing the stick in his hand. With a growl the Yanish backed, dragging its meal through the grass. Lindarg's whole body was tense and alert; he raised the cudgel as the animal edged nearer to the bush behind which he was crouched. 'Just a little more…' ran through his mind. The animal came backing into the bush. Lindarg raised the stick with both hands. 'Stay still!' was the thought in his head; the Yanish froze, then the branch crashed down, crunching the beast's neck and it lay dead.

Two days later Lindarg came face-to -face with the wild scattered plains north of the Forest of Dorn. The trees had dwindled quickly and now, suddenly before him was the brighter light of a cloud-dappled sky, and the scrub with the north wind bending it; beating on his skin.

He had no desire to leave the forest. Squatting in its sheltering eaves, he looked long over the bleakness which revealed the North Chain far in the distance; and yet he could not go back in there; back into the forest – the way he had come. His mind was turned that way; in it still the tatters of an empathy with a greatness which was even now beginning to evade him, as were other memories. Was Nayella a dream? Was there a reality of an existence behind him? The forest tracks did lead somewhere – or did they – was that too but a dream, a transient memory? Yet in him there was a deep past and stirrings that he could not place in his life – life? What had been the life in which he was trying to place them? More important, when?

But while his mind pondered wild thoughts and his heart strove to bring clarity to his purpose and existence, the needs of the flesh overcame them and foisted their own purposes. He was cold. It was darkening. He was hungry. Casting aside perplexities he immersed himself in the task of building a shelter. Bare hands tore and worked at branches, saplings and bushes; shaping, weaving – creating an aegis to cheat the wind. When it was done he did not rest but instead went forth in the darkness and frosty wind to find food and wood to burn. Later he slept in greater comfort than for many days.

For several days longer he lingered on the margin of the forest with a fire for company while the sleet battered ceaselessly on his refuge and the animal skins dried for covers on the icy nights. But one night, the warmth brought no comfort; the morning thrust him toward the mountains with the skins tight about him.

The shell that was Lindarg wandered ever northwards like an animal. Now there were no thoughts of Nayella – only those of the beast which creeps along the ditches keeping out of sight. Night was his domain; the time of the non-human and he felt at home; yet there was something in him that wished for other things. It drove him but seemed content at present for him to go unnoticed in the shadows and the tall plants but ever it threw him northwards – to what there was no guessing. And so he journeyed on, striking silent terror into the living things of the land, clambering slowly into the foothills of the northern mountains. Clothed now in many skins and eating always rich meat; always moving; the cold of the season did not encumber him and the woodman's body healed and toughened.

This was the first time in the history of Endworld that one such as this wandered free. Deep in the very weft and essence of life's forces there remain yet rules; the breaking of one causes ripples through that essence. The ripples are felt and they create some small disturbance somewhere that has repercussions – no more perhaps than a slight feeling in some Nether creature's mind – a tilt of the balance or status quo which has endured; endured because of its fineness and its dependence on other balances. Within the change, forces held in check on one side of the pivot, Old Ones – forgotten since their suspense – work again. Some say 'it is written…' which means it is part of that weft and essence and it is given to few of mankind – perhaps none – to know the reasons. These forces are also known as 'fate' and 'destiny' but whatever they are called, they are ordained and they operate only when the need for their actuation has been generated. That they will have an effect, therefore is inevitable; that they will work to redress the old balance or strike a new, inescapable. In troubled times many deeds may be done which defy the logic of the doers but their seeds have been sown round the pivot and in answer to one deed another is automatically fermented. None can say when or where the first seed was set, or by whom, nor the last…

But Lindarg was watched. Mighty though Venain was, there were other entities in Endworld about which he knew nothing. When he had claimed to be a god, finding everlasting life through the stone; when the Deathling had gone free; Endworld had felt it and Sylee too had sallied forth northwards to glean for himself what had been done. Now Sylee looked down upon a strange sight from a high crag.

"A man – or perhaps a man," he thought to himself, chuckling with the irony, struggled northwards and was now turning east – with no purpose – or perhaps he had? "Ah the riddles! What fun! A woodman of Dorn, yes – Lindarg, or perhaps not Lindarg. Deathling! Ah, again the irony!" Sylee was a picture of mirth. "I wonder who is the one that knows, the woodman and where his body goes?" Sylee laughed stupidly at his poetry and uttered more to please his mien.

"I wonder who is the one that knows -
The woodman and where his body goes?
And what aid is fate to lend
To befall that body's end?
And as it goes along its way,
What will it forge on each new day?
Mayhap 'tis beyond the world to tell
The errand of the Deathling fell.
So to you 'My Liege' – good speed
It isn't I who knows your deed!"

"Oooogh – eeegh – ha -ha!" Sylee laughed and continued to laugh as he turned back southwards. Lindarg had already disappeared over an eastern ridge; as Sylee, he knew nothing of the future – nor was it any concern of his.

Like the forest, Lindarg made the moorlands his home; so too the snow; he drank it, burrowed in it for shelter and tracked animals over its white softness – but always they came to him. Often there were days without food but then, after the days without, it was there; he knew hunger but never starvation. Hidden resolve ploughed him on and never did he falter until the morning he saw the Baeths following his tracks through the snow. They were far behind but travelling much faster than he on steeds and Lindarg felt something akin to confusion and panic. There was nowhere to go; nowhere to hide, no forest, no trees; only the snow-sprinkled foothills of the northern mountains. There was no escape so he ran – but his pursuers came faster and closed in. Lindarg heard the hot breath of the steeds on the slopes below him as he collapsed, exhausted in the white coldness of the snow and again his wrists felt the bonds of captivity.

4

BAETH MINES

L indarg was roughly thrown in; behind him, the iron grating clanged shut. After the silence following the receding steps of the laughing Baeths he became conscious of many other prisoners around him breathing regularly but otherwise noiseless in the dungeon's gloom. The chamber was large and full of captives like himself his mind's eye showed him bodies strewn about the floor, pressed together, his own body touched at least two others. Nothing stirred; far to the left a low moan drifted over the warm prostrate forms. He nudged one nearest to him but there was no response; a kick to one lying at his feet produced no more success. They were not to be easily wakened – and probably would not welcome it either. He slept with them in the inky blackness which descended with the coming of night beyond the grating.

First light brought noise and confusion into the dungeon. In moments, alert, disgusting travesties of human creatures writhed in a miserable heap where food had been cast through the bars. The cavern echoed with yells and unintelligible grunts as more scrambled for the food. Some ate; most didn't and two were crushed amid the threshing melee. More food was wasted than consumed, while the two dead bodies were dragged out beneath the partially lifted grating. Shortly afterwards a frantic baying in the distance suggested rather than confirmed their final fate. Lindarg shuddered.

These men were not men he recognised, not the hefty woodmen, but Gulleners. Then he found himself wondering;

'Gulleners? Who are they?' He had never heard of Gulleners but instinctively he knew that some were from that city. 'City?' He knew of no city in the forest kingdom. Then he wasn't sure about a forest kingdom either.

He regarded them, debased, filthy wretches of men; haggard, broken, shattered spirits; animals – or worse! And yet they had been fine men once; some among them had been proud Farislanders but Lindarg could not fathom how he knew. He felt the urge to speak and selected one near to him.

"You…" but the man shrank away, clutching a few morsels. He turned to another who seemed yet quite strong and who had grabbed the most food. The man glared defiance and ate faster as their glances met.

"Who are you?" demanded Lindarg. The man's jaw dropped.

"… Ah…"

"Speak!"

"D… D… Durnor."

"I am Lindarg." The jaw fell open again.

"L-Lind – argh…" But he was interrupted and the flicker of interest which had crossed Durnor's face was extinguished by a mask of horror and despair. The grating scraped open; outside were Baeths and Yanish, sleek well-fed animals with rows of glistening teeth.

Like weary machines the captives filed out through the opening, pushed and kicked on their way by jovial Baeths whose trained Yanish glared threateningly at the file of effaced, emaciated men. Lindarg watched as they withered further in the stare of those creatures; their fear of them was a phobia. In terror, the line shuffled over the dusty bare earth red with ore, tatters of clothes flapping as they bent into the biting wind. There were no shackles or ropes to prevent escape and the Baeth masters had no whips or sticks; the obedience of the prisoners was absolute because their terror of Yanish ultimate. Lindarg followed behind Durnor, keeping close to his one contact but shuffling like the rest. He passed a Yanish, ignoring his presence and the animal became uneasy. Its attendant Baeth sensed its disquiet putting it down to the presence of a new and healthy captive. He gave the beast more rein and was satisfied when Lindarg cringed and shook as it moved toward him. The captives shambled on into the gaping red mines of Baeth.

Filing into the dusty darkness they came upon the others labouring out encrusted with a clinging red grime, pushing heavy wooden carts piled as high as the stone roof would allow, with rich, heavy ore. Lindarg could not understand how such beaten wraiths of men could toil so hard but he was soon to find out. As the tunnel narrowed, those coming up were closer to, trudging with glazed eyes. To one of them a Yanish was leashed; snapping at his calves, bloody gashes where teeth had closed on flesh too weak and too slow. Another fell and died, fighting to control the burden that was too heavy and Lindarg caught his breath as the truck began to roll back on the steepening slope, but it jerked to a sudden stop. There were ratchets on the wheels; these were the cause of the incessant clanging sound they made. The man in front of Durnor was pushed across. Automatically he took up the cart handles and began to continue its journey out of the mine. Lindarg breathed a sigh of relief; he had nearly lost Durnor. He realised too that whoever had designed the carts, knew in what circumstances they would be used and had shrewdly guessed at the state of the men who would push them. Not a single lump of ore was spilled, nor was an inch of ground ever lost.

The noise from below was reaching a crescendo; scores of picks hammered and reverberated; carts clicked and creaked; smoke filled the galleries as yellow torch flames flickered and guttered in the foul air, but there were no more guards and no more Yanish. Lindarg marvelled that the toil went on unabated. Frail, exhausted men hacked and shovelled; the pace never slowed and there were no rests. It was unbelievable. Momentarily he broke away from the line to draw a man's attention but the man merely cast his glassy eyes upwards and returned to the ore.

Sometime during the day, they left their work, returned to

the surface and were given a little dirty water and a few morsels of equally dirty food. Lindarg gave his to Durnor, seeing beneath Durnor's glassy eyes a spark of life which did not quite die as it had before.

Then a hideous thing was done. A wandering captive, nearly blind with fatigue, stumbled into one of the Baeth guards who cursed and grasped the wretch's arm angrily. Other guards nearby chided him, aggravating his ire. He kicked his dozing Yanish sharply and it sprang up with an aggressive yelp. The poor captive froze in terror, shaking uncontrollably as the animal menaced him. With a cruel smile the guard took up the beast's rein and using its free end, tied the man's hands behind his back. The tortured anguish of the hapless man was obvious, and the end, probably inevitable.

Some animals delight in toying with a victim before delivering the fatal blow; this was true of these Yanish. In its first bite there was no poison and it was only a nibble, but its effect on the man was devastating. Screaming and dodging he ran helplessly in circles; fell; ran more, pitched; ran more, then fell again. Eyes sparkling, the animal had paced him effortlessly and now, meanly, it sidled up to bite him again. This time there was a little poison – just enough to give a searing spasm of pain. Again the man was galvanised into action; running, falling, gyrating, screaming, moaning.

Lindarg did nothing.

The pain of the third bite drove the man completely beyond sanity and he threshed and foamed in a cloud of red dust. The Yanish was wrenched a few times by flailing arms which seemed to be everywhere at once – despite their incapacitation; but the animal was only stimulated by the struggle, revelling in the final throes. Finally, it crunched open the man's head as if it were no more than a bird's empty egg.

It was already dark when they were returned to the sleeping chamber after an endless tour of labour during the rest of the day, Lindarg knew Durnor was nearby.

"Durnor." The hissed urgency of Lindarg's voice was

absorbed by the mass of prostrate bodies. There was no reply. "Durnor!" This time he shouted.

"Aah... Lin... dargh -" It was a shattered sound but very near. Lindarg moved toward it and could just make out Durnor supported on one elbow.

"Are you alright?"

"H-h-ungry... t-t-thirs-s-ty..." The voice in the dark face before him tailed off.

"We must talk," pursued Lindarg.

"Talk -? No strength... dus-s-st -"

"Then we must eat."

"Eat? How...?"

"I will get food, Durnor -" But as he said the words, Lindarg was unsure himself where the food would come from.

He regarded Durnor's dim shadow, feeling the pity for these men surge within him. He was tired and worn after one day's toil – how often had Durnor and the others been through this circadian hell? Then he knew that, not only must he escape, but so too must these unfortunates. He did not know how this would be accomplished, but was certain that he must try. The thought gave him purpose; the purpose, strength to proceed.

"Come," he said to the dark shape. Stiffly, Durnor followed Lindarg's lead to the grating. Side – by – side they peered beyond its bars. A dull night glow showed them the guarding Yanish breathing quietly in the stillness; ideas began to form themselves in Lindarg's mind.

Suddenly the Yanish was bolt upright and staring straight at them. Its lightning movement caused Durnor to cry out and cringe back into the shadows. Forcefully Lindarg retrained him. Durnor struggled and shivered in his firm hold but lacked the strength to break it. In an instant Lindarg knew the Yanish and it knew him and was held by the man's glare. Slowly it turned and effortlessly bit through its tether, padded demurely to the grating, through it and into Lindarg's hands which quickly wrung its neck like a damp cloth. Durnor was wild-eyed, gazing from Lindarg to the dead animal and back again. Finally, he plucked up courage and gingerly prodded the warm fur. Then he smiled in wonder.

At the rear of the chamber, away from sleeping captives, they drank warm blood and tore at stiffening muscles.

"Do not eat too much at once – it will not stay down." Lindarg cautioned. Durnor hesitated and Lindarg continued. "We have all night – there is no hurry – and there is much we must discuss."

After a long pause punctuated only by the deep breaths which followed hasty mouthfuls, Lindarg asked:

"Most of these people are of Gullen and the Southlands – but not you – where is your land Durnor?"

"I… and some of my friends…" He hesitated, looking over toward the dark mass of bodies, "are from Farisle."

"Farisle?" Lindarg had heard of the place but only in some distant memory. He knew nothing about it.

"It is far to the north, past the boundaries of the Baeth lands, beyond the further mountains and out into the seas." Durnor's eyes moistened with recollection but his sorrow was a secret in the darkness as he mumbled, "A fair land I fear I will never see again."

"Indeed it sounds a fine place." consoled Lindarg.

"Ravaged by Baeths!" Durnor spat those words into the red dust.

"What is torn may be re-made – and none can say of the future who is to see what for the first time – or again." Lindarg caught his own words and wondered at them. They had been spoken in the Farislander's tongue, not the pidgin language common to Endworld and they had issued, unbidden from his inner self; he shuddered. Durnor was taken aback; questions surged into his mouth.

"Who are you to know our tongue? And the Yanish, it was like a furry frinnet in your grasp – and less dangerous. You are more than you seem, from which land are you?"

"I – I cannot say…"

"But I cannot trust who I do not know!"

"Then I must answer as I can, though I am not sure. Perhaps

40

I am Lindarg of Dorn, but the name means little to me. My past is like a sea of mist and there have been changes; now I am as uncertain of my name and origin as I am of my purpose and what has led me thus..." Lindarg's voice broke off, trying to think of more to say in answer. Durnor gave no response and at last, after a quiet in which both were lost deep in their own thoughts, Lindarg said, "We must escape."

"It was tried at first, but there is no hope -" Lindarg ignored Durnor's despair.

"You mentioned 'others' -"

"My kinsmen lie among them." Durnor motioned to the sleeping forms; the gesture lost in the blackness.

"Then they will join us?"

"They have not the strength or will -"

"Had you before today?" Lindarg's question was finely put, Durnor paused.

"No it is true. But you have given me heart!" There was gratitude in his eyes; Lindarg could almost feel it in the dark between them.

"Then we must work together and make whatever plans we can. Each must know his part but our captors must not suspect!" Lindarg paused for a moment then added, "Your kinsmen from Farisle -" but Durnor was ahead of him.

"-I was their leader -" Durnor's voice was self reproachful and bitter, recalling their defeat at Baeth hands. "I must do what I can do to repay the debt of that defeat. You have offered me opportunity Lindarg; I will grasp it gratefully!" Lindarg felt a firm hand on his shoulder reading courage and determination in its grip. Momentarily the grip faltered. "But what of the Yanish? Even fed, my folk and the Gulleners will make no move to escape."

Lindarg's reply was sympathetic. "We must do what we can to break down that fear – are you as afraid?" He tossed the question to Durnor.

"It would be easy to say that I am less afraid now, having half eaten one and with you here… but out there – alone…"

"You will know tomorrow," was all Lindarg said.

The following day was little different from the one before. Lindarg wondered whether Durnor's apparent fear of the Yanish was real or well-feigned. He didn't ask, and was not told. But the day did bring luck. It rained so hard that water running into the mine turned the red dust into a treacherous, slippery mud and no matter how much goading was applied to the hapless toilers, they were unable to push the carts up the incline out of the mine. Even the Baeths realised that the task was hopeless, and after the carts had all been filled below ground, work was halted and the captives returned to the chamber to sleep.

The incident gave substance to Lindarg's vague notions of escape and lent time for preparations. As the Baeth guards finally wandered away, they failed to notice that two of their prisoners were far from asleep. Farislanders were being moved to the rear of the chamber. Durnor was firm with his fellows; any who resisted, preferring to escape back into the soft release of sleep, were cuffed and dragged back to reality by Durnor's curses.

"Andur!" he screamed at one. "You cannot end like this! I will not let you! Move, you sluggard!" Then he turned to Lindarg. "We will need more food." Lindarg saw his eyes moist with anguish at the state of his kinsmen.

"Stay with them. I can see to the animal alone."

"Good luck – and be careful!" The hissed voice full of friendship and hope warmed Lindarg.

"I will!" He smiled to himself in the dark. He had been thinking about slaughtering another of the awful beasts for a little while and was quite looking forward to the confrontation. It came sooner than he expected. Long before he neared the grating, two yellow-green eyes appeared ahead of him and the animal which he had been going to kill padded silently up to meet him.

With the Yanish dead at his side, Lindarg sat in the passage reflecting on what had happened. It needed to be thought about. Had he willed an animal he could not see? Could merely thinking about a Yanish bring those nearby? The one in the forest – had it been alone in that clearing by chance – or had his own thoughts brought it there unknown to him; for him? The possibilities which this power presented were chilling, and worse, not understood.

By morning Lindarg knew the names and voices of the seven others whom Durnor had gathered around him, leaving their faces for the daylight.

Like Durnor, Andur too had been a leader of men – a small force which had been swept off the face of the earth by the Baeth might which had whirled suddenly like the wind off the seas. Eisdan, Fanor, Karil and Turg had been among those few skilled fighters of a beleaguered land; as Durnor and Andur they were adept with swords, highly trained and swift in close combat. Durgel and Durgol, Lindarg learned, were brothers both in blood and craft. They too had been skilled swordsmen but their main task had been to oversee the forging of weapons to defend their home, a task soon ended by the ignominity of surrender. Eisdan said little that night but when their spirits had risen and they discussed the plan to escape he had said; "I see little hope in such a plan, yet without it there is none. Death only, awaits us here. If the chance to gain some recompense from these murderers leads also to death, then so be it. Vengeance at least will make it sweeter." His voice had been fatalistic but Lindarg had drawn heart from the depths of its vehemence and the muttered agreements which cemented their resolve in its wake. "Aye," rejoined Andur, "That is a satisfying thought at least!"

The mines dried at last – except for the lowest tunnels – and work was resumed with added vigour. The extra days' rest was being used to great advantage by the Baeths who, with more Yanish than usual in evidence, were demanding increased efforts from the captives.

All morning Lindarg and the Farislanders worked steadily,

if slowly; after the food break they stopped altogether. Andur led Durgol, Durgel, Karil and Turg into the water-sodden parts of the mine. Using cupped hands, they cradled water back to the working level and threw it over the lower portion of the ascending cart-way tunnel. After several journeys the slope was made impassable by carts, though the captives ever more frantically tried to push them up, often several to a cart. But it was no use.

Lindarg, Durnor, Faran and Eisdan had remained in the galleries trying to discourage the workers and alert them to the plan. Lindarg had quietly disposed of two Yanish, he wasn't ready to display his powers yet. They had guessed rightly that they would not be able to persuade the captives to stop work or understand the plan, but the meat Lindarg offered did more than words could hope to do. The wetting of the cart-way gave them no choice; no ore would leave the mine; all there knew what that would lead to and panic set in with the realisation.

Men hacked away at rock feverishly – as if somehow they would thus avoid the retribution which snarling Yanish would wreak upon them. Others milled around helplessly; none dared to escape up the tunnel.

"Stay close!" Lindarg shouted. "They come!" The noise of the animals' approach could now be clearly heard and it was joined by the whimpering of the men in the mine. Carnage was imminent. Lindarg placed himself a few paces before the opening; behind him were the eight Farislanders; he felt, rather than knew what to do.

With a final slithering and baying six ferocious Yanish issued full pelt from the sloping cart-way, saw Lindarg, and stopped as instantly as if they had run into the rock itself. In his stare, their eyes lowered and their mouths closed, then they padded around listlessly in the torchlight.

"Kill them!" yelled Lindarg. In the silence that followed the shout, the Farislanders, showing no fear, butchered the animals with picks and shovels.

"Give me a sword!" muttered Karil spiritedly as he lanced

one with a shovel, slicing its side open with ease. "Then I would settle some scores!"

"We!" Andur enjoined, casting him a meaningful grin. "If there are swords above we will have them, Karil."

The captives always ate when they were told to; now they were being told to and they ate. Lindarg and the Farislanders went among the feasters, nursing and coaxing spirit, making the noises of speech; slowly arousing decaying minds and leperous bodies. More Yanish arrived. This time one or two of the Gulleners killed and they marvelled at Lindarg's power. 'Wizard', was mentioned by more than one among them.

With the second wave of Yanish eaten, time became of the essence. Lindarg called the Farislanders around him.

"I think perhaps we have little time left. Soon the Baeths will send soldiers down – little though they might relish these dark musty tunnels – we have forced it upon them and alas, I have no power over men. But first, talk to those who will listen, talk of escape and hope, find out what you can. Seek leaders; those who know; those who might show spirit in the end. Tell them to take up their picks – not for hacking away at rock – but for slaughtering Baeths!"

"If it can be done, we will do it!" Durnor hissed for them.

"Also," continued Lindarg, "There is little enough light left above in this dark Coldseason, and we would be helpless in the dark. Make haste!"

Catching Lindarg's last words, they swept off among the men. At last many began to talk and think; the babble of voices gradually rose in volume – soon it would be heard above.

"Lindarg!" Durnor hailed from a distance along the gallery. Lindarg joined him.

"This man has news." Durnor motioned to a large and probably once proud man whose face was alive, quivering with eagerness.

"Our queen," blurted the man, "she is held captive also…"

"A queen captive?" broke in Lindarg, his face changing a little

45

before he added distantly, "Then we must save her as we may. Where is she held?"

"There is a stone room by the Baeth guard quarters, I think she is there." The man's face displayed revulsion and he looked away with moist eyes. Lindarg read the meaning in his expression; some of the captives would probably have seen or heard her being used. The thought set his heart pounding. He must rescue her; he had to – there was a reason – it would be humane, yes but there was something more – a bond? He did not know why this Southern Queen was so important to him, yet he knew what had to be done, his whole body thrilled with the idea.

He guessed there was no more time. Gulleners with little to fight with and as yet little fight in them could not meet Baeth soldiers down here and survive; it would be a massacre. They needed room; they had to go now. He must rescue the queen himself.

"Durnor, Faran…" The finality of Lindarg's tone told them what he was about to say, and as Lindarg entered the bottom of the tunnel to the surface, they incited the Gulleners to follow.

There had been no time to think of further plans; everything was chaotic, Gulleners surged after Lindarg up the tunnel; carts were cast aside and Lindarg heartened to hear and feel the fury awakening in his followers. He himself was afraid, afraid of what might await them at the entrance of the mines; a whole Baeth army might be ranged across the red earth, ready to thwart the escape as if it were no more than a brief rush of stale air. He could hear the Farislanders behind amid the Gullen cries; the drive gathered speed; then the entrance was upon them.

As they coursed out into the light, hope rose in Lindarg. Only a score or so of ill-prepared Baeths faced the fierce tide of captives who poured from the red hell-hole in his wake.

"Kill them and flee south!" he yelled jubilantly, sending Yanish scurrying from their path. Suddenly bereft of their animal weapons, the Baeths stood transfixed; confused before the

46

onslaught of embittered men. In moments they were ruthlessly hacked by the mob and their bloodied bodies scattered underfoot. Durnor and Durgel felled a Baeth each but the escaping throng needed no further encouragement. Again Lindarg's shout rose above the tumult.

"Go! South! Their army must soon follow!" He rushed to the stone room by the empty guard quarters and halted at the door.

There was a Yanish inside, wary and frightened by the noise. At his unseen command, the beast bit itself and died quickly. The door was firmly locked. Lindarg charged it but it refused to budge. Suddenly he felt helpless; somewhere in the blood-soaked, trampled earth where the Baeths had stood was the key. Frustration overwhelmed him as he surveyed the scattered, pulpy bodies; the keys might be trodden in – or snatched – he would never find them in time alone!

The last of the Gulleners were disappearing over the unkempt fields and out of sight to the south, the noise of their passing fading. But as he looked, eight figures were returning. Recognising the Farislanders, Lindarg waved them away.

"Leave with the others – that is your only hope – fly south!"

"No!" It was Durnor who spoke and the breathless word was final. "You need help – we will give it." Their faces would not be argued with and Lindarg's mind flashed back to the queen.

"The key! It must have been on a guard but I cannot find it!" Faran and Eisdan smiled, gripping their picks more tightly.

"We are well practiced with them," intoned Faran as they ranged on the massive wooden door. The sound of their blows was deafening but the wood gave only slowly to their pounding. It was ancient wood from the Great Brown trees – perhaps grown eons past in a forest long gone in these lands. Andur and Karil took over from them, but it was not until they were all exhausted that the door finally gave way.

Inside, the queen lay in rags on a straw mat, chained

47

restrictively to the rough wall. In a glance Lindarg noticed the bruises of her ill treatment and his heart was heavy for her – yet strangely, it was lighter than it had ever been since he could remember. When their eyes met, in the same glance, there was something deeper – perhaps recognition, desire, gratitude, which passed between them. But the fleeting moment was gone as soon come, Andur was hacking at the wall fastenings with Eisdan. As they jerked free, the queen whirled out of the door and away from the mines, carried by the Farislanders.

Fleeing across the first open field, they could hear the clamour of Baeth soldiers from behind the hill, readying themselves for pursuit. Soon they would swarm in their wake… At last, the queen spoke between hurried breaths.

"I will run as you, we will cover the ground faster that way." They let her feet drop and to their amazement she ran faster than they – lithely for all her sufferings – over the grass, chains rattling about her. Lindarg and the Farislanders paced her, thudding southwards toward Gullen as dusk began to fall.

Already they were meeting stragglers from the fleeing rabble; then the rabble itself, worn out and spent; the feebly-sloping ground had finished them; they had no choice but to rest. Some already slept on the cold earth, flight forgotten.

There was no food, they were poorly clothed and the Coldseason night was closing in fast. Lindarg scanned their rear. Seeing nothing, he thought it probable that the Baeths would hold their pursuit until first light the next day and reflected bitterly that the few hours' delay would not affect the outcome of their hunt. It was a small comfort that they might have one long, cold night of freedom.

It took a long time to herd the Gulleners together, where at least they would be warmer and safer in the bleak dark hours, but Lindarg's heart was leaden. Ahead were the marshes – given away by lush waving grasses and wispy trees – already the ground underfoot was damp. They would have to climb into the foothills to skirt it. Many would not make the climb and those who did would only run until the next day or the day after when they either fell with exhaustion or were overtaken by the Baeth army. It didn't really matter which he reflected. The queen too was crestfallen as she regarded the forlorn leader of a battered and beaten rabble.

"You should not have stayed for me," she said. "Precious time was wasted. I can be of no use in this venture and I will be thought dead by those in Gullen. Perhaps that would have been better."

Lindarg was at a loss for words. "What difference would there have been? Still these people would have come no further than here – indeed, many may go no further. And if they had, how much longer would they have kept their freedom – another day?"

"True -" She broke off searching for a name.

"Lindarg," he offered; the queen resumed.

"True Lindarg, it is far yet to the Southlands where Gullen lies – many days' ride, and on foot; who knows?" She pondered awhile as Lindarg stared at the ground, then continued; "But I do not feel that we are finished – more, that this is a beginning – and yet our position seems hopeless."

"A few could perhaps escape and hide," suggested Lindarg, but his heart was not in such a venture.

The queen sensed his lack of conviction, but said, "You, and these men here -" She indicated the Farislanders who were sprawled on the meadow grass. "There is a chance you might survive to warn Gullen and seek help."

"Gullen?" Lindarg was again helpless. "I do not know where it lies, except south from the Baeth mines, and if it is as far as you say, then in this wilderness we would soon lose our way and perish in vain."

The queen's amazement showed plainly but she hesitated to comment, then; "Surely Gullen is known to you?"

"No – and neither to the Farislanders, they are from the sea lands north of Endworld."

"And you...?" The queen's face was questioning as she spoke.

49

"I... I am... Lindarg..." he finished, unsure.

"What is your land?" pursued the queen.

"I am not sure – a forest I remember, but that is all."

"Then you are not a great leader?"

"No, my Queen, just Lindarg."

"You have no past?"

"None that I can remember."

"That is strange, Lindarg, but of your future I may be able to help you in time."

"How?"

"I feel our futures are bound together and that they are not at an end here, but you puzzle me much." Her eyes were thoughtful as she regarded him. "I have never seen a Yanish bite itself... except..." She saw his wry smile. "It was your doing, wasn't it?" she stated.

"Yes, but I don't understand how, or why -" Lindarg tailed off, unable to explain further.

"No," she agreed musingly. "Few people are given to understand themselves and you, it seems, less than most." Lindarg could see that she could have said more, perhaps ached to say more, but for now she remained silent.

"My future; you said you might help but have not said how, and I cannot conceive that you should know more about me than I do."

"Aah, Lindarg, not I who knows; there are things more powerful than we in Endworld."

"What things?"

"Gems, perhaps, or a spell; but our great wizard is feared perished at the hands of the evil sorcerer Venain a season ago, and without his guidance there may be no help..." She stopped abruptly as if a sudden thought had occurred to her, then continued. "But this speculation does not help us now. The present problem is more immediate and without its solution the future is likely to hold nothing for any of us." Suddenly she looked up, deeply into Lindarg's eyes and said, "Why did you lead an escape?"

"I am driven from within by a force I cannot reconcile. Even now it is becoming restless and will doubtless compel me upon some action which is without merit, plunging me into yet another hopeless situation as now – but if I did not heed it, then I fear I would do nothing, even be nothing." His voice was soft, far away as he spoke the last words; thoughtful; turned inward.

The queen caught his mood, making guesses at its meaning and stared long at Lindarg searching for answers, knowing them to be there, feeling their importance. Something deep in this strange man keened at her; plucking at her senses. At length she said, "Then let it drive you. Those men who have spoken are full of praise for you. It drives you well."

Lindarg had to agree. In a short time, he had achieved much and gained acclaim in the eyes of these men of Gullen and Farisle but the strength came from within. It was not his.

Karil had been listening to the conversation.

"Lindarg," he broke into their thoughts, "our position seems hopeless and will not be made any more so by lighting fires, hunting and eating – if food can be found – and at least some will have the strength to face their end tomorrow." Eisdan and Faran nodded nearby. "Some may even have the strength to be lucky," he finished.

5

THE CHANGING OF THE WAYS

The Farislanders did much that night to bring comfort and a little cheer. Little enough there was of each, but that little given then was worth half the riches of Endworld to those who received it. Lindarg did nothing all night but emptily watch the goings-on and the fires, hearing distantly the few voices as a tuneless accompaniment to his brooding inner dark which shunned the outer dark of night. There seemed no drive – only a void within. He marvelled that the Farislanders could behave as though preparing for life the following day, when that day could only bring certain death. Among the gatherings round the fires talk steadily dwindled: rest came uneasily and with an air of finality. Alone amid them all, only the queen kindled some spirit – and that fading as the mist became white over the swamp with daybreak.

Weary, but somehow with a liveliness the eight Farislanders stood in the early light and regarded Lindarg sitting, head in hands. He had hardly moved since the dawn. Next to him the queen, more awake than he, peered into their faces, sensing something. It was Durnor who spoke.

"Sire." There was no response from Lindarg. "Sire!" The tone was urgent now.

Slowly Lindarg's head rose to meet their gaze and Durnor continued: "We of Farisle have talked this night and are of one accord. You have saved us from the Baeths and their mines, from Yanish and from our own despair. In doing this you have given hope mayhap to our people – though they may never know. For these things we have elected to serve you as liegemen in your fight with the foes of Endworld. Your death only will release us from this vow save our own passing – and that only grudgingly." From behind him Durnor produced a gift and eight hands offered the wooden sword to him over the dewy grass. In the daze of being little more than half awake, Lindarg took it as it was offered, marvelling at its making amid such chaos. The first gleam of the rising sun was captured and thrown off the polished wood; once a shard of the Brownwood door of the queen's prison; before that part of a mighty tree felled in a forest whose memory only remained beneath the soils of these times and places.

Momentarily Lindarg's heart was lightened and he bore the flicker of a smile; within him something stirred at the touch of the old wood. He opened his mouth to speak but the moment was cut short by a shout from below.

"Baeths!"

It was a fearful shout, as compelling as inevitable; desolate in the damp air. A massive column of fighting men appeared from the thinning mists. There was no choice but to stagger above the marshes and blindly they did so, following the vanguard of Lindarg, the eight Liegemen of Farisle and the Southern Queen.

It was hopeless. Remorselessly, weary men forced worn bodies up the slope but the Baeths were closing fast and all realised that there was no time left for flight – a flight that gained little ground and sapped whatever vestiges of strength were left. Agony was blazoned on the faces of those who ran, stumbling upwards, more slowly with every step; despair on those crawling. Some distance above them Lindarg's fleeter party stopped and turned reluctantly to look down as the first of the Baeths brandished their weapons and prepared the run the straggling Gulleners down. The queen wept as the slowest Gullener twisted round, helpless as a trapped frinnet – to face and fight the Baeth soldier who had caught him up. Even the small branch was too heavy for the man and as he swung it toward the soldier's head the point of steel appeared through the man's back, blood soaking the rags that he wore.

Andur raised his sword – stolen from the body of a guard, fury and grief etched on his countenance. "Let us fight!" He yelled to the other liegemen. Karil started forward with him.

"No…" Durnor stayed them but Karil stared defiance.

"With a sword in my hand I will not stand and watch while friends are slaughtered by a common foe!"

"That is my feeling also," interrupted Eisdan, "I too thirst for Baeth blood but I will spill it here, beside our liege; together. Let them come – the wait will not be long; savour it!"

Durnor's glance thanked him for his support, but the liegemen were torn. They would have descended to meet their attackers; descended to their deaths on the valley floor but they would not leave Lindarg and he sensed their dichotomy from their wretched faces.

Only moments separated their bid for freedom from an end of butchery and carnage. Lindarg was sick inside; anger, frustration, guilt and dejection devastated his being.

Then Lindarg changed. Those near to him looked upon a placid countenance with furrowed brows – beneath which eyes burned and narrowed as he stared down into the valley below.

Now the Baeth army rushed headlong over the meadow grass by the swamp toward them following a clear beaten track curving up the hillside which seemed to promise an inviting course to their goal. But no – the track divided before a sheer scarp and veered into the swamps. Not swamps! Where the swamps had been was meadow, and over it the paths and tracks ran in the open. Baeths divided with the tracks and poured onto the paths. Some leaders followed a path upwards across sloping meadowland and it changed back into a swamp as they ran over it. Screaming and floundering they were enveloped in the very real, sucking mire. With their unaccountable demise came utter chaos among the Baeth ranks as apparent meadow, paths, tracks and cliffs became a flux with the swamp and apparent swamp was revealed to be meadow. No way was safe, none as it seemed.

The broadest track of ancients would turn back into swamp and engulf; a branching path would promise a way out of the mires – only to be replaced by swamp. Swamplands black and deep revealed themselves to be real meadow but they had been avoided by the assailants and the reality beneath the illusion was only realised as the once-firm ground gave way to a wallowing death under their stamping feet. Ways changed with increasing rapidity until the valley was a fitful blur of changing terrain and floundering bodies. The air was rent with the screams of uncomprehending, terrified men scattering hither and thither over ways which came and went – illusory and real.

Some who fell grovelling and wailing into apparent swamp found themselves on the green grass of the meadow but they were maddened, shattered by their fear. The lucky ones were those whose chosen way changed back to swamp and who never saw the light of evil days again. Luckier still were those who froze with fright on the real meadow and heeded not as the illusion perched them over treacherous bogs – then back onto the meadow: they hid their eyes and it was their own eyes that deceived them. A blind man walks on firm ground – not that which looks firm.

And so the Baeth force was routed – a handful fled in terror – but most were swallowed up by the swamp and a dead silence fell upon the valley as the flux faded into reality and those who had watched tried to believe what they had seen. The queen caught Lindarg as he fell like a withered, fallen leaf of Dundellin. He too had seen – and could not believe – the impossible.

For two days Lindarg slept, nursed by the Southern Queen as if he were her own child, never leaving his side. The liegemen gathered scattered Gulleners together and arranged a makeshift camp with fires and food to strengthen frail bodies for the journey to Gullen.

A short distance from the leafy shelter they had built for

Lindarg and their queen, Durnor, Durgel and two Gulleners sat on guard beside a warming fire. Always there were two or three of the Farislanders watching over the shelter and their liege. For their nearness and concern the queen was deeply grateful; Lindarg oblivious. Again their conversation went over the events of the previous day as if trying to confirm or establish what had happened.

"The changing of the ways," mused Durgel aloud. "Surely it must be the only battle Endworld has ever known where the victors have never lifted a weapon, spilled not one drop of enemy blood – yet won as surely as if their foes had never been!"

"And perhaps your very words carry a deeper meaning," added Durnor. One of the Gulleners broke in:

"It is certainly Gullen's first victory over a large Baeth force."

"And how it was achieved!" burst in the other. "Surely you serve a great wizard, Durnor!"

"He says not."

"They never do – for in secrecy, it is said, lies much of their power," the Gullener retorted, adding, "I too would serve such a worthy liege to the death. You have chosen well and have already earned much esteem among our people. Gullen will honour you – of that there can be no doubt. Much you Farislanders have done for us!"

"We bear a deep gratitude to our liege and sense that he works toward an end that even he does not or cannot see. We have vowed to aid him; that is how we feel." Durgel nodded, then Durnor continued; "It may be that Gullen is – or will be – part of these things; is bound up with our future. If so, then Gullen we will serve also." He paused, regarding the Gulleners' faces – set with respect for the foreigners, these Farislanders: determined men, proven leaders among them. Eisdan joined them to warm himself.

"But we do not know that Lindarg wrought our victory," suggested Durgel though there was little conviction in the statement for those who had been closest to Lindarg had seen the change. They had seen the anguish, doubt and indecision vanish; in its place had been power: steadfast, irrepressible.

"Who else then – the queen?"

But the other Gullener answered his own question. "I do not think it was her."

Eisdan regarded him. "Perhaps not -" he paused and looked fixedly at Durnor, "but she knows more than she says – or she suggests more and whether it was Lindarg or not she has paid him very close attention."

Durnor nodded agreement. Eisdan always seemed to have considered things which others had missed.

"I have heard of such a thing happening before," said the first Gullener, "but so far in the past that the account is but a story for children – and one which they quickly forget."

"It might be the valley itself – there is something about it…" Durgel's tone was reverent as he gazed at the tumble of terrain below them.

"And why," challenged the Gullener, "should the land so favour us? It is not our land – nor would we want it to be – these northern parts are cold." He shivered in the short silence, then went on. "The Southlands have been threatened by Baeths for some time but we are scattered on the lands, loving peace: to grow our food; living quietly in villages. In these times we need a great leader such as Lindarg to build an army and marshall our defences. Perhaps that is what he will seek to do." The Gullener sighed, then went on: "Once we had little need to fear the Baeths and they left us alone but our wizard – Virdil – left the city for distant deeds beyond the Forest of Dorn not long ago. The queen was with him. Our small force was a rearguard for their party but we were attacked by Baeths. Massively outnumbered, we were swiftly captured. The queen's force and the queen herself were also taken while our wizard was elsewhere. What remains of those two forces is here. Our wizard is feared lost and doubtless Gullen now lies defenceless." His face was a mirror of despondency.

"We too were taken unawares by the ever-greedy and cruel Baeths," enjoined Durgel.

"Then our meeting here could surely be a changing of the ways for the honest folk of Endworld, perhaps fate has brought us together to rid Endworld of the Baeth blight."

"There are doubtless other evils waiting to replace them – some even of our own making," broke in the other Gullener. "Whatever Virdil sought was important and might have destroyed him."

"If that is so then Baeths might be the least of our worries!"

"This wizard, Virdil," whispered Eisdan, "Did the queen know him well?

"Yes, they were often together – they and the council were the guardians of the Southlands and Gullen." The exchange was followed by silence. Durnor was puzzled by Eisdan's enquiry but knew he would have good reason. Finally Durnor spoke.

"There is much that you Gulleners must teach us of these lands, their stories and peoples. Already you have mentioned Dorn, Virdil, the Southlands, the council and now you hint at something worse than Baeths!"

"Of the latter we know nothing more than we have already told, Durnor," said the Gullener, "but of the Northfolk, Eastfolk and Westfolk; of Gullen itself, the magnificent Forest of Dorn – its king and the woodmen who live there -"

"Hold!" yelled Durnor good-naturedly, "These tales must do another time! For now, let us rest!"

Despite the haunting mist over the marshes and the evening shadows: despite the bodies beneath its mires and the drift of the damp night air, sleep that night was strangely peaceful and secure.

On the third day after the changing of the ways, Lindarg awoke. The queen and the liegemen displayed their relief and joy but Lindarg had forgotten the shattering of the Baeth hordes and how it had happened, disbelieving their accounts. He was utterly ashamed that he had passed out as soon as things fared badly. He brooded alone and would not look anyone in the face, saying nothing, always restless and ever looking south. He avoided looking at the marshes. To him they were sinister and he was no less fearful of them than others who could remember seeing, who all recounted the same tale of the fate of their foes. A tale of the land in riot beneath them and as they told it their eyes spoke of his part; said that he, Lindarg, had set that chaos: had changed the ways; had saved them all by wizardry. Lindarg could not accept that meaning in those eyes.

That same day, Andur and Turg had captured four beasts to ride and had departed with two Gulleners southwards to Gullen for help and with news – news which the city could hardly hope to hear in these times.

"We hope to meet you on our way to Gullen," said Durnor to them as they prepared to leave. "Be careful, ride fast and stop for no-one."

"It is you who have the difficult task and should be careful!" Andur threw back and casting a glance at Lindarg added, "You have our liege to guard – more from himself I fear; we have only ourselves! And mark this, sore will be your trials should he be lost when we next meet!" The threat was friendly; sporting, but beneath it was the meaning.

Durnor slapped Andur's exposed thigh heartily, "On, precious cur," and watched as the riders receded becoming mere dots lost in the tumble of the horizon, then vanishing from sight. He approached Lindarg. "You are rested well, Sire?"

Lindarg grunted but said nothing.

Durnor persevered. "Andur and Turg have left for Gullen with two Gulleners to tell of our coming and bring aid, but we for our part must make an effort and start south: the Southern Queen is becoming impatient to see her people again."

At the mention of the queen and confronted by Durnor, Lindarg softened and said, "You are right. I should listen to those who care more for me than themselves; I am being selfish and stupid. We will go now – there are lands to be traversed. Tell the men to carry what they may but not to overburden themselves."

Lindarg visibly brightened as he thought to himself; 'south, yes, south to Gullen with haste. If the queen desires to be there then so do I: in Gullen; with her: together'.

The changing of the ways had a sublime but subtle effect on Endworld. The working of such power so openly was felt in other places. What exactly had happened, why it had happened, where it had happened and who or what had caused it to happen, were obscure to all but those who had blindly seen and could not understand. But in distant places there were stirrings; a rumble under the Plain of the Great Stone; a long sigh in an ancient tower; a stirring in Gullen itself which went unnoticed and west of the Forest of Dorn Venain was pensive anew, cradling the Knavestone; doubt returning. Even Tromillion, the Dreaming Man, woke to ponder awhile under a grey earth; to wonder why the seas shivered a little and the winds had forgotten to blow that day over the canopy of the Forest of Dorn. Most people blamed it on the weather.

"You can't trust it these days. It does whatever it wants to do, no more, no less." ended a woodman's conversation in the Great Dome.

And on the Old South Road there were murmurings among the old ghosts: Tristenval called to Sylee and when Sylee came to their meeting said: "Aah, Sylee, there has been a disturbance in the north – what does it mean?"

Sylee laughed wickedly, "I know not." He laughed more as if pouring ridicule on the very suggestion. "No, do not ask me, never ask Sylee about such things for Sylee doesn't know – and yet maybe he knows too much. Or perhaps I just guess." The little man's frame shook with mirth; "Yes, that's all Sylee does – he guesses!"

"Is it good?" pursued Tristenval patiently. "Does it bode well for the balance?" His voice was tremulous and Sylee gleaned from it the fear ever present in the Old Ones: that they will be unsown from the balance of Endworld as it was then. They trod the past, always fearing that the present, one day, would forsake them, blasting the delicate forces of their being from memory; crushing their tentative grasp on their Southland haunts; dispelling them forever.

"Aaahh," mused Sylee sadly – then lightly, "too many questions – and who knows what is well – and for whom? Ha! Ha! For whom indeed? Not Sylee." Maddeningly he giggled again as if sharing some secret joke with himself. "If you say it has happened in the north, then that is where it happened; and if it bodes well, then good; but if not, what then?" He grinned at Tristenval's annoyance. "Yes, what if not? What would you do, lost in the wastes of these warm lands?"

"But have you not been in the north recently-?"

"He has," another man said, interrupting.

"Then…?" Tristenval's face was anxious, pleading, but Sylee chuckled, moving his gaze to the man who had just spoken.

"Really?" He retorted sarcastically, then laughed. "Tell me then, why would I go to such a cold place – and where, pray, in the north was I exactly?" The man grunted and looked away. Tristenval's face still held the question and Sylee, controlling his glee spoke to him. "This and only this will I say – for I merely guess at more – yet perhaps I know more – more than I should. Yes, Tristenval," he laughed again, stupidly, "the balance is tipped – not far – but how far is far? And how much further may it be? Do not ask, for I cannot – dare not know."

"The old fool knows nothing – leave him to his riddles!" said the other man to Tristenval.

"He is right!" agreed Sylee bursting with glee. "Sylee knows nothing – nothing at all!" With that he bounded away, cavorting idiotically along the margins of the Old South Road.

Tristenval called after him but he was gone.

6

GULLEN

Of the march of the Gulleners, their queen, Lindarg and the Liegemen south from the battle of the Changing of the Ways, much can be gleaned from the ancient Gullen records of that time. Shattered men found themselves, friendships were struck, and probably for the first time in long eons Eastfolk, Westfolk and Southfolk were drawn together under one banner against a common foe. They survived by hunting and gathering whatever wild things would afford them sustenance, but they did not ravage their path – which was to their advantage since later it was less easily followed by Baeths.

They took from the land thankfully, as men with new life sampling those natural things which man ever chooses to shrug off as he busies himself in cities and behind walls. They took only what was needed; there was no waste, and the land repaid them their forbearance.

Those men sampled the delights of the evening smells, night mists, warm cheery campfires with shadows behind them on the cold nights, songs, poetry, tales; of camaraderie long lost; of what lay over the next hill or round a further bend. But yes, many craved to see their loved ones – and perhaps their joy was tempered – though still a primitive joy. Most of all those men became, somehow, a part of the host of living things. They depended on the web of life of the land, every bit as much as it depended upon and trusted to them, its integrity. Many 'lost' things were revealed anew, small things that were part of the natural bounty of Endworld:

The sun tumbles from the sky – awry,
Mist shivers over marsh.
Trembling reeds tinkle the lake – awake,
A night mist rolls from the wood.
Tree shadows lengthen, pass you by – and die;
Repose by fire while
Fragrant flames of the Byrill – spill
Their sweetened tang across the grass.
Breathe deep the scented air – that's there,
Let days of trouble gently pass.

So recorded Phlack in his account of the march of the Gulleners from Baeth, and similarly the healing virtue of the Rherindel bush, the exotic flavour of the nuts of the Green Tree, the refreshing smell of damp wood and dew-sodden moss, the succulent crunch of the Little Laybower (Carapellin Beetle), the soothing balm from the resins of the moorland scrub. These and many more things were found there – and were always there.

The land worked its will over these folk who must live from it, hardening their hearts to the mining and other destructive plunderings of others such as Baeths who were its enemies; nursing back an empathy in man for that from which he had emerged. More than Gullen were these men living to preserve, their fight was as much for that great entity which was Endworld, which lay before them, around them, and deep within every man.

At last, Endworld itself had made a move in its own history, but in retrospect only was this ever realised, and then by only a few.

There was no pursuit by Baeths, and the journey, though full of many wonders and much sadness at the passing of a good number of the company, continued at the easy pace of the slowest. The weather too was kinder than it customarily was for the waning of the Coldseason. The snows would only just be melting on the northern hills, but here, sheltered by those hills, it was warm, and becoming warmer the further south they went.

"Our liege and the Southern Queen are growing ever closer, Durgol, see, they sit together most nights now," said Faran.

"It is good to see them so," replied Durgol, firelight dancing on his rugged features. "I feel there is a bond between them, more than just that of her gratitude for her rescue."

"Last night," broke in Faran, "they talked of Gullen – or rather, the queen did. I heard much about the city; a fine and mighty place it seemed from what she said."

"Then how was she wrested from it?" asked Karil disbelievingly, carelessly casting a faggot into the dwindling fire.

"Ah," replied Faran, "that she explained-" Then Faran stopped to look at the faces of the other liegeman.

"Tell us then," scorned Durgol.

"It was simple. She was not in the city when she was taken. She was in distant parts of her realm and far from aid when the Baeths came." Faran looked down sadly, hesitating before continuing, "She told of her treatment in their hands; foul deeds that I will not mention, and her voice betrayed that she owed much to our liege." There was a quietness over them for a time while they pondered those deeds which Faran would not mention and about which none would ask.

"What else did they talk of?" It was Durnor who finally spoke.

"I did not overhear all!" retorted Faran indignantly. "I was on guard, not spying! Perhaps Durgel and Eisdan will have more to tell when they return from their watch!"

"But you did hear more?" Durnor's statement was questioning; challenging.

"Yes-" He left the word on the air as he stared into the fitful embers beneath the new faggots until their eyes bored into him. "The queen told of the council of Gullen and what may have happened in her absence; of a general called Fanor who hates Baeths and of other generals whose names I forget. She spoke of the Southlands around their city, of the continuing war with the Baeths who covet those lands; of their denizens who are ever wary of Baeth plunderings, but have been slow in answering.

Our liege, though says very little – as if he is not a part, quite, of this world, and yet he answers and comments oft times amusing the queen. It is good to see them laugh."

"Is he a wizard?" queried Karil. The question was on all their minds.

"None, it seems, knows," stated Faran, "Least of all himself."

Speculation concerning the identity of Lindarg and his growing relationship with the Southern Queen increased daily and was doubtless high on the conversation priorities of all campfire circles in those days as the survivors from the Baeth mines drew inexorably nearer to Gullen.

Then, in mid-Astellin, as the southern weather was warming to the promise of an Achemin of glorious sun, riders came out of the south.

"It is not Andur and Turg. There are too many." said Karil shading his eyes and peering into the sun. Eisdan stood beside him.

"But they would hardly come from Gullen without others, after all, we do bring their queen!" Eisdan's tone was indignant; his companion seemed to have forgotten that there were others in Endworld who would have more than a passing interest in the company which slowly approached Gullen from the north.

"Yes, but many of the beasts have no riders." Karil was not convinced.

"It will be Andur and Turg with Gulleners and many days' supplies on riderless beasts for us," concluded Lindarg, joining their conversation.

So the journeying Gulleners, the queen at their head, with her Lindarg and the six Liegemen of Farisle, awaited the meeting. Not long did they wait. And the meeting was glorious. The light from its fires could be seen from the walls of Gullen that night. Some even swore they heard the sound of uplifted voices over that great distance, but the less perceptive argued that it could not be so, it was too far for sound to travel. Nevertheless, it was as if something of the meeting did reach Gullen that night, something deep, hidden and not understood.

Four riders – two of them unknown – had brought news, but that had been many days ago. Not all in Gullen had believed their story; the defeat of the Baeths at the Changing of the Ways, was of course, the ravings of madmen. Even Gullen itself had cringed a little under attack from marauding Baeth bands out for their own ends; a whole force destroyed without trace by unarmed slaves must be a pathetic travesty of the truth. Nearly the four had been put to the sword but they had stuck to their story. Fanor had sensed a Baeth ruse to obtain supplies and had decided to use it to his advantage by allowing the supplies to leave Gullen and following them with a troop of the city's finest fighting men. But now those men were not fighting. Now Gullen did believe – or rather felt – that truth. The city seemed to hum with a vitality and purpose. None slept. By the next day it was somehow accepted that nearing the city was a great part of it which had been lost; returning in glory, and that its leaders and followers alike would be honoured and led with pride into its inner halls and its highest places.

And they were. No man was denied from the feast of welcome. It was held in the central place and those honoured were received in the massive central hall with its enduring pillars – erected perhaps before the men of Gullen were conceived. From far and wide others came and were gathered in the courtyard which surrounded it and made the building monumental in its solitude. But for the feast, and that once, it was dwarfed by the effort, noise bustle, merriment and sheer numbers of the hosts of Gullen and the Southlands.

Thus the feast of Astellin was established on the nineteenth day of that season to celebrate the return of that which Gullen had lost. Many sons came home; many fathers too; hearts were uplifted with reunions and friendships re-made. In later years the only essence of that original feast of Astellin which remained, was that of reunions and the joining of families together. Some even came to call it the prodigal feast, perhaps the only time in a Starseason when they would see a son or daughter, for it was both bad luck and great discourtesy to miss it.

To those there, that first feast will always remain different. It was the only year that has permitted its holding in the open so soon after the Coldseason, thus others, perforce have been smaller, needing to be confined within walls, cosy round the fires of the Byrill, with nuts of the Green tree and walks on astellined evenings. Too, it was the only time when it was confined to Gullen; in later days, the feast spread to the whole of Endworld and in the minds of those who honoured it, came to signify new life in the land and a new path for the development of man in Endworld. It was said that anything planted or sown on the nineteenth day of Astellin would grow and produce with greater vigour, repaying a hundredfold.

In that central place were gathered the queen and her household at the highest table, noblemen including the Lorist, certain musicians, and officials of all kinds including the treasurer, the townsman, gatekeepers, mayor of the council and others. There too, at the queen's left side, would have been Virdil, but the place was empty, marring the first feast of Astellin. All around and before them were set the tables of the warriors, generals and the Gullen Guards. Among these were Banor, general of the Westfolk army and Fanor, general of the Gullen Guards whose aversion to Baeths was second to none; his swarthy face, hard, dependable but not without an air of humour. He was by far the largest of the Gullen leaders, topping even the Farislanders and he led his men fairly, but with a personal force which was universally praised and respected. Beside Fanor was Darg, one of Fanor's trusted commanders, a smaller man but well able to equal his leader in both combat and strategy. With these were seated Lianor, general of the Northfolk and Danig and Raydel of the Southfolk.

Also in that central hall were the special folk of Gullen and many from other parts of the Southlands; freemen, men of renown, great valour or skill, some aged, some young; many of those in fact which Gullen had honoured at some time for some reason. This host within the hall spilled out and mingled with others who spilled in from the courtyard outside, and yet somehow it was orderly, and that order was accepted by all.

In this setting, on the first day of the feast, with foods, wines and beers being freely given and consumed, Lindarg was called to the high table. He stood humbly – but straight – while the queen rose to address the gathering.

"Gulleners!" Even amid their noise the queen's voice was heard and a cheer was raised which lasted many long moments; tears of joy moistened her cheeks. "Gulleners," she continued when the cheers began to die. "We are here to celebrate and remember great things-" Another long, loud cheer greeted her words, cutting them short. At length she continued; "There are powers in Endworld working for Gullen and its lands. Mighty these powers are, but we must do our part. These days are to feast, recount and enjoy, but the future will be different. The Baeths have suffered a defeat-" more cheers. "But they are not beaten. Virdil has not returned, and so we may take it that the greater evil of Venain – his sorcerous enemy west of the Forest of Dorn – still remains, perhaps waxing as we speak. Soon it will be I fear, that he comes here to claim Gullen and the Southlands for his own." There was a commotion of shouts from the throngs.

"Never!"

"No!"

"Gullen cannot be taken!"

Agitated people murmured in protest; the queen waited.

"By now you will know of our escape from the Baeth mines and those things which followed." She motioned toward Lindarg; "Lindarg it was who saved us, and he also who turned the Baeths at the Changing of the Ways, bringing us safe to Gullen."

A cacophonous roar of approbation rocked the very foundations of the central walls, and the longer it went on the less Lindarg found stomach for it; such acclaim was not his wont.

"To Lindarg!" shouted the Southern Queen raising her jar.

"Lindarg!" echoed the multitude as they stood to drink with respect.

"And the eight Liegemen of Farisle!" she added and the Gulleners rose once more.

When they had settled, the queen continued, "Gulleners, it has been decided that Lindarg should be acclaimed Lord of Gullen. Let any man speak now who feels this honour should not be."

There was a long silence in the great hall, then; "I would ask a question." It was the Lorist of the city. The queen looked enquiringly at Lindarg. He gave a barely perceptible nod.

"Then ask it, Lorist. It is your right." A tense silence preceded the Lorist's question.

"It is said of Lindarg that he changed the ways and destroyed an army; it is further said that he controls the minds of beasts. I have in mind, my Queen, another who could do these things…" The intonation was heavy, serious, demanding. "I would know from whence he and his powers are come."

The peoples of Gullen murmured as if in agreement; it was only right that they should know the nature of who they were about to honour so.

Something inside Lindarg squirmed, but he said levelly, "Many men were re-born from the despite of those Baeth mines – perhaps I too was one. Before it I can only remember running. I am driven from within by a force which I understand no more than you. It has driven me toward Gullen and for Gullen; to what final doom I cannot see. The powers are not mine, and from whence they came I know not; they came unbidden and seemingly to the aid of Gullen rather than just myself. I do not ask for them, but I cannot deny them. Perhaps it is you, Lorist, who should tell me?" The last statement was quizzical and the Lorist rose to respond, but the queen checked him.

"Are you satisfied with the answer?"

The Lorist hesitated a moment, then said, "I am, my Queen," and sat down.

No other voice was raised except in the uproar of appraise which followed as Lindarg was led to the only vacant place at the high table; that which was once Virdil's at the queen's left arm. The Lorist smiled inwardly, and smiled outwardly at the queen's pleasure as, humbly, Lindarg accepted that place. 'It could have been set for him,' the Lorist mused to himself.

The liegemen in their turn were honoured along with many Gulleners of those who had come out of Baeth; the stories were re-told of each deed, songs of Endworld were sung – and many new ones including the 'Song of the Byrill'. Room was made for oaths and games, laments, ballads and a myriad of nonsense songs which filled the spirit with life, for in the fires was the wood of the Byrill and on the tables the nuts of the Green tree, and with them – the memories and the tales – came a little of the old spirit of Endworld back into every man; so too a goodness and wholesomeness that lasted those people through the bitter seasons to come and was never again forgotten while the Southlands that were then, endured.

Long 'ere that first feast of Astellin was over, the queen, turning to her left, said, "Come, Lindarg, Lord, we must talk alone – for you seem restless within – as ever you have become more restless on our journey from Baeth, and there are questions to be asked between us."

Almost unnoticed they slipped away, but the liegemen had seen, and after the two had entered them, they put a guard on the queen's rooms. A guard which was never relaxed until they departed from Gullen.

Together and alone the Queen and the Lord of Gullen sat by the fountain. Without, the feast progressed toward its close, but within, their own thoughts were lost in the shimmering lights of the water, the sounds of those thoughts mingling with the soothing tinkle of its movement. Together they were as never before; for long hours, words were of little importance as they were borne by the blissful reverie of caress and nearness.

It was the queen who spoke at last, seemingly from far away. "We have grown close since Baeth; closer than I have been to any man, save perhaps one called Virdil; and yet little do we know of each other. I have said, and feel deep within, that your place is here and mine is with you by your side; perhaps it is love, and yet..."

"My Queen," protested Lindarg, "I am not worthy of such from a queen, I am not even of Gullen!" But there was a dreaminess in his voice.

"It is customary in these lands for the name of the queen to be known only to those few who must know it; it has been part of the Lore that has persisted through time, and perhaps even yet there is great wisdom in its caution. But now I tell you, Lindarg, that my name is Syntelle."

"It is a great honour for me, and a name of beauty, my Queen-"

"Syntelle, Lindarg, Syntelle," she interrupted.

"Syntelle, Tell me..." But the queen silenced him with a wave of her hand.

"I will tell you of the Southlands and myself, rest here awhile and listen."

Then Syntelle told of Gullen, the Eastfolk and Westfolk; many names of fathers and sons; many places and deeds; of customs, beliefs and traditions and on into the night as the dim light of the building's stones took over from the softening daylight of dusk. Then she talked of Virdil.

"He was a powerful wizard who worked well for the Southlands, Gullen and perhaps foe Endworld itself. His house is in Gullen and is sealed by spells which none save him can penetrate or undo, except maybe the evil one called Venain. It was that same sorcerer whom Virdil left to lay a Starseason ago, and from whom he has never returned, though some are not sure..." She hesitated, looking intently at him, his eyes on the fountain's waters, but the names meant nothing to him and he gave nothing away to her stare.

"Lindarg..." He looked up into her eyes. "Who are you? A forester of Dorn I feel you cannot be. No, you are more than that. I feel it; there is affinity which I cannot fathom; it is as though I have known you."

"No, Syntelle, until my capture by the Baethfolk, I was…
I was…" Lindarg strained to think for a long time. "I was a
woodman – still I feel the lure of those astellined glades, the soft
damp and the quiet…"

"I am sure you are more, Lindarg, much more…"

There was a pause. Syntelle moved to a stone seat and leaned
her back against it as Lindarg continued.

"I can remember nothing of my past. It is as if I never had
one before the snow-covered hills of Baeth." He forced his mind
back to the forest before the snows, but it would go no further;
there was nothing more before that. "I came on the snows from
a forest, perhaps Dorn, perhaps not, but before that there is
nothing – not even a glimpse of who I am or from where I came
– and yet I have the name Lindarg…" He tailed off, thinking of
little else to add.

"You can remember nothing?" asked Syntelle, repeating his
statement as if he might revise his memory at her bidding. Her
face was sympathetic, tinged with a little sorrow.

"Nothing."

"Not even…" continued the queen. "What has made you
forget?"

"Not even that, and yet there is one thing I have – for no
apparent reason – so it must be from-" he hesitated, "before-"

"And that?" encouraged Syntelle.

"I have this inner force which I cannot control or
understand. It prods me and fires me with a drive I cannot
resist. When I do certain things and travel certain ways I can
be happy and feel fulfilled; it leaves me alone. But when I turn
from the path it desires, when I turn other ways and do other
things – and as I sit here – it urges me ever more strongly. Its
power it was that lurked within me in the Baeth mines, and
its power too which makes the Yanish quail and-" Syntelle cut
him short.

"That power which threw the Baeth army into confusion?" It
was a questioning statement.

"I am not sure, I can remember little of that and what I can is painful."

"Aaah!" exclaimed Syntelle, "Not painful – wonderful!" He caught her long, fine hair and ran it through his fingers.

"Since then Syntelle, has been wonderful. With you I have found much happiness and wish it could go on forever, you and I in the Southlands. But I fear it cannot be and I am sad, for my inner self is restless, though it does not tell me where to turn. It is a vengeful force I fear, for from hate springs the fiercest emotion of all, and it is fierce. It will not allow us to live and love as we have, and I must obey." There was the trace of a tear; he loved Syntelle and she knew, though she knew not who had stolen her heart as none had ever done before. They embraced in the entrancing reflections of the water. For a while their thoughts were only of each other.

"The world is cruel at times, Lindarg. You are not yourself; the evil Venain is not slain I fear-" Syntelle hesitated. "Virdil has not returned and the Baeths are ever at our door; our recent victory will only delay them and serve to whet their appetites." Her face was hard now as she continued. "But I have not been idle. To me falls the guardianship of these Southlands and Gullen, and no more than you can I rest while they are threatened. Once, nothing could have assailed these lands and this city save the gods themselves, and long since have they departed from Endworld, leaving it to men. Now, without Virdil, with evil rising in Dorn, we are weak and my task has become greater, greater perhaps than I. But I must do what I can. Before Virdil departed, these things he said to me: 'There may be troubled times ahead, Syntelle, but weaken not; things may not be as they seem, but trust in the stone.'"

"Stone?" queried Lindarg.

The queen pulled at a golden chain which was around her neck. At its end, buried deep beneath her tunic, was a glistening oval gem. "I have not told you of my gem, I had to be sure; and though I am still not sure after all these blissful days, I can see no other course."

Lindarg regarded the silvery stone. It was smooth, hard and with somehow independent depths which seemed unfathomable, as if one peered into a bottomless crystal pool.

"Few know of this, Lindarg, and fewer still of its powers. It can show you what you ask of it – speak a name and it will show, but the name must be the right name – and even then it might not show. I fear it perhaps grows weaker or we have lost the wisdom of its use. I have seen things in it; Virdil also. Through it he found Venain in his castle far to the west and went there." For an instant her face showed bitterness and sorrow. "He should not have gone…"

"Is this true?" cut in Lindarg.

"Yes."

"Then surely you have seen the future of the Southlands and Gullen – are they seized?"

"Though the stone may show, who knows when it is? For the Southlands will go on forever and always the stone shows and always those visions are the same."

"Then it is worthless," Lindarg brooded.

"No!" Syntelle was emphatic. "I have asked it of Lindarg and its depths go blacker and deeper. That is surely death! And yet you are not dead!"

"But…"

"Wait," interrupted Syntelle. "There is something more. Your powers; the Yanish, the changing of the ways, are not new to me. Virdil's were the same, I have seen him use them. I thought that perhaps you might be Virdil, in some way disguised-"

"This is madness!" Lindarg broke in. "How could I be?"

"I remembered what Virdil had said," Syntelle went on, ignoring Lindarg's outburst, "'Things may not be as they seem.'"

"It's-" But Lindarg was ignored again.

"And then I thought that Venain – only he could it have been – had killed Virdil, robbed him of his powers and come here as you, to toy with us for his amusement. It was possible perhaps. So I asked the stone of Virdil, fearing what I might see, but again I saw only the dark blackness of death. Nothing more would it show. I asked it too of Venain, but it was as if Venain had never been, for it showed nought, remaining unchanged by the command."

"I do not know of this Venain." Lindarg was sullen and indignant at the mistrust.

"I had to ask, Lindarg, I had to. Little good it did me!"

Lindarg nodded slightly, seeing her quandary and said, "Then you discovered nothing?"

"Not quite. I feared the stone had lost its power with Virdil gone, or that I had asked it too much; then I asked it of the Lord of Gullen – I knew you had that name at least – and only one thing would it show; a vast valley of smoking stone and rubble. Over those stones clambered a lone figure in the distance; the Lord of Gullen. I do not know where or even when that vision might be."

"And it was me?"

"Alas, I could not tell, the figure was too distant, but I believe it was the Lord of Gullen because I trust in the stone. Know this Lindarg, there has never before been a Lord of Gullen – and who can know whether or not there will be another one after you."

"I must see this vision." Lindarg reached out for the stone but Syntelle withdrew it suddenly.

"No. To see oneself in the Queenstone is not wise; death tomorrow it might show, and who would wish to know that? To me it shows one thing – but what would it show to you?"

"I cannot say."

"And are you sure you would want to know?"

"No." But there was tension in his voice.

"Then never dare ask it." Lindarg relaxed a little.

"What does the vision mean?" he asked Syntelle.

"I do not know. What it showed was truly the Lord of Gullen – perhaps only for an instant – and then maybe, forever. Nor can I say who the figure was. It might have been you – or it might not."

"A fickle gem!" retorted Lindarg angrily.

"Fickle perhaps, but true; and yet things are not as they seem. The true Lord of Gullen must be of the lineage of the Queens of Gullen – my family. You are not, therefore you cannot be truly Lord of Gullen – it is only a title."

"I don't follow."

"We named you Lord of Gullen."

"That is so."

"Then you must have had your real name before that."

"I cannot remember if it is not Lindarg."

"And Lindarg does not exist according to the stone – perhaps never existed – who knows? And yet here you are. I believe in the stone, but I know otherwise. Long have I wrestled with this conundrum!"

"This gets us nowhere but further into riddles." Lindarg's voice was patiently philosophical.

"Which I may yet solve!" Flashes of light from the water danced on her face, "These nights when we have lain together, I have been plagued by dreams – your restlessness may affect more than just yourself. These dreams were all of the Dreaming Man, Tromillion of Thae – a land far to the east. Long have I puzzled over their meaning until this day. I asked the stone of Tromillion, and with him you lay on a bed of gold."

"That is in my future?"

"Yes, if it is not in your past."

"How can I know that when my past is hidden to me?"

"Why did I have the dreams? Why did I ask the stone? Why did it show Tromillion when you were with him? I cannot answer these questions, nor yours."

"It seems then, that I must seek out this Tromillion," said Lindarg, then thought to himself, 'why I wonder?' As if sensing his thoughts, Syntelle said softly, "Perhaps you will dream with him the answers to questions which it seems you cannot even ask yourself, let alone answer. Too little do I know of the mysteries of Endworld, Virdil might have known, but not I."

He knew she was right. The idea gripped him – or part of him; an urge welled up inside him and his moroseness vanished as quickly as it had come with the riddles. At last; a purpose; a direction. They both smiled as if a weight had been lifted from their shoulders; a smile of release and peace of mind. Syntelle took the stone from her neck saying.

"Take it, it does little enough for me and I do not know the name of the one I would most wish to see in it." Lindarg caught her meaning and they kissed by the stone chair. Night-time whispers fuelled their desire for each other, filling them with abandon and a passion which they could not ignore…

Later, in the early hours, they lay together, both reflecting on the irony; the decision that might tear them apart forever, had brought them closer and more happily together; Lindarg to journey far to the east where none had ventured in memory, and Syntelle to stay as she must within Gullen to do what she could in its hard times.

The liegemen too found solace, comfort and friendship within the walls of the city, while the Warmseason caressed the land and the Achemes bloomed far distant in the Forest of Dorn. Theirs was found among the ranks of the warriors of Gullen and their leaders, with whom they sported and laughed; visiting the taverns to drink ale and sing. They joined their training also; exchanged skills – skills of Farisle for those of the Southlands. Much enthusiasm and competition was brought to the warriors of Gullen by these liegemen from a far land and soon they were organising tournaments; matching contestants. These things were seen to be so by the wise of the city and the Gullen generals. The liegemen were accounted worthy and given commands.

Throughout the Achemin, they plied the forces of Gullen; their men growing in skill and stature as warriors, and with this came the awakening of the spirit of the city – so shattered by the loss of their queen; so bemused and beset by events which hitherto had rapidly overtaken them; shattered by eons of peace in the Southlands, then shattered again by the attack on Venain from which few had returned. There had been no time to reconstitute a force from those that remained.

Many were the bonds of respect and allegiance wrought by the liegemen then, and through many trials to come did they endure.

7

TROMILLION OF THAE

T he morning was cold, as if the Coldseason was upon them. The liegemen were silent and mounted, their heads turned against the chill wind. Perhaps they wondered why their lord should decide, so suddenly, to leave Gullen; why he should go east. Certainly for them Gullen had been a welcoming place, where they would have stayed longer and where they and their liege were needed. There was still much to do in advance of a possible Baeth attack, and probably even more when it came. Faran had found Layna, from whom even Andur and Eisdan had struggled to wrest him early that very dawn! They had drunk and sung with the Gullenfolk in their old, cool taverns, exchanged tales of Farisle for those of the Southlands and had made friends easily since their outlook was jovial; also their entry into Gullen had been glorious.

Mayhap though, their distant expressions pondered upon the future that might have been theirs in the Baeth mines; a dusty red death of slow starvation and overmuch toil far to the north. From that fate they had been saved indisputably by their liege, Lindarg who now dallied with the queen as they patiently waited. Or they were resigned that all good things must end, or not ending, be interrupted in order that their essence can be re-lived once more. But whatever, they would ride with their lord, they had pledged that much and more, to them it was important and hardship had strengthened that purpose. They had been the right hand of Farisle, and perhaps they would be yet again, but for now they had another task at the right hand of their Liege-Lord, and they would not turn from it. Such was their respect and love for a man that none could understand, not even himself.

Only their faces were exposed to the cold and as Lindarg approached, Durnor's and Eisdan's were turned toward him displaying the gaunt features of these men from Farisle. Their northern faces were taut and a little sallow; cheekbones prominent; chins hard and thin set; features reflecting the northern clime, beyond the mountains and Baeth. They were of lesser build than Lindarg, but beneath the swathing cloaks their bodies were wiry and powerful; a keen and delicate poise with swift reactions and cunning to make them fearful adversaries in any combat. In the morning light Lindarg could see the serious set of their mouths, the thin whiteness of clasped lips, and above them the burning black of those northern eyes. Awesome, honest faces, and there was sadness there; determination, loyalty and caring.

"Greetings Lord, we are ready." Durnor's beast shuffled uneasily beneath him as he spoke. Lindarg rode toward them, fresh after his times with the queen, she smiling while she walked beside his steed, her face happy, yet not so. She had no wish to see Lindarg go and neither of them could guess when – or if – they would meet again; he had to go, she knew, and was resigned to – though scarcely content with – that fate.

"Farewell, Lord," she said, "Return as fast as you may."

Lindarg gazed warmly down at her as he caressed her hair, saying, "You shall be forever in my mind." Then he whispered so that none could hear, "Syntelle. Do not worry while I have the company of my friends, it is not necessary." They moved toward the gate of the courtyard.

"Good luck to your venture, my Lord," called the queen, lowering her eyes as Lindarg led the way out, turning his steed east.

Durgol saw her tears and guessed at her anguish. She watched until long after they had vanished over the brow of the East Gullen Road which led to the Eastway, she felt, as land long since harvested, bare, useless and empty.

For several days they journeyed eastwards with the setting

sun always behind them, moving from one warm inn to another. Slowly they approached the edge of the Eastlands and the inns grew thinner, their days longer and a comfortable night less and less certain. The end of the twelfth day found them at the Brushwood Down.

Brushwood was an outland village which romped drunkenly among the undulating farmlands – Gullen depended on the produce of such places – but trade and news were slow to come and go. Not only did the company travel in advance of the news of their passing, but here in the eastern out lands they were even far ahead of the news from Gullen concerning the rout of the Baeths at the Changing of the Ways and the return of the Southern Queen. So, as they entered the Brushwood Down after sunset, they were just travellers, and travellers going east were very rare – rare enough to engender immediate suspicion and distrust; thus was there welcome.

"We are full at the moment – always are after harvest time, and harvest is later here than away west." The Landlord cleaned glasses fervently behind the bar, nervously eyeing their swords.

"Is there another inn in Brushwood then?" asked Lindarg.

"No" The landlord was rather curt. "The nearest one – east of here that is…" He hesitated. "You are travelling east, aren't you?"

"Indeed we are," replied Lindarg, trying not to show his dislike for the off-hand treatment they were being given.

"Ah yes, I thought so. Well the next one is two days from here – maybe three – at Wetland."

"Then at least allow us a meal kind, Sir," cut in Faran, shivering slightly. "We have come far today."

Lindarg tumbled a gold coin onto the counter. Its Yanish, head motif gleamed iridescent in the smoky light of the bar. A nearby drunkard's eyes fell open, though the head behind them seemed still asleep. Torn for no more than an instant, the landlord made up his mind.

"Nine suppers!" He yelled through a door behind the bar.

There was an exclamation and a shuffle from the back room, then he turned to Lindarg and the Liegemen once more. "Please make yourselves comfortable, gentlemen." He motioned to a room behind them and followed them in. "Perhaps you would like drinks?"

They ordered a large pitcher. The landlord hovered beside the table that served as a bar in this room, taking too much notice of the weight of Lindarg's two pouches. "You say you have travelled far – from the west?" He intoned the question at Faran who was warming and busy removing layers of clothing.

"Why yes, landlord, we have been on the road for several days."

"Have you any news from the west – from Gullen maybe?"

Lindarg answered, "We have heard little since our stops have been short, but we did hear of a Gullen victory over an army of Baeths…"

"That is good news. When and where was the battle? Who led them? Perhaps Fanor – he hates those plunderers."

"We have heard no details, though perhaps as you say it was indeed Fanor." The landlord seemed pleased.

"There are also rumours of a new Lord of Gullen. Have you heard them?"

Durgel answered, "We have heard that too, and maybe the rumours are true, but we have seen no proof."

The landlord was a little confused by the faint smiles which slid across nine faces, but before he could ply for more news the supper, steaming and savoury, whirled in.

He left them to eat while he saw to other customers. Lindarg reflected that he had seen inns more crowded, the Brushwood Down did not seem full… Then he could not decide where or when – or even if he had seen inns more or less crowded; so much of memory did not exist!

As they were finishing the meal, the landlord reappeared with more drinks. He seemed much more breezy and addressed them generally.

"It's a long way to Wetland and a cold night; forgive my previous inhospitality – strangers like yourselves are not common in these parts, especially now. People stock up for the Coldseason and stay at home. You are welcome to stay the night." Then added hastily, "But I cannot offer you beds, this room is all that is available, but at least it is warm."

"Thank you, Sir. A noble gesture and much appreciated. Will you join us in a drink?" Durgel held up the full jug which the landlord had just brought in, then continued enthusiastically, "Your ale is the best we have tasted – an excellent brew."

The landlord reddened a little saying, "Very kind – er – yes I will – thanking you." He seated himself on a nearby table and poured himself a drink from their jug. He encouraged their drinking and as the party warmed, more jugs were brought.

Laughing with them the landlord reintroduced the topic of travel. "You say you are going east – to Wetland then – what might be your business there so late in the season?"

Lindarg was wary but said nothing. Faran answered, "Not to Wetland, but beyond…"

"Beyond the Outlands then?" queried the landlord interrupting, his face a little incredulous.

"Thae," volunteered Lindarg. The liegemen sharpened, until now they'd had no inkling of their ultimate destination.

"Thae," muttered the landlord, "I have heard the name but the place is of no consequence. I have heard in tales that it was once a beautiful and magnificent land, rich and verdant – but everyone knows it has been wasted. Wild moor, winds and grass; nothing more; no-one goes there now…" He stopped himself, realising that these travellers were going there.

"Is this place easily found?" asked Lindarg.

"Can't miss it!" was the reply. "When there's nothing else, you're in Thae." He chuckled a little at his joke, then asked, "But what would gentlemen like yourselves be wanting in the barrenness of Thae?"

Lindarg glanced sidelong at the bulbous smiling face. "There are other tales too," was all he said in reply.

The liegemen men were alert now, but Lindarg was not giving anything more away just then. "We will search to find whatever there is that may be found, there may be more in Thae than the eyes can see…" They all sensed that these were his final words on the issue.

The landlord changed the subject yet again, but to one they could all follow easily. "Let's drink," he said, pouring from yet another jug which had miraculously appeared.

They were all becoming rather drunk. Lindarg did not begrudge them the opportunity, but part of him rued the time which would be wasted recovering and warned against the possible dangers of relaxing vigilance in strange parts, particularly after the landlord's most sudden 'change of heart' earlier. Lindarg smelled a rat – a rat which Eisdan already had by the tail beneath his inebriated exterior. The landlord's voice cut into their thoughts; "You intend to stay at the Wetland Down tomorrow or the day after?" The question was addressed generally.

"Yes, it lies east and so does our path."

"It is owned by a cousin of mine who will be even more suspicious than I." Their merriment subsided a little. "But I will give you a letter for him which will set things to rights." He beamed at his own good-heartedness.

"That would be very helpful," observed Eisdan more than a little too pleasantly.

Again the landlord offered profuse apologies for his lack of welcome when they had first arrived, adding, "But I start early and perhaps you also and it is late already." He left; they settled down and the lights were out.

Eisdan did not sleep. Lindarg slept lightly. He had avoided most of the plied drinks but the large potted plant by the table had not – and certainly hadn't complained. He wondered what effect several jars of strong ale in one night would have on a plant, he would remember to notice in the morning.

A slight noise in the room brought Lindarg fully awake, alert but unmoving. He was immediately aware of the noisy sleeping of his companions, and a presence. The room was very dark but he could just make out the blacker outline of the landlord's hefty frame. By his feet was a small furry creature of a kind which Lindarg had not encountered before; he experienced it rather than saw it, and felt its perfect discipline. Both shapes remained motionless for a long time; Lindarg sensed a growing rapport with the furry creature which fascinated him. So intent was he on the creature, that the landlord nearly had the pouches in his hand before Lindarg had even considered what he was going to do.

Suddenly the furry creature sank its teeth into the landlord's wrist and his face became a tortured picture of pain and surprise as he struggled to stifle the yell that waggled his tongue. Frantically dragging off his pet, he careered as quietly as haste would allow from the room, snagging the door catch noisily and banging into a barrel in the passageway. Once there, there was a squeal and a thud followed by a low, vehement curse. A door closed; silence again.

Lindarg grinned almost aloud, imagining the confused and frustrated cursings which would now be taking place in some other room out of earshot. Deciding finally that the gold was now safe, at least for the night, he went to sleep.

At breakfast the landlord was not in evidence. The company were all still very groggy but Lindarg knew they would soon be alert once they had sampled the cold morning rain; outside was grey and dismal with its falling. When the landlord did appear, his eyes were averted and his wrist bandaged; traces of blood had soaked through. There was no sign of the furry thing. Lindarg made no comment and the others appeared to be in no state to even notice.

"The girl has prepared a lunch for your journey. Here is the letter as promised, and I have seen to it that your mounts were fed and watered ready."

Lindarg gave him another gold coin to the sound of the landlord's gushing thanks and protestations that he could not accept; that his efforts had hardly been worth such handsome recompense; but he took it all the same. Lindarg heartily refused the proffered change and tucking the letter safely under his belt said,

"I shall ever remember the Brushwood Down for its good hospitality and ale Sir, and its night's entertainment." Lindarg looked very pointedly at the bandaged wrist, but could not discern whether the landlord had caught his meaning. He turned to the liegemen, "Let us make way."

Hastily they took their belongings out onto the track where their steeds waited.

The cold rain was cruel on their faces as they waved farewell and set off eastwards. As the inn fell from sight, Lindarg reflected that these lands seemed as barren as Thae was reputed to be.

"Sire," Durnor broke into his thoughts. "What do we seek in Thae?"

Lindarg regarded the liegemen sympathetically. "I have been unkind bringing you on a quest of unknown purpose," he spoke to them all. "We seek Tromillion of Thae, often known as the Dreaming Man. The gold is for him." Eisdan smiled wryly.

"Ah Sire," he said, "How well you dealt with that grabbing landlord last night; it was difficult not to laugh!" Lindarg was genuinely surprised, the others puzzled.

Eisdan described the night's attempted thieving amid their raucous laughter. "A better sight I have not seen on a fat face," he concluded, spluttering with mirth.

Lindarg laughed too.

"No Sire, your burden was not unguessed by us. Hard it is for one to guard so much; for eight it is easy in turns, and for nine, easier still!"

Lindarg laughed again saying, "You are right Eisdan, I should have told you at least about that, forgive me! It seems you protect me in spite of me – and even from myself!"

"Ah, that is another thing!" threw in Andur thoughtfully. "Gold is easy to watch!"

Lindarg cuffed Andur heartily and said, "On! And I shall tell all."

They continued in a close group round Lindarg, listening intently.

"It is said that if you scatter gold on a hillside in Thae, Tromillion will collect it and take you to dream with him. In these dreams you may find answers to questions of your past, and even future. I go to dream, because I feel I must, perhaps to find my identity and the answer to why my mind – if it is mine – does not always behave as my own. Even now it drives me and I can scarcely guess at its motives."

"All these things can be dreamed, Sire?" asked Karil enquiringly.

"With the Dreaming Man, it is possible that all things can be dreamed – I cannot say. But I have no other plan than this – which the queen herself suggested. Nor do I know what dreams I seek, therefore I cannot know what I might find."

"Ever you were a puzzle, Sire!" broke in Faran.

"Indeed, that I can sense," he replied resignedly.

"What is this land like, and who lives there?" asked Durgel.

"How far is it?" added Durnor.

"Wait, my liegemen, these are all questions I cannot answer. The innkeeper said it was barren and no-one lives there, perhaps he is right…"

"But what of Tromillion?"

"Ah…" Lindarg's voice sounded distant, "Tromillion. He may only dream there, or maybe he is his dreams – or your dreams."

"This speculation is confusing," summed up Karil.

"Then," replied Lindarg, "let us wait and see."

They rode on east into the grey rain.

The Wetland Down was comfortable; there was no trouble; the landlord, having seen to their needs, left them alone and sleep was peaceful and undisturbed. In the early morning as they prepared to leave, Lindarg approached him for many days' supplies and a spare animal. The former he charged highly for; the latter he parted with only grudgingly and charged the very earth.

They were ready to leave when Lindarg turned to him. "We are going east – how much further does the road lead?"

"East you say, Cousin Frind did not mention that in his letter…" He thought hard for a while then, "The road goes for another two or more days' ride into the Hinterlands, then there is no more."

"And after that, how far to Thae?"

"Who can say? Those who have been 'beyond the road' never returned."

"There are stories?"

"There is nothing. Old stories, yes, but now there is nothing."

"Why don't people go there?" asked Faran perturbed.

"Why should they? There is nothing to go for." The landlord seemed a little irritated and ended the exchange by adding, "You will know when you are there, there is nothing but wild moor, winds and grass." The hint of a dubious smile crossed his face as he ducked into the Wetland Down and once more they turned east.

Sure enough, the road dwindled and reluctantly faded under moss and scrub. This was the Hinterland; terrain faintly undulating, unkempt and broken only by small streams and trees here and there which seemed to struggle in a beaten world. Their first night was spent huddled under a group of large trees in a sheltered valley – almost pleasant, with a gushing, clear stream. There was no danger here and they all slept well, indeed they all agreed wryly that the only possible death to be met here was one of boredom; an ironic thought that made them all laugh.

The days and the lands passed by and neither was affected by the passing of the other, except that their trail was left in the damp earth. Always they were up at first light, putting the eastern glow ahead, then pressing on… and on… the weather becoming colder with the season.

"Surely we must be in Thae – or these wasted Hinterlands are endless!" complained Turg on the eighth evening as they settled after their meal.

They were sheltered from a strengthening wind by a rocky crag and some stunted trees; the fire was cheery and warming, but the feeling of distance and desolation was a dampener of thoughts.

"I do not think we are there yet," replied Lindarg matter-of-factly. "Renar said we would know when we were."

"But we have no way of knowing," protested Turg.

"You are wrong, my friend; 'there is nothing in Thae but wild moors, wind and grass'," re-quoted Lindarg.

"Then we must be there – there is nothing more than that here!"

"Look around you; rocks, trees, streams, valleys…"

"Then if Thae has less than this, it must surely be a void."

"Exactly!" snapped Lindarg. "Nothing."

They settled to sleep and Lindarg waited patiently for their regular breathing; in this land they had long ceased their pointless terms of vigil. In the silence, Lindarg turned away from them and took out the Queenstone, laying it in his palm. There was a slight glow in its depths as if the light were a purring response to the caress and attention. He looked long and hard into it, then said quietly,

"Syntelle." In the stone she appeared, standing as he had last seen her in the courtyard at their departure.

So young she looked to be queen. Black hair, long and waving streamed in the breeze, dancing around and behind the faintly blushing countenance which bore a wistful smile but was saying farewell. Sparkling eyes with a depth of love which had as yet barely been fathomed, invited him to return. His eyes were drawn downwards drinking in her lithe body caressed by the short silken shift of white she had worn for him; its hem partly covering – yet revealing – firm thighs as it was pressed wetly against her by the wind and rain. Weathered, yet delicate skin followed the curves of her calves, smooth, supple; her stance steady and erect.

He felt desire within him; a wild surging attraction to her magnetic beauty and he remembered their frenzied nights together; that she had been irresistible; had teased him; had awakened buried responses which had been lost with his past; taunted him with her body so that he could take no more without ravishing her. Together, helpless in each other's grasp, they had wrestled and loved; neither in control of the other or themselves, for the queen could no more help herself than could Lindarg; it was as if their destinies had been inextricably entwined during those warm nights of the Sunseason and fate had set a spark to their tinder.

He saw the lips forming words and longed to kiss them; then it was a dark room and he was with her. He felt more than saw, him and her together, nor could he decide where or when it might have been. Soon the vision faded and for a long while he gazed, transfixed into the crystal's heart, then whispered again, "Syntelle." The stone showed nothing. Then he remembered what she had said, that the stone did not always work, and sighed, looking ahead into the gloom of the Hinterland. Returning his gaze to the stone he said, "Thae."

Thae appeared to him, and that vision was unforgettable; Lindarg knew they were not yet there; this must still be the Hinterland, again he whispered Syntelle's name, but the stone remained clear and dark and he reflected bitterly on its limitations, putting it away and out of sight.

But Lindarg did not know that Syntelle was only Syntelle in his presence, to all others and at all other times, she was Queen of the Southlands; nor did he know that in the old language Thae meant 'nothing' and that before Thae was Thae – before the spiteful quarrels of the gods had torn it – laid it waste, it had been a great forested land called Eastelsane, and that after Thae it would be re-named… nor that the stone had been made for omnipotents to whom all things then had been known, which wisdom enabled them to ask the stone correctly. The stone itself had no limitations save those imposed upon it by its user.

The following day brought them into Thae. At midday, they rose from the Hinterlands and they knew they were there. Before them it stretched, hill upon hill and by hill; grass on them and between them; an even, ancient, grey grass, hard and bent beneath the cold wind which met and chafed their faces.

Lindarg looked at his companions. "Thae," was all he said; they nodded. But as the word was spoken, the wailing wind whipped it away and shredded it. "From here," continued Lindarg shouting above the wind, "five of us will go on so that the rations will last longer into Thae. Durnor, Durgel, Durgol and Turg, I ask that you return across the Hinterlands for supplies, our trail should be easy to follow. Collect them from the Wetland Down then return to here. Do not go on into Thae, just wait, and though long may that wait be, do not waver. Harder I fear will such a task be than ours."

"We will see that this is done and await your return, Lord," said Durnor, only the merest trace of disappointment showing through his tone.

With that, they turned their backs to Thae and melted once more into the Hinterlands, leaving Lindarg and the others with the spare animal and all the supplies that were left save what was needed to carry the four back to Wetland.

Lindarg, Andur, Eisdan, Karil and Faran rode reluctantly into Thae. The land felt eerie and hostile, the wind cold and daunting.

After a long silent while of faces twisted against the wind, Andur voiced his thoughts. "This place is unsettling, its absolute nothingness harrowing." Lindarg and Eisdan agreed and Andur went on; "An enemy can strike fear and that I can bear, but this land is suffused with a fateful fear – which is all the worse for having no apparent cause."

91

"Perhaps there is more to this place than can be easily perceived."
Lindarg caught his own words – the very same he had spoken before
at the inn. They all shuddered; it was like a nightmare.

Suddenly Faran stooped from his steed and plucked a small
thing from the ground. "Look," he exclaimed, like a child finding
his first Astellot, "a Wailberry – and there are more!" But they
were cheated. The berries were woody and held an unpleasant
bitter taste which screwed their faces.

They travelled on; a grey sky hung over the grey grass and all
around the grey hill-hummocks lay.

Night came with an amorphous dark which seemed to seep
evenly from the sky.

"We will have to rest the night in the shelter of a hill, we have
seen no better places," suggested Lindarg.

Eisdan pointed. "There's a larger hill over there which should
afford better protection than these others."

The wind had cooled even more with the night and the
thought of being free of it spurred them on, as shivering, they
made their way into its lee. But there was no lee; the wind howled
as strongly as before.

"It's no bigger than the one we have just left!" scoffed Fanor. "In
fact it is smaller and certainly doesn't provide as much shelter."

Eisdan was annoyed. "Well it looked bigger from over there!"
he contested.

"And that one looks bigger from here," countered Lindarg.
"Perhaps they are both the same."

It was dark now and they tried to settle at the foot of the
hill, but the cruel wind cut from the sides and swooped down
from the top. They moved round, but the wind was everywhere,
hugging the hills and the grass, blowing incessantly. Again they
moved, but it was no use, the wind could not be escaped in Thae;
worse, it was insistent, had no respite and could not be ignored.
All night they lay awake buffeted by it, huddled with their restless
animals, wrapped in all they had brought, but still it was bitter
and they gained no rest.

When the grey dawn came they were tired, hungry, thirsty and cold. With nothing to burn they ate cold food as they shivered in the wind and the light revealed the land they dreaded to see.

They did not linger long over that breakfast and that was as well for there was little choice and even less comfort. Lindarg persuaded his steed to stand against the wind which had not yet warmed from the night.

"Let us ride," he said. "At least the movement will warm us!" Stiffly they mounted.

It was Eisdan who voiced their thoughts first. "Which way, Sire?"

A sudden chill of realisation spread through the company; there were no tracks; in the hard grass and earth, they had left no trace, nor had there been any 'eastern sky' which had brought them thus far.

"Which way is anyway?" spat Andur bitterly.

Karil broke in, pointing into the wind, "The wind was in our faces yesterday, that is our way."

"But it changed last night," Eisdan argued. Andur agreed.

"Perhaps, but it is our only hope," muttered Karil looking quizzically at Lindarg.

Lindarg's face brightened as he said, "I may be able to solve our problem, wait." Though his inner self had remained hidden since they had begun their journey, Lindarg hoped that it would not lightly allow him to travel the wrong way. He tried four directions, a further four, then returned to them dejected. "It is no good. Until now I have been able to sense where to travel – here there seems no sense of direction; I cannot guide us… We are lost."

A long silence followed his words and the emptiness of the land was a sickness.

Andur broke their melancholy. "We cannot go back, so we have no choice but to face the wind as Karil suggests." And this they did.

"There is a flatter way in that direction too, at least the going will be easier," observed Karil. They agreed and set off.

Once again they were deceived. The 'flatter' terrain felt steeper and they struggled hard to cover little ground. Then another way invited them – but that too was no easier. Choosing a path, they realised, was a complete waste of time; the nothingness that was Thae was evenly distributed, and there were no easy ways through it.

Sometime later the wind changed. They halted, regarding Lindarg helplessly; the question hung on all their lips but Lindarg had no answer. The wind wailed between their dejected faces.

"Are we to wander this accursed place until we die?" Faran voiced all their thoughts with his frustrated cry of anguish.

Andur was furious: drawing his sword he threw the gleaming blade deep into the grey earth shouting, "Damn this cursed land! Damn you wind!"

But the sound was lost and the withdrawn blade was grey with the lifeless dirt. Sheepishly he rejoined the others, but they all felt the same and did not blame him for his futile outburst; there was no glory in dying for nothing, in nothing, doing nothing; and the despair of this land could not be fought.

For days they wandered without hope until one day found them dismounted and huddled, shivering in the wind; Lindarg left them and went to brood a while on another hill. Nothing passed between the liegemen until Lindarg rejoined them.

"What now, Sire? Will we ever find Tromillion?" Faran's voice held despair as he continued. "And if we do, how will we return – and to where?"

"Our supplies will not last much longer, Sire. Soon we must ration them," Eisdan said.

"Then soon is now," snapped Lindarg. "And as for Tromillion, I did not know where to look when I came – now it doesn't matter. It is said that he is to be found on a hillside…"

"But this whole place is hillsides and every one is the next, and that its neighbour!" protested Andur, interrupting. "The task was ever hopeless!" Now Lindarg was bitter. "I have failed you, led you to your deaths on a mission without purpose. You should end me here and now."

"I suspect little need for such a hasty action. Death is only days away – but do not think us faithless – we would no more slay you now than when you led us from the Baeth mines!" Andur's tone was philosophical, attaching no blame to their liege.

There was no point in moving further, and the darker grey of night with its bitter wind found them hopeless and helpless where its changing had left them in the darkness. Lindarg slipped away, desperately clutching the pouches of gold. Hidden from them, he took out the Queenstone and whispered, "Syntelle." Its depths showed her in the courtyard again saying farewell. Lindarg wept in misery, but through the bitter tears came a ray of memory; then a flood. He recalled Syntelle's words: "Tromillion… you were with him." She had seen Tromillion and he, Lindarg, together – but when? How? And was the stone always right? Lindarg forced into his mind everything that he knew; everything that had been said about the Dreaming Man. "Gold scattered on a hillside will bring him," had said Syntelle, remembering her dream, but which hillside? "One hillside is the next – and that its neighbour." Andur had said.

"Perhaps any hillside," Lindarg thought. "Yes!" He was jubilant. "It must be any hillside; there could not be a special one – not here." Then he recalled his own words – or were they his own? "There may be more than the eyes can perceive…"

Forgetting the others, he began tossing coins wildly into the air, handful after handful, and as the last of them fell onto the grey grass, breaking its dismal monotony like discs of fire, he saw a bent old man collecting, methodically, his coins. A wizened old face looked deeply into his and said, "You wish to dream? Come." He was led by the man to a cave in the hillside, large and resplendent was its opening, lit by a glow from within. Incredulously, Lindarg wondered how they had missed such a thing in this land – and so nearby. They entered the subterranean vault and Lindarg's gaze fell upon two golden beds; beds of

95

coins, bracelets, chains, cups, armour, helms, swords, rings and a myriad of other treasures from countless ages; every item was golden and their glow suffused the cavern. "Of what would you dream, Lindarg?"

"How did you...?"

"...Know your name?" The man's eyes flashed mischievously as he completed Lindarg's words for him, then; "I know many things – from another's dream perhaps – I cannot be sure."

"Who's dream?" Maybe it had been Syntelle's, Lindarg thought as he posed his question.

"Dreams do not belong to people!" The voice betrayed the man's indignation at the question. "They are part of the ether of the land; anybody's; everybody's; who knows who's tomorrow? They exist in spite of us and sometimes we are fortunate – or unfortunate – enough to be visited by them in the night. Since time immemorial when Thae was not Thae, and even before it was Eastelsane, I have dreamed with men the dreams of this world..." He tailed off wistfully, then went on; "But mostly the last eons I have dreamed alone, my services forgotten in these times."

There was a long pause before the old man said, fatefully, "Would you know past, present or future – and of whom – for I can direct the path of your dreams?"

"I wish to know myself."

"Aah, wise, wise, for who are you who is known as Lindarg, who or what are you to become? You have travelled into the heart of Thae to know yourself; truly you shall! Are you not afraid? Do you know what there may be to be learned?" He scrutinised Lindarg closely, then added, "How did you know of me?"

"Syntelle, Queen of the Southlands, she dreamed of you and..." Lindarg stopped, not wishing to reveal the part played by the stone, but Tromillion went on for him;

"And she looked into the Queenstone?" he queried with a sly grin.

"Yes, but how-?"

"Aah, how did I know? The Queenstone dreams and

96

sometimes they are shared with me. I have been expecting you, Virdil, now drink and lie."

Lindarg started at the mention of Virdil but accepted the tiny chalice of clear liquid; it tasted vaguely sweet but its power could be felt. He reclined on the bed of golden treasures and sleep came; the gold seemed to melt around him, suspending him in a calm fluid...

He knew he was Virdil and all that Virdil had known was known to him. Now he, Virdil, directed the dreams and sought what he sought.

A raging furnace for an instant gushed molten rock and amid the noise of the great roar was the sound of a hammer on cooling crystal; distant words deep underground; but the scene was unclear and it swam brilliant vermillion like the molten rock; changed to a blue-lit cavern whose vastness hid its limits; there was confusion; the air charged with conflicting powers; men vied and chased; screams and cries replaced the roaring of the furnace; he was there himself, desperately searching for treasures; on the floor was a gem – he took it, hiding it from sight; the Book? Where is the Book? He must have it – Venain. It was open; he was reading from it; stop him! Get the Book! Virdil himself reached out to it; Venain snatched, ran, was gone; Virdil read the tatter of paper that had torn from the page;

for one so riven,
soul so taken another is given.

and he knew that sliver of script lay hidden in Gullen.

A great hue and cry was taken up; things were missing; the most important was gone; people had departed; anyone could have taken it – the hammer! It must be found! Virdil searched, others searched. Was it destroyed? Where was it? Darkness now – and with it uncertainty; the plunder was divided – but among whom?

Then the scene was a ruined castle on a forest hill in Dorn; Venain entered and claimed it, sealing it with spells from the Book. Virdil knew that now he had an enemy, for always had Venain sought power. Time passed; visions, places and names; lakes were formed and dried; trees grew and fell; a snatch of activity in the castle; some visitors; a captive. Horror! A woodman! Lindarg! Attack Aaagghh! The fire of Eq. Eq; the Tower of Koryn; Eq; a mighty tower... Eq; a fading vision of a tower atop a cliff face; monumental, awesome in its sentinel solitude... Eq; Koryn; Eq.

Then he was back on the grey hillside in the chill wind of Thae. A glimpsed spell from the book fleeted in his mind and he said it amid the nothingness that was this land; knowing his predicament; then it was forgotten. Around him the grass smoked and reluctantly burned. The circle widened and the flames increased in height. Thae burned.

But those muttered words carried echoes far. Their power had no measure in these later times and the message of their utterance reached beyond the confines of Thae, finding rest in dark places. Eq heard his own words once again but they were uttered free – was his power loose? He quailed impotently at the thought, but there remained nothing he could do; meddlers were touching the very core of the weft; jousting with the balance that had endured while he lay entombed by his own devices and carelessness...

Tumbling blindly through the fires came figures. Caught unawares, shaken but unharmed; they left prints in the black ash as they approached their lord and the wind blew warm in Thae!

"Lindarg, Lord! We have searched and given up twice – and searched again for days!"

"Hail, liegemen. We have succeeded. You will be rewarded!"

"It is enough reward to find you safe and well; but the fire, it does not burn!"

"Do not fear the fire, it burns only Thae. Hope that Durnor and the others see it and come to look for us, for without their aid and the food they must bring, we cannot hope to reach the Hinterlands."

"That is true, Sire, the supplies are finished – they must be quick!"

The finality of Eisdan's statement contained hope. In sheer joy they hugged Lindarg in turn, though they were weak from their many days in Thae with dwindling rations. Lindarg knew they would never make the journey from Thae alive, even if they had known which way to go.

"Rest," he said. "We must wait and hope that Durnor is reckless and seeks to find us."

Even as Lindarg spoke, Durnor and the other liegemen were regarding those flames, far into Thae.

"Perhaps they need help," suggested Turg.

"We were told to remain here whatever happened. The food we have is needed for the journey back through the Hinterlands, do not forget that," cautioned Durnor

"But they may be in great danger!" Durgel agreed with Turg's point.

"Surely we must see," Durgol said.

"What good will food be if they do not return? We will wait – and eat it – and then if they do appear, there will be none left for the journey back anyway," cut in Turg.

"Maybe they started the fire as a signal," suggested Durgel.

Durnor was thoughtful; "All that has been said contains elements of wisdom – therefore we must do both."

"Both?"

"Two will go into Thae and two will remain here with enough food to take us all back through the Hinterlands should we return." The sense in the decision was obvious, but they all wished to go. "We must decide."

Durnor took four stones and scratched a mark on the side of each. The figure was a letter of the old language of their homeland – the first letter of their word for fortune, 'crelas'. Solemnly, they each took a stone and tossed it saying, "douam crelas" which meant 'fortune decides'. Durgol and Durgel were chosen. Durnor wished them well, saying, "We will remain here until the food runs out – or you return before – either way, we will still be here…" He smiled.

Durgol replied, "I know." It was a flat statement with a wealth of meaning and trust buried deep within it.

He and Durgel turned their steeds into Thae, smelling the cold, acrid reek of the fire on the relentless wind which came at them from there.

They tried to skirt the fire, but always it was there in front; to the left; to the right, barring their way and always nearer. Soon they were upon it, but through it they could see the black calm which it left. Durgol looked at Durgel, "We must go through, the others travelled straight when they left the Hinterlands, we too must go that way." But their beasts would not go through that thin veil of fire.

"We must go first and pull them through after us," suggested Durgel. They tied lengths of rope to the animals' tethers and ran through the fire. Numbed by the shock of realisation that the fire did not burn them – wasn't even hot, they stared disbelievingly at each other.

"The fire…?"

"Ask no questions, we are safe and we need our steeds; pull! Pull!"

They were small animals and probably not the best that could have been sold to them; it was a struggle, but eventually the poor beasts leaped through and stopped short on the blackened earth, shaking and stamping angrily. It took precious time to calm them enough to continue their journey, but soon they were pressing on into Thae, behind them their hoof prints in the black ash.

There was no wind now; things were changing in Thae and as they rose to the top of a high hill they could survey a vast land, blackened and raw. From behind them now came a sweet, gentle breeze from the Hinterlands carrying with it the last seeds of Dundellin onto the earth of Thae.

They had journeyed non-stop for two days; far in the distance and to their right was another high hill.

"We will head for it and hope to see more from there." said Durgol, pointing wearily.

"That is the best plan," agreed Durgel. They forced themselves on with only brief stops to eat and drink sparingly. By evening they were ascending its slopes – even as from the other side, Lindarg and the others were also. To those who are lost, the highest place is home, and they were all come there in Thae. That night they feasted – though meagrely – in that high place and it was the first such held in Thae since the coming of men into Endworld. Mingling with the tinkle of carefree laughter was the patter of raindrops on the black earth and they saw the gleam in Lindarg's eyes as he felt the drops on his skin.

The morning was full of a wonder which silenced them all as they turned westwards. The tracks were gone, but the breeze still blew from the Hinterlands and the slanting rays of the early sun chased them on their way. Durgol and Durgel had been told of the Thae that had been, but only the others had felt it; only they could deeply know the difference which had no words to describe it. Even as they watched, the night's rain was trickling down valleys dwarfed and shaded by crazily – pitched mountains and hills.

Far away to the north and west, deep under the Plain of the Great Stone, the change was descried and a mighty force which dwelt there yet, remembered times long past and wept with joy for the land that was re-born and self pity – for he would never see it. Beneath those tears though, the great deed kindled a light of hope which had all but faded eons past.

The wind did not change but it rained again before they reached the edge of the Hinterlands where Durnor and Turg waited. Already, as they took a last, long look into Thae, seeds were beginning to grow, lifting their tender green shoots to the bright sun. With high hearts they turned and headed once more west with their company re-formed, but before they had gone but a few paces, Lindarg suddenly stopped and dismounted.

A stunted old tree, no more than waist high grew there and on it were two large fruits, hard and brown, but within those cases, tender new trees. A whole Starseason – perhaps two the tree had struggled so near to Thae, to produce them, sacrificing its own growth. Lindarg plucked the fruits of the Great Brown trees of the Forest of Dorn and threw them into what had been Thae. His liegemen watched in silent awe as he faced Thae and looked into the Queenstone, saying quietly, "The entrance to the Forest of Elsane…" There was a pause; nothing happened, then; "The entrance to the Forest of-" he thought a while, recalling the words in the old language, "-Yirfurnelle; re-born!" In the stone they all saw the image of two spreading Brown trees with a track disappearing into the depths of a verdant forest.

Lindarg looked up and the stone paled again. "The land that was Thae," he said, "is now Yirfurnelle. It has been re-born and re-named; perhaps in time it will nurture a forest greater than the one of Dorn and here will be the entrance to the Liegeman's Track." He handed the stone to Durgol. "The stone will show what you ask of it. Ask it of the Liegeman's Track into the Forest of Yirfurnelle."

Durgol did so. In the stone was a black landscape with two sets of hoof prints in the black, dusty earth heading straight into what had been Thae. Lindarg was amused at his surprise.

"But Lord-" he stammered.

"Once through the fire," explained Lindarg, "you were setting the Liegeman's Track through the Forest of Yirfurnelle. Already it has been travelled twice and the new land is but a few days old!"

The liegemen were filled with wonder for they could see that their leader had gained in stature and wisdom. They could all see as well that he looked much older – indeed he was nearly 'old' – but none said so. Lindarg went on, holding up the Queenstone which Durgol had gingerly given back to him, "This stone knows all the future, and all the past 'til its forging when Endworld was still young, for everything after its making was once in its future." He smiled at their bewildered faces. "One only has to know what to ask…"

Together they turned west. Andur asked, "Tell us, Lord, of the Queenstone and the Dreaming Man – what did you dream?"

"Of the Queenstone I can tell you little more than I have already said – and perhaps that is too much! But my dreams aaah, I dreamed that I am – or was – Virdil. He in the woodman's body of one called Lindarg. I have lived the past that once was Virdil's and truly I am Virdil again, but the years of that dreaming has aged me." They avoided his glance but Lindarg knew what they thought and continued; "Yes I am no more Lindarg to whom you are pledged; I am Virdil, Wizard of Gullen and the Southlands. Henceforward you are released from my service, for it was to Lindarg you gave your allegiance-"

"Sire," cut in Durnor, "Whatever your name, it is you to whom we owe our lives; it still holds that only death will release us." They had stopped now to face their lord; swords scraped lightly from sheaths and the eight liegemen made to reaffirm their vow.

"Hold liegemen!" Lindarg's voice was commanding, "There is more you should know before you rashly sell your hearts once more to a man so unworthy of your trust.

"I also dreamed of my struggle – that inner force is now known to me – though I do not yet fully understand it myself. I have an enemy and it is hate for that enemy which drives me. Hear this, liegemen, hear it well," Lindarg paused, eyeing them. "He has destroyed me once, yet somehow there was a... mistake perhaps, or a twist of fate which has brought me thus, and I know I must meet him again. I fear for myself in this destiny but more do I fear for you, for Gullen, its queen and the whole fabric of Endworld. I cannot turn aside from this – nay I am here because of it. That enemy is the sorcerer Venain. Powerful he is; poised to seize Endworld; nor will he stop when it bows before him, he will reach beyond the seas to other lands..." Again Lindarg paused to emphasise the import of what he had said to them. Now his voice lowered, "There is much I do not yet know; many imponderables which bring doubts and fears – it is already as likely as not that nothing remains in Endworld mighty enough to unseat him; that I go a second time to my end. You are young and strong, think not to follow me into death – already I have led you near and you have wrested me from it – this has been but the beginning!"

Sensing the end of his declamation, Durnor spoke for them all. "Lord, no more than you it seems can we understand or know all the reasons for what we do and have done. We did not vow liege-service to a mere woodcutter but how could we know you were more than that when you didn't even know yourself? No! We will not take release." With that, Durnor came forward, sword held high, "I serve 'til death."

Each then did likewise, reaffirming their pledge against the backcloth of the barren, tumbled Hinterland.

Lindarg laughed, but his eyes were moist. "I am served by eight fools! Eight fools who ever guard me from my own follies, protect me and give me strength; eight, courageous, comforting fools." The voice was suddenly serious again, "But I wouldn't swap one for all the powers of the ancient gods of Endworld!" With that he urged his steed westwards.

Humbled, but light-hearted the liegemen followed, bursting with a myriad of questions and not knowing how to ask even the first one.

Lindarg rode aside from them most of the time, deep in thought. He needed to think. All that he had dreamed had to be sorted, important things remembered, pieces placed in the puzzle; but much didn't yet fit. Venain was master of potent forces. He could summon legions of Nethermen, dead men whose death was a joke since they 'lived' only to add to the number of times they had 'died'. For ordinary men they were angels of death offering no escape. Lindarg shuddered; he had faced them once as Virdil, several were daunting, a legion could scour the length and breadth of Endworld in time. He had assumed that they could not be sent far from where they were summoned, now he was not so sure. Time, if anything, enhanced a wizard's prowess. Lindarg knew he could not encounter so many and survive. Then there was the fire – the sorcerous fire – he had used it to burn Thae. It burns only that which it is sent to burn, and cannot be turned or quenched until it is finished. That fire had vanquished Virdil and he knew it was a power he could not hope to fight; the Book might tell, but Venain must have that too. Yes! The Book, he would not lightly give that up! What Venain's powers had been before he gained the Book, Lindarg did not know – nor did he know yet of other stones and their uses – at least not all of them. Starseasons ago he had guessed that Venain had acquired one, though from where he had not been able to fathom then, the wise in Endworld had thought such things lost. Foolishly, he had seized an opportunity which had not been his, and utterly failed to banish his enemy. Sheer folly it had been to attack then, knowing nothing, but suspecting much. But then maybe that had been predestined...

He looked across at his liegemen. They at least were happy for now – and with good cause for it is not often that men can change lands and save wizards. He wondered how much he could tell them; had he perhaps told them too much already?

At least he knew what to do next. The dream had shown him that. There could be no forgetting the vision of the tall desolate tower shouldering mountainous peaks, peaks which could only have been the Southern Chain, impassable except in legends from a bygone age; the Tower of Koryn... and Eq. Lindarg presumed Eq to be an entity, but of what kind there had not been the slightest hint in all his dreams; so who or what was Eq? What would he find in the Tower of Koryn? Would it help his own quest? He had no answers to these questions, but knew he must go there. In all his new-found wisdom, there was no knowledge of the Tower of Koryn, but there were many dusty books in Gullen which had lain unopened even in Virdil's long history. Lindarg sensed that the time to return there seeking such knowledge could not be afforded; he would have to learn for himself.

At once he felt the need for secrecy, at least for now, so he kept his thoughts concealed as they picked their way through the first snows on the widening Hinterland track and entered the Wetlands. It was bitterly cold now and they were huddled in cloaks whitening with flurries of flakes.

Their return through the Hinterlands had been uneventful, but as the days of Coldseason dragged by, gloom had assailed them on that weary journey. A foreboding, unbidden had stolen upon them after the elation of Yirfurnelle; had silenced them, turning each one inward; abrogating conversation. Their silence was only relieved by the sintering sound of snow falling on frozen ground and the wheeling of the wind keening round bare branches. Each of them looked resolutely ahead to the imagined warm fire and cheer of the Wetland Down; anticipation rising with the slowly lessening distance.

8

BRUSHWOOD

Rounding a hill, they looked upon the Wetland Down. A swift glance halted the group, dismay gripping their faces. A shattered and burned travesty of civilisation lay tumbled before them; the tavern cold ashes and snow. Grimly and silently they sped to its remains and what they saw there told its tale.

"Baeths!" Faran glared wild-eyed and spat into the snow. "Is there no limit to their molestations?"

Renar's bloodied face rested askew among the charred timbers and snow; blistered features staring at the sky; a frozen expression imploring and fearful. Lindarg and the Liegemen were assailed by a deep sorrow and at the same time a melancholy anger which promised to brood beneath furrowed brows. They had much to thank Renar for; goodly company and hospitality for a night or two and a never-ending stream of supplies which must have placed the innkeeper near to his minimum Coldseason stores.

Amid the snow several other bodies could be discerned but their faces were hidden; many would have been familiar. The onlookers wept, gripping their swords, faces averted upwards.

In a firm, low voice Durnor spoke at last. "Lindarg Sire, this cannot go unavenged..."

"The Brushwood! Frind! He may have striven for my gold but I would not see him meet his end at the hand of Baeths – we need swift steeds!" shouted Lindarg.

In answer to his call, powerful beasts were upon them snorting hot breath; stamping the ground.

"On!" he cried and in a whirl of snow, with no thought for

provisions or plans and with minds bent on action; fighting, vengeance and death, they thudded away west on the thin trail to Brushwood. Into the night they sped – their animals knowing the track – though it lay now beneath a thickening cloak of white.

"Sire," gasped Andur. "Our mounts – they will never keep the pace!"

As if in answer, their steeds seemed to grow in stature and sucking in great gulps of cold air, increased their speed. Grimly the Liegemen and Lindarg hung on as their mounts tore through the muffled dark: Lindarg's eyes gleamed with a demonic fire and they knew Virdil was there with them and the right way was ahead.

Pre-dawn was paling the sky as they thundered over the brow into Brushwood – sleeping still under the snow.

Lindarg was exultant, "In time! In time!" His relief was echoed in their steeds and they slowed.

The commotion of their arrival had wakened Frind: an upstairs light was lit and his face, bleary and shocked by the cold, appeared from a window.

"Wha' – th'…?" was all he managed before Lindarg's voice stabbed upwards.

"Frind, stir yourself. There is likely trouble afoot – and alas, we bring sad news." In that voice was command and sincerity.

Moments later the main door opened and an oily light spread across the track as the riders shuffled to a stop.

"Back from the east… I did not expect-"

"Never mind what you expected," returned Lindarg as Frind peered more closely at him in the light of the lantern – as if trying to make up his mind who he might be. He was about to say something when Lindarg began again. "Frind, prepare yourself and listen – listen hard." Lindarg solemnly yet as quickly as he dare, told of Renar's end and the destruction of the Wetland Down.

Frind's face contorted with grief and anger but he heard

Lindarg out as he finished. "The town must be alerted and made ready, we will aid as we can."

Hardly had Lindarg finished than Frind filled with air like a huge balloon. He turned and charged back into the inn flinging throaty bellowing curses through its very foundations. It seemed he would warn the dead!

As Frind's orders rolled through the building, Andur's voice came from behind them with a fateful sound. "They are here!" With those words they all heard several muffled yells and the dull sound of hooves over the snowy ground. At the same moment, the huge red face of Frind reappearing at the door but calmer now – caught the news.

"Are they… aahh." He disappeared again.

"We must fight, a sleeping town cannot!" Durnor clutched the hilt of his sword to his own call; seven others followed suit. Eisdan's features were grim as he turned and spoke to Andur. "A pleasure I have long awaited! Let us choose our ground."

Andur nodded, his hard-set smile filled with assurance. As one, the liegemen's swords rang defiance; glittering blades thirsting for blood.

"Farisle!" shouted Durnor, his sword raised to the morning light.

But their gallant steeds were finished and could move no more; dismay tempered their defiance. That same moment they saw a ravening horde of two or three score fighting men descending on the quiet little town and felt themselves – a mere eight – weak and hopelessly outnumbered. Too soon was the attack; Brushwood could not be ready in time; it could only be a massacre. On foot with swords drawn the liegemen spread out across the snow to face those who came to slay. None of them thought of the morrow.

But even as their foe's fiendish grins became white and clear, Frind was with them, seemingly larger than ever and grinning like the attackers; a crazed but calculating visage. Already he aimed and placed the tube to his lips then blew with explosive force. The leading rider clutched his throat in surprise – then his grin was transformed into an agonised rattle and ended as he pitched lifeless into the snow. Frind loosed five more Yanish teeth darts in quick succession with seemingly no effect – then the Baeths were upon the liegemen.

Two of Faran's opponents fell dead before his eyes: the Yanish poison had worked slowly; their faces contorted with agony but paralysed muscles unable to scream. Then Faran was hacking away at anything that moved. With a leg sliced off the mount of his next attacker crumpled awkwardly, throwing its rider brutally onto Faran's upturned sword. The snow reddened. Turg took a blow on his sword arm; four Baeths had singled him out – in a moment he would be a memory. But his anger flared and still he held them in check, loosing their blood to join his own melting the snow.

Durnor's robe was slashed; blood oozed from several cuts but four riders lay dead in the snow around him; still his blade was a blur of sanguine. Eisdan's fury grew, his battle cry accompanying his lunges as he rushed among the disquieted steeds of the enemy, his blade flashing from one kill to the next. The Baeths around him milled in confusion unable to organise counter-blows and range upon their elusive, deadly quarry. But Eisdan knew that for every Baeth he slew there were several others to fill the breach and each one fresh, while his own strength would inevitably fail. The others fared likewise; none would last the battle: it was all but lost. They were too exhausted and disadvantaged.

Frind had run out of darts and looking round frantically for a weapon, he tore up the inn sign on its stout wooden pole and charged, bellowing, at his nearest antagonist. The 'Brushwood Down' caught him full in the face shattering both the sign-board and the rider's neck. To see this iron countryman bellowing and killing with a mere piece of wood fired the hearts of the liegemen and they rallied anew, taking more riders down; melting more white snow with warm red blood. Then from the trees up the slope appeared another horde of Baeths; their malevolent, spiteful chorus freezing even Frind to the spot. Behind the defenders the town had awakened – too late…

Lindarg leaned on a door post, weary and spent after the night's headlong rush, but the battle would be lost without his aid; he tried to summon strength… In the town behind he could hear the smashing of doors as Baeths who had skirted the fighting took their raid into homes with women and children screaming in terror.

Suddenly in the cold, early light, chaos fell upon the ranks of the riders; steeds pitched and threw; snorting and wild they cavorted like crazed bulls across the battlefield and through the town. Many riders were thrown; others were whisked bewildered through the snow and out of sight. One animal ran at full speed into the side of the inn and its rider was catapulted through the window smashing several tables and an inside door, where he came to rest; dead. Swords were forgotten; the once besieged and nearly crushed liegemen breathed easily once more as riderless beasts calmed and those to which riders still clung hurtled beyond sight. A shrill voice drifted back to them:

"Gargol will hear of this – wizard -." Then was gone. Barely perceiving, Lindarg fell exhausted into the snow. Some of those who had seen ran to his aid and he was carried into the inn with Andur and Eisdan at his side. Around them villagers murmured, "Wizardry?"

"Virdil?"

"But Virdil has not returned…"

"You saw those steeds – how else would they have behaved as they did?"

"This Lindarg then – could he somehow-?"

"Did Virdil have a son?"

"Timely though, whoever it was!"

The battered Baeth body was thrown back the way it had entered – such was the custom in these parts for those who were unwelcome and the bar-room was refurbished. Outside Frind had vented his last vestiges of wrath finishing the life of a raider with his pole. Bleeding and weary the liegemen limped toward the inn. Hurriedly Frind replaced what remained of the pole and sign, looking at it a trifle wistfully and welcomed them in at the door saying:

"I regret gentlemen, that my hospitality has been a little delayed – but for as long as you wish it will be yours," and added, "pity about the sign, I'll have to have another one made and charge it to the Baeths."

They all smiled rather weakly as Frind hobbled into the back, obviously in great pain. Andur stared after him and muttered loudly, "I'm glad he's on my side!"

For the next two days the Brushwood Down appeared to be the hub of activity for the little town. Most of the townsfolk showed up several times a day; everybody and everything seemed to be coming and going from the inn. Already Frind, now much recovered and some others of the menfolk had warned outlying farmers of the danger and persuaded most of them to move into the town where the innkeeper provided them with the best accommodation he could offer. Another group of men had left for Wetland to see to its remains and bury its dead. Frind went with them and when they returned two days later, grief for his cousin and family was clearly etched on his face. There were no survivors.

Frind became looked to for leadership, a responsibility which he discharged with increasing fervour and he had gathered together a small army of 'blowers' who were ready at a signal to bolster the town's defences should the need arise again. Supplies and stores were brought in from far and near and cached safely against the rigours of the Coldseason. All around Lindarg and the Liegemen there were preparations and bustle, yet still Frind managed to see to their needs and recovery. The inn had been turned into an arsenal of blowing pipes with garish missiles and collected boxes of Yanish teeth darts; rusty swords, heavy axes, pikes and the like.

In the evening after the second day of the battle of Brushwood,

Lindarg emerged, recovered and restive, Frind met him as he came down the corridor to the bar where many were gathered making plans and preparations in case of further attack. Actually a good deal of ale was being drunk most of the time and people still marvelled at, and re-told the stories (many exaggerated already) of the battle.

"Aaah – er -" Frind was at a loss for a name.

"Lindarg?" suggested Lindarg.

"Hmm – yes, yes it is good to see you are rested. Er – we owe you much – Brushwood is grateful to you, for it was you, was it not who turned the fray in our favour?"

"Perhaps – and maybe not," replied Lindarg. The liegemen smiled; he was being evasive again and was surely himself once more. Lindarg went on; "It is as likely that you owe as much to these Farislanders." He motioned to them scattered by the bar and smiled the smile of a wise wizard. "And from what I heard, you made as good an account of yourself. You must teach us the art of 'blowing' sometime – for all the lore and knowledge that there lies in Gullen I fear the skill is lost and that is a great mistake!"

Frind's face reddened: as if to hide his embarrassment he raised a tankard calling, "To Lindarg and his liegemen!"

"Frind of Brushwood!" came the answering toast accompanied by a chorus of cheers somewhat drowned by good ale. Music was started and the gathering made merry well into the night.

But before its end, at Lindarg's bidding, Frind, the liegemen and himself slipped quietly into a back room. Once settled, Lindarg caught their attention, his countenance troubled.

"Brushwood was a good victory – yet I fear ill may come of it in time. Gargol's men once more have been rebuffed and it is likely that we have but succeeded in stirring him afresh." He hesitated; the others remained silent as he thought about his next words. "Know this: you must not call me Virdil. I lay it upon all of you never to use that name; Lindarg I am and will remain…"

"But Sire," objected Turg. "What harm is there in a name?"

Your dream showed it, even Frind suspects…" He cast a quizzical glance in the landlord's direction.

"I guessed," responded Frind to the unspoken question, "But how? Virdil was lost I heard-" Lindarg cut in on Frind's speculation:

"It doesn't matter how and in any case I do not know myself – there is much I have yet to learn. I just feel it is wise that I am not known as Virdil." Then he added, "The time may come for that." They accepted the statement and Lindarg continued; "Gargol of the Baeths will soon know that I have Virdil's powers – some of them as least. 'Til now he has though Virdil slain else he would never have sent men and beasts into battles. Now he assuredly will not."

"Then we are in great danger here," said Frind.

"No Frind, I do not think he will waste time on Brushwood again – unless, when Endworld is finally his, he comes in person to wreak revenge on this tiny thorn; but no, at the end of things it will not be Gargol that remains. Brushwood I think has little to fear from Baeths in the times to come…"

"From whom, then?" asked Frind suspiciously.

"Ah, there is another enemy whose hand has not yet touched the Eastlands, for now he has more important things on his mind-"

But Frind interrupted him, bushy beard vibrant, "He!" he exclaimed incredulously. "There is only one then?"

His voice, full of scorn challenged Lindarg who stared back saying, "What if that one were me?" Frind gave no response to the question and was on his heels, but Lindarg pursued him, "What if he were more than I; much, much more?"

A tangible silence hung in the room, eyes glanced between them until Frind lowered his face and said, "Is this true?"

"Yes, there is another – of that I am certain at least," replied Lindarg darkly. "Our fates must surely bring us together… again."

"Again… then…?" Frind was silenced by the realisation of what Lindarg who had been Virdil was suggesting: its conclusion inescapable. So too Frind realised that they were embroiled in struggles far surpassing Baeths in their importance in Endworld; beyond his reach and comprehension; he saw then that his part would be of mortal men and steel – and to eschew these less palpable conflicts.

Lindarg's face was heavy with responsibility as he interrupted their grim thoughts. "What we decide here, this night, may be of the greatest import to the outcome of what lies ahead and all of you must be on your guard in the seasons to come. I regret that I can see little more than you of the dangers which assuredly are in prospect. Your own counsels must guide your actions as the need arises."

"What then must be done?" Durnor it was who broke the monologue but Lindarg waved him into silence, brows furrowed.

Finally he said, "Long have I wrestled these last two days with exactly that question and I am no nearer a complete answer now than then. Indeed, what I propose may be utter folly but I can do no more than follow the dictates of my heart."

"Well?"

Durnor's response showed impatience, but Eisdan stayed him with a knowing glance muttering, "Hasty answers compromise truth."

But Lindarg ignored them and resumed his monologue: "Gargol I think will set grandiose schemes in motion – no less than the taking of Gullen." Frind was dumbstruck.

"Surely Gullen is too strong to fall!" he intoned indignantly.

"Was," corrected Lindarg. "Much I think has happened since you were last there. Virdil's house lies empty; the queen mourns and the city's armies are depleted from the battle of Dorn. Gullen has lost its head for a fight and I fear it would fall easy prey to an army of Baeth fighting men."

"Then we must aid it as we can!" Faran's statement was a stark demand.

"And so you shall!" answered Lindarg, "Indeed it is my plan. Liegemen, you must leave for Gullen at dawn with all speed.

Seek there one called Farg, for his life is wrought against the Baeths. Frind – you must gather those men Brushwood can spare and ride to Gullen also. See to it that the Eastlands are scoured for valiant men as you go and that they take with them their worth and weight in supplies. The city will need both should the Baeths lay siege. Every hand – or mouth," Lindarg gave vent to a wry smile, "may be called upon to fight: Gullen must not fall." His commanding tone could not be gainsaid.

"It will be done vowed, Frind," and the liegemen nodded their assent.

"But what of you, Sire?" asked Eisdan.

For a moment Lindarg was silent – then evasive, "I must go south."

"South?" exclaimed Frind. "Will you not aid Gullen?"

Lindarg regarded him sympathetically. "I am needed elsewhere and for other reasons; stout men can face Baeths – men like you."

The statement sounded final and Frind, catching the look on the liegemen's faces, said nothing more of Lindarg's own plans, but Lindarg volunteered; "I will tell more when we next meet…" He broke off then but there was hope in that assertion.

Then he stood, indicating that the meeting was at an end but Durgol stopped them. "Six will be as good as nine in Gullen and we are more forgers than fighters, will you not let us ride with you south? Durgel and I will not lightly let you go."

Lindarg was touched. "Your loyalty is beyond doubt and perhaps it will be hard for you to let me ride from you into greater dangers – but I must follow my dreams." The word 'my' was heavy with emphasis. "I am more than the Lindarg who first came here with you. Forgotten lands lie to the south – my way lies through them and I foresee that sinews and swords would be worthless there." He paused long enough to grasp hold of their arms, "Besides, Gullen will have need of skilled forgers -" He left it at that and they retired to steal from what remained of the night as much sleep as they could.

The relief of those few garrulous days of ale and stories at the Wetland Down was harshly broken by the crack of a stinging cold, early dawn. Even at this hour, Frind, with others were long gone and already leagues away – his band swelling with recruits as farms were shut up against the Coldseason and children and lady folk were ushered together in safer numbers with men who stayed behind.

Lindarg and the Liegemen headed their new mounts westward along the Eastway and with great sadness the townsfolk of Brushwood waved them away and were left behind; their part almost played out – but long remembered as an early blow to the Baeth plans.

For the large part of that first day they rode in silence, knowing that Frind and his band would soon be hard on their heels heading for Gullen. Later in the afternoon they came upon a barely perceptible crossing of the ways and Lindarg stopped.

"My way is south along this forgotten way; it will be hazardous – but fear not for me. All speed to Gullen with your news and swords; tell the queen that, in my heart, she goes with me. Farewell until we meet again, for we shall – must!" Before they could respond he was well into the scrub of the old way and was lost from sight. Andur turned his steed toward that track;

"Come, Faran, we will follow."

"No!" Andur checked and looked at Eisdan who had spoken. "For once let him ride alone – we would probably be a burden at his side," Eisdan finished.

Reluctantly Andur turned back to them. "You begin to be like him!" he snorted as they started back on the Eastway to Gullen.

9

GULLEN IS TESTED

Few words passed between the liegemen as they sped westwards until they became aware of the noise of fast-approaching steeds from their right.

"Halt!" shouted Turg in a hushed voice. "Riders!" In an instant they were still and the noise easily heard.

"Baeths perhaps?" muttered Durnor.

"Into the trees!"

They melted into the woodland to the left of the Eastway just in time. A horde of armed fighting men surged into view little caring of the commotion of their passing as they clattered onto the harder surface of the road a short distance behind where the liegemen had stopped and turned from their path. As they did so, Durnor recognised the leader as one from Brushwood – but there were no others he knew. These then, he surmised, must be Eastfolk mustered from further villages and towns.

He stepped out into their path. "Ho, friends!"

The leader slowed, those behind him following his example as he said, "Hail Durnor – and liegemen," he added as the others emerged from the trees.

"'Tis a fond meeting once more," came Karil's voice. "But where is Frind?"

"He has sent many of us to outlying towns and villages, there to seek further aid and supplies and to muster the Eastfolk who are still ignorant of what turns in the Southlands – but will be eager to join us in our cause. He has sent many others from the road to find support also. Frind himself is ahead but has pledged to await us short of Gullen so that the Eastfolk may show well at the gates of the city and enter them in great numbers and honour."

"Then let us ride together to Gullen," said Durnor. Further words were unnecessary as they turned and headed again toward the city which was at the heart of the lands and culture of the Southfolk of Endworld.

On their way westwards there were more meetings as men came from other parts of the Eastlands. Large and small groups joined the swelling throng which journeyed to Gullen; stopping fitfully; moving determinedly. Soon they met up with Frind and many others who had set up a makeshift camp a little aside from the Eastway less than a day's ride from Gullen. Here they stood by for those who had not yet joined them until the muster was well-nigh complete.

That evening before sunset Andur and Durnor had climbed a hill above the camp. From their vantage point they could see the city but a league or so to the west with the low sun glowing on its roofs, its dust and vapours hanging in the pale sky. The walls of the city soared sentinel from the southern plain; rising dark and sheer stone upon stone forming a squarish plan with rounded corners; the buildings of Gullen ordered within. At each corner rose a round tower commanding views across the city, the surrounding plains and the whole rake of ramparts which were like giant teeth set against the evening glow of the western sky. From where they stood they could make out the quadrately curved roof of the central place looming starkly above lesser structures, its atavistic petroglyphs – which they guessed had endured since before the time of man – clear and admonishing even at this distance.

"Surely such a place is invincible!" whispered Andur in awe.

"While its defenders live..." countered Durnor darkly, adding to Andur's statement; then went on. "A siege would triumph as surely as if the walls did not exist. Defenders have

119

but three courses – to fight, surrender or starve. Had they been able to prevail in a fight then they would not have incarcerated themselves behind walls where, daily, they will agonise between attack or surrender; where each day that passes will diminish their strength and bring nearer the inevitable. Thus defenders can never win; they may only avoid defeat for a time – and that perhaps not long. Even in 'victory' they have nothing to gain for what they defend is already theirs. Defence is a desperate plight from wherever the stand is made."

The chilling truth of Durnor's words made Andur shudder as they were bathed in the glow of the decaying sun and turned down from the hill.

The following morning, they set off on the final stride to Gullen itself; the mighty snake of the Eastfolk on the Eastway. At their head rode the van of Frind and the Liegemen as they came into the view of the watchers on the walls. Frind shouted first as the column came to a halt before those high walls, short of the barred east gate.

"Hail Gulleners! The Eastfolk come to their city's aid in these troubled times, bringing fighting men, supplies of food and weapons, we seek entry to the city."

"Welcome, liegemen lords and Eastfolk." The reply drifted down from above the gates. "The queen asks of the Lord of Gullen."

Now Durnor answered: "Lindarg had taken other roads though we know not where or why – and we have news for the queen." He paused for a moment then; "Frind," he motioned to the innkeeper whose face still showed surprise and consternation at the titles afforded to the liegemen, "has brought this host – a good man with good men; his story will be told."

The gates were flung wide and the first of the musters of the Southlands entered Gullen causing a mighty stir, for Gullen itself was barely aware of the threat which Lindarg had foreseen. Though its denizens had been vigilant and even with the numbers of Baeth raids on outlying villages increasing, since the taking of their queen nearly two Starseasons ago and the changing of the ways, the immediacy of the Baeth threat had seemed to decline. Thus had Gullen been lulled into a time of calm…

Close up now, the liegemen took in the detail of Gullen's exterior, noticing the massive stone blocks that made up the walls, each painstakingly dressed; the length of a tall man and twice a man's width in height. Andur imagined the scores of men who would have been needed to move each block; the tackle and gantries to place it – or had sorcery been used with its power beyond the imaginings of men? In each wall was a central gate – one for each of the cardinal ways; fashioned from the wood of the tough Brown trees of Dorn; solid, resilient, imposing. Above the east gate which they now neared, an angular tower – not as tall as the rounded corner ones, straddled the gate's arch and from which the gates could be defended and controlled. Pock-marked with slit windows, defenders could deal death upon any who threatened the gates. Inside the gate tower geared wheels turned by men worked the gates and above them a stout bar of metal could be lowered to lock them once closed.

Soon the liegemen and the queen were together in her chambers and she plied them for news:

"What happened in Thae? Where is Lindarg? Where has he gone? What did he dream… Did he dream…?"

They all answered her many questions at once.

"One speak for all," she said desperately, raising a hand, "else I will learn nothing amid the banter of eight good voices!"

"I will speak," said Durnor casting a quizzical glance at the other liegemen who tacitly agreed.

"Then speak on – there is much that I and Gullen must know. The coming of the Eastfolk is a harbinger to Gullen; time may be short."

Durnor began. "Thae is no more-"

But the Queen interrupted, her face incredulous. "But that cannot be! A whole land cannot disappear!"

"Thae did not disappear, it was consumed and changed from

121

that barren waste – inconceivable to those who have not known it – to 'Yirfurnelle'-"

"Re-born!" muttered the queen, half to herself.

"Just so. It is soon to become a forest as Dorn – perhaps greater."

"How do you know this, Durnor?"

"We have seen it in the stone and Lindarg says that the stone shows the truth – but only if you know what to ask of it."

"Ahh – I have heard that before… And you saw this yourself?"

"Yes, my Queen."

"Then he has shown you the Queenstone which I gave to him?"

"He has; we have seen its power – it was a fine gift."

"What of Tromillion? Did Lindarg dream?"

"He did – and was greatly changed by those dreams. Not all of them did he understand – and probably very little did he tell us of what he dreamed."

Syntelle smiled at Durnor's wistful statement, recognising the wisdom of a wizard's silence: information is knowledge and in sorcery, knowledge is power.

Durnor continued. "But he did say that he dreamed he was Virdil."

"Virdil? But… how?" Syntelle blurted.

"He could not say himself – or would not. Lindarg he was, yes, but in him also is Virdil and his is the inner force which drives him."

"Many things are made clearer to me by what you say – though by no means all; this is good news for Gullen and Endworld and maybe we should not ask how this has come to be. Oh! It makes me happy beyond all hope, liegemen; but I see from your faces that you know little of this Virdil."

"Only that he-" Durnor groped for the right tense, "er, was a wizard and that he had an enemy called Venain."

"Dark is that name, liegemen," she whispered grimly.

"Aye, Virdil was destroyed by him once," added Durnor,

"Lindarg told us that much. He told us too that he must never be known as Virdil – that must remain hidden from all ears; he is Lindarg."

Syntelle's eyes were bright with excitement. "If this is true, liegemen, then he knows more than we can ever know and we must do as he wishes: he is Lindarg. But I will tell you of Virdil and what he was... or still is."

They listened incredulously to what she unfolded of Virdil and his fate. It took long in the telling but none there missed a word. At last she finished:

"So now it is clear that there are two enemies of the Southlands: Baeths most immediate and an awesome force; Venain, more remote for now but of greater power than the combined might of all the Baeths in Endworld – and who may, as we speak, draw nearer. Fate has wrought that we meet them both 'ere they meet each other; 'tis a cruel pass indeed but for a while at least, Gullen rejoices." Syntelle paused while her recounting was mulled, then, "But lords, I am selfish, let us eat; time enough for more news after!"

Frind was called for and joined them as they ate and the queen said, "He is now here whose story you said would be told, Durnor, now tell it."

Durnor recounted the sad end of Wetland and the Battle of Brushwood, Frind's valiant part in it and his mustering of the Eastfolk at Lindarg's bidding. He also repeated what Lindarg had said that grim night in the Brushwood Down; that Gargol would turn to Gullen; that the city must be defended. At the end, Frind stood a little unsteadily, un-used to such acclaim but with determination said;

"My Queen, already we in the east have suffered at the hands of these Baeths; many a homestead and village has been ravaged by them in their search for supplies and sport: peace-loving people murdered, defiled and tortured for their foul pleasures; we would not see Gullen fall to these same filth. We have come from our homes in the east to fight; to defend our kin; to help protect the Southlands and all its peoples. I swear a hundred of their kind will die for Renar – a good cousin who probably never even woke to see what it was had come to slay him. There are many of us, my Queen, hard men, good fighters and true; we are yours to set against foes – death or victory 'ere we turn aside…"

His oration finished Frind glanced about him sheepishly. Lords of Gullen and the queen with them had risen to respect his words; now the queen spoke;

"Gullen thanks the Eastfolk for their aid, the offer is treasured and gratefully accepted by Gullen hearts. Eastfolk are ferocious men they say – oft considered suspicious and taciturn – they will need a leader who understands them – a leader they can respect; one of valour, courage and proven worth," she hesitated, finding Frind's eyes and looking deeply into them. "Do you, Frind of Brushwood, accept this charge?" Frind, looking as though he wished the floor would swallow him up stammered;

"B – but I – I am no warrior I have no experience in such things…"

"You have met Baeths, fought them and prevailed; alas, there are few in Gullen who can match even that brief experience and there may be time yet to learn about 'such things'," interposed the queen.

Frind saw their confidence and esteem: with but one choice he answered, "I accept."

With those two words, Frind became and took on the burdens of a general of a large part of Gullen's gathering forces: leader and commander of all the Eastfolk who had come with him and others who would come late from the Eastlands, of which there were many.

The queen continued, "Farg, Frind, you should seek with all speed for he is the general of the Gullen Guard. Together and with the other generals and the liegemen lords you must make plans to defend the city, for as surely as Lindarg warned, I fear the Baeths will not long leave Gullen alone – and we must be ready."

"It will be done, my Queen!"

Frind left them then to find Farg.

Sitting once more, the queen turned back to Durnor. "Now, liegemen, what of Lindarg – where has he gone so secretly?"

"Secretly indeed – he would not tell us!" returned Durnor, then, "But he heads south. Not long after we had left Brushwood he turned that way and forbade us to follow."

Syntelle looked puzzled. "South?" Her question was rhetorical, "What lies there? It is long since that road was used; it is but a legend in the minds of old men – it is said that a man may travel that road for an eternity and still not reach its end," she mused, remembering what Virdil had once told her.

"An endless road that goes nowhere?" Eisdan was perturbed. Syntelle nodded vacantly as if trying to recall more. "Who would build such a thing and why?" Eisdan queried.

"I cannot imagine, but the stone may have shown – or perhaps a dream… But we have neither and maybe it is better that way…" She paused, lost in a reverie, for a moment fancying Lindarg as a shining silver ghost travelling in slow motion through distant times. At last she broke the silence. "Rest well tonight, my lords. The days ahead will be full and as Lindarg speeds south to his fate, we must do as he bids and see to ours."

Gullen easily absorbed the Eastfolk as those in the city opened their doors to them and they were made welcome in every home. Welcome too were their supplies – ample to support them and more in the hard times to come. By the second day, several score more had come from the Eastlands, swelling the host already there – yet the flow was not ended.

It was not until the third day after the Eastfolk's arrival was full that a war council of lords and generals was held in Gullen for the first time. It was attended by the liegemen, the generals including Frind of course who had already drummed up enormous enthusiasm for his army of 'blowers' – though as yet few were convinced that it would prove any potent force in defending the city. There also were certain of the city's wise including the Steward, the Lorist and Syntelle. Mainly the council would be for talk of fighting men and others merely needed to know what it was that they planned. Farg called the council in his role as co-ordinator of Gullen's Guards and his was the duty of its presidence.

Though, on their first visit to Gullen, the liegemen had been hailed lords as Lindarg and though they had mixed, revelled and laughed with Gullen's men; had been accepted and trusted, Durnor rose first at that council and spoke for them.

"My Queen, lords and Gulleners, we liegemen are pledged to the service of Lindarg, Lord of Gullen. Likewise and at his request we serve also this city and its peoples who have warmed our hearts and spirits with their kindness, making the Southlands a home for us far from our torn lands. Our hearts are stout and true; not quailing in battle nor in hardship; whatever is ours to do we face it together and no task will thwart us 'ere death itself intervenes. Farisle was a fair place where we grew happy and free; proud too. It was ravished by Baeths long before they turned south – and few survived those ravishes unscathed. The Baeth mines where we toiled added fuel to our wrath – though but for Lindarg the fire in our breasts would have been long since quenched in those dreadful places. Even now new captives will toil to their deaths and that hardens our hearts the more."

"Well spoken, Durnor!" Farg's teeth gleamed hard and white. "To start a task with one accord is to hasten its completion – the city will be prepared the sooner and that is our commission – for in Gullen many of the last treasures of Endworld lie protected. The wise tell us that it is the role of Gullen to dispose of them wisely – not of invaders who would scatter them piecemeal over Endworld. Thus our duty is laid upon us. No less do we have a similar duty to ourselves and the denizens of the Southlands. Nor should we think that the Baeths would stop here, Dorn would follow, then they would sail from these shores to other lands which exist. To all these peoples we have a clear incumbency." He paused, then finished, "Where is the Lord of Gullen at our time of need?" There was barely a hint of contempt in his last words but they were marked well.

Durnor was indignant and his sword rang as he replied to Farg's ill-considered words. "Our liege rode into danger – not to caper on the southern grasses!"

But Syntelle interrupted them. "Stay these words – they are worthless to our plight. Already Lindarg has been through more than you or I could conceive and I would guess that it was with no light heart that he forged a different path from those whom he loves and serves. Virdil knew of mightier forces in Endworld than were even guessed by us and were he here now perhaps he would be talking of seeking them himself. Maybe he has already sought them and failed once…" She broke off, not sure how to continue, then, "You are right, Farg, our duty is clear – and it could be that another's charge is clear to him but obscure to us. We know that Lindarg has powers with him and we must think that he intends to use them. In the very secrecy of his deeds my lie their success."

Farg was apologetic. "I spoke hastily in the heat of the moment, my Queen – I intended no discredit on the Lord Lindarg. His liegemen may freely seek redress of me as they please."

"We accept the apology and will take no recompense for hasty words." said Durnor, "Indeed we rarely understand our liege ourselves and therefore cannot resent your question." His sword now sheathed, he gave Farg a hefty cuff on the shoulder. "Come, what is to be done? Time is wasting; we are eager for action now."

With that the council began in earnest and Farg continued, "The city walls are solid and will not fall easily even to an army of thousands – a few can defend them comfortably. In that lies both good and bad fortune; inevitably a long siege would crush us though we might ward off the invaders time and again. As I see it, two things must be done with all haste. Firstly, fighters from all corners of the Southlands must be brought to Gullen and toughened for battle; trained as fighting men – not farmers or craftsmen. They must be the equal of the Baeth might – man for man. That will take time but the walls will give us that time: time also to forge weapons for we have had need of few of these for many ages – and men can achieve little without steel – however stout their hearts."

"With this we can help," cut in Durgol, motioning to his brother. "Our skills in Farisle were as forgers – these we made when first we came to Gullen–" He drew his sword and motioned to those of the other liegemen.

"A fine blade indeed, Durgol! And many such will be needed," observed Farg.

"Then set us that task and it will be done!" The two brothers stood proud.

"That is settled then," stated Farg, a sureness in his voice, then continued, "Secondly, and equally important, supplies must enter Gullen too. Food, water, wood, metals, cloth, building materials – all those things needed to support the hosts which will be gathered in the city. The preparations will be hard for all, but dangerous will be the lot of those who rouse the Southlands gathering men and supplies; the commotion of their passing will not escape Baeth eyes and they will surely try to thwart those plans."

"Send us then to stir the Southfolk," volunteered Andur, "and Frind also."

Before Frind could speak to agree or otherwise, Farg broke in with a smile, "No, not Frind. It is his wish to form a special unit – and he shall have his way – maybe Gullen will learn something it has forgotten…" Farg's voice contained little conviction.

"Thank you," was all Frind said in response. He knew – oh yes, he knew what he could and would do – a hundred dead for every one in Wetland Down was in his mind.

Farg went on. "Liegemen, if it your wish, then the task is yours. Gullen does not lay this upon you. Some who know the Southlands will go with you."

"But the band must be kept as small as possible so that it may

128

more easily go unnoticed when it is expedient to do so," rejoined Andur.

"That is true and well said," replied Farg. "There will be no more than a score altogether and you may take those whom you know best and who wish to go; it is imperative that the gathering begin tomorrow."

"Today we will go; we have been prepared since our coming to Gullen – so also are those who would ride with us," said Durnor.

Farg looked surprised – but pleased, marking their initiative well. "Then tarry no more; remaining preparations will be attended to by the captains and townsfolk: the city will be in readiness for the men and supplies you bring. Good speed and luck to your errand!"

As the liegemen turned to go, hard faces set to their duty, the queen rose to her feet and said to them, "If by chance you hear tidings of the Lord of Gullen, send word speedily for I am vigilant for his return. Good luck to your venture, return safe that in Gullen you may yet again be honoured."

Not long into the afternoon the liegemen were ready to ride: Banor and Fanor with them. A weak sun did little to assuage the still cold of the day; Gullen around them was alive with anticipation.

"Greetings once more this day – I hope the liegemen are well rested. The days ahead will be full and sleep scarce." Banor's tone was querulous as he aimed his words at Durnor.

"And to you Sire," the liegeman replied, then added pointedly, "We have been strangers to sleep before-"

Banor's voice cut him off, "Of course, I am foolish to speak to you of dangers and travail." Banor was sincere. "Come, we will start from the city and talk as we journey."

They wheeled their mounts and cantered between dwellings lining the long avenue from the central place to the western gate; their passing echoing hollowly off stone walls and down alleys. They talked little over this distance, noticing the change in the city and its people; the hurried bustle obtrusive yet not so. At the westgate Durgol and Durgel bid them farewell and good fortune as they passed through and onto the Westway between fields which surrounded the city.

Andur regarded Banor and Fanor. He had barely met them during his first stay in Gullen after the feast of Astellin and the following Warmseason; now he pondered their impressive appearance.

Tall and erect, proud men of Gullen they were with the wavy flaxen hair common to Gulleners flowing from beneath the steel helms they wore. Hard-set noses stark against their lean, weathered faces set with a fair bristle; alert, brown eyes beneath imposing brows – furrowed above by the task ahead: stern and determined faces they were. They wore tunics of rough cloth – Banor's blue and Fanor's green – which left tough-muscled limbs covered only by a light, silvery mail contrasting with a breast plate of luridly gleaming metal of a grey hue. A broad, woven belt of stout hide was clasped at its front bearing a crest of the same metal. The detail of their crests differed but in common they had the twin boughs of barley – the mark of Gullen. Attached to each of their belts was a long sword of steel with a hilt of silver and gold, deep in a polished wooden scabbard: two knives in sheaths; a food pouch, skin gourd, hide thongs, a small horn and other essential items such as flints and salt – each with its own place and container. Both good, useful and true men to have on one's side, Andur thought. He was glad too; they would need with them someone recognised and respected to convince those who might doubt; though the Baeth threat was now well known in the Southlands, so too was the coming of the Lord of Gullen and his liegemen. But their faces were not yet known and even though they wore the helms and insignia of Gullen, many would have been suspicious and would not have heeded the call to muster had only the liegemen sallied forth.

They left the gates behind; Andur was aware of Banor's voice scattering his thoughts. "The plan is simple. We will split into two parties for speed and ease; one will take the main route west, the other south. At each village the message will be spread and riders sent from that village to its nearest neighbours and so on. This will ensure that people who are known alert those in outlying areas and that we will be spread less thinly. It is essential that any Baeths are avoided and that for as long as possible this gathering is done secretly." They all nodded assent, then Banor continued, "Who will accompany me to the south?"

"Faran and I with Danig and Raydel will," suggested Andur, alive now with the thought of swift action ahead.

"Good, then Fanor, Durnor and the others will ride west. All roads return to Gullen and may we be well met there once again in the days to come!" shouted Banor, turning south from the Westway.

"Good fortune, friend!" returned Fanor, "We shall meet again – look to yourselves well and take care." Fanor, Durnor, Eisdan, Karil and Turg watched as Banor's party thundered away over the meadows beneath the Coldseason Sun.

"On!" Fanor shouted with an upraised hand, "We must make Corindel by dusk and the ride is long."

The final convening of the Southlands had begun while Gullen herself prepared for those who would come and for the conflict which would as surely follow. War! What did this city know of war? Short was its time to find out!

Such mustering did not pass without mishap, since Baeth scouting and raiding parties were more frequent after the ignominity of Brushwood and the changing of the ways than any in Gullen had guessed. News was slow to travel when village peoples were reluctant to leave their homes. Only the first – though perhaps the most bloody – of these encounters happened at Corindel on that first night.

As the Gullen party approached the town they could see a fire to its north side and around it even now they could hear the commotion of the fight as fiery sparks scorched into the night sky.

"It looks like a farmer's timber home is burning," observed Fanor, slowing.

"Baeths?" uttered Durnor, the same question on all their minds.

Fanor stopped then said, "If it is then we must skirt round and make for the town – our mission must be of greater importance than one farmer's home." But there was little conviction in his voice, their instinct was to go and help.

"Surely," said Turg, "more than one or two families fight there."

"Aye," agreed Karil, "it sounds like many from the town have turned out."

"There may be too many Baeths – we might perish, then what of our quest?" Durnor cautioned them, "Perhaps we should not investigate."

"Then the town too will be unsafe soon – and there will be less men to muster," argued Turg, adding, "And if we do help them they will doubtless help us the more."

"I say Turg is right." Eisdan spoke now. "We must go to their aid and anyway, I hate Baeths!"

"Then pray that we are successful!" Fanor's voice boomed as he turned his mount and began the headlong charge toward the blazing farm.

Turg had been right. Corindel had been alerted; scores of folk had turned out of the town to forestall their attackers. Poorly armed – but incensed, they painted a ruthless, desperate picture in the glow of the flames and wild smoke but they were faring badly. As Fanor and the Liegemen drew near they could see knots of townsfolk with forks, scythes and the occasional blunt sword – cutting and hacking but being felled surely and swiftly with trained blows from shining steel. Baeths hooted over their butchery; this was what they enjoyed doing. They had sampled the rewards of pillage before; after the victory came the womanising with crushed submissive souls to do their every bidding: nubile girls – too young for these men – but used nevertheless; women to torture and beat; surviving men and boys to kill slowly. They looked forward to the food – more than they could eat – wasted while their starving captives struggled, helplessly bound, awaiting their fate at the pleasure of their captors. Drink too they relished; gorging themselves to insensibility. With glee they fought for their right to these things and equally, with a wild, terrified, desperation, those of Corindel sought to bar them from the town that they would so plunder and lay waste in their wake. Valiant was their attempt but doomed; ten at least of them fell for every Baeth who died.

The hearts of those who came in aid were stirred; in their minds the wonder that they had arrived here just now; that they had nearly made another decision. Gullen blades rang amid the din, throwing back the fire's glare from their honed steel: fighting blades these; well-balanced; slick in their hands: held aloft they charged into the fray. Westfolk were heartened by the sight and gained strength – perhaps thinking that these were the fleeter scouting party of a larger body of men who could turn these raiders; that those others would come on their heels to scythe down Baeths like wheat; crushing their helms like empty eggs. But alas! Only those five swords were there but behind them narrowing eyes, keen warrior judgment and timing; experience of the ruses of battle and conflict; hate, courage – and perhaps even a fragment of Endworld itself.

Then the blades descended and in the swiftness of a single shout, five Baeths lay dead. A cheer was heard above the cries; Baeths turned to meet this new and very real enemy which drove at them from the dark. In moments Fanor and the Liegemen were beset but Baeths found them harder to kill than the townsfolk they had been butchering. Fanor skewed his body aside while a Baeth sword rattled his mail; bruising without wounding; his own blade leaping upwards deftly; swiftness belying the power of the blow. A jawbone crunched, the point of the blade rose deeper; the body stiffened and fell. Already Fanor was pulling the sword downwards and backwards slicing to the bone the thigh of another Baeth who bustled from his right. Blood pumped vermillion onto the tanned skin – only just did the injured man parry the death blow which followed the slice. Fanor's sword whirled again – too swift for the dazed man – cutting his tough hide armour like cloth and burying itself deep into his abdomen. The man hung, stricken, folding slowly, but already the blade was clear and entrails oozing the gap as Fanor took yet another Baeth with a clean thrust through the heart. Durnor was at his side saying; "A blow to be remembered long, Fanor!" His voice was low, determined, encouraging. "I am glad to fight again!" he continued, wheeling round to face the Baeth leader.

The leader's blade found Durnor's right shoulder, dinting on the mail, sending a shock of dull pain through his arm. Durnor's sword leaped into his other hand in time to clash with another blow from the Baeth, his sword sliding down that of his antagonist, tearing at the hilt and severing a finger. The man did not seem to notice, intent on curving his blade beneath Durnor's thrust. Durnor hammered it down from his body and it glanced painfully off a leg but the man was too slow; before he could bring his blade up the two mounts closed together as eager villagers pressed into the battle, trapping it for an instant. In that fleeting moment the leader died; Durnor's blade swept across his throat like burnished lightning and the body gurgled a last cry into the grass.

"Ha!" came a cry from Eisdan some distance to the right of Durnor. Three Baeths had singled him out and were upon him. He ducked – then swerved his mount with a swiftness that threw only one reflected flash of firelight from his sword. Two blades clashed together above his head; the third man, expecting to deliver only a final unchallenged thrust from behind, found a blade leaping for his throat. His duck was fast; the blade sounded loudly on his helmet and while that stunning ring still whirled in the man's head, he died as the sword bore down cutting deeply into the side of his neck. The other two had now turned to face Eisdan but he was ready and moved in to attack. Feigning a sudden lunge to the man on his right who moved his sword to the defensive, the slight was followed through with a twist of Eisdan's body, glancing cruelly into the face of the attacker on the left of his own striking sword. Blood seeped from beneath the helm as the man groped blindly, his sword raking a red, oozing wound the length of Eisdan's left arm. Eisdan gasped in pain, recoiling from the wildly-flailing weapon. Then the man was drawn down and the townsfolk took him. The last of the three wavered and in that moment of indecision, Eisdan's sword raked his sword arm; severing tendons. After the blow it hung limp, the weapon useless at his side. As Eisdan prepared to strike, a fork flashed into the man's abdomen – its fine prongs easily forcing a passage through the mail.

Those from Corindel rose into cheers and led by the fighters from Gullen, took the battle to the remaining Baeths. Under this unexpected onslaught their resistance withered and with their numbers lessening ever more quickly, they searched with frenzied back glances for an escape to the rear but the townsfolk were all around now. Father and son from the burning farmhouse were behind them, rueing their loss; vengeful eyes burning. A Baeth turned his steed suddenly to crash a way through to dark freedom beyond the melee; instead he fell into their arms as they scythed the leg tendons of his beast and it collapsed beneath him. When he reached the ground he was dead and within minutes, the last of the Baeths had joined him, lifeless in the dirt.

The warriors from Gullen were cheered to the head of the throng which marched with triumphant and grateful acclaim into Corindel. Heroes they were and welcome they were made; their message, half expected by the men of the town, greeted with approval; they would go to Gullen. The man whose farm had burned and who had fought well said; "Gullen is the hub of the Southlands. Without its tenure our times would be short and these lands might not see peace as we have known it ever gain in our time. Corindel will surely aid Gullen!"

The townsfolk, still together in their fighting horde, greeted this brief speech with tumultuous approval, Fanor smiled.

Quieter now the farmer turned to Fanor saying, "But for you-" he gestured to include the liegemen, "and the Liegemen of the Lord of Gullen, there would no longer be a Corindel to leave. Gladly we will come."

"We thank you, Gullen will welcome you but we must travel as a small band to further places – that way suspicion of the Gullen plan will be less. Send your men to alert those nearer; the farms and the smaller villages; send them to gather the supplies and harvests that Gullen will need in the times to come."

"It will be done, Lord Fanor; nothing will be left here for the Baeths; what we cannot take we will destroy – though our own sweat be in it!" His tone was low and sincere, "Come," he continued, "Tonight we will have our fill of what the tavern has to offer; we will drink to the Southlands, Gullen and its lords: to our victory here this night and for those of ours to come."

Through the night, Corindel reverberated with celebrations – celebrations with an air of finality about them. Ale and wines that could not be carried, had to be drunk – in the morning they would be poured away. Fanor and the Liegemen joined with the songs and merriment but drank little; theirs would be the testier job of the morrow; further west they must go; Corindel and its near neighbours could be left to those who knew it best.

Within days of Banor, Fanor and the Liegemen leaving Gullen, the peoples of the Southlands began to pour in; a mere trickle at first, swelling as the days passed into hordes from every direction save the east and north from where most had already come in the earlier days of the conflict – though more did come from those places. The city absorbed them; elders taking supplies into store; taking men for their armies and work parties; allocating shelter and homes. For the first time in the long history of the Southlands – lands that had lain protected by wizardry and before that by the dictates of the gods – Southfolk met together and were united by, the threats which were poised to overtake them all and plunge Endworld into chaos.

Despite the early snows in the Eastlands, that Dundellin was long passed, the Coldseason had not yet struck Gullen. Throughout the mustering the season had been kind as if Endworld was working perhaps for the city and the denizens of the Southlands. Now Gullen was filled and ready. Farg was reporting to the queen that the preparations were complete.

"The men are trained and stationed, my Queen." He bowed slightly, then continued; "The gates have been further secured, supplies rationed; now we can only wait."

"It is well done Lord Farg," intoned the queen, though wearily, now heavy with child – Lindarg's child.

She was grateful that Gullen had been distracted. Had circumstances been different, she may have had to lose the child, though she wanted it. She had not been taken for a wife, thus, by the traditional ways of the Southlands, the child should not exist. The elders of the city, though disquieted, had pretended not to notice – partly because they had been too busy to be concerned with such matters but more importantly because it was unprecedented in the royal line of Gullen; an embarrassing anomaly.

Syntelle had sent the liegemen out into the Southlands as soon as they had returned from the musterings – to scour the lands for Lindarg but they had failed and now, with the final closing of the city's gates, she felt her last hope was gone that the Lord of Gullen would arrive in time to claim her and the unborn child: it would be born in his absence. For long she had remained hidden from all but those with whom she must confer and they had kept their knowledge secret. When Gulleners had asked of the queen they were told, "she is in council with the elders," or "she meets with the generals – there are secret plans afoot – perhaps wizardry." Thus the questioner would be placated and given succour.

But she ached to see her peoples – many of whom had never seen her – walk among them; talk to them, comfort them and give them hope for the villages and farms they had left. She

137

longed to say to them that Gullen would aid and repay them when it was over, even though she herself could do little but guess at the outcome. She longed to visit the guards and warriors on duty to brighten their day as she could; and the women who prepared the meals as their menfolk prepared for war. The city – her city – was active about her, full of her peoples but she was set apart.

She snapped out of the reverie which the generals' reports always brought upon her; Farg was still there, she lifted her head and said to him, "He will be called Virlin, for I am certain that he will be a son."

"Lindarg will surely come soon," comforted Farg. Syntelle had already told the Liegemen of Lindarg's child and the name upon which she had decided. They at least were glad for her and their liege. They were not of Gullen and Farisle was a freer place where tradition was not so cruel in such matters.

"Thank you, Farg," she said. She could see that he found it hard to accept and that she was somewhat diminished in his eyes. In fighting men traditions were, of necessity, a firmly established part of their psyche; she could not dislike his well-hidden disdain and sank again into her own reverie.

She thought back through the events of the near past, all seemingly had happened so recently and so quickly and yet it seemed like long ago that the first Baeth attack had found the Southlands basking in the Sun of Warmseason. She had not been in Gullen. Virdil had taken her from the city to Glaydelle in the north west parts of the Southlands at the edge of the Great Forest of Dorn. From there they had intended to go on to the Great Dome to visit the heart of the Woodman's realm and to accept the hospitality of the Forest King, Fordyne. Virdil had said that she should see the splendour of the forest and its inhabitants. Even then she recalled a hint of haste in Virdil's notion as if he might have added: "For they may not endure long…" But time had caught up with Virdil; in the stone he had seen Venain; a sign which he guessed would come – when his sorceries were set aside for greater designs and he lay unprotected. Virdil had left her then to collect men and march on Venain. His last words to her had been: "Do not go to the Great Dome in the forest yet; go back to Gullen in the next days and when I return, maybe then we will visit the Forest King. I will leave the Queenstone in safe-keeping in Gullen – for I have great need of it now. Later it may be of comfort to you and bring you news while I am gone." Then he had caressed her fine hair lovingly – perhaps longingly – a trace of sadness deep in his eyes.

She had felt his deeper anguish and said with the assurance that she sensed in his own mind; "This Venain is a dangerous foe-"

"More dangerous than I, Syntelle," Virdil had interrupted, but while there is a chance I must take it for he threatens the peaceful web of Endworld with his greed and shamelessness. I cannot turn aside from this opportunity which fate has offered to me; this may be why the Queenstone came to us from the depths of time – but there are other stones – other depths and questions; though for all the wisdom in Gullen, some of these things remain hidden." His countenance had turned dark then beneath long, flowing locks of black hair as he looked hard into her eyes. "I sense troubled times ahead and that grieves me for I have set my task – my charge is to still these troubles – and if they continue, then I must needs have failed."

She had begged him not to go: "Why must you lay this burden upon yourself? Gullen does not; I do not; the elders do not," she had pleaded tearfully, "If it is hopeless, do not attempt it."

"Aaaah, Syntelle, beauty of the Southlands," Virdil had replied. "Those whom you mention do not know as I do – it has ever been hopeless and ever will be so – but now, yes, now, there is but a moment of hope. It is in the stone, but even as we speak that time of hope may be drawing to a close and I must act and move swiftly. I am the only one who knows the true depths of the task; I am the same who has recognised this time of hope –

so brief in the history of Endworld, therefore," Virdil had risen before her, tall, erect, important, "I have vowed and the vow is sealed."

Syntelle had ceased to argue then. She knew that when a wizard sealed a vow his own words left him but two choices; to achieve that goal – or perish in the attempt. Were he prevented from discharging that vow, he would as surely die as with a sword in the temple; a wizard's vow was set against death itself. Seeing the truth in his eyes, Syntelle could not and would not stand in his way. Just before his departure from Glaydelle to Gullen that day, Virdil had said; "In times to come, things may not be as they seem – but trust in the stone!" Then she had bade him farewell, wishing him success and that night, cried herself to sleep.

The day after, as she was about to leave for Gullen, the Baeths had attacked. It had been quite a large force and they had taken the village, herself and other prisoners easily. Obviously they had been watching; waiting – perhaps futilely as they had done before, for Virdil to be absent. He was feared by Baeths more than anything else they knew of in Endworld; they had seen his powers; imagined others yet more ruthless and did not wish to experience them again. Now they had seen the wizard leave – riding like the wind for Gullen; a dark – perhaps distant purpose beneath the black crackling hair – and they had attacked the next day.

Somehow she remembered little of that harrowing journey through that Dundellin to the mines; even less could she remember her mistreatment – the cruel blows that she knew she had endured – but had forgotten their pain. Those days of brutal visits, lashes, the half-depraved guttural laughs of the men atop her; her Yanish guard, trained to kill; enjoying to see the terror of its victims. All these things were shut in the dark recesses of her mind. Then had been the release and the joyful trek to Gullen; hard – yet bountiful with empathy; the joys of her peoples in the land; the strange attraction of Lindarg; the Warmseason in Gullen with Lindarg restless and herself happy – yet strangely

140

sad as Dundellin hurried in; deeply sad as hope for Virdil's return had finally faded, yet still inexplicably laden with hope somehow.

That Dundellin, with Lindarg gone, leaving her with a child which she knew Gullen could not accept, she had one day been drawn to the quiet of Virdil's house – and entered. At first she had thought that the sealing spells had been broken and that it was a sign of the wizard's death finally. She had wept there, some tears of genuine sorrow; some of self pity. Then she had seen that the spell was not broken when Banor had come to comfort her and had not been able to enter, though he could see her within.

"Come, Banor," she had said and he had entered without hindrance; whereupon she had told him about Lindarg's child; to keep it secret among the Lords of Gullen, for, she had said they should know of an heir to their city. But Banor had not been sympathetic and from then she had been left alone save for the city's business which required her attention.

Long had she wondered why the seal of Virdil's wizardry did not bar her – but had found no answer. Much time had she spent thereafter in the soothing quiet of Virdil's house: she had cleaned it – as if for his return – and to take her mind off the problems which beset her. All the time in her mind she had tried to piece together the many 'things' which were 'not as they seemed'. In doing she gained much inner succour but no answers. Happenings in Endwörld seemed to her to have overtaken Gullen and particularly herself...

A new voice, breathless and fearful in the room, jolted her. "They are to the north, general." The soldier was bowed before her but his head was turned to Farg, "They will be here by nightfall." He paused, then added in an awestruck, drawn breath; "There are thousands of them!"

The news against which Gullen had prepared so long but which it dreaded every day that passed to hear, had come. That they could be helpless against such might with no sorcery had occurred to them all many times; now the reality of those fears was to be tested. By the evening of the next day, Gullen was surrounded.

For several days neither side made any move; the Baeths did not attack; Gullen remained sealed and adamant – watching the foe building siege towers and other impedimenta of war. Then Gargol's ill-timed haste was made clear to him. On the sixth day of the siege, Coldseason shattered the Southlands, plunging them into a wind-tossed icy waste. Water froze – even within the glow of a fire; the Baeth tents had to be shored up against the northerly squalls which lashed across the bare Gullen Fields. The building of rams, towers, shields and engines of war which had so far kept men busy and in good spirits was halted: men could not pull frozen ropes tight with withering hands; eyes could not be turned against the wind without being scraped raw. Wood for towers was re-directed for fires as Gargol's men abjectly shivered in a frozen hell of their own creation. Gargol himself saw his own hand forced into the open: when this freeze had passed, another would follow – already frost bite was wreaking havoc with many men – the lethargy of exposure with others. So at the waning of that first fierce tendril of Coldseason, rations were doubled and everyone was allowed fires; half-finished towers and ram-carts were dismantled and burned. Compared with those which had gone before, that night the Baeth army lived again, fighting back the raw chill with full bellies, warming bonfires and rising spirits; sleep was welcome and refreshing.

But these things had been noted in Gullen and their import guessed. No-one could maintain the use of wood on that scale for long without retreating to a forest for more. Gullen quite rightly did not envisage that Gargol would just walk away, bested by cold; they now anticipated and were ready for, an early attack. What was not seen from Gullen was that behind the glare of the night fires, the forces surrounding Gullen were moved to the north of the city – all except a few score men and those enormous masking fires which were smoky in the dawn light. Gullen therefore defended no wall any more nor any less than any other...

Soon after dawn the onslaught came like a holocaust from the north. Gullen eyes were set agape by the might which surged toward them. All the impedimenta of war which had been finished swept like a tidal wave at the one north wall; behind them a sea of eager men roaring the Baeth battle cry – a mighty howl like a storm through the tree-tops of Dorn. As soon as the attack was heard, those few Baeths left to the east, south and west of the city, sped easily over the fields to join it, keeping safely out of range. In the city, overcrowded, its streets alive with activity, strewn with cooking fires, racks of weapons, shelters, camps, stores of food, log-piles and cashes of a myriad of things, swift movement was impossible. Gargol had been quicker than Gullen to realise its internal plight and thousands of stout Gullen hearts pounded with frustration as they scrambled through the mess to aid the defenders on the north wall.

Frind and the Liegemen led the defence of the north wall and every man there quailed at the tide of death which surged toward them. Once the enemy drew near enough, the arrows began; a murderous rain of shafts; Eastfolk died; screamed in pain; cursed disabling wounds. No man showed plainly to those arrows; Frind's horde of blowers clung to the stones, revealing a tube and just one eye; by each man a box of the deadly Yanish teeth. But their compatriot bowmen had to display more of themselves just to loose one arrow: many died on their first fleeting attempt. The blowers were the only ones who could counter the avalanche of bodies below. Frind shouted the order; Durnor saw a swathe of death overtake the nearest Baeths, those atop towers – hitherto unchallenged – were taken first. With every breath, each of the scores of Frind's men set flight to a deadly tooth; Baeths fell willy-nilly in their hundreds but the Yanish darts quickly diminished in the boxes.

Frind called runners. "Go to the other generals. Tell them the north wall cannot hold against this – they must aid us if they can – and soon!" To another he yelled, "Take ten men, bring more teeth." Frind turned without seeing one of the runners he had sent fall to an arrow.

Already some of the blowers had run out of darts; uselessly they awaited supplies. Beyond the wall, the flow of attack which they had temporarily stemmed was renewing afresh. Grapples flew aloft faster than they could be cut away; towers were nearly abreast of the wall and still arrows clattered around, finding marks. Frind urged bowmen to show themselves so they could deal death but of those score or so who did, death was dealt to them far quicker than the time to level their bow. As if he himself had slain them, Frind was stricken with grief and fury in equal measures; he personally rushed darts to his men, muttering encouragement. Many of them were becoming breathless; their shots veering wide; falling short; soon they would lose the strength to pierce even the skin – let alone clothing or hide.

Then he saw the Gullen Queen by him, heavy with child, carrying full quivers and boxes of Yanish teeth from the stores; a thin, silken tunic clinging wet-whipped about her in the bitter wind. Gratitude flooded the faces of those to whom she threw the supplies of war and a snatched, desperate word of encouragement. The sight of their queen, her great valour and sacrifice stirred many men to rise afresh to meet the foe on the north wall.

The first Baeths appeared on the walkway of the north ramparts; leaping from the first tower they came to Gullen jubilant, breathless, perspiring with the heat of conflict; more appeared up grapple ropes. Liegemen's blades rang to greet them: scythe them down: send them back from whence they came. The rain of arrows was quenched as they came, now the Gullen bowmen could display themselves to wreak havoc on the Baeth towers – three more were dangerously near – but the number of defenders were few and the blowers were not good with swords. The enemy wedge on the walkway grew rather than diminished until the whirling blades of the liegemen entered the fray – crowding the foe with little room to fight. Then another tower fouled the wall; eager men pulling it closer with grapples, then leaping. Eastfolk swordsmen, dour, stern, hard met them;

steel upon steel rang the length of the northern ramparts; valiant, desperate hearts cut and clubbed with waning strength.

Sheer weight of numbers was overwhelming the paladins of the north wall – still no help was in sight.

Only then did the truth fall upon Frind: "The city is too full! They cannot reach here soon enough!"

Eisdan heard his frenzied shout and said through the blood on his face, "Fight, Frind – though there seems no hope – we must at least gain a little time; fight for Renar, Wetland, Brushwood; your very life!"

Fired by Eisdan's words, Frind shrugged off the responsibility of command and threw himself beside his eastern comrades against the slowly, painfully, advancing front of the Baeth assault.

As he did so he was dimly aware of other things about him. The distance was greying and he could feel ice crystals stinging coldly against his skin; then melting with the heat from his thrashing form as soon as they touched. The wind too had waxed; its distant lashing roar audible above the din of battle – and closing. Far over the Gullen Fields he dimly perceived trees bending below the fury of a raging, bitter storm – and there were Gullen cries from below! To the right and left of the Baeths came Banor and Fanor with their men racing into the flanks of the enemy.

"It will be death out there for them," muttered Frind grimly.

"Then we are equal and fight together – for it is death up here too!" came Eisdan's dark rejoinder.

But the aid brought with it hope. The Gullen bowmen without were fresh, their quivers full and long since had the Baeths abandoned their bows for the grapple and sword. Standing off, Banor and Fanor's men shot death shafts into the milling flanks of the attackers. Valiant though their stand, to the Baeths it was but a hindrance and would not have turned the battle: they would have been crushed by a single unit of Gargol's ravening army.

Just at the moment Lianor cried his support from the streets below the north wall – too late and too few to staunch the enemy drive – his voice was shattered by a sudden lurid pink glare which bathed the dimming scene; illuminating the ice crystals which seemed to halt their descent for that instant – and the deafening, roaring crack in its wake. The storm – as no other before or since – descended and ravaged the scene, raging its fury across the Southlands.

Ice crystals like jagged shards of clear rock – some as large as a man's finger – raked the flesh. Friend and foe alike cowered, braced against the violence of the tearing wind; beat into submission by its unrelenting ferocity; fear stark on their faces in the sudden lights; heads trembling to the reverberations of the thunderclaps. With blood-fogged eyes and flayed faces battle was forgotten; no man held an advantage; no man had an answer. The commotion of the hailing shards was drowned by the tormented cries of tortured men clamouring for shelter and retreat. Out in the fields Banor and Fanor urged their men from huddles and turned them back into Gullen – into the shelter of solid stone and wood. For the Baeths it was worse – their turn was into the driving wind from the north and lacerated tents.

Gargol saw that he had lost the chance for victory – even though it had been within his grasp. There remained no opportunity to re-group and repair with such depleted supplies, sundered equipment and devastated men. He saw too the folly of his haste to crush the Southlands in the Coldseason. He had been lulled by its lenity and was now left with no choice but to withdraw in humility.

In the gentler morning whiteness of snow, Gargol had gone. Only the debris of battle and frozen bodies remained; shapes and lumps in the clean brilliance. Gullen began the work of salvage from abandoned stores, burning and cleansing and the healing and resting of her own injured within the walls.

Two days later a son was born to the Southern Queen, Syntelle, and he was called Virlin as she decreed. The birth was not acclaimed in the city – though there was no secret now of the queen's indisposition – since her appearance in the battle. Many Gulleners had assumed it rightly slain at birth since there was no father: that there was no announcement and that the child was never seen by most, merely served justification to that notion.

Among the generals and the elders of the city who had seen Virlin there was much debate and it was Syntelle's impression that the omnipresence of the liegemen alone created the narrow way along which the child's life stumbled for those first few days.

"He is the son of our liege and we will guard him as Lindarg's own flesh and blood…" Durnor had said to them when they had come with tradition on their minds. The unspoken threat was all too clear and the elders shrank from hasty action in the matter for reasons of both 'prudence' and 'diplomacy'. That they undoubtedly wished to remain alive did not overtly enter their deliberations! One or two who claimed visionary powers intimated that there might be a sign in such a birth – that perhaps it was prophetic within the changes which were taking place in Endworld. Suffice it to say – as in the words written in the annals of Gullen history – 'The boy Virlin was in part suffered to live at the time by more or less equal measures of speculation, suspicion and caution on behalf of those in charge of such matters.'

He was, however, dearly loved by Syntelle and the Liegemen of the Lord of Gullen.

10

ON THE OLD SOUTH ROAD

A while now had passed since Lindarg had bade farewell to his liegemen. With them had gone some of himself, for he knew that their task in Gullen would be hard but then, perhaps, they more than any could succeed. Again he wondered what drove them; then remembered how long he had not known what drove him. He knew now, but then he was wise and a wizard.

The track was very gradually narrowing but beneath its veneer of grass and scrub could be made out the shapes of long neglected but expertly laid stones which had once been the surface of the Old South Road. A rustle in the bushes to his right stopped him. Lindarg listened intently, but the sound was not repeated, nor could he sense an animal presence to send on its way. He forced his steed off the road in the direction of the sound, casting around, but found nothing; returning, he shrugged the incident away and turned once more south.

He had been this far along the road before, further even, in his past, but time had changed it; masking it so it seemed like a different journey. Sadness tinged with a melancholic elation touched him frequently, dragging his thoughts into the past. Those ancient travellers; rich and hearty, would have trundled carts laden with gems, armour, fruits, spices – even spells and perhaps more potent ware still. Feasts would have been arranged en route with merchants going different ways meeting and, as had been the custom, spending two riotous nights by the road.

Two nights because it was done for each to invite and entertain the other; it was considered unworldly not to return the favour however inconvenient, but life had been much richer and slower then. Old ways and traditions had gone on and on unchanged and unbent, those ancient peoples of Endworld had continued as their traditions, thinking foolishly that they would continue to go on in the same way forever.

The sudden noise cut through Lindarg's thoughts jarring him to an abrupt halt. There had been that rustle again but this time followed by an animal-like laugh. In the ensuing silence Lindarg shivered slightly, seeking an animal presence but once more, finding none.

"Who is there?" His thin vice was lost in the tumble of low growth leaving him alone with only the echo in his mind and the silence deepening, yet he sensed no threat. For a long time, he listened and strained his eyes over the still bushes; again he challenged the wilderness to no avail then resumed more slowly, warily, his southward way, certain now that someone – or something – out there shadowed him.

Soon his thoughts returned again to the earlier days of these lands which were long forgotten. They had not endured in perpetuity.

Once change tilts a single scale of the balance a fraction, from then on it always and seemingly irrevocably gains momentum. So Lindarg could not join in the sublimity of those days; they were gone; the road only knew them, and it was a furtive attempt to recollect those times which moistened his eyes. He did though, feel a bond with this past on which he reflected, knowing much of their customs and ways. They might have been proud and edifying times – but Lindarg knew that nothing was perfect – or it just wouldn't change; or would it? Perhaps the land and world itself needed to be exploited in varying ways through the ages and that each new way, each change, was merely a precursor of the next in some great cycle of events. Of one thing he was sure; things were longed for that could not be had, and experience of the past as it had been, with the people that had been there, could never be had.

Again he was rudely reminded of the present by the primitive cry he had heard before; not animal, yet not quite human; not hostile, yet it dogged him, unseen as he moved along the road. This time it came from a distance but was clear in the cool quiet. Lindarg tried to ignore it but found that he couldn't. Brooding over its importance he stopped his mount and let it graze while he himself rested, wrestling with enigmas. He decided to allow himself an indulgence and took out the Queenstone. It was vibrant in his hand, he looked deeply into it naming the 'Old South Road'.

A brief glimpse of what he had imagined it to be shot through the heart of the stone but was immediately replaced by the violence of men, reminding him that those times had been just as much sanguine as sublime. He looked away, a tear in his eye, avoiding the scenes of death the stone portrayed, then returned it to its pouch. Shadows were lengthening and he had come far; here the snows were scattered and thin and Lindarg decided to rest for the night rather than push on further.

After eating some provisions, he dozed, without thought for a fire since, though not exactly warm, it was still and not quite cold. In the comforting atmosphere he felt content; somehow it seemed a good place to be, with the merest rustle of shrivelled leaves a damp, caressing quiet surrounding him.

Soon the whispers began. They were happy sounds which filled the heart with gladness and his open eyes caught the dancing of firelight on the trees, his face felt the warmth of their glow. Singing too could be heard, in the elder tongue long lost; though not understood, its sounds were joyous and their metre satisfying, relaxing. Fully awake now, Lindarg moved among the campfires of those ancients and could not believe what the Queenstone had showed him as he experienced – almost perfectly – that which could not be experienced. He sang with them, talked, ate and drank with them; they were there with him; there were no strangers, the great and the small were equals and their contribution to the whole equal in proportion. He was equal to them, though they knew him and addressed as a wizard, knowing him by a name other than Virdil, Sandrinfal he was called, and as they him, he knew them, their names, songs and customs. Here was that enchantment of the past which he had longed to see.

The days whiled away shading into nights, all perfect in that olden way, but all very different, with changing peoples, new conversations, fascinations and pathos. Lindarg had no thoughts of continuing his journey so he tarried longer, day by day becoming less and less able to even recollect Koryn or his purpose. Soon merchants he had first met going north were returning south and the re-meeting was more rewarding than the last; brimming with bonhomie, news and gladness.

Had some quirk of fate not taken a hand, and not too late – for he had dallied many days – Lindarg, Virdil, Lord of Gullen who was Sandrinfal of old, would have been content to wither away on the Old South Road and join the ghosts of its travellers forever, and perhaps, as they, he would have been happier if he had.

He was talking with Trindledine, a great friend and the subject was the Queenstone. It was considered as a gem only, for in those times, unknown to the people then, such stones were still in the hands of the gods and their existence unguessed by men. Trindledine said; "Ahh, `Fal, little did I suspect that you had such a beautiful forging, let us all see!" In Lindarg's hand it glittered and shimmered with fractured light, glancing coloured rays into the air and onto their marvelling faces. "I have a lovely girl in mind to whom I would give it – if you wish to barter it." The tone suggested that it was just a thought. Lindarg ignored him but Trindledine persisted, "You may have the pick of what I own and as much of it as you may carry!" Lindarg was tempted by such a generous offer but did not show it, eagerness was never a part of bargaining – unless you wanted to lose on the deal. But Trindledine went on, trying to seem disinterested in the outcome of the exchange though Lindarg could sense that he would probably give anything and everything to gain what he desired! Such was the skill of the merchant – and Trindledine had lost it.

"She is the most beautiful woman I have seen, it would be a fitting gift, she lives in the Castle of Eq in Dorn a…"

But Lindarg was no longer listening. In the stone he could see Venain's castle and from its ramparts the sorcerer grinned widely, almost exultantly. The old ghosts dissolved with the fading of that stunning vision in the stone and Lindarg was there on that very real and lonely road. He was tired, but alert; leaner and older looking; by him, his provisions were long mouldy and all but rotted away. He was also frightened. Never had anything so innocently pleasant – even blissful, been so potentially ruinous, so totally unavoidable. He had learned a lesson; the 'safeness' of these old places was a dangerous veil over the truth, they were only 'safe' because their danger went unrecognised.

'Why was Venain smiling so?' He thought to himself furtively. He could only surmise one reason for that, but at present, no explanation; he must move fast! His steed returned from its wanderings at his call, "At least some things are easy!" he muttered to himself. A new day was just beginning as he hammered away south, his mind too full now to dwell on the Old South Road again, but he would never forget his sojourn and perhaps in better times, or when his life was fading, he would come to join those old ghosts again. They would always be there – as maybe they would always be everywhere for those whose minds can seek them out and whose hearts are sympathetic and receptive to their whispers.

By the fifth day after his dalliance with the traveller – ghosts, Lindarg could see far in the distance the looming white summits of the Southern Mountains. They were, he knew, impassable now, and he supposed that Koryn must lie on this side. Somewhere nestling in the shoulders of those peaks was that tower, the glimpse of which, in his dream, he would never forget. Now his mind was firmly fixed on that objective; something was there for him, and he suspected, for him alone. What it might be was only a vague notion in his mind; nor did he know where the tower was; those mountains thrashed across the whole of the southern margins of Endworld; the great road divided before them and was lost to the east and west in the jumble of their foothills and chasms. Nowhere in these long abandoned parts of the Southlands was the influence of man in evidence. Few had been this way since the ancient travellers and little was known about its once magnificent cities and palaces. Again the memories of those elder days assailed him, but he pushed them aside – perhaps another time he would wander aimlessly and steep himself in the mystique of this land – not now.

He reached the fork of the Old South Road as the evening cool was descending. The Coldseason did not seem to touch this place and he was reminded of Dundellin, the season which, strangely, he liked most. But which way to turn? How was he to find a single tower in all that rose before him? The questions turned his thoughts to the Queenstone. In his palm it was seemingly alive with a vibrance; Lindarg felt excitement, it had never been like this before…

"Koryn." But the stone remained blank. "The Tower of Koryn;" again nothing appeared. He was at a loss and wondered if the strange feel of the stone was affecting it, perhaps it would not work so deep in these ancient lands. "Venain's castle," he commanded with a slight tremble in his voice, but only a lake, large and serene appeared in the stone; then the lake dissolved and was replaced by a raging fire which filled the whole sky and with it came noise – a roaring cacophony; the stone shook, and within it a terrible scene bounced and danced wildly, burning trees flew through the air, their crackling loud in his ears. With the sound came the smell – unmistakably that of burning flesh and with that emanated the destructive emotion of hate. All these things surged from the stone as if it was opening a door to another time and allowing it to pour through. Soon it was hot in his hand and suddenly he had dropped it. Retrieving it from the grass he noticed it was still warm; never before had it done so much; never before had there been sound, smell, and feeling! Gingerly he put it away, confused.

Had that been Venain's castle? What of the lake – certainly not a castle? If it was, WHEN? The stone had undeniably worked, but had it worked correctly? Lindarg now doubted that Koryn existed and then wondered whether Koryn was not its real name, so the stone would not show it. Even the wisdom of Virdil had no answer and he wished he had never looked.

His confusion was sundered by a high-pitched laugh; a gangling body shot, somersaulting from some bushes and across the track.

"Aa ha – a traveller! A real, live traveller!" The man came to rest and sat upright on a rock, then dissolved into another spasm of gurgling merriment. Lindarg was speechless; beneath him his animal was alarmed and he struggled to calm it. Suddenly the man leaped up, prodded the animal once, then collapsed into further peals of idiotic laughter.

"A traveller of the present on our road of the past…"

"Sir!" shouted Lindarg indignantly, "I am Lindarg and I-" Once more the man folded into a fit of laughter on the track, cutting short Lindarg's words. Lindarg was furious but something bade him to be patient. Suddenly the man was quiet and to all intents and purposes of normal disposition.

"Lindarg you say-" Lindarg was amazed that the man had registered anything amid his idiotic glee.

"From – er – Gullen," added Lindarg.

"Gullen?" The little man's eyebrows raised slightly. "Or from Dorn, you say? No you did not say from Dorn did you, my pardon. And you travel south?" Before Lindarg could open his mouth to reply, he went on; "Of course you travel south – that is why you puzzle here at the fork! Were you going north there would be no problem – ha – no problem at all!"

"You-"

"But then you couldn't have been going north, since there is no way from the south – yes?" Utter glee spread over the fellow's face and Lindarg resigned himself to another seemingly endless spasm of laughter, but it did not come. "East, perhaps – aah, you could have been going east-"

"I-"

"No. To be going east you must needs have come from the west – and who comes from the west?"

"Who-?"

"No-one comes from the west. No; there is nothing in the west from which to come – not in these lands, oh no. Nothing comes from there." Lindarg was beside himself, words clamoured within him as the man babbled on; "Aaah, but you are so clever, Sire. Yes, 'sire' does suit you – or perhaps 'my liege'? You are definitely both, Virdil." That was too much.

"I did not say my name was Virdil!" blurted Lindarg insistently.

"Ah, no; my pardon once more, Sire, I should listen much more."

"Indeed you should!"

"But I would miss so much Sire, if I were to listen! Oh, yes! What is said is one thing – and can be heard; what is not said – now that is another, a different story – and which is true?" He broke into laughter but Lindarg kept his patience if only because this very odd little fellow was making nonsense out of much sense and at least he himself was learning by listening.

"And your name?"

"Aaah, my name – of course, you do not know!" The voice was loaded with incredulity as if he considered that everyone should know his name.

"That at least is true," intoned Lindarg, "There you have a distinct advantage over me!"

"That wrong, Sire, I shall right this very moment; I am Sylee. Yes verily, Sylee." His laughter rolled along the road once more.

Sylee could have been quite young. Certainly he was small, bouncy and mischievous looking with eyes that flashed attentively yet one could be excused for supposing that one looked upon a simple man. In contrast to his young looks, the hair was grey – more white and his skin ruddy with the outdoors; bits of grass clung to his rather tatty clothing which could once have been shiny and plush. Generally, he had an abandoned, unkempt aura and as he again degenerated into a gibbering giggle on the track, Lindarg's feelings for the man were a mixture of sympathy, interest, distrust and an odd excitement.

Then Sylee straightened, faced him, and suddenly said, "The stone will not show it – yes?"

"That is also true."

"And you do not know which way to go? That is true as well!" imitated Sylee gleefully. "Then you will need me to go with you – I will lead you."

Lindarg wasn't at all sure that he either needed or wanted the company of Sylee. The little man sensed his hesitation. "The tower does not easily show itself, believe me. Yes; it is hidden, very hidden. But Sylee knows where it is – or perhaps I guess. But Sylee knows what he guesses. Yes, Sylee can take you."

"Who are you and what are you, Sylee?"

"I am myself and happy. You have felt the joy of these lands? These lands are my lands and I dwell in their memories. I have laughed for an eternity with those memories and wish to continue to laugh; but I have guessed. A season ago Sylee heard the rumblings in the earth and the laughing stopped and Sylee was sad for a while-"

"Go on…"

"Why was Sylee sad? I was sad because the ghosts were and they were sad because the land was unquiet-" He paused, lowering his voice to a whisper. "Venain-"

"What do you know of Venain?" demanded Lindarg, interrupting.

"Nothing, I just guess. And myself, I don't care – or perhaps

I do. I am content to play here in these southern lands the way they are; but maybe he would not leave them this way and the world would be a worse place for that! You know of him much more than I-"

"Tell me-"

"Come, we must fork right for Koryn, and mind, we cannot rest at night. Never rest at night in these old places."

Lindarg was already tired from the day's journey, the thought of continuing all night was daunting to his spirit.

"Must we?" he argued.

"We must."

And with that, Sylee started off westwards with a grin and a chuckle, capering along the road faster and with greater ease than Lindarg's animal. Every-so-often he would grab a berry or some leaves and munch them displaying a gourmet's pleasure with each mouthful. Lindarg tried some, but found them bitter and nauseating; he didn't have much food left.

Lindarg welcomed the morning. The night had been pleasantly cool for travelling and he had seen no danger, but then, he realised, that meant nothing here – and there was always that unreal feeling – almost agreeable, but at the same time disturbing since it had no apparent cause.

Sylee stopped by a perfectly round mound at the roadside; "Rest here my liege – it is a dangerous place – therefore it is safe…" He laughed again but soon stopped. "There is something you can do for me Lindarg."

"Then ask, you can be certain that I at least will listen." said Lindarg pointedly.

"I would borrow the Queenstone, Sire."

Lindarg was obviously going to refuse, especially since its mention reminded him of what Sylee had said the previous evening, 'the stone will not show it', and that there were still a thousand questions in Lindarg's mind.

"You cannot find Koryn without me and I have pledged my help. The least you can do, Wizard, is to afford me entertainment."

The disgruntled voice was pleading slightly and Lindarg could find no way of saying no.

Reluctantly he drew out the Queenstone and offered it.

"It will be safe with me," promised Sylee, seeing the hard stare in Lindarg's face. Clutching it tightly, Sylee peered into the gem and said, "Show me the death of Toombril, blood, Scoth's severed head, the fight of the stones…"

Gore splashed red in the crystal and the sounds and smells of butchery, treachery and misery, sickened Lindarg. Tactfully, Sylee moved away from him and out of earshot, continuing to gloat. All day he made the gem work and Lindarg knew why; without horror as contrast, joy is degraded and these lands had forgotten such miseries that were in their making once.

In the evening they set off again westwards; Sylee was somewhat sombre as he had returned the stone. It had felt spent, as if there were no life in it after its work of the day; Lindarg seized the opportunity for talk.

"Sylee." The little man looked up – for once without mirth on his face. "I am hungry, are there no animals to eat round here?"

Sylee screwed up his face. "Animals, my liege? No. There are no animals here, these lands are no place for ordinary beasts – and to eat them?" The look of disgust on his face finished his last statement adequately. "You will have to eat berries."

"Their taste is displeasing!" groaned Lindarg.

"Displeasing, yes, perhaps; but you will eat them – ha ha, yes; you will eat them. There is nothing else."

Sylee offered him a bunch which he had just plucked. Lindarg swallowed some quickly and was surprised by the speedy way in which they quelled his pangs, and the taste was soon gone. He pocketed the rest, then ventured, "How did you know what I asked of the Queenstone at the fork, Sylee?"

"I saw what you asked – or rather, no, I didn't see; at least not quite see-"

"That will not do for an answer, Sylee, you know that since the stone showed nothing how could you have seen?"

158

Grinning gleefully, Sylee did not answer immediately, but at length said, "Did you, wise wizard; ah yes – did you, wise wizard, know which way to go at the fork?"

Lindarg did not like his mocking tone. "No, I didn't."

"And would the stone have told you which way to go if you had not asked it of where you were going?" But he did not wait for an answer: "No, of course not, how could it?" Lindarg said nothing, always Sylee was right in an odd sort of way. "So you had to ask it of Koryn if that is where you wanted to go-"

"But I could have been going anywhere in all these lands for all you knew-"

"Aaaah, ha ha!" cut in Sylee. "Where else then, in all these lands might you have been going, Liege-Lord – where else?"

"That you would know better than I, Sylee." He thought for a moment, then, "Perhaps a ruined city or some other olden place; to the mound we stopped at – uncounted places I could have been going to." But as soon as he said it, Lindarg saw the trap; confirmed by the mischievous widening of Sylee's huge grin.

"And how many of those uncounted places, wise wizard, could you name?" The question was deliberate, pointed and without an adequate answer. Lindarg was silenced.

Nothing more was said until they came to a multiple branching of the way; faint routes scurrying away from them on all sides, losing themselves amid the tumbling scape of scrub and hills. All the while Lindarg felt belittled – even threatened by the casual profundity of the little man Sylee, since he knew everything else it seemed, he must be aware of Lindarg's powers with both mind and sword; it was hardly credible that he thought himself safe from Lindarg – no safer than the idiot-child which he feigned to be; yet he was ebullient with assurance and confidence, revealing no suspicions or fears. It rankled Lindarg deeply.

"This way – I think." said Sylee, apparently looking in all directions at once. Lindarg was not convinced – didn't want to be. "Are you sure?"

"Sure? Yes, perfectly sure, do you doubt that I can lead you to the tower of your dreams?"

'There!' Thought Lindarg reproachfully, 'He's at it again; knowing I dreamed of Koryn; so off-handedly.' Lindarg's rancour rose forcefully. 'Next thing he'll be saying he's had a chat with Tromillion about Syntelle and I!' He didn't doubt that the infuriating little man could lead him to Koryn – he'd managed everything else so far – but he certainly wasn't going to let it be easy. So, as Sylee turned to skip off along his chosen way, it vanished to be replaced by a gigantic rock. Lindarg smiled at his handiwork, 'Let's see which way the weevil goes now!' he thought, triumphantly, holding the illusion. But Sylee capered straight through it and did not once falter to take the illusory way; nor did he comment on the change, he seemed totally oblivious to it!

Such a negation of his powers subdued Lindarg and he decided that, whether he liked it or not, he would have to depend on Sylee as it seemed he was powerless to affect him; in fact, he reflected, Sylee appeared to be a greater adept than himself. His insight and wit, the way he had handled the stone, his 'immunity' to Lindarg's wizardry and that aura about him as if he created an image of himself that was much less than he really was – a regular wizard's guise. And yet the simple explanation that he was such just did not fit. Lindarg pushed the enigma to the back of his mind, he would have to await further events – if there were to be any – to answer those questions, there were plenty of simpler ones to be going on with…

"Tell me what you know about the Queenstone, Sylee."

"Only what the ghosts have told me, and they never tell all, never."

"Tell me then, who owns it?" Sylee shot him a remonstrative glance;

"Ah ha! who owns a gem which is thine? Syntelle perhaps?"

"Wha-"

"She gave it to you?"

"Yes."

"Of course she did. I asked it to show its giver – for generally it has been taken in the past – or ownership 'assumed'. Know this, Lindarg, it has only been freely given twice, and the new giver it shows is Syntelle, Queen of the Southlands and Gullen. It is yours."

"Who was its first giver?"

"Its first giver? Soon you will know. Soon you will know more than I and more than these ghosts; and the other stones too, yes, those too. They are why you are here and why I lead you; but even now I fear the blind is leading the blind. Ha, yes, the blind leading the blind – and so far to go." Suddenly Sylee broke off and laughed, looking aside from the pathway. "Continue on this way Lindarg," he said, "I will be with you again before the day." With that he bounced off into the bushes and was gone.

Sylee reappeared none too soon, for it was full light and Lindarg was tired of hearing the murmurs he knew he must not listen to.

"Rest well today," said the little man, "Tonight will take us to the entrance to the Vale of Koryn, tomorrow you will enter it… tomorrow you will enter Koryn Vale. Yes, rest well tonight."

11

THE TOWER OF KORYN

Koryn Vale was an awesome sight, even to one such as Virdil who had travelled and seen much. More imposing still, was the tower: perched as it was, seemingly teetering on the brink of a sheer black cliff, smooth and shiny in the evening light. Still half a day's ride away, even now it loomed over the landscape as if trying to thrust higher than the white-topped peaks behind it. At the top of its column there appeared to be a circular wall wider than the rest and within this wall a building uniquely square on the roundness of the column and walls. Surrounding it were jagged peaks, across the vale from it, sheer cliffs and between the two, the soft verdant vale; almost flat, narrowing and sloping upwards into the mountains.

Lindarg held his breath, realising only now how much that vision of the Tower of Koryn in his dream with Tromillion had not shown; but he realised that what had been shown might only have been a memory of what Tromillion had seen, or what he had dreamed. This was the real thing, as it stood, now.

Crazily tilted stones were scattered around giving the valley an untidy air, yet at the same time adding to it as if they belonged – just as they were. Instinctively he knew their name: Styne stones. Laughing, Sylee seemed oblivious to the sight and was scampering about in his usual mad way behind Lindarg.

"Sylee?"

"Yes, my liege?" he answered, then, "Ah ha, perhaps you have found the tower?"

"Of course, there it is, see." Lindarg pointed along the rising vale before them.

"There, Sire, you have the advantage over me, Lord of Gullen, you see I am quite blind. Yes, my Lord Virdil, hee hee, quite, blind. The ghosts lead me; they are kind to me and through them and with them I travel; they are my eyes and ears in Endworld."

Lindarg was almost surprised, it helped him to understand Sylee; maybe it explained why the Queenstone had done more than show when he was nearby – and why he had ignored illusory ways.

Then Sylee continued, "I cannot go with you into the vale for it is shunned by the ghosts and I would be helpless and lost, but tell me what is it like?"

Lindarg described the valley, tower and precipices as well as he could.

When he had finished, Sylee said, "How much the sighted miss, but I thank you, Lord, for the glimpse. What else do you 'see' in the valley?"

Lindarg was puzzled, the emphasis on 'see' was poignant.

"Nothing," he answered, "but a few Styne stones."

"Ah, Styne stones; 'nothing but a few Styne stones'," he mimicked, then burst into uncontrollable glee. "Beware, stones, here comes a great wizard; mind him, he eats stones! You are nothing in his eyes! No, nothing in his eyes." The chillingly mocking voice faded with the receding Sylee; then was gone and only the echo reached Lindarg's ears; 'beware stones, here comes a great wizard – he eats stones'.

Though Lindarg knew what Styne stones looked like, he had no idea what they were, and amid Sylee's last ravings he had been given no opportunity to ask about their significance; now he was apprehensive, unable to free his mind of the nagging question: why didn't the ghosts go into the valley?

As Lindarg entered the vale, he knew it was not the same. That is not to say it was evil; it wasn't. Nor was it inviting, nor nostalgic like the Old South Road. It was negative, disinterested, but it did make Lindarg, the Lord of Gullen, feel very small. 'There is a power here,' he thought, but it wasn't one he knew or recognised, nor had he felt it before. It was very strong, but moved in no direction and appeared not to threaten. Lindarg's animal was so alert for itself that it seemed to disregard his soothing command, unspoken and apparently unheeded – the beast breathed heavily and was very nervous. Lindarg too was on edge, but lulled; not anticipating trouble; quiescent.

In the stillness, their paces on the soft turf were a sin and they echoed dully even across the vastness of the valley entrance which undeniably felt much narrower than it looked, making Lindarg feel cramped as if he entered a narrow pass. He passed the first of the Styne stones and turned aside to regard it. Smooth with age, it was slightly leaning and pointed at both ends. Most were about half as high as a man, some a little higher. Lindarg could not put his finger on what was odd about them, but certainly there was something 'not right'. Uneasy, he moved on wishing that he still had Sylee's inexplicable insight with him. 'He would have seen right through them!' He thought, ironically, but they were unmistakably odd.

Time passed but the day did not change much. It remained still, became no warmer and no colder; the sun moved overhead but that didn't seem to make any difference. The sea of Styne stones were on all sides now save to his left where a sheer cliff paralleled his way only a few paces distant, and they were disquieting. He noticed a cave in the cliff face near to him; he peered hard from where he was trying to fathom its extent and debating whether to stop and investigate. Its opening was several times his own height from the ground but there seemed a clear way up of foot-holds chiselled into the rock. Behind him he was suddenly aware of a sound; a dull, heavy thump on the ground and he turned his head...

He could see nothing but Styne stones. In that same instant he realised that one of them had fallen down – and knew why they seemed so odd. The fallen one was pointed at both ends and now he saw that they were all balancing impossibly on those points. There was nothing embedded in the ground. A cold sweat burst on his forehead and fear gripped him. How did they stand so crazily off-balance?

Suddenly the fallen one was moved upright again, then fell over toward him with another dull thump. Three more fell down and with the first, raised and fell, thumping their way over the grass, leaving no mark – but the vale shook with each unnerving sound. Others followed suit until the whole valley's stones were on the move. Two of the nearest leaped into the air, thrusting their pointed ends forward, backwards and to the sides like lances, cleaving the air with a swish. Then they would fall and thump nearer to jump up again and repeat the thrusts, deftly at random heights, always edging nearer. Lindarg panicked, in less than moments he would be battered, sliced and crushed to a pulp. With a fleeting sorrowful thought for his mount he slid down and ran for the cave; scrambling desperately, then turning in the entrance, hating to look back into the valley.

So bewildered was the animal after being abandoned by Lindarg and by the thumping which now shook the ground, it had not moved. The first stone thrust far into its side with a crunch, smashing bones, spraying blood and knocking it several strides sideways. As it collapsed, three other stones fell on it with a sickening squelch; the remains were unrecognisable.

Lindarg wept with anguish and fear in the cave-mouth as the grey sea thumped ceaselessly against the cliff below. There was no escape; bones littering the cave floor testified to that and with the thunder of the striking stones ringing through the cave and the rattle of old bones, Lindarg sank to the floor in despair, cursing his own folly and ineptitude and cried like a whipped child.

The stones continued to hammer against the cliff, making a noise but causing no damage – they would only destroy – intruders. He regarded them below, throwing themselves around like toys; a quick search in the back of the cave had confirmed what the skeletons had already told him – above; it was shiny and smooth with not a crack as far as the eye could see from the cave entrance. He noticed a warmth by his chest, instinctively he raised his hand and felt the Queenstone. It was glowing with warmth and life even before any command.

He knew then that it could find an answer – but what to ask it; why hadn't he asked it of the stones before? He agonised for a long time, clutching the gem closely, then said into it, "Syntelle…" She was there in the courtyard, her farewell echoing in the cave; he could feel the love in her face which was rosy with the cool morning air. Tears welled up once more and his whole being ached to be with her again; his tortured psyche screamed to be free of his hopeless predicament; free to go to her; free from the Styne stones and their unquenchable thirst for his destruction.

"Will I ever see you again, my love?" He found himself whispering desperately, but even as the words were spoken the stone was misting; Syntelle fading, fading. "Syntelle… Syntelle…" But she was lost in the shadowy mist, mist which darkened and began to assume shape. Unbidden the stone was responding, choosing its own course; Lindarg's eyes were drawn into its depths. A dusty tome formed, darkly bound, ancient; pages turning to his gaze; olden script, indistinct, flickered by. Then the leaves were still, the mist cleared and Lindarg could read what was written.

At the cave-mouth he read from the book, falteringly in the old language, the stones calming at his words and lying quietly down on the grass. One-by-one at first, then in ever-increasing numbers, they lifted and fell back the way they had come – each to its own niche in the Vale of Koryn, thudding away from the cliff. As the last one rose to go, Lindarg climbed down and scuttled off in the direction of the tower which was his goal, passing many more Styne stones on his way, all now silent and still.

Soon the tower was high above and he was nearing the base of the soaring cliff on which it teetered. So far, he could discern no way up that sheer face, but as he drew closer to, the way to the tower was plain. An archway had been hewn into the rock and in its dim recesses Lindarg could make out a stairway leading upwards into the dark bowels of the mountain. Round the mouth of the opening flickered a ring of fire barring the entrance; over the arch was carved the legend; 'Koryn Gate – let none seek to enter who cannot douse the fire'. Evidently no-one had ever managed to douse the fire for it still burned, probably as it had always done for millennia, the guardian of Koryn Gate.

Instantly Lindarg knew that this was the sorcerous fire of Eq. It had consumed Virdil once, finishing him in an irresistible flare like a torch to tinder. He had burned Thae with it – a land which had resisted all the natural forces since time immemorial had been powerless in its acrid grip; he had seen it in his dreams, and never had it been quenched until its job was done. Only he who set it could turn it, and now Lindarg wondered whether the author of this fire still lived. Fatefully, he wondered too whether such a fire would continue to burn after its author's death and if such was the case, how then could the world ever be rid of its curse? Wisdom held no answer.

The fire guarded Eq's tower; it was his fire, set by him. But those times and their gods were gone – no part of Endworld now; Eq was no more, but his sorcery endured to plague mankind 'til the end of time. The enormity of it was harrowing; tore at the mind, negated the Law, confounded the balance and Lindarg knew that the Queenstone could not or would not aid him. Its rules were fixed into the crystal, irrevocable, invariant. As Lindarg pondered the flames, he could feel their hot glow and though the dew on the grass beneath remained cold, he knew the flames would consume him as surely as if he were a dry blade of grass.

The vale too, with its Styne stones, repudiated that same balance, powers left un-rescinded; active in perpetuity – a desperate toe-hold on eternity by the vanishing power of the olden immortals. Irresponsibly, Eq had set a deed in anger which he could not undo – as a dying man releases the arrow into the heart of the slayer.

For days Lindarg searched the precipices and mountains for another way up or round, but deep down he knew there would be no other way; the tower remained, as Eq had designed, inaccessible, inviolate by the mortals who had cast the gods down.

Now Lindarg – exhausted from his vain searches, regarded the flames, despair clouding his thoughts; the Queenstone, fickly, dead to his words, nothing from his dreams gave hope or help – was gone beyond hope into the depths of despondency.

But Lindarg did not comprehend the fact that he himself was a unique event in Endworld – 'the first time it was that one such had roamed free'; Deathling. His very existence was a denial of the Law and the seeds of his coming had been sown deep in the past when gods tumbled; Eq set his guarding fire; Graggan was entombed and other gods were lost to the memory of man – 'none can say when or where the first seed was set – or by whom – nor the last…'

But in the Vale of Koryn, Eq had placed a different stone. It was much larger than the others and stood uniquely stark in the verdure near Koryn Gate; a giant monolith, erect, unmoved. Lindarg had failed to notice it before, now he seemed unable to ignore it. No ordinary Styne stone this; never had it moved and yet it had been assigned with power and words; it had been Eq's evil joke – a parting shot as he faded and set his bridges afire to ward off the mortal predators who would try to follow. Eq had left the stone to destroy, not mortals, but other beings who might seek to reach him across those bridges, 'others' who might well have succeeded otherwise…

Deathling! 'A man, yet not a man – ah, the riddles!'

Lindarg's eyes were drawn to the monolith, enigmatic and sentinel behind him but could not descry why he had so unexpectedly noticed it… no! He was assailed by the truth… it had noticed him. Finally, its power was awakening and it could not be ignored.

The ground hummed, the hum turning to a rumble, ominous and deep; the giant stone shook and became unsteady. With a mighty roar, the great finger of rock tore from the earth scattering debris, then fell toward Lindarg. The shock of its fall shook the ground; Lindarg's legs were unsteady with the tremor as he rose, terrified by the awesome threat that was coming for him.

There was no time to ponder why it had not remained still as the rest, for with each rise and fall it covered many strides and would soon be upon him. Grasping the Queenstone he shouted, "The Book! The Book!"

Panic welled up within him as the stone remained blank.

"The Book! The Book!" He continued desperately.

The gem was cold and the stone nearly upon him, closing faster than he could hope to run. In desperation he changed the ways in its path, so that he appeared to be where the arch really was; the stone hesitated, then changed course. As it started its last fall to the arch, reality reappeared and it fell with a reverberating thud across the fire and did not move again. In an instant, Lindarg was over the stone, through the gap it had made in the fire and at the foot of the dark stairs. Breathing heavily, but unscathed, he began to climb.

The dark closed in, gripping and squeezing all round; the echo of his soft paces were hollow, resounding. The steps wound upwards steeply but not evenly, turning sometimes to the right, left, and once, over themselves so that in the bend the steps suddenly changed from one side to the other and for an instant hung over the space below. Stale breath seemed to cling and follow him along in the stillness so that breathing was laboured. Several times he stopped and after the third such rest the passage narrowed alarmingly then, without warning, he was aware of a fork. To the left was a wider passage – still going upwards and with steps; a slight draught flowed down it then up into the roof

169

at the junction. Lindarg guessed that there was a hole above for ventilation. The wider, breezy passage was altogether the most inviting and Lindarg ached to take it. Instinctively he decided to follow the narrow one – so far everything had been designed to deter entry to the tower – surely this was but another obstacle and the more inviting way would lead to impossible catacombs in which he might wander until life expired. He forced himself into the narrow passage and continued resolutely on upwards, thankful that in ascending the sloping tunnel it was easy to avoid its roof – which he realised was much lower than at the start.

The steps disappeared and he was obliged to scramble on all fours in the full knowledge that the further up he went, the further would be his relentless slide down should he slip. A flatter part gave him time to stop, rest and consider.

The tunnel was very narrow now with barely room for body and limbs side-by-side, forcing him into a confined, prostrate position all but wedged in a solid tomb of utter dark, and though it would be difficult to climb down, the temptation was there to return to that fork and even now take the easier route. Perhaps not temptation – perhaps good sense; returning would only become less and less thinkable from now on and at least from that flatter part he could make a start. It was a terrible choice to be faced with there; buried to an unknown depth in solid rock and surrounded by dead blackness with a painfully long and arduous twisting tube his only known way out. He willed himself on.

As if the hewer of the tunnel had guessed that this flatter place would be the last for a change of heart, the tunnel suddenly twisted doggedly then opened out with returning steps marching upwards and out into the light.

Even the strong wind of the cliff-top was warmer than the cold bowels of the rock as it whistled mournfully round the ancient base of the Tower of Koryn. Far down below from the narrow causeway on which Lindarg now stood, the vale was a mild green ribbon, untouched by the winds which whipped at his clothes. The tower seemed to sway, and here, so close, loomed awesome and impossibly top-heavy.

A stone door at the base of the tower was slightly open, as perhaps it had been for eons. Lindarg leaned on the wind as he fought it across the causeway to that opening. Once inside, the first stirrings of disappointment invaded his mind. Dust lay everywhere; wind-blown debris scattered in corners mixing with the grit from crumbling stone. Dejected and weary with toil, Lindarg abandoned himself to the lonely decay, feeling the ultimate safety of his complete inaccessibility, he slept, relinquishing his body completely to oblivion and peacefulness among the spires of the world, he had come so far... so far...

For how long he slept he had no idea, but he awakened stiff with the aches and bruises of hard stone; he was hungry but had no food at all, such things would have to wait. Examining the room, he discovered a small passage which coiled up from the far side and disappeared into the ceiling. How he had failed to see this earlier he could not imagine – then he was in that passage, spiralling with it up the Tower of Koryn.

It was steep but the going was easy until he realised that light was filtering from ahead. Cautiously he rounded a corner and there the steps passed outside the walls of the tower; to go out there needed courage. The passage was only a man's width and the wall on its outermost side only waist high; beneath it, nothing between him and the green valley far, far below. For a long time Lindarg did not move out into that narrow, spiralling ledge; somehow he had to make himself ready; somehow he must come to terms with that insecurity. When his mind was finally calm, he stepped out allowing himself a glance at the overhanging ledge above him, but not looking down. As he edged round, the wind caught him and he froze, pressing into the stone of the tower as if he might force himself through it and back to safety within its walls. He inched further, hugging the wall behind him but his nerves were failing; irresistibly his gaze was being drawn outwards across the void and down beyond that low wall. With agonising slowness and tension in every fibre of his body, he lowered himself onto the steps so that he could crawl. Below the level of the wall it was easier – his mind free of that emptiness which was below him – surrounded by those high far mountain peaks which betold the precariousness of his perch.

Tentatively he crawled on, upwards, turning, turning, eyes fixed in a forward stare. Then, in front of him, the wall carried on unbroken, seemingly suspended in mid-air, but the ledge on which he crawled was gone and the valley was leering up at him through the void. His head swam with panic as his eyes misted and he felt unsteady; he knew he would not be able to turn round – and to go back? His mind was a dim blur but he forced his consciousness to hold on and doggedly he fought that dark panic and the nausea it brought with it. With closed eyes, he found for a few minutes he could think. Was it an illusion? He reached out a hand without opening his eyes and it went through the hole. No illusion! Immobile with fear, he edged his hand back forcing thought. It was possible that only the first stride or so of the gap was actually not there; that the rest was an illusion. He could not bring himself to reach across that gap with the wind rushing through. He began to inch backwards, then stopped; he could throw something. Carefully he reached behind him and drew out his salt pouch, then, clinging desperately with one hand he raised the other and threw the tiny sack across the space, forcing himself to watch. It landed over the open space some two strides in front of him – without falling through! Almost he laughed; so nearly had he given up all hope and so obvious had been the answer to a wise person. With eyes firmly closed once more he crept over the gap, feeling the air press his cloak against beaded skin. At only an arm's length he felt the other side, invisible, but solid to the touch. Summoning all his control he heaved himself across the gap and felt for the salt pouch. Nothing would have persuaded him to open his eyes now – suspended helpless over a drop to the valley of unfathomable distance.

Progress for the blind was slow but while groping physically, Lindarg found his mind was drawn away from morbid thoughts of heights and falling, always his hands worked to discover any alteration in the ledge, for there could easily be another gap in the invisibility. For what seemed like an eternity he crawled in the self-imposed darkness and was then aware that the light and the wind were lessening; that he was surrounded by substance once more, and he opened his eyes.

The spiral ledge had gone up through the floor within the top circular wall of the tower and his head was in a walkway between the topmost square building and that outer wall. Relieved, he allowed himself a glance downwards from where he had come. Below him there was absolutely nothing – even the ledge's wall had disappeared and he knew that, had he opened his eyes there, he would never have survived the shock. Hastily he drew himself onto the walkway and sank back down to the stones with his back to the outer wall; he could only dismiss the thought of ever going back.

For a long time he made no move as his mind rested from the ordeal. It was the Queenstone which brought him slowly back to reality – a stark reality on that lonely, inaccessible Tower of Koryn; its warmth stirred him and clutching it, he entered that high place and long he gazed on the scene that met his eyes.

Save for a pebble and two small pouches in the centre of the floor and the dust of time, the room was empty. The Queenstone, though was alive and hummed with a vitality which surpassed anything before. Lindarg held it, instinctively calling.

"Eq." A wavering spectral figure appeared, darting from side to side within the gem and its power waxed; the figure broke free into the room, growing like fire, spreading, taking shape over the pouches on the floor. Vermillion features spread a radiance and warmth; deep eyes, unfathomable, stared down; old white hair shimmered silvery-orange but the body – if Eq had ever had such, remained indefinite beneath the visage.

Even before the features were sharp and complete, the god's voice echoed in the chamber assailing Lindarg from all sides, emanating from the air itself.

"Who are you who has dared to summon Eq through time?" It demanded.

"I am Lindarg, a simple woodman of Dorn…"

"No!"

"It is true!" insisted Lindarg.

"You are more. Brazenly you have challenged the sanctity of my repose and defiled my tower; it is a lie!"

Lindarg sensed the violent power around him, gathering to strike, threatening.

"You have defied the stones of the vale – and the fire, my fire – or perhaps they are memories in these times." The last words held doubt.

"They serve you still-" Lindarg felt the force increase as he said it, primed to rend him from the face of the world.

"Then you have come for me mortal."

The voice was menacing, Lindarg knew he would not be able to resist the onslaught which now readied itself.

"You have crossed my bridges, now you reach across the very chasm of time itself-"

The god's eyes flared a satanic red. Power heaped upon power charged the air; Lindarg was numbed by the ambience of its poised ferocity.

"You will not succeed…!"

Cowed beneath the impending fury, Lindarg waited for the blow, but the words and eyes faltered, their intent unfulfilled and the power hung impotent between them.

"I-I-cannot name you…" The god's voice, quieter now, was incredulous, its power withering; "What has been done? You do not exist – yet I speak with you. You are surely more than you say."

"I am also the Wizard Virdil."

"Sandrinfal – it could only be!" The power surged – and died a moment later, before Lindarg had fully sensed its onset.

"Not he…" came the god's perplexed words, almost whispered and clouded with doubt, "Then who?"

"I have told you the truth."

"Yes, I can feel that you believe it to be the truth, yet such is beyond belief."

Lindarg made no response to the assertion since he could think of nothing to say; he comprehended only that the power which had threatened was gone, that Eq's wrath had somehow been deflected and he was grateful for that. Then Eq continued. "You possess a Queenstone. How is it yours?"

"It was given to me by the Queen of Gullen."

"Given, then it is truly yours – is this she of whom you speak?" The gemstone flashed red and from it the spectre of Syntelle was formed in the chamber as vibrant and beautiful as herself in the flesh. Lindarg caught his breath in wonder, but before he could answer; "I see you speak true once more – it is she. Aaaah, but she is fairer than memories; my goddess I would have made her. No, mortal Lindarg, Virdil or whoever you are, she is safe, I will not harm her," said the ghost as Lindarg jerked in anger at his suggestion.

Eq's voice was warmer now and more distant. "I merely suggest that you have chosen well Sandrinfal." The vision of Syntelle was fading; "Yes truly beautiful… You who have been given the stone are welcome here, though I do not relish the intrusion and I despair for your name. Why have you come?"

"Tell me of the six Equilstones which you forged at the beginning of time."

"Aha, you ask much. Six of them I snatched from the hot heart of the mountains and as they cooled I fashioned them. Many Starseasons I laboured in the great heat, for the longer they cooled and the more they were worked, the greater their power. But why should I tell you more, Virdil? Answer me, why?"

"Whatever I own is yours – though I have little enough to offer."

"The little of a poor man may often be a greater gift than half the kingdom of a king; the Queenstone, would you trade that for information?"

175

"Willingly."

"Ah the trust! Know you its powers, Lindarg?"

"Only that it may show what you ask of it."

"Then you do not know. It can also make a man immortal! Once the gods held such stones and through them the souls of mortals sacrificed to their deity gave them immortality to continue their great works. Would you still give it willingly?"

Before Lindarg could say yes, he was overwhelmed by another thought; "Venain's stone! Venain has one!"

"Perhaps," enjoined Eq. "There were six; I have three, you one, Graggan… hmmmm… These are strange times when mortals walk with gods' stones; simple wizards use the tool of the gods, perhaps the twilight of our time is finally at an end. But I have no need of your gift, for the stones on the floor are Equilstones." As it was said, one of them shone a brilliant white as his now shone, the other two were enclosed in pouches of animal skin. "And yet there is a small thing you can do for me."

"I have followed my dreams thus far and from here I will continue whither fate leads; whatever is your wish shall be done if it is in my power to do so."

"One thing I need, Virdil. Bring me this thing and I will give you much, fail and… if you fail, you will have failed yourself also I think, and therefore Endworld too…"

"I will strive to do this thing. I will bring you that which you desire."

"Then hear me, Lindarg, hear all and listen. This much I will tell you now, and when you return you may ask whatever else you wish to know.

Great were all six Equilstones for each has the power to transfer souls and thus enable eternal life. Two Kingstones I forged, two Queenstones and two Knavestones;

The Kingstone destroys unwary beholders,

The Queenstone is fickle – but may tell what you willed,

The Knavestone enthrals a name into 'slave',

An Equil of three and their powers are stilled.

Separately each can work great deeds, together, in an Equil, they are nothing, for eternal is their triangle and within it they struggle together to no avail, their ceaseless banter being heard through time. I kept three and gave three to other gods – that their work might last forever, but that was not to be. Thousands of souls they stole and after thousands of Starseasons, they became weary with the certainty of life, degenerate and careless in their ways, thus their works dwindled and mortals less and less saw the need for sacrifices; soon there were no more and we gods passed quietly away out of the minds of men. As the gods waned, two of the stones were lost. Thurgelle, goddess of the rains and winds and the air was toppled – now the weather is its own master for there is no-one to guide it; Fairgot, goddess of water, rivers and oceans; Graggan, god of the earth who created swamps, barrenness and plenty from the land, who wrought the heights, valleys, chasms and labyrinths of the world, fed and nurtured the green life that was rooted in his domain – his were the great forests when Endworld was young." Eq sighed with recollection and quieted. Lindarg waited patiently for him to continue.

"Fairgot, graceful and shimmering, her elegance was unsurpassed in Endworld, constantly shifting like a million ripples reflecting the sun, she too was ruined, though what happened I know not." The voice wavered, the orange face, wistful and saddened suddenly fixed on Lindarg. "Know this Virdil – the stone you carry was hers!" There was a pause, then; "Aaahhhh, Sandrinfal, would that you could see the hand which once cradled that gem." Eq paused again, deep in recollection of times past. "Also there was I, Eq, god of fire, forger for the other gods. Ahhh, the power and magnificence that once was mine, you would never suspect what I was – when I really was, for now you see only the merest vestige of me, protected and comforted in decline by these stones. They are also my folly." The god's tone was bitter; "I cannot truly rest and join the ghosts of the past until what I have done is undone; I cannot form the equils to allow the stones to fade as ourselves, because I cannot find and bring them – nor even am I certain where the others might be. I am helplessly bound, a slave to the stones while they endure, a useless memory in Endworld…" The voice broke off, laden with self pity and reproachfulness…

"Then I will help," interrupted Lindarg, "to form those equils and allow you to pass, for I know the goodness of the life with those old ghosts, and perhaps I may join you there one day."

"You understand?" There was a hint of hope in that wizened orange face; Lindarg's heart was filled with sorrow for him and for those ancients he had met on the Old South Road. Now he knew that they missed the gods who could not come. There was a long silence. "You must bring to me a Knavestone. In return, you may take a Kingstone – for it is of little use to me – and you must pledge to destroy the others so that this wraith life of mine can be finished."

"You have my word that this will be done, but where will I find-"

The god of fire broke in; "The two Kingstones and Queenstones lie in this chamber accounted for. Perhaps your – er – who was it? – Venain, has one of the Knavestones." Lindarg caught his breath at the mention of that name. "I see you fear this person – perhaps with justification Virdil, but remember this, if he has and even if he knows all its powers, I do not think it can be used against you."

"It is not for myself I fear, it is my friends and those in Gullen who he will seek to control."

"Then let us waste no more time here, I will say what is left to say and you must go whither you feel is best; these are not my times and I cannot wisely counsel what you should do."

The god paused for a few moments as if summoning strength to continue, then went on, "The other Knavestone I gave to Graggan, god of earth and he has it yet. I know he still lives, and more, I know why he still lives. He burns with a consuming inner hate for he was imprisoned in his catacombs while sleeping carelessly; his guarding spells were uncast and now he rages impotently, trapped, until he runs out of souls and passes. But I fear the thousands of Starseasons of animals' souls will have made him ugly and squalid. The land of the Great Stone under which Graggan lies entombed is barren; no magic can work there now. A man stands alone for what he is and the powers of gods are forfeit; Graggan cannot break this void."

"How-?"

"Think not that he will release his stone to you lightly, since in staying alive for as long as possible lies his only hope of revenge. His bitterness drives him and I fear his rages are unreasoning, perhaps too he would relish a human soul! This land lies far to the north and east…"

"The land of the Baeths!" uttered Lindarg.

"Baeths, who are they?"

"They are a plundering race, oblivious to and despising the ways and customs of Endworld; they are bent on bringing it to its knees, maybe even as we speak they are taking Gullen."

"Does this Venain control them?"

"I think not – they have yet to find out about Venain!" Lindarg managed a flicker of a wry smile and added; "They will find that there is not room in Endworld for two masters."

"Then surely your problem is half-solved?"

"No, most of Endworld lies between them and will be torn 'ere the one meets the other – or the peoples of the land must lay them both – there is no other way." Eq frowned.

"The land cannot – must not fall, certainly it will not easily fade or be overrun, it is too old for that. It will stir yet, but we waste time! More will I tell you on your return." The vermillion visage trembled weakly; "My strength fails, but I say this; I am elated more than for a long time and I feel much may come of our meeting…"

As the god said these last words, he faded from the chamber and the stones darkened; Lindarg heard the wind outside the tower walls and gazed once more onto the dust of its floor. Gingerly he reached for a pouched Kingstone...

12

THE RAISING OF THE WILD THREE

Venain knew of the Baeths and their intentions, he knew also that Graggan, the god imprisoned long ago was still securely entombed under the Great Stone and that his life – more, its life – was dwindling, soon to be but a memory in Endworld. Graggan had wrought nothing for eons and had not been missed when Venain's forefathers had bound him with sorcery beneath the stone.

Of Gullen and beyond Venain knew frustratingly little except that there was likely nothing left there of greater power than himself and those ancient, mighty artefacts which he now possessed.

In fact, Venain's knowledge was accurate but deficient in one small detail: he had nudged the balance; sent a small tremor through the stasis that was Endworld since the fall of the gods – a tremor which nurtured his doubt. In the complexity of that stasis, that shudder could not be identified or named and vainly he had spent many hours searching through Endworld with his mind. The familiar things still endured as before: Graggan, the steadfastness of the Forest of Dorn, the dark pit in Gullen which had been a wizard's home – Virdil's home – still guarded by powers which should have faded with their author but of that author he could find no trace. Here perhaps lay the enigma – a Law of sorcery unaccountably unconsummated.

Nor in his searching had he discovered the whereabouts of the body whose soul had been taken – who had been Lindarg. It seemed to have stolen from Endworld and vanished. The

Knavestone could find none of these names, neither could his probing far-sight.

Dorn was quiet, the only wizardry alive there was his own, the woodmen of the forest realm becoming ever more heedful of the Lore in its shadow, leaving Venain alone – a loneliness that aggravated his restlessness. But the Southlands were in disarray; caused, he knew, by the Baeths who had long coveted them from the cold north. It was toward this upheaval that his mind now turned and there he decided to look for amusement and benefit. Most of all he sought information. He was little interested for the moment in the skirmishes between Baeths and Gullenfolk; rather he was keen to discover any of the important things that were happening in Endworld that made him uneasy. Others might uncover deeds of interest to him – if not to themselves. What he needed was the name of a Baeth general who could know things. With that name he could use the Knavestone and begin to work his will beyond Dorn; begin to control the tide of events.

Venain; the god; would bring all the powers and peoples of Endworld unto himself and before him, in the end, they would be forced to cower beneath his omnipotence; quail in the face of the ultimate might that he held: sanctify his deity. The age of the evil god Venain was impending.

"Jarquil!" Venain's silent command from his tower was irresistible. Below a minion set aside his task for a while to answer that call; Jarquil came. Without words, Venain's orders were clear to him.

"Bring me three stout woodmen. Select them well. I do not seek woodcarvers or tree minders with wives and children, I want tough adventurers of steel who would travel in my service for wealth. They will be hard to find. If, once you have found them, they will not come, call me; I will make them. Give to me their names. Then they will come. Do this thing speedily but without haste. Go; take whoever you will to lend help."

Before the sun had moved enough to trace, Jarquil and four others had entered the Great Forest of Dorn and already Jarquil had a plan which he was sure would please, amuse and honour the sorcerer Venain – and Jarquil lived only to gratify his master. They followed the paths and tracks to the Dome at the heart of the forest. Their passage was watched and noted by many woodmen but none dared interfere with messengers from Venain. Once there, an announcement was made to all denizens of Dorn and sent down tracks and paths – some long forgotten – to reach all ears that would listen in the forest and many more beyond.

"Men of Dorn hear this: Venain has sent me to you and is sincere. He invites all men of good fortune and body to a feast and bouts of mutual tournaments and games on Castle Hill. Gold a-plenty there will be for those who honour him and show well in these tests of strength and skill. And by his leave the greatest three of those who gather will journey into distant lands to seek reward and adventure for themselves and Venain. The tournaments will be held on Astellin day and after. It will be a good event."

It was soon accepted among the more wayward of the woodmen that many would go. 'It will be a good event' meant it had better be – they knew that at least. They knew too that Venain was always 'sincere' – if it wasn't a good event then his wrath would surely be felt by all those in the Forest of Dorn. And there were those who heard and saw opportunity in the invitation; young men in distant parts of the forest – gone astray from the normal course of woodman life; tough, independent, hardy – as unshakable as the sturdy forest trees themselves. These were the ones whom Jarquil sought and no other way would he have found them as swiftly nor as surely.

Jarquil and a lesser minion tarried at the Great Dome in comfort as 'guests' of the Forest King while the news was passed through the forest. The runners had been given gold to add glitter to their words and this too was well done for some eyes were opened to the brightness which might indeed lie beyond the forest.

Outwardly Fordyne had welcomed them, but beneath his regal exterior his heart was heavy with foreboding as he saw fine men fall before the lure of gold and turn away from the Lore; watched fathers leave their families and young men – their lives in front of them – walk away. Worse, he was craven. Venain's men had treated him with contempt – as if they were the forest's ruler. He had let them; offered no resistance; had actually welcomed them.

"Will you not refuse them Fordyne?" A councillor had whispered privately.

"How can I oppose the wizard?" he had replied. "Father tried – to no avail. The power in the castle was far too great." As if to justify his weakness, he had added; "Were I to do so I fear retribution that would cost many lives – I dare not risk it."

The other two minions had returned to the castle to begin the preparations and to alert their master of the plan. From his tower Venain sought Jarquil in the Dome saying into his mind; "I am much pleased. You have acted wisely Jarquil and have discharged well the special trust you bear from me. It is long 'ere I was publicly honoured or amused. I thirst to see a truly animal spectacle, aggressive, sordid and… blood…?"

The question was left in Jarquil's mind.

'Oh yes,' came his own thoughts as soon as Venain's had gone. 'There will be blood – but dearly rather than needlessly spilled!' Well did he deserve the praise of his master – and well he knew it!

For once then, the minions and the resources of the castle and its wizard worked, apparently, for the good of woodmen and those who began to gather there early were treated with respect and hospitality; being housed in pavilions which had been erected around a large open space on the gentle slopes of Castle Hill. They saw the food, drink and other pleasures being prepared and stowed safe for the day; the marking of arenas and courses,

184

frames, weapons; tests of strength and skill for both greater and lesser men. All those who saw the preparations marvelled at them.

Kel, the lonely one from north of the forest was one. He knew Baeths and feared them not. Many had encountered him but none had ever lived to tell the tale. Kel had learned to kill without reason or remorse – his justification the dead bodies of his kind who had deliberated first. Around the pavilions he was just another woodman competitor – as was Dranubinal – but the latter loomed larger and meaner. None knew that but days before, at the sight of gold, he had slain his wife with a single blow of one hand, destroyed his forest home and walked like a giant to Castle Hill. Now he stood squarely, a contemptuous smile creasing his face. As far as he was concerned there would only be one supreme victor at the tour's end – there was no room for three! He slept in the open on the hard earth and when it rained he grunted and turned over in the night.

Dorn held many strong men and many gathered there; some had left wives and children. None would never return to them. But there are other men – not strong of body – but well able to look after themselves. These too were assembled and there was an air of competition even before the day dawned and the feasting began.

It was cleverly planned. The first few days were riotous with few competitions – save small games of skill for amusement but with prodigious amounts of food and drink and a few glinting gems for the victors. Neither Jarquil nor Venain deigned to attend these events; instead they feasted in the castle and schemed about the days to come.

The third day was the first with organised bouts. Comely, half-naked maidens added to the rewards – each helplessly bound at the mercy and for the use of the victor. The addition of such alluring extras greatly enhanced the endeavours and numbers of contestants, elevating their exertions beyond previous bounds. That night and for many after, plaintive screams of abject submission betold the fact that such spoils were well-accepted and deeply appreciated by cruel and violent men at their worst. Few survived to see the tour's end.

Men stripped and wrestled; there were no rules save for the honouring of submission and many a fight ended bloodily with several deaths that day. Always there is one who will strive beyond his limit and be crushed; few heeded such passings – they could have yielded at any time.

There was a log-breaking competition where each contestant was given a two-edged axe and a tree trunk the thickness of his body which had to be hewn asunder in a given time – that being the time it took for a volunteer to drink a large vessel of ale. Only two contestants had won a gold coin and those only because the drinker had been bribed to 'choke' on the draught as they hacked. Now a barrel of a man stood with vessel poised. He downed one on no time while a competitor was awaited then held aloft another as a challenge.

"Drink!"

The command was obeyed instantly and the draught half consumed before the great hulk of Dranubinal picked up the axe, threw it into a nearby tree, selected the thickest trunk and with a mighty roar lifted and whirled it onto the axe-head embedded in the tree. As the log was cleaved its free end tore into the crowd pulverising a man in its path. Many others were felled – but recovered – probably suffering little more than a few broken bones. The axe shattered and the tree tumbled atop the drinker, crushing him with a third of the drink still to go, spilling ungainly entrails and yellow ale into the dirt. Venain was not slow to notice how Dranubinal had succeeded – by using the axe differently – where others had failed. He liked that. Nor had Dranubinal showed the slightest concern about the innocent bystanders killed or maimed by his methods. Venain liked that too.

There was Yanish slaying too: their baying was incessant on Castle Hill throughout the day and scores crowded to witness these bouts. They took place in a stone paddock in a hollow with walls twice a man's height – from which neither beast nor man could escape. A large stone slab moved by four minions closed off the exit. This was a fight to the death and it was soon realised with the two agonising first deaths that the Yanish were half-starved and bloodthirsty. Only brave or foolish men felt that stone scrape shut behind them and faced the trapped beast. Nor was poison any respecter of strength or wit; the first blood had to go to the man. Jarquil himself presided over this game and often Venain watched from his tower over half a league away – but to the sorcerer it was no distance – from there his vision showed him every tooth mark and graze and he amused himself by guessing the time it would take for the man to fall after the first bite. He was usually right.

Since dawn a lissome, dark haired beauty had shivered and whimpered barely-clad at her post and still, at the cold sun's height, she remained unclaimed. Men had tried – for it was no coincidence that Jarquil had saved such a beauty as the prize for this contest – but the Yanish, cruelly and swiftly had vanquished all comers.

Now Kel stepped forward to the post; eyes lustful; drinking in her sinewy curves. He tore at the shift as she cringed, withdrawing from his unrestrained appraisal. The garment fell to her waist, the revelation drawing an involuntary intake of breath from the excited throng and a raking leer across the woodman's face while the taut, well-honed muscles which abounded on his naked torso rippled in anticipation. He turned, selected a trident from the available weapons, pushed the minions aside, rolled the stone gate alone and stepped into the arena to stare fixedly at the waiting beast. Around him the onlookers quieted for the man who displayed not a trace of fear for the most cunning, swift and deadly of all Endworld beasts.

Faced with this redoubtable edifice of a man, the Yanish slunk one way then the other along the base of the furthest wall. Never once did it take its eyes off the man as it padded unceasingly back and forth but it would not attack. Kel advanced on it, trident poised forward as his body; a low snarl deep in his throat. The distance between man and beast lessened until the Yanish had room to do no more than sway uncertainly from side to side as panic rose within it and its eyes widened like twin flames. The tension in and around the arena was tangible; Jarquil and Venain from afar – could see and feel it. All there knew the coiled ferocity with which the cowed, fear-crazed animal would erupt at any moment into a paroxysm of whirling death.

Its leap was like lightning but the three prongs as fast. In the air they met – furry fury and cold steel. With a speed and violence that defied the eye, the animal twisted free of the points which had raked its belly, ripping its own flesh further as it turned frenziedly downwards to come at the man from above. With mouth agape, poison teeth dripping and an ear-splitting evil howl it dived at bare skin. At the same moment the weapon whipped across its path slamming forcibly into the side of its head with a sickening jolt deflecting the jaws which snapped shut on thin air as it was hurled to the ground. Lithely it rolled upright, blood oozing freely into the fur on its snout and neck, then powered its back legs against the dirt to lunge at its foe's leg. But Kel had not steadied his weapon after the sideways swipe; he had let it turn, gathering speed and now the slick points were whisking down to greet the animal's charge. Too late it saw the flashing tines; too late to draw back from its fateful lunge and with a dull, wet crunch, two fingers of steel seared through its neck impaling it immovably to the hard earth. The beast's eyes protruded and glazed; legs thrashed wildly and poison jetted harmlessly to the ground as it squealed out its death throes and the cheering crowd parted between the victor and his prize.

Hot and violent he crushed her against the post; claiming her in the heat of his conquest, then dragged her screaming away and silenced her with one thrashing blow.

Next the man with mad eyes went into the paddock and Venain knew this bout would be different: even he could feel those eyes and the madness behind them. The man had no weapon and no vestige of fear – and the Yanish knew it! The man's eyes stared and he chuckled as the animal whimpered and made for the wall. But the man was behind it and leaped on its back with a shout of glee; hands closed round the neck; mad fingers squeezed and twisted and as bone snapped the man's face turned skywards and mad eyes bulged at the sun.

Elsewhere a game of forfeits was being played – a sly game of the mind with wood patterns on the ground. When one player gained an advantage by walling up his opponent's counter, that other took a sleeping draught which first stimulated the mind to greater ploys then, after the third, fourth or fifth such, brought an unconscious sleep to the defeated from which none ever woke. Jarquil had used a slow poison. The game was of particular interest because it contained and element which no other game there held: a big man could take much more poison before ill-effects; a smaller man much less and the weakling only one or two draughts. Thus, those who played men of greater stature had to be very much cleverer since the poison selected greater size and the game, keener minds. Dranubinal took forfeit several more times than his opponent but still won – walking away after seven drinks while his opponent 'slept' with four. Kel would have nothing of this game; he thought it an unfair test of a man's fortune and was sure the forfeits were poisoned.

In this manner, over the following days, man was weeded from man. There were many other games and tests – some painful with victory hard won – others not so. Venain knew all that went on and noted names – of those at least who would give one. Kel didn't; neither did the madman who knew of no name for himself anyway, though he must have had one.

With but two days remaining the tour had become ever more violent. Not without evil intent had Jarquil goaded and rewarded the contestants with gold – and fairer spoils – not only had the competitions themselves taken their toll but so too had greed and covetousness. Men had fought over prizes, slaying and stealing, avenging and goring; suspicion, tension and mistrust had increased with each passing day and in the confines of Castle Hill, led to blood-letting night and day. This had also been part of Jarquil's plan to eliminate the lesser men and unknown to those who stayed, any who sought to leave with spoils by melting darkly into the night forest had met their deaths in the hands of a fell grey foe which unceasingly hunted the lands around Castle Hill. No gold or other rewards left that place, neither did any living soul save three…

By the final day of the competitions Venain was nigh sure of the outcome. This day the three would be chosen. He appeared on the battlements, shining golden robes reflecting the morning sun. The cheer which rose to greet him, led by his minions, was caught up and amplified by the Woodmen of Dorn.

"Hail Venain! Hail Venain!"

"Mightiest in Endworld! Hail Venain!"

The echo was flung between the castle walls, the forest and back. Venain revelled in the acclaim which was his.

"This tour," he shouted to them, "has shown many men of excellence, good spirit and worth. Many have been rewarded for valiant deeds and well-deserved have been those rewards!" His declaration was interrupted by cheers but he let them cheer for many moments before raising his hand; "Those who wish are free to leave with their gains." He swept his raised hand in an arc as a gesture of dismissal then continued. "This day I have reserved for the greatest contest of all. From it will emerge the three mightiest to be famous in Endworld and rich beyond measure. Today will not be for leafy hearts – nor hearts of tough wood," he paused for effect, "No!" He shouted, "Today is for the steel-hearted among you – for those who would rend the world with me and grasp its last great wealth and power!" Again he paused, scores of men below hung on his every word and he gazed over grease-shining, muscle-taut bodies – barely clothed but uncaring of the morning chill which chafed their skins.

"Forget the games of past days!" Venain's voice was thunderous; "Today will be the greatest test of men seen since the sun rose on the coming of men into Endworld and from them will arise the three most fearful men of Dorn. They will become of all men, supreme in the world; they will ride on steeds to far lands; into great deeds – deeds to be blazoned onto the face of the sun itself 'ere it finally sets!" Venain spoke well for he knew that he must if any men were to fight through this bloody day.

"Decide!" The challenge was flung down. "Let only the bravest remain for only those mighty three will ever leave of those who stay!"

Scores of men began to collect their spoils and shuffle down from the hill into the forest; each in his way content with what he had gained. The promise of death to all but three had not cheered them since they knew from past days that there were men they could not best. Many took their fairer spoils too – maidens no longer – some bound like slaves, others 'free' to walk at their victor's heels.

Beside Dranubinal a small man wavered.

"Surely you will not stay?" Dranubinal sounded disinterested, but he was surprised; the man had no chance at all.

"No-"

"Then begone."

"But I have heard that death awaits those who enter the forest…"

"Are you sure this is true?" queried Dranubinal.

"N-no-"

"Then there is but one way to find out." Dranubinal's statement was flat. Then, seeing the man still hesitating added, "What did Venain promise that made you come?"

"Gold, riches, rewards."

"Do you have them?"

"Yes-"

"Were you promised life?

"No…" The voice trailed off.

"Then you can merely hope that Venain will be merciful – you cannot expect it." Dranubinal turned away then, thankful that his own decision was easier and sure that the man was right.

Eight men were left, standing tall on the hill, while the rest melted into the forest – and out of the memory of man at the hands of fell grey killers.

Minions now worked anew on the hill. Venain had to be amused properly; this was to be the best spectacle since the short-lived but stimulating battle with Virdil over a Starseason ago. Five frames were built consisting of two sturdy uprights supporting a thick spar across the top with a notch in its centre. Between the two uprights of each frame a small fire was lit directly below the notch. Each fire was tended by a minion and was fed from a huge woodpile. Kel wondered at these wood piles – they were big enough to keep such fires alight for many days yet this was to be the last day of the tournaments. Not far down the slope from the five frames an arena was laid out and marked.

With the preparations complete the castle gates opened and from them emerged legions of grim, grey-faced warriors on magnificent steeds and those there wondered that the castle could hold so many. None had known of an army within its walls and for many it was the first glimpse of the real power of Venain. Dranubinal stirred – some evidence at least that the sorcerer was able to do all he spoke of. Kel too was pleased – though uneasily when they and the whole arena was impenetrably surrounded. A cruel smile twisted Venain's lips as he noted their suspicious discomfort.

"You eight have chosen, so be it. Each will meet another in combat; the combatants will be chosen by me. Also I will decide the order of the bouts. There is one rule only: the cry of 'yield' is to be honoured. No fighter has the right to take the life of another unless I decree so."

Two sets of assorted weapons were placed several strides from each other within the arena; a spiked flail, a huge axe and a smaller one, a long and short sword, a spear, a long knife and a pole as thick as a man's calf. At the start of each bout, contestants were stood their own body's length behind their weapons, facing each other.

Kel's opponent was shaking and sweating profusely. He was one who knew he should not have stayed and Venain had chosen him to battle first; knowing the outcome; the better to demonstrate to the others his word – and the fate of the loser.

"Fight!" The order was crisp and clear from Venain himself and obeyed before its echo had died away.

The two men dived simultaneously for the weapons but Kel did not stop to select one. His dive was right over them and into a roll on the grass between, then powerful thighs lunged Kel's head and shoulders into the abdomen of his opponent just as the man unbent with his selected weapon. The man was lifted his own height from the ground and the sword, round which his hand had barely closed, spun skywards to fall outside the arena. The man crumpled, remaining insensible while Kel unhurriedly chose an axe and raised it above his victim's head. The man grovelled and cringed and this was taken as a yield since no sound issued from him at all. There was a cheer from the host of minions and warriors but it was not joined by the six contestants who remained.

"And now you shall witness the fate of those who fail. May it harden beyond all imagining your own resolve to succeed." Venain's foul tones were gleeful with evil as minions bound then dragged the loser to a fire-frame. A thick rope was passed between bound wrists, over the spar and the man was hauled up to dangle over the fire beneath. Minions kindled the fire afresh with more wood and as the pain shot through him from below – so the man lifted himself clear of the flames with flexing arms and taut, cracking muscles. There was no sound from the cruelly-crammed mouth but the face, a garish-beaded red picture of torment betold the searing agony. Slowly the arms gave way and the feet were back in the flames. Renewed pain brought renewed strength and the body lifted again – but more slowly. Rivulets of sweat ran down the legs where black sparks had clung to the

193

damp and flying ash had settled; drips hissed into the fire below.

Minions allowed the fire to die a little and the body rested from its exertions but still writhed and struggled in pain; feet still only red. Then a little more wood, tiring arms, more pain, more drips and up and down went the man. It could go on for a day – even before the drips of salt sweat were mixed with fat to kindle the fire; long before the feet blackened – and the legs – how long would they take? How soon – or late – would death come? No man could guess. A tougher man might take two days... perhaps longer...

A grim, dark realisation visited those who watched and their faces were as stone; nerves and sinews taut and ferocious. Surrounded as they were by Venain's legions of death, they were left with but one course. The silence was broken only by the crackling of fires and the creaking of the fire-frame with the man like a travesty of some gruesome ancient yo-yo set against the sky.

Dranubinal fought next: his opponent gone beyond fear – to fight was all his mind would countenance except that a chance blow might end him before the fire. This prayer was answered for Dranubinal whisked up the pole faster than the eyes could see – even Venain missed the blow – and the head lay in the dirt in a rain of blood. Nearby the madman laughed as blood spattered on his leg.

"Blundering fool!" Venain's voice was charged with anger. Warriors and minions alike tensed for a command but Dranubinal cast his head upwards and said; "Hear this wizard – I slay all who pass between me and my goal; that goal is set; I will not be restrained! Set me against any, – nay, set me against them all – I will fail you not!" The booming voice had almost defied Venain.

"Brave words and well spoken, Dranubinal. Perhaps you are right and I must look no further – yet I shall."

Half-satisfied, Dranubinal shrugged his huge shoulders and left the arena to the madman and his opponent.

The word was given and the madman's eyes shone bright as he laughed a demonic laugh to match their stare. The sound sliced through his opponent's composure like a fiery sword and reason left him. Crazed, he cavorted and ran as the eyes laughed and watched him go to his frame like one who was dead already – or one who preferred pain to life or death just then. More did the madman's mirth resound at the sight of the burning, rising, falling, dangling man. Even Venain shuddered a little and under his breath murmured:

> "A madman to frighten even the dead -
> From whom the bravest men have fled.
> Even I dare not enter that head -
> So let his name remain unsaid."

The final duel between the remaining two closely-matched woodmen was only really noteworthy in that it lasted through the night and in those dark hours was lit only by the glow of the waiting fires. Venain slunk from his keep to hear loud the crunching and tearing of bone and ligaments; breathe deep sweet smell of warm and over-hot flesh; to see close the blood, filth and gore of that long and evil night.

Mercifully dawn brought an end. Broken weapons and a broken man lay around; a beaten man still stood, swaying uncertainly. Though the loser was close to death, the last vestiges of pain and suffering were wrested from him by the fire. But with sinews and muscles torn and blood raining onto the fire, his life was ended swiftly. His scream though, reverberated long after in the minds of those who had heard it – chilling their hearts anew.

Now the minions melted behind the grey warriors. Four of the fell creatures came forward to meet the four men of Dorn and the circle closed about them. From close-by came Venain's voice, almost a whisper in the dead stillness.

"The three men who remain will be those who ride the world!" No sooner had the words faded than the grey men bore down upon their prey and the clamour of battle rang on Castle Hill.

The madman's laugh seemed to whip up the wind and even grey eyes avoided that stare to drive at an easier target. Kel and Dranubinal struck deep and with fury; slaying their foes at a stroke – but they would not die! Instead they turned and came on with added vigour, down again on their quarry, striking cold their hearts with the stench of the inhuman, striking hard and straight with burnished steel. Nethermen! The undead! The battle would not stop until a woodman perished! Each man was not going to be that one and each fought as he had never done before in his own world and in his own way: the mad laugh, the mighty slashing bellow of Dranubinal and the cruel, fleet, deadly, thinking menace that was Kel. These three were left when the last of the greatest ordinary woodman fell and was dragged away to his place.

The three had been chosen and Venain was much pleased as they entered his castle to do his bidding. Behind them minions still tended three fires but now tortured mouths were freed and far off their pitiful screams echoed mournfully through Astellin-lined glades in the Forest of Dorn – the plaintive sound a grim harbinger of darkness to come…

The next day, the Wild Three, resplendent in fine mail and burnished helms; riding magnificent steeds and bristling with weapons of honed steel – the finest in Endworld – waited restlessly for the castle gates to open. For once Venain had spared nothing to equip his warriors and they in their turn were bolstered by the finery with which they had been regaled. Few indeed were there in the whole of Endworld who could match their magnificence and now they were eager for conquest. Venain knew their names and through the Knavestone he entered their minds – save for the madman – he would follow the other two – and directed them into the Southlands to do his will there.

The thunder of the three beasts shattered the stillness of the forest's edge as Venain drove them hard eastwards through and beyond the Forest of Dorn.

They had been gone many days before they encountered a few score Baeths who had been plundering some abandoned, far-flung homes of Westfolk; their denizens long since departed for the safety of Gullen. The meeting took place in a wooded glade; it was a pleasant place to parley – soft sunlight, warm, sweet-tinged, damp and peaceful.

"Hail Baeths! Who is your leader?" greeted Kel.

"I am." The voice was sardonic, confident, assured.

"We would speak with you."

"Then speak – they will all hear." The Baeth leader motioned to his band of fighting men sprinkled around the clearing and spilling from the trees.

"I would know first to whom I speak." Kel's voice did not disguise his impatience.

"Surely," said the man, "it is enough to know that you speak to a leader of three score men or-"

"Your name!" The Baeth leader pondered the demand unhurriedly, provokingly.

"One word from me and you are…" He drew two fingers across his throat; the scattered men grasped their weapons. The Baeth leader was enjoying the taunt and was looking forward to the carnage which would be dealt out to these three upstarts when their silly demands and provocations were over.

He was right. Carnage there was but it was the Three Wild Men who emerged and only the woodland benefitted from the meeting and then only when the worms and other crawling things had feasted their fill on the Baeth remains.

Baeth, Woodmen and Southfolk alike were cut down like chaff in a swathe across the Southlands. A score here, ten there – but there were a few who survived – the clever ones who hid and lived to tell the tale. One such was close to and a good friend of Gargol. Thus, as Gargol re-marshalled his men, hell-bent on the destruction of Gullen, news came to him of these 'Three Wild Men who were invincible'. Thinking them to be of Gullen and that they must be of some importance, Gargol took some of his army and went out to meet them on the Kronan Plain.

With Kel at their head, the Wild Three slowed; Baeth soldiers were ranged in ever-deepening lines stretching across the plain before them. Dranubinal turned to Kel and said flatly, "We cannot fight an army."

"Then we must talk," concluded Kel.

The madman merely laughed across the grass.

"Halt Gulleners!" Gargol's booming voice was a directive.

"Not Gulleners," corrected Kel. "To whom do we speak – a great general perhaps at last?" he queried sardonically, facing Gargol squarely and eyeing the vast array of men ranged behind him.

"Indeed, I am Gargol, general over all the Baeth forces who commands and directs the fight to deliver Endworld from the clutches of the Southern degenerates. And you, if not of Gullen, then where-?"

"Have you not heard of the Three Wild Men of Dorn?" Dranubinal's voice thundered out.

"I have heard rumours-"

"We are the same – and the rumours are true." But behind the eyes of Kel, Venain was gone.

Back in his tower he muttered the name 'Gargol' into the stone and now his will was behind other eyes. The Three Wild Men were now free to do their own will in Endworld and Gargol said to them, "If it is riches, fame or power that you seek, then to Gullen is your path. Do not think it will fall to a mere three – great are the rewards which lie hidden in that city – so the harder they will fight to defend them."

"And still we will take what we desire!" resounded Dranubinal.

"Then your road from here is south."

"South then!" rang Kel's voice and the mad laugh was with them as they turned and thudded away into the sun.

Venain was jubilant and chuckled long in his high tower. In but a few days he had wrought more than the Baeths had achieved in several Starseasons – and he might yet learn more by the Wild Three in Gullen and what he learned there would be of more use than having the names of a thousand Baeth generals!

For now though, he began to mould the mind of Gargol, finding it not an easy task for the general had many advisers and Venain could not be in all heads at once. Also he found the logic of Gargol's mind very different from his own – it was the blind logic of patriotism, discipline and duty – both to his men and Baeth; a mind with very set and limited horizons with which Venain tussled, kneading and melding it to his purposes – and much time it took until finally, succeeding, he took control.

And while Venain struggled to work on the general's mind and weave different plans within it, three men failed to turn from their road to take the Eastway to Gullen but passed it by on the Old South Road and when next Venain did search for them, the stone was blank to their names.

The Three Wild Men loosed into Endworld by Venain had, seemingly, vanished in the flux of eons which was on that old road through the Southlands and beyond... where they encountered very different 'foes'...

13

LORD OF THE SOUTHLANDS

Even after a furious struggle, Lindarg had not been able to lift the Kingstone. Eq would not relinquish it and it remained as firmly fixed as if it were part of the very stone of the chamber floor. At first he had felt cheated; not trusted and that Eq in the end did not intend to keep his word, but reason had brought enlightenment.

If the god had spoken the truth about wanting, more than anything, to be freed from the deeds he could not undo and allowed finally, to pass away, he had to be sure the Knavestone was brought to him. So, Lindarg realised, the Kingstone was to be his bargain counter; its ultimate power the ultimate lure – Lindarg would wish to use it at worst to become all-powerful himself, at best to aid his friends, their city and Endworld itself against gathering forces. If Lindarg had taken the stone now, the god would have reasoned it unlikely that he would return with the Knavestone, but would keep both for good or ill – or just because the temptations were great. Eq's wishes would then be forgotten. In his way then, Eq not only ensured that his own interests were served, but also those of the greater good of Endworld – and Lindarg could not resent that.

Thereafter, Lindarg had slept long and easily in the tower relieving the aches and exhaustion which recent toils had wreaked upon his ageing frame and though his leaving Koryn was unimpeded by obstacles and the guardians of the tower – since it was not in their words to bar exit – it was many days before he emerged from the vale. Sylee had gone but vaguely Lindarg could remember the way – though not all the dangers.

Not long after leaving the vale he became suddenly aware of a presence – an animal! A steed! Not daring to wonder how it came to be in these lands which animals shunned, he probed its spirit, coaxing it to come. Inexorably it was drawn to him until the smooth snout nuzzled its master. Praising his fortune, Lindarg climbed slowly onto its back, gripping damp fur tightly and turned it toward the Old South Road. On foot he could never have covered the distance to Gullen, now there was at least a chance, though he was weary… weary…

Behind him the cold from the mountains had spread down into the lows and valleys, nights were bitter with frost and the east wind tossed the bushes of the plain. Lindarg drew his jerkin and blankets of Yanish skins around himself, cursing the snow-laden sky. There was little food to be had and none of it was to his taste.

With the coming of evening the old ghosts were abroad and their fires were warming to the soul. Night and day it was harder to resist the welcome of their whispers – easier to slide from life into their eternally warm arms; to relinquish responsibility; to achieve their karma out of life. By day Lindarg tarried more and journeyed slower as his body aged and faded with the final southern flurries of the Coldseason and on into Astellin.

But one evening the voices were busied with news. Lindarg had not resisted the lure of their fires and in a glade his body was taut and still atop his steed; he had joined them to warm his soul.

"Welcome again, Sandrinfal! 'Tis good to meet a second time – and so soon. Where have you been since we last met? You look older. Aaah, the weather out there is bitter, is it not?" Trindledine was offering him hot food but not the food of mortal bodies. Lindarg ate greedily answering,

"It is the cold of the bones which I have felt – and the chill of loneliness in these southern wastes."

"Then it is good that you have joined us – tonight there will be a great meeting since I hear that Akryanl from beyond the Southern Mountains has at last found the old way through them and will reach here this very day from the south and from the north approaches Vanuryl with goods from the oldest city of Endworld – even I do not remember its name – but nobody forgets Vanuryl once met! You must join the feast, then afterwards perhaps you will journey with him – we think he might traverse the Southern Mountains if he can bargain with Akryanl for the route. Aaahh! It will be a magnificent meeting, have no fear."

The two conversed for long over ancient matters – those things which were always discussed. Two travellers bargained for the Queenstone – but Lindarg would not part with it – nor the soul of his steed which waited, grumbling in the melting snows with his body in the world of flesh.

"It is not here," one of the travellers had said, "but it will come if you call it, then we may have it." They offered much gold for the beast but Lindarg had been adamant; he would keep it in the world until there was a better bargain to be had. The travellers shrugged their shoulders and went on their way. Trindledine said, "You were wise not to trade for so little – your beast will live long in the world yet and its considerable value may be saved for a better bargain in the future – unless it is killed before you call it, then it comes with and belonging to, whoever chances to cross with it. But less of such matters, come sing with us a welcome; the scouts of Vanuryl are coming – see them!"

Lindarg looked to the north and saw two gold and silver banners of metallic lace, shining black steeds, polished helms on leather, silver sword and golden flail gleamed in the evening Sun; behind them – far behind but visible now, beasts high-piled with ancient merchandise; opulent; glittering; spectral. Lindarg was filled with wonder – surely half the wealth of Endworld was approaching – but when the scouts arrived, they brought news as well: "We passed three travellers in the world, great men they were. They heard us but would not come."

"They were travelling south?" asked Lindarg, suddenly interested.

The first scout regarded Lindarg quizzically; Trindledine caught the question in the glance. "Forgive me," he blurted. "You have not met Sandrinfal?"

"We have seen his body and beast – he is not yet here!" The voice was indignant, "A man should choose-"

"Perhaps he is coming!" There was an unmistakable edge to Trindledine's retort. "And you would do well not to forget the old customs of welcome for he is a great wizard – might even take your goods back into the world – fear that and respect him!"

"Then, Sandrinfal, be welcome and also at our meeting this eve but if you seek to know more of the travellers, then a bargain must be set – the first perhaps of this sojourn."

"Bravo! Bravo!" Trindledine cut in. "That is much better."

"What then wizard have you to bargain with – perhaps your steed's soul to keep me company for an eternity?" Lindarg considered the suggestion – but not for long.

"In giving information you lose nothing since you still retain what you have given – therefore I offer nothing in return!"

"Well said and true! What is your answer to that, Vanuryl-scout? Trindledine was much pleased with Lindarg's opening gambit.

"I answer this: it is true that I lose nought, but what is also true is that you gain the information and I gain nothing. In a bargain both sides must gain – what will you offer?" The scout was gleeful with his argument.

"He has a gemstone," interjected Trindledine; Lindarg shot him a remonstrative glance.

"Ah, then show it," But his eagerness faded at the sight of the Queenstone; "Look behind me Sandrinfal, are our packs not loaded with such trinkets? I would not trade for ten of them. It is not enough."

"I can only trade what I possess," murmured Lindarg and continued sarcastically. "Maybe all of that cannot be enough for someone as you Sir – who has everything…?" The scout did not miss the intonation.

"I do not have everything-"

"Then name something you desire."

"I have named it and now you must bring him to me from the world."

"That is too much; already this day I have turned down many bags of gold for the same trade – and it may be that the information you have is useless to me – I cannot see it as you can see what I offer."

"Good, good," muttered Trindledine.

"How can I show you information and still have it left to bargain with?"

"Ha, you cannot!" came Lindarg's retort, "And I think that makes your position somewhat precarious."

"A cruel blow 'Fal," bubbled Trindledine. The scout's brows were knitted in thought unable to find a counter to his opponent's assertion, but Lindarg suggested,

"You could reveal to me a small part, then I could decide on its worth."

"How do I know which part to tell?"

"Answer just this: to where were they travelling?"

"That and no more: they journeyed to Gullen." Lindarg called his mount and it appeared, warming itself by the fire.

"The bargain is made, we must celebrate!" exclaimed Trindledine, "And hear the news of these travellers." The scout's face remained impassive as they waited for him to speak. "Come, speak man, 'tis your bargain," said Trindledine impatiently.

"Yes – with Sandrinfal only. What will you offer to hear?" Trindledine's mouth hung open;

"Isn't the steed-soul enough?"

"Indeed, it is a most gracious price – from Sandrinfal -" The unfinished statement was no suggestion; it was a pointed dig.

"I have no need of the information," protested Trindledine awkwardly.

"Then don't listen." But a sudden thought brought a smile back to Trindledine's lips.

"Sandrinfal will tell me anyway."

"That's his business." The abrupt words were a dismissal and Trindledine had no choice but to wander away.

'I suppose you don't amass such wealth by giving it away,' he thought to himself philosophically, knowing the scout had been quite right to send him away, after all, why should he, Trindledine expect something for nothing? 'Worth a try though,' he chuckled to himself by the fire regarding Lindarg and the scout.

"One was a madman whose name is not known, the other two were strong and determined. Three powerful men who might easily take a city in these times; in their heads was only slaying and gain. Hundreds of men they had already slain – and ready they were to take on a whole army – for they had met one but rode it by to reach the city ahead of it, they said. Venain had sent them into the Southlands but-" Lindarg was no longer listening. The mention of that name stunned him, sending tremors through his frame as he faded from the firelight into the snow of the Southlands where he remembered he had to go.

The cold was biting – though it was well into Astellin now. His mount lay dead beside him in the melting snow. Summoning all his remaining strength he rose doggedly, facing the wind, forcing his body into it and onwards toward the road's fork which lay yet many days away on foot. There was no thinking beyond there – to a distant Gullen…

While Gullen licked its wounds, the liegemen sped to where their liege had turned aside from the Eastway to go south.

"Halt!" It was Durnor's voice from their front. "This is the place – and three have ridden this way not long since." The others drew up, mounts snorting hot breath white into the chill air. Eisdan spoke,

"The tracks have come from the north and they were moving fast, maybe our lord is in danger – Baeths perhaps?"

"No, I think not," replied Banor. "Not just three."

"Then who?" queried Faran darkly, half to himself. None of them could guess.

"Our duty is clear – we must follow our liege and whoever 'they' are, south." Durnor's voice had hardly died away when, from far off down the old road, came a laugh; faint – yet clear and somehow unnerving. "Let us ride!" was all Durnor said as he turned, thudding onto the Old South Road.

Little was said on that journey. Night and day they pelted and always the laugh was ahead of them – atavistic and stark amid the silence of these forsaken lands. They felt observed; surrounded by presences; stoically they surged on; their thoughts ahead and on their duty; sensing danger but intent upon their self-appointed task. Soon the tracks were fresher but still the laugh was ahead of them, mocking their progress, spurring them on ever faster – but faster still went the laugh. Exhaustion threatened to overtake them and their steeds as the days and nights flowed past, thrusting them further and further into the wilderness of these southern wastes.

"Have you not heard them?" Andur had said suddenly to Eisdan as they rested one evening.

"The voices?"

"Yes – their whispering never quite stops-"

"Do not listen Andur, they are not of this world."

"You mean-?"

"Yes," Eisdan's voice was a whisper itself. "I fear they seek to cheat us of life. Heed them not – they have nothing to offer the living."

When they reached the fork before the Southern Mountains they stopped. The laugh had gone and the tracks had turned east – very fresh now in the dwindling snow: the thaw came early this far south. Beside the fork sat an old man, haggard and diminished. Only just had he found the strength to change the ways before the three who would surely have killed him for sport alone.

"Lindarg! Surely it is – yet how can it be?"

The old man looked up at Eisdan with relief deep in his eyes and croaked, "I am Lindarg, or perhaps Virdil – and yet I am Sandrinfal, liegemen. Yet again you save me, yet again you work for Gullen and Endworld. Take me to your queen, I would see her."

He did not speak again.

Lindarg's return to Gullen plunged the city from the elation of the Baeth retreat, into a fateful and morbid foreboding. Their lord lay dying, the queen mourning at his side – powerless to prevent his wasting away. The child Virlin – their lord's child – was presumed slain at birth by ordinary Gullenfolk and now, with Lindarg's return, they shared the guilt of that over-hasty and shameful deed, adding to the grimness of those days. The few elders and leaders who knew that Virlin yet lived agonised over their deceit but could reach no decision. They could not relieve the citizens of their guilt without revealing that deceit and the indecision which had beget it: thus exposed, they could hardly expect a continuance of unwavering loyalty – and they dare not risk such disunity in these imperiled times.

The physicians of the court had been and gone leaving little hope in their wake; Lindarg's life was slipping away and there was nothing they could do. He had even been unresponsive when his son Virlin was secretly brought by Syntelle, Andur and Karil.

"This is our son, Lindarg," Syntelle had whispered, lifting his wizened hand to touch the baby's soft skin but Lindarg had remained motionless, uncaring. Karil had said sadly,

"He does no more than breathe, I fear it is a forlorn hope that he will stir again." The truth in the sentiments which Karil had voiced had assailed them with the dread of impending grief; there were tears in Syntelle's eyes.

"But while there was a chance that sight of his son might help I had to try," she pleaded. The empathy and sorrow in their faces had spoken more than words, but Andur had said comfortingly,

"Yes, it was well tried-"

Woodenly, Gulleners and their armies toiled to ready the city for the onslaught they knew would soon come from the Baeths. Their mightiest force with Gargol, spoiling for retribution at its head would come at them again now the snows had gone; come better equipped and with the hindsight of previous failure and with Achemin creeping up from the Southlands, Gullen knew there would be no help from the weather a second time. Yet those preparations were made; the queen ordered it, though perhaps she too could raise little hope that the city would last through the Warmseason with its hot, rainless days.

Nor had their wizard returned – most reckoned that he never would – and only time separated the city from inevitable defeat and subjugation at the hands of the foe.

The liegemen helped as they could but always – though listlessly now – they guarded the queen's quarters where Lindarg was passing his final days and from where Syntelle rarely emerged.

'Thus,' so it is written in the annals of Gullen history, 'the integrity of the city, its denizens and their lands, hung by the finest of threads in that dark Astellin when hope faded… '

"My Queen." It was Durnor, in the open doorway. "There is a traveller who requests an audience, he says it is urgent – vital that he sees you." For long moments Syntelle only sobbed, then said quietly,

"Who is this traveller?"

"He will not give his name."

"Then make him! And make him tell his purpose!" She burst into more tears and Durnor left but got no further than a few paces from the door.

Bouncing down the passage was the traveller; so easily had he evaded Durgel and Faran that he was still giggling. Before Durnor could give vent to his incredulity, the traveller said, "Aaahh, Sir,

208

your friends-" He broke off into a fit of laughter which echoed along the passage. "Your friends, I fear, are quite blind!" There was more mirth. Durnor's sword rang, but before the blade was clear, the man went on; "I am glad the queen has agreed to see me for it seems she is not safe without me. Oh no, not safe at all!"

"The queen does not wish to see you – leave this place immediately!" Durnor's voice was firm and final. His sword barred the way.

"But that is not what she said – or perhaps she did, but it is not what she meant. No, mark me – I know what the queen wants because I guess – and I know what I guess."

The sword was at his throat now, anger flooded Durnor's features – his face livid behind the hilt.

"Your name then – and purpose!"

"Ah yes, she asked that." The little man thought for a moment. "Tell her I bring her that which she most desires and as for my name, tell her I am myself. If that does not satisfy her tell her to ask the Queenstone of 'myself'. Ha ha – yes, tell her to ask it that and see what she sees."

"I will not ask it that, traveller." Syntelle was in the doorway behind Durnor.

"Of course not, my Queen, for only the foolish would see themselves as they really are and not as they wish themselves to be. You are no fool," he chuckled wryly. "Of course not!" The traveller bowed much lower than he already was, then added, "Neither am I."

"Put down your sword, Durnor," said the queen. "The traveller who is himself may enter."

"Aahh, my thanks."

And the traveller walked straight in, cast a glance toward the shrouded bed and bounced into a chair. Syntelle followed him noticing that he had already settled comfortably.

"Perhaps you have journeyed far and are hungry?"

"How far is 'far'?" asked the traveller philosophically, half to himself and half out loud, but before Syntelle could respond he continued, "I like Maeberries, Shord hips, Sweet Mellia – and oh, I really adore the leaves of the Tuvril and Wailberries – what a delicacy!"

Syntelle was perplexed, "We have none of these."

"Ah, my Queen, there I'm afraid you are wrong – very wrong. We are still in Endworld?"

Syntelle nodded imperceptibly.

"Well yes, I thought we were – knew really-" The unkempt little fellow looked as if he were going to burst with glee.

Syntelle did not share his amusement. But then he steadied himself.

"As long as we are in Endworld, then all these things will be around. Send the oldest hag that can be found in the city, she will know of them and find them."

And she did. Never had she moved so fast since she could remember; a request for her services – from the queen herself! The traveller was overjoyed for they were all in prime condition and he ate lustily as the hag watched, grinning across her cracked face. Syntelle turned to her. "You will be rewarded, no other could have found these." The grin widened displaying rotten teeth and there was a new gleam in her eyes.

"Yes, by all means reward her, my Queen," suggested the man. "But to have been of use once more is likely reward enough!"

The hag laughed sharply and left. The traveller also laughed – but with a ridiculously full mouth, then quite suddenly said; "To our business then."

"I think, traveller, that you are here because you know already what I most desire – not just for myself and Gullen, but for Endworld, Farisle -" Syntelle hesitated, "And yes, the Baeths too."

"You think I can help you in this?" queried the traveller.

"No, I think you do." Syntelle's voice trembled with reawakened hope.

Glee spread over the man's face at the queen's display of wit.

210

"Ah, yes, I like that, very good; I thought I could help and that is why I have come. Always I try to help, but who do I help? Better ask who I do not help!"

"But can you?"

"Perhaps." He paused for a while, then, looking toward the bed. "The door is closed?" he asked.

"Of course."

Syntelle motioned to it impatiently and the traveller nodded then said, "Who is this man who is dying?"

"He is Lord of Gullen."

"His mother was Queen of Gullen then?"

"No."

"So his father was king?"

"No-"

"Then he cannot be Lord of Gullen. Perhaps he is – who was it – Lindarg?"

"You know him?" The tremble returned to her voice.

"I have met him – but you ask if I know him – I ask, do you really know him?"

"It is true I do not."

"Virdil, maybe," continued the traveller.

Syntelle started at the suggestion but had given up being surprised. "There are similarities," she answered.

"Indeed there are…" The man thought for a long time and there was silence in the room save for the light breathing – now becoming irregular – coming from Lindarg behind the drapes.

"It will not be easy for you to do, my Queen. Oh no. Such things are not easy – and this thing in particular – perhaps you may decide not to do it."

"If I can I will."

"Stern resolve and a stout heart but how much stouter will it need to be before the day is through? How much indeed!"

Syntelle made no answer.

"If you wish to save him there is only one way. You must make him Lord of Gullen!"

"But you said yourself that if not born of the queen or king he cannot be Lord of Gullen, who can change the past?" Her voice was despairing, hope fading.

"None can. You must ask the Queenstone of the 'the Book'. In your mind as you ask will be the thoughts of what you seek. These the stone will obey also. Read carefully the pages it shows. Be sure you know what you must do. The Book will tell – but be sure you know! Only you must know; do this thing alone. None must be told…"

"If it is to be so hard for me and you are so wise, will you not do it for me?"

"Aaahh," sighed the traveller wistfully. "Would that I could – but I am blind and the Book has to be read."

Syntelle was aghast. "Blind? But you have walked into a strange room unaided, seated yourself as if the chair were your own and sifted through the food before you-"

"And now I am rising to go – ha ha – and yes, I will show myself out of this strange building. No, no, don't get up on my account – there is no need for didn't I find the right room in this place first time? No-one would show me the way." He was half way to the door, "And the chair – who sat in it before you or your father – or perhaps even Virdil? Who made it? Who built this palace in Gullen?"

"I-I do not know," replied Syntelle bemused. "They are dead and gone-"

"Dead, yes…"

The insinuation in the unfinished statement made Syntelle cast about her almost fearfully – as if expecting their spirits to appear. She shivered, but before she could reply, the traveller said his last words.

"Farewell, my Queen," and was gone through the doorway. Moments later Durnor entered.

"The traveller has left, my Queen."

"Did you show him out?"

"There was no need – he knew the way."

"Would you believe Durnor, that he was blind?" said Syntelle, musing.

"No – how could he-?"

"I didn't think he was either."

Durnor's face was perplexed for a moment, then he shrugged and asked, "What was his news?"

"I am not really sure myself." Syntelle was thoughtful.

"Is there in some way hope then?" Durnor hardly dared ask.

"Perhaps – but I cannot be certain – at least not yet. Now you must leave the lord and I together. See that we are not disturbed, not by anyone for any reason at all. Will you do that for us?"

"It will be done, my Queen, and this time none will slip through – unless they are invisible – and maybe not even then!"

"Thank you – I will call if I need you – and tell the other liegemen what has happened."

With a nod of assurance, Durnor left.

Syntelle regarded Lindarg's face – old, careworn and so peaceful that she wished she could just let him pass away quietly – and yet she did not wish that. She had loved him – but then he had been young; now, so soon after, he was very old. It was cruel. A lifetime seemed to have been frittered away in but seasons and now there was nothing left for her or Gullen. Everything his life had led him to do seemed to have aged him; now, before anything he had started to do was complete, he was too old to finish. She knew then that she had to do whatever she could – not for herself, the love she was losing, Gullen or Endworld – but for him.

Syntelle reached for the Queenstone. Clutching it in both hands as Virdil had shown her many Starseasons ago, she whispered.

"The Book." One page only appeared in the stone and that page was complete; its words frightening as she read;

Practice ye no magic for one Starseason.

Let menfolk gather ye willingly a soul...

It was clear what had to be done. The traveller had been right; she had to be sure she wanted to do it for she would indeed need great strength.

"Durnor!" But Andur greeted her call and as he approached she went on: "He wishes to see Virlin – perhaps for the last time – bring him and hurry!" Andur ran off, returning shortly with her baby son and Durnor. "Thank you, liegemen, do not think that you are forgotten – you may all see him before his death finally releases you from his service."

"That we would appreciate; to be there at his side."

"Then keep together and near; I will call again when the time comes but for now the time is for his son and queen – we should be together and alone!" Durnor caught the intonation.

"We understand, my Queen, the whole of the city will wait until you are ready!" As he turned to go he saw fresh tears in Syntelle's eyes and realised that there were some in his own too.

But it was not to Lindarg's death that they were eventually called, nor was the queen's call first...

It was twilight of that day when the city brooded over their dying lord. None spoke of it but it was in all minds and people sat quiet as the fading of the day seemed to echo the fading of their lord and of many hopes for the future of Gullen. Through that fateful half-light came a dread voice from a high tower.

"Baeths!"

For long, agonising moments that one word echoed through the city being caught up by hushed voices and passed on its way, leaving in its wake a silent dread.

"Their whole force is upon us!" Thousands of eyes cast from the city walls upon that sight – at once awesome and splendid; malevolent and threatening. Here came the great might of the Baeths and as surely as men continued to pour from the furthest forests onto the plain, it sounded the death-knell of Gullen. The liegemen watched, their inner hearts re-living the dread of the

Baeth mines which seemed to open like a dark red chasm before them; grasping the hope that they would fall swiftly in battle; knowing now that Farisle would never be rescued; feeling a helplessness they had never conceived.

Before darkness fell, the city was hemmed in by the foe and their watchfires sprang up all round. Down from the north gate was Gargol's fire and behind it sat the general himself – come this time in the assurance that the Southlands were his. A captain drew by him and saluted.

"When do we attack, Sir?" The voice was respectful and genuine, the reply curt.

"There will be no attack."

"But-" Gargol's look silenced the man.

"I do not want a burned-out shell – fool!" An evil smile creased Gargol's lips, the soldier before him was taken aback. "There is power within." The words came with a sneer. "I want it – would you not rather walk through the gate?"

"Of course, Sir."

"Then let us wait for them to open it – or let them rot!" The last words were a screamed challenge issued over Gullen's fields.

"Very good, Sir."

"More than very good! Sublime!" Gargol's eyes were set with a demonic glow; the captain cringed away, his general was not himself; he had no wish to be near. "We wait. That is all, you may go."

"Thank you, Sir."

The captain wheeled away, glad to put distance between himself and the man who led them – who seemed to have been changed by his obsession with the Southland City and what lay behind its walls.

Already the trumpets of victory were ablaze with the noise of fanfare in Gargol's mind. Not a single item of his latest plan had failed to work. Other attacks on the Southlands and his latest on Gullen had only been made to alert his enemies to the threat. Gullen was the obvious 'safe haven' and he had planned that the men of the Southlands would go there. Cunning he was when he allowed that mustering; cunning enough to have shown some opposition to it – and after the Coldseason, when food of all kinds was in short supply, with Warmseason coming and thirsts rising; with less rain and hundreds of men – and those outnumbered ten to one – he had all the fighting men of the Southlands in one pot!

From Gargol's mouth issued a fell laugh across the space to the great gate and the cowed city quailed at that new sound.

The liegemen feared to go to the queen's call but her face was serene.

"Come, liegemen, he lives!" Hardly daring to believe, they met him in the queen's room; a youthful Lindarg greeted them, eyes glittering.

"Hail liegemen!" He could see disbelief on their faces and sought to assuage their doubts. "Aaah, think not that a wizard would die so easily – and with his work undone. Endworld stirs the more each day – in time you may hear of the powers which have worked this day and what they have wrought – but now is the time for action. Gargol…" He hesitated for a moment, wondering, speculating inside himself. "… has forced our hand. We must do what we must."

"But Lindarg, what of your journey-?"

"And you were so old-"

"And the blind man who came-"

They all clamoured at once.

"Now is not the time for tales but I will tell them soon – blind man, you say, now that is interesting!"

"Who was he?"

"One called Sylee I think-" But Faran interrupted;

"What was he then?"

"Ah, now you ask a difficult question or perhaps it isn't difficult really – maybe the only difficulty is explaining what he is to those who would not understand the words-"

"You speak as if you were he!" exclaimed Durnor. Lindarg laughed and their reaction to that laugh told him that they had heard Sylee laugh. 'Then he has been!' He thought to himself, 'that explains much.' But to the liegemen said, "Come, find the generals, summon the wise, there is a council to begin. Make haste, meet as soon as you can. I will join you when I have done my work."

With that Lindarg left them hurriedly, their mouths still agape with wonder and questions and vanished from the eyes and clamour of Gullen as he entered Virdil's house where only two had set foot since Virdil himself had left to challenge Venain. A glance told him that Syntelle had been there; things were tidied; the dust new and thin. In there he found much wisdom – much of what he wanted – particularly maps. But he did not find all he sought and that made him uneasy.

As Lindarg entered the council Banor had just asked the Queen of Virlin.

"We have ever been ready for this day Banor, Virlin is now far gone on his way to the Great Forest of Dorn where he will be safe. The moment the cry was heard, he was taken south from the rear of the city before the siege was closed, then if we fail, the line of the Gullen-lords will not be broken and even though the city be in ruin he may return to claim from those ruins the magic that was Virdil's."

Though it was hard for her, she lied well. It brought calm to the council and deep within, those there were glad and the wise nodded – at least one problem had been solved expediently.

Lindarg was greeted with great honour and even greater surprise and though Syntelle had warned them of his miraculous recovery, they were not prepared for the youthful visage upon which they now gazed. This and his vibrant, assertive grin flushed them into silence and they waited for him to speak.

"Gargol himself lies outside the city walls. He has come to see Gullen fall and we must hope that for now he will be content to lie in siege not risking men in attack. I fear too that it will not be long 'ere Venain stirs – indeed he may already have done so and know even at this moment what fate awaits

217

our city. If he does, our plight will please him and he too may be content to wait since he cannot himself leave his defences to approach the power that lies yet within Gullen." Lindarg raised his voice, charging it with the fire of rhetoric. "The time we have left must be used wisely. Gulleners have fought well with swords and their tale will be told as long as the Southlands remain: now they confront a host which would crush them as eggshells; now Gullen must fall quiet in the face of adversity. Most of all it must endure for as long as possible and while it endures things must go unnoticed until the time is ripe." Lindarg lifted his head to the generals, then continued, addressing them; "Your task has been hard and the rewards few, always there were more enemies and less supplies; always your men have fought and gained little. Now that task will be even harder, you must wait and conserve all you have. Those in the city face lean and leaner times; you must face them and wait; nothing must be squandered: secrecy must bathe all things." He paused again to allow the message to sink in; "Do nothing but defend and survive, time yet remains for valiance."

Lindarg's eyes narrowed and flashed fierily so that none would gainsay his words. "My task is now clear to me – though not all the reasons or the likely outcome. Venain is the real enemy. Virdil fought him once and was slain – yes, Virdil has truly passed away. Whether the Baeths are defeated or victorious is unimportant for Venain will sweep before him all in his path and drench the Southlands – perhaps the whole of Endworld – in evil forever." But those there wanted to hear more of Virdil.

"How can you be so sure that he is dead?" asked one. But the queen answered first.

"I too know this; Virdil's name in the Queenstone is blackness now."

"But this must mean that the wizard's house is open and its sealing sundered-"

"-Or that none will ever enter there again," finished another.

"Neither is true," Syntelle replied, "There is yet Virlin, try to enter and see." For the moment the voices were satisfied, allowing Lindarg to continue.

"The time has come for me to reveal much of what I know – but not all. Safe will be that knowledge locked up in this besieged city, some indeed may be of use." He paused for a long moment, all eyes were on him. Behind his knotted brows the vestige of a plan was forming – one that must be kept hidden, only some things could be disclosed at this moment.

He waited for the murmurs to die down, his face grave, demanding attention, then announced:

"Venain has unlocked the secret of immortality: unless he is destroyed he will live forever." The council was dumbstruck, so too were the Farislanders. Then raised voices were all talking at once. The queen, the only one seemingly unaffected by the enormity of Lindarg's statement, held up her hand for silence and they quieted – but one voice insisted,

"What you say must be impossible – how can you know?

"If you are asking 'are we certain?'," said Syntelle, "Then the answer is no; nothing is certain. Virdil suspected this much long ago and so left to prevent it. We are forced to assume that he failed for Venain still lives and Virdil does not." They seemed placated, if not all convinced. Lindarg went on,

"Many of you know the power of the Queenstone, well Venain has a stone with a different power – much more sinister in these times – the power to control a named mind; to look through its eyes; to control its speech. All he needs is a real name and that person is as a slave to him." Another stunned silence passed over the council as the meaning of what Lindarg had said assailed them. Into the silence he continued; "Do not let any names reach the enemy for already Gargol might have been named to Venain, use only titles or familiar names." He stopped and surveyed them, ensuring that each there comprehended the enormity of that demand, then said: "It will be hard – perhaps impossible – to avoid those names but everyone must try their utmost, lest we end up trusting no-one, suspecting friend and foe alike to be his slave." Lindarg paused for breath noting the looks of fear and despair etched on the drawn faces of those about him. "He has another power too; more evil than the Knavestone; more destructive and deadly than a thousand Baeth armies: Nethermen. From within his defiles he commands their legions out of the depths of the dead; grey men from a grey hell. They cannot be slain for they are dead already; merciless and no less sharp is the steel they wield; men cannot stand against them; Southfolk and Baeths alike will perish before them."

When Lindarg finished, a fearful quiet enveloped the council as dread gripped their hearts and the gloom of abject despondency shredded their resolve. The chill voice of Lianor, frightful in the hush said, "Then we are finished – and Endworld with us finally-"

The statement hung over them like a shroud of doom until Lindarg said, "Perhaps not-"

But was interrupted by Lianor protesting; "But you have just said that these Nethermen cannot be slain!"

"It is true, they will not die but what is also true is that they can be sent back from whence they came. That is the business of sorcery not of valiant men and swords."

Some there nodded at his words, Syntelle and the Lorist prominent among them, and some of the gloom was dispelled but Lindarg had not finished.

"But even as these may be his greatest powers, I fear he has yet others; others which may in time wax more evil than those foul ones of which I have spoken – but I cannot be sure. It may be that he will keep such things so well hidden that I cannot discover them until it is too late." His face was grim now and his voice lowered to a deep snarl; "Despite this – nay, because of it – I will defy him to the last!"

The words were a vehement promise; Syntelle marked them, recognising the vow set within and knowing this she trembled as she spoke.

"I too," was all she said from behind eyes which moistened even as her knuckles whitened on Lindarg's arm.

"Hopeless though it may be in the end, we also will have tried!" Durnor's voice came on the heels of Syntelle's and she was grateful to be rid of the eyes which probed her ill-concealed emotions. Frind too made it clear that he would not be left out and others nodded their support, binding themselves inextricably together with a common resolve.

Lindarg saw now that the council's crisis of despondency was over and he sank down into his seat with a sigh of relief. So easily it could have gone another way, shattering what little hope remained; he'd had to take the risk; no longer could he have shielded them from those awful truths which he had borne alone until now. Cleverly he had used Venain's ultimate despite to convoke the opposition against him. He stood again.

"It is to seek an answer to these powers that I am forced to leave this city once again before I come to its aid-" He suddenly raised his voice over the clamour of protest which followed the statement; "I wish it were otherwise, since at any time Venain may strike – and should he do so, it will be a fell blow."

"Then you cannot leave us!" said a voice flatly.

"Must not!"

"We will not allow it!"

"Not again!"

"Never!"

"You are needed here-"

"I must, there is no choice open to me. Venain will not be beaten by men and swords, perhaps not even by all the sorcery that can be found in the end, but I have to seek what I can!"

The council was in uproar, loathe to let their lord ride away again to return a hapless, wizened shell. They appealed to the queen to urge him to stay but she would not, saying only, "We must look to, and save our city from, the more immediate threat of the Baeths at our door. If they overrun the city, first we will no more have to worry about Venain – and the rights and wrongs of who goes where will be of little consequence – if indeed we are allowed any choice in such matters by those who would be our new masters."

Despite their continued protestations, the decision that their lord would go was held. With him would go Andur, Eisdan, Karil and Turg; the other liegemen would remain in Gullen to aid its defence.

One question only remained: how could they leave the besieged city and pass through the closed ring of foe undiscovered?

"It can't be done," said the same flat voice which had insisted Lindarg stay and it seemed to echo the thoughts of many.

"We will find a way!" was all Lindarg said as he wheeled round motioning to the four liegemen to follow him and they left the hall with the coming of the night, Lindarg's eyes saying all that was needed to Syntelle on their parting.

14

TO THE PLAIN OF
THE GREAT STONE

That same night, not long after the council, Lindarg and the four liegemen wormed their way from the city in the deeper shadows of a stone wall and ditch which ran alongside the north road out of Gullen.

Soon they were near the inner edge of the Baeth army's encompassing circle; a few paces in front of them stood two sentries, conversing but vigilant. Their replacements approached.

"Seen anything?" asked one.

The two sentries pointed at each other and with a grin said simultaneously, "Him!"

"Very funny," muttered one of the others adding pointedly, "Nothing of any importance then."

The two sentries they had come to relieve shook their heads, yawned and walked away. Eisdan and Karil clutched a long dagger each and with bellies against the soft damp grass of the ditch, inched their way toward the two new sentries. There was no sound as the two Farislanders rose as one, left hands over Baeth mouths, knives thrust behind the ribs, blades angling upwards toward the heart and the bodies folded slowly down into the ditch with barely a rustle. Swiftly the two donned the uniforms of the dead soldiers and hid their half-naked bodies in some reeds behind the wall. They also bundled and hid their own clothes.

Time passed as they waited for the next changeover and none

too soon was it in coming. Both soldiers died in shocked silence as those they had presumed to be friends buried cold steel deep into their breasts. Their soft sighs rattled slightly but that was all. A fifth uniform was provided by a man from a nearby tent who, much the worse for drink, staggered groggily into the bushes to relieve himself – his non-return passing unnoticed by the tent's other noisily sleeping occupants.

Even wearing Baeth uniforms they had decided that they couldn't possibly hope to just walk through the Baeth lines even at this hour without a challenge and any such confrontation would inevitably foil their intent. Instead, they were following Eisdan's plan and were now spreading out so that there was quite a distance between them. At a given signal each of them set surrounding bushes and grass alight. The scrub, dead from the Coldseason and dried by the Astellin winds, caught and soon blazed, the chill night wind chasing the smoke and flames toward the Baeth encampment. The Liegemen and Lindarg, as sentries, raced with it into the camp to alert the Baeths of attack.

Andur rushed from the area he had lit to the nearest campfire remains shouting; "Wake! Wake! Gulleners attack! To your weapons!" As soon as they awoke but before bewildered bodies emerged, Andur had moved away to alert others of the danger, leaving the fires and whirling smoke to do the rest. In this way each of them separately and safely sped to the outer perimeter of the Baeth army leaving blissful confusion in their wake – to be added to presently when the fires were out, five dead bodies discovered and no intruders were to be found anywhere.

By now the uniform-clad companions had met on a small tree-covered hill and were hardly able to contain themselves with glee. Behind them the shouts and yells were everywhere with torches and light from the fires throwing shadows off running forms scuttling hither and thither. They could make out at least two tents which had caught the flames adding no doubt to the notion that the Baeths did indeed face an attack.

In fact the incursion caused more disruption than they

imagined. Gargol assumed that since the sentry's uniforms had been taken, the intruders were still disguised within the camp and a full-scale question search was instigated to no avail, leaving Gargol with grave doubts – and very annoyed – that something had happened and he didn't know what. He even suspected treachery among his own men and issued a statement to the effect that any suspicious behaviour on the part of any soldier would be 'rewarded' with a summary death. With this, he finally but unsatisfactorily closed the affair. Behind his eyes, Venain too had to be content with nothing.

Dawn was paling the horizon as Lindarg led the liegemen away saying; "There is still the unsolved problem of steeds – did you not notice that there weren't any to be seen?"

They nodded and Karil said, "Can you not-?"

But Lindarg waved the suggestion away; "There have to be some around for that, we will have to walk."

They set off northwards wearing still the Baeth uniforms which they considered might be useful again and still smiling over the success of their ruse. At last Karil spoke;

"I see we are travelling northwards, Sire, but to where?"

"To the land of the Great Stone – it is a plain beyond the northern hills and in its centre lies a gigantic stone laid there by the forces that shaped the very earth – where it will still lie when the earth is unmade somewhere in time."

They were surprised to receive an answer so quickly but realised just as quickly that their liege wasn't about to elaborate any further.

"Past the Baeth mines then?" Turg's question brought a chill to their hearts.

"We will pass them by well to the east but in any case I doubt that there will be much activity there since Gargol has marshalled his forces to take Gullen – we should be safe in those Baeth lands."

"What is it you seek there?" pursued Karil. Lindarg looked sidelong at him as if in warning, then said,

"I have never seen it before – therefore I cannot describe it.

Only its name I know and that would be of little use to you but to another it might – so it will not be said. Think me not untrusting of you, liegemen – I have trusted my life to you before – and still I live but I fear already that I have said too much at the council, so for a while at least, I will say nothing more."

They accepted the explanation resignedly and pressed on, talking of more immediate things while their liege, they could tell, was probing the land for steeds.

Several times they passed places they recognised from their trek to Gullen after the hell of the Baeth mines and the changing of the ways. Campsites barely perceptible – disguised by two Starseasons of new growth as the land recovered; fire places now mossy green; toilet areas a riot of colours as a multitude of flowers lifted their nodding heads to the Astellin Sun and the trampled way a verdant swathe along each side of the north road. Here and there were marked graves of Southfolk they had come to know well then lost too soon.

Half way through the second day of their journey, Lindarg waved them to a stop. "I have located some steeds – there are many but they are far away and have men with them from whom they cannot break free. Perhaps if I work on them they can be made to veer our way but we too must do our part to meet them, come."

He turned them a little east of north and they followed in silence as Lindarg fought to draw the roped animals inexorably in their direction.

Toward the end of that day they met a score or so of Baeth soldiers. Evidently they had been collecting mounts – probably for use in supply trains – since there were many beasts with them all riderless and tethered following behind. The leader of the foraging party hailed them over as soon as he saw them, his face a pleased smile to see a change of company. As Lindarg and the Liegemen moved over to the stopped Baeths, Lindarg hissed quietly, "Leave this to me!"

They were within talking distance now and the leader's

mouth opened to greet them but no word ever came out. In an instant the Baeths were fighting to control their animals, then Lindarg drew his sword shouting, "Kill, liegemen! None must escape to Gargol – he thinks I am in Gullen and perhaps also therefore does Venain."

It was a bitter struggle and brutal in its swiftness. The confusion caused by Lindarg's sorcerous strike enabled the four liegemen to cut down several Baeths before they could return a single blow. Then combat was enjoined; Baeths knowing that no quarter would be given – that none would be allowed to escape – the attackers that none must. Andur was faced by two Baeths who both raised their swords at the same time. Andur's sword flew upwards between them severing a hand – which still clung to the harmlessly-falling weapon – at the wrist. The other blow he dodged easily, so surprised was the man at the effect of the upward cut on his comrade – and Andur's deadly blade came down behind on the fellow's neck, severing vertebrae with a crunch. The other, still nursing his wrist in disbelief, was quickly finished with a thrust to the chest. No sooner had the skirmish begun than it was over, with dead Baeths scattered in a small area around them, their animals and the others that followed, scattered widely, checking as Lindarg drew them back. They selected the best five and were soon on their way toward the distant hills – faster than before and jubilant at their good fortune.

Since the encounter with the Baeth foraging party they had travelled like the wind for three uneventful days to reach the foothills of the North Chain. Now the terrain was more difficult and often they were forced to walk.

"Is there no way round these mountains?" Turg pleaded as he peered at the forbidding, jagged rocks ahead which towered higher and higher the nearer they struggled.

"They can be skirted," admitted Lindarg, doubtfully. "But it would take many more days than we can afford. There is a pass a little to our right at a guess which should take us through them to the plain beyond. It is called the Pass of Teeth, but I have not been that way before. I can remember it from the maps in Gullen though, it should be easy enough to find."

The others nodded and they pressed on grimly. Soon the animals became a hindrance and they left them – happy to be free once more on those northern slopes and Lindarg grinned, knowing they would breed undisturbed here for a long time, gracing those slopes with their splendour and agility.

"It cannot be far now to the pass," observed Lindarg as they continued upwards over jagged terrain, cold winds finding them where it could and waiting for them to emerge from hollows where it could not blow. Then a grey curtain could be seen rushing up to them from the slopes below, above it the sky darkening.

"Rain!" exclaimed Lindarg vehemently and in the next few moments it was upon them; lashing their jerkins against shivering bodies, spattering chill drops on the liegemen's bare legs. With the seeping cold wetness, their spirits soon began to fall; still the Pass of Teeth had not loomed from the greyness. Their progress slowed and the grey curtain began to turn a darker grey with encroaching night – a night which each of them knew they could never survive up here in the cold without shelter. But equally they could not go on indefinitely in the dark, stumbling blindly, perhaps missing the entrance to the pass, or in the wrong direction – or worse still into some concealed ravine, there to await an inglorious and wasted slow death. No, they had to stop.

Then Andur waved upward to their right – there was a semi-circle of jagged-topped rocks with the rain deflecting around them – raising his voice he said, "There may be shelter behind those rocks." His tone echoed the desperate plight of them all and eagerly they scrambled upwards to reach them. Behind the rocks there was indeed some shelter – meagre, but welcome, at least they became no wetter in their lee as they huddled together for warmth, taking turns to be on the outside of the cluster and trying to snatch a little sleep when on the inside. It was a long, testing night, the kind which saps the will to survive in a dreamland of imagined warmth when the body, ignored, slowly goes cold; hard it was to move from the inside to the outside for that chill grey hour before dawn.

But the light brought with it unexpected tidings; behind them, now clear in the lessening drizzle, was the pass they sought. Unmistakably, the rocks where they had sheltered were the 'teeth' and those teeth blocked the view of the pass from below.

"But for the rain," muttered Lindarg, "we might have passed below those rocks without affording them a second glance..." He trailed off but the others knew what games of fate were in his mind and saw how, in unexpected ways, they still worked for him.

That afternoon the plain appeared as they reached the end of the pass. It was a parched, forsaken and dusty brown expanse; at its centre lay the huge grey stone, so totally out of place and yet so perfectly positioned in its centre. The stone riveted the attention. It was mountainous in proportions and perfectly block-shaped being much much longer and broader than it was tall, pock-marked with holes and entrances; obscenely rectangular against the surrounding eroded mountains and hills with their mixtures of curves and crevices; it was a paradox and a supremely poignant one. Down from where they stood on the pass, swept an ever-widening skirt of gently sloping dusty brown land all the way to the plain and the stone.

The liegemen passed between two large boulders marking the egress from the pass and began the descent onto the plain but Lindarg did not follow and they turned to call him, their mouths falling open in mute surprise at what they saw. Their liege, struggling against a mighty but invisible force, was unable to pass by the great rocks.

Unknown fears gripped the liegemen when they realised that they had been separated from Lindarg by some unseen

229

power. Eisdan screamed, "Lindarg!" and ran crazily toward the barrier drawing his sword as if he thought to cut through it with a blade. Behind him ran the other three, faces twisted with incomprehension and dread but Eisdan had run straight through and was now beside the bemused Lindarg trying to help him through. Then Karil added assistance by pulling from the other side and in their haste and terror between them almost succeeded in squashing the unfortunate Lindarg's face who yelled at them to stop, then fell back watching, perplexed as the Farislanders crossed and re-crossed as if no barrier existed.

And yet to Lindarg it was, inescapably, there. He tried going round the boulders for a good distance each way but he could not pass; he was barred from the Plain of the Great Stone as surely as if he had never come. At length he sat down to think, the liegemen at his side.

"It is sorcery; but a kind I do not recognise. Why does it only hinder me?" he mused, thinking aloud, then, "Perhaps it was only set for me, maybe Venain's doing – but how could he know I was here – or would come? Or it might only proscribe those who seek what lies beyond; among us only I know what that is. It may only work against Southlanders – there may be a thousand reasons why it bars me and not any of you. I am left only to try them all and see."

He placed himself close to the barrier and began a tirade of words, actions and curses that should have shaken rocks and trees, every now and then he kicked it with a foot but nothing seemed to move or even slightly weaken it. Exasperated he stopped for a while to consider. Eisdan approached him.

"Can we not try something else?" he suggested hopefully but with no ideas. "We have wasted hours-" but he was cut off.

"You have wasted hours, I have used them – perhaps futilely – but every idea discounted is progress of a sort. These things take time." He waved Eisdan away but the day was waning and still there was no movement.

At last, as darkness fell, Lindarg moved away from the barrier and joined them; he was exhausted and perplexed.

"I do not understand it. It seems to be the ultimate sorcery which cannot be broken by anything I know."

"Tell us what you seek and we will go in your stead," suggested Andur.

"No, I must go myself and alone." Lindarg's voice was final and the liegemen declined to argue the point further. That moment Lindarg remembered the Queenstone. "Of course!" he shouted exultantly, "The Book!" As he said it the stone was in his palm and in its depths the book, open. But the page was blank. His hopes were dashed in an instant; he knew there would be no answer there but he was reminded of Eq. Was there something the fading god had said? Lindarg fought to recall all his words... 'Graggan lies imprisoned... his guarding spells uncast... no magic can work in that land... a man stands alone for what he is... ' "Yes!"

The liegemen saw the change in his countenance; even in the darkness his eyes shone.

"Liegemen!" he cried out. "The barrier is there to bar things of power; it nullifies wizardry; it is the ultimate abrogation of sorcery. The Queenstone cannot pass – nor I – unless I relinquish my powers!" He handed the Queenstone to Karil saying, "Guard this well until my return." And to them all he said, "Once again I ask you to stay behind and patiently wait – but it must be. I shall not be long – or perhaps I shall never return." The last words were darkly spoken.

"But Sire-"

"Farewell." Lindarg waved away their protests, turning from them to face the barrier. Loudly they heard his voice; "I stand alone for what I am – a man." Then the tall moonlit figure passed silently between the stones, shrank onto the plain and was lost in silver-lined shadows.

Somewhere before him lay the great god Graggan.

15

GULLEN BESEIGED -
THE WESTGATE FALLS

With Lindarg and four liegemen gone, Gullen set itself to face the siege, holding fast within its walls; food and water carefully rationed and stored. Work had been completed to hollow the city's three wells deeper as the heat of Achemin approached. It was estimated that the swollen population of Gullen could last fifty days – perhaps a little longer with tighter rationing – but that was only providing there was no fighting. Any conflict would take its toll on those provisions unless many Gulleners were killed – which would enable the supplies to last longer. But no-one would wish for a companion's death to lend their own life more days.

The Baeth hordes were watched constantly from the walls; training and sporting on the sunny grasses of Gullen's fields – heedless of any threat from the city, knowing there would be none, sure in supremacy and victory. Their campfires glowed into the nights and the sound of merriment drifted up to the city walls on cool breezes while within those walls the heat of the day was rarely dispelled with tempers often enflamed in the cramped conditions.

As Gullen sought to improve its lot, so did Gargol. The west gate of the city was approached by the Westway, a broad well-worn road which dipped down to the city gate from a small hill. The road was straight from the top of the hill and from this vantage point it was nearly possible for the Baeths to look down into the city. It was while he peered from the top of this hill that Gargol decided upon a simple but effective idea to provide amusement perhaps more than any advantage but if it worked well the siege would be over much sooner and with less loss of Baeth lives. Sending men to scale the walls was, he reasoned, merely a way to kill a few Gulleners and many hundreds of Baeths; as far as possible his men were to be preserved. The days needed to prepare and plan could easily be afforded, so behind his lines, out of sight from the city, those preparations went ahead.

Some days later, while Venain looked to the north, his attention on the Plain of the Great Stone, Gargol, himself once more, decided to attack.

From the onset of dawn, it had been obvious that an offensive was about to be launched. Gullen responded in readiness.

"Ah, Farg," said Lianor the general of the Northfolk as Farg approached from the garrison quarters, "A fine morning it would be without those scum." He motioned over the battlements.

"A good day to test us," sighed the general of the Gullen Guards, "What do you think they are up to?"

"So far they have moved scores of men to the east side of the city carrying much equipment with them."

"He isn't keeping the move secret, is he?" commented Farg dryly. "There's a trick here I suspect..."

But Lianor continued; "Frind says there are men on the hill to the west as well – though there appears to be few – he thinks there are many more behind the hill."

"Hmmm, a two-pronged attack – but will it be that simple? I wish we knew more!"

"See! There are more men moving over to the east – that is where the main attack will come," Lianor stated.

"Or that is what he wants us to think, while the main force waits over the hill to the west."

"Or maybe he wants us to think that instead!" burst in Frind joining them.

"We're just guessing!" Farg cursed. "Has anything more

happened in the west?"

"No, but those that can be seen are sitting tight and ready, armed to the teeth."

"Talking of teeth, Frind, how are the stocks of Yanish darts?" It was Lianor's question.

"We have fair numbers but will need a thousand times that amount for the numbers which we face."

Frind's reply was despondent. "Is there any news from Banor and Danig on the other walls?" he asked.

"There appears to be no change on their sides – still as many as ever there has been, they wait as we," answered Farg.

"But where, then do we place our men, Farg?" queried Lianor.

The Gullen general though for a moment; "The north and south walls are well covered by Banor and Danig, we will divide our men between the west and east walls."

"Neither might be strong enough!" protested Lianor.

"It is a risk, granted, but that is not all of my plan. Our three forces should remain as three; you, Lianor and your men on the east wall, Harfin here at the west-"

"What about us? Where will we be stationed?" Frind had cut him off.

"You, Frind, with the Eastfolk will wait between the two in the heart of the city. Your men are stout and can run; their effect in a swift onslaught is devastating. If the main attack comes from the east, then as soon as we know, the Eastfolk will aid that place quickly; likewise to the west. Should both offensives be equal, then Frind, you can split your men and aid both."

The two others thought for a moment, then Lianor said, "If the attack is swift will Frind be able to aid us in time?

"That may depend on how soon we can determine which is the main point of attack-"

"-And how fast we can run!" cut in Frind. Farg eyed him cautioningly.

"What would you do then, Frind?"

234

"I would split three ways as you but place the other third at the west out of sight."

"And you, Lianor?"

Lianor reddened a little. "Errm, I think they will attack from the east and the west is to distract us-"

Frind was indignant; "The east is most obviously the lure! That is why we are being entertained so by the cur's movements!"

"Then," interrupted Farg, "we shall be undecided in a prepared way – my plan goes?" They each nodded assent – though grudgingly. Farg straightened; "Ready the men, Gullen will meet the enemy as they come – even as it may yet be – from the north! And it will not be long!" Farg drew their attention to the foe. They had quieted now; movements ceased – a tense calm before the storm… then…

Sound of horn shatters dawning sky;
Red flare in the east and red fanfare above.
Startling birds falter in flight over fields
Casting a fiery eye in panic;
The sounds stabs shock into the hearts of the men -
The blast they have long awaited, cowed,
Has come at last.
The fear of the thrust -
The sickening pain of the blade
Is imagined and lived in hot minds full of red blood -
Their own blood;
Red as the eastern scape;
Red as the sound of the horn.
Scarlet terror as the fiends draw near,
Then the vermillion flare of fear flushes each frame:
Before staring eyes duty unfolds – a crimson road to death;
An arrow in the throat or a thrust and twist of cruel steel
     in the gut,
Life gushes out carmine:
Horizon fades with the anguished glare of sanguine pain.

Then the nausea is gone -
Ready now for the slaughter to come.

And the battle began from the west. From behind the hill reared huge wooden shields carried by many men; each one concealed and protected a score or so others and a cartload of arrows – enough to bathe the city from end to end with deadly shafts. Small slots had been cut in the rough wood, enabling the bowmen beneath to shoot from almost complete safety right under Gullen noses. The barrage of shafts soon began; chance shots taking their toll; defenders on the west wall were pinned down without ever time to aim well enough to secure a slit. No foes stepped beyond the wooden shields. In the western streets of the city, womenfolk darted hither and thither collecting arrows which fell everywhere. One woman was hit in the leg, another shouted up to defenders on the wall; "We have sacks of arrows for you, come down and collect them," but was dismayed by the voice which replied; "Keep them! They are useless with nothing to shoot at!"

Farg heard the attack and spurred his steed to the west wall and Harfin to survey the fray.

"Hail Farg!"

"How goes it, Harfin?" though he knew the answer.

"Badly – we can make no ground and slowly they pick us off. If they break the gate we will not be able to stop them coming on – they are too well covered."

"The gates will hold – there are many men above them – none will get through," Farg assured him. Harfin's face betrayed the doubt he felt but Farg continued, "The shields are near – we must get oil onto the wood – then burn them."

"But how?"

"Fit arrows with pots of oil and bung them. Smash them onto the wood, then send fire."

In response to the suggestion, Harfin called several of his best bowmen over and explained the idea. They nodded and went away to collect pots. When they returned, Farg took over;

"Send the oil first – all at the nearest shield – then follow with fire." The pots soared away and down smashing onto the wooden frame. Even as they landed the fire arrows were with them and the oil burned. Several Baeths beneath screamed as the lighted oil dripped through slits. One ran from the shelter of the shield and was cut down by Gullen arrows hungry for a mark. Now the wood itself caught and scores of Baeths were slain as they scurried from beneath it to the safety of others. More pots were tied and loosed but as they flew the other shields moved back out of range of the laden arrows and the oil fell short while Baeth bolts continued to rake the parapets.

At that moment the roar of the enemy hordes sounded from the east of the city. Multitudes of them surged forward behind shields. At the same time a horn sounded twice from the east wall – the signal from Lianor that the main attack had come to the east. Frind heard the double blast; turning to the Eastfolk he cried; "Lianor is beset! To the east!"

"Luck to you!" It was Syntelle shouting to him and he waved his sword in salute, yelling once more; "To the east!"

It seemed to them an overlong pelt through the streets as they surged to aid the east wall but Frind pushed them:

"Faster men! Before the walls are taken!" The rising cheer of their charge neared the east wall; "Faster!" Now Frind could see Southlanders beleaguered; being slain, falling from the walkway like rag dolls: still they ran and yet they seemed too far way.

At last they were there; the Eastfolk on the wall with Lianor. The liegemen too had come from their posts – swiftly on steeds – the horn's howl their agreed cue also; together they formed a phalanx that would not waver. Blowers showered Yanish teeth with deadly accuracy hurling pain, panic and death through the shield slits into the milling Baeths beneath. The few attempts to scale the walls in that first onslaught were easily thwarted – though so nearly had they succeeded; the timely aid had saved Gullen for now but Farislanders and Southfolk alike were poised with swords held high for the next thrust which would surely follow.

A single note from the west struck Frind cold to the heart. "Harfin's call!" But he could not go – not now; Harfin and his defenders in the west would have to stand alone. Desolately too the liegemen's heads were turned to the west...

Farg gazed over the one blazing shield to the hill. There, the Baeths wheeled a giant ram cart. Scores of men pushed from behind – the roar of their chant withering; others pulled from the front with ropes. Those behind were protected by a solid wooden shield and each of the cart's wheels was twice the height of a man. Along its centre was a tree, pointed at its front end with the great weight of its bowl and roots behind. On the trunk were piled the branches held in a wooden framework. The ram dwarfed the toiling men around it; was menacing and final as it was poised before the slope from the hill down to the west gate. Gullen could only watch with dread as the marching men flanked it all round and were still rising from behind the hill in its wake.

"The gate!" yelled Farg, "Defend the gate!" Men hurried from the further ends of the walls to aid the Gullen guards on the west gate – ducking and dodging as they ran bent; some falling to remain still, until Gulleners thronged the gate in readiness. Harfin blew his horn a second time to call the Eastfolk but he knew they would have already answered the double blast from the east and could not now come to the aid of the west.

A mighty cheer from the hill challenged Gullen's very walls; behind the cart, hearty men heaved on the poles; safe behind the shields and branches a thousand thighs thrust – sending doom to the gate. Slowly at first but down the dip ever faster, the cart gathered momentum until at the last moment torches flared the oil-soaked wood. A blazing pyre of flaming fury tore down and crashed into the west gate, rending it asunder; scattering blazing Gullen bodies from above; searing the very foundations of the city wall. Baeth fighting men remained on the hill: they would wait for the fires to cool, then walk over the pile of ash.

"Bring water!" Harfin's words were harsh above the roaring commotion. "The fire must be doused else the gate cannot be held!" Already Farg was organising a chain to pass water from the city below to the gate tower now shrouded in thick, acrid smoke, yet no water was loosed on the flames.

"Now!" screamed Farg, "Before the flames take hold of the gates themselves." Still no water was thrown but a few badly-aimed pots. "Why do the men not use the water?" yelled Farg to Harfin.

"They cannot – if they show but an arm it is impaled by Baeth shafts and the smoke and heat blurs the eyes." He returned from the walkway. "We cannot get near enough." Farg looked up and saw the fusillade of arrows renewed from below. Filled with dismay he stopped the chain; water would only be spilled and wasted – and already the mighty gates were crackling, their flames licking above the city walls, black smoke billowing away to the north. Soon the timber would be burned away and the ashes cold; then Gullen was finished; the enemy would walk in; there would never be enough time to build even a barricade to delay them.

But even as the fire bespoke Gullen's doom, the attack on the east wall was renewed. Harfin and Farg heard the commotion from across the city.

"Will he ever draw us from here to there?" There was abject despair in Farg's voice as he went on, "Frind cannot be spared from there now – not even a few of his men – and I fear Lianor will be sorely tested." His voice betrayed the hopelessness which he felt.

"But we can defend the gate for a long while; few will be able to come through at a time and we shall be ready for them!" Harfin's words were valiant but rang hollowly.

Farg peered momentarily over the battlements nearby and turning back from the fateful sight replied; "Who then will guard the walls? As you say Harfin, the gate must be defended but the wall cannot be abandoned for no sooner than there were no heads to be seen on it would the Baeths scale it and with no opposition or warning, be upon us from above."

A breathless messenger arrived from Frind and Lianor. "I bear tidings from the east and seek news – has the gate fallen?"

"It burns as we speak, shortly they may begin to enter," said Farg.

"Then my request is useless."

"Say it," said Farg desolate, knowing what it would be.

"Lianor asks for support if it is possible. Banor and Danig have sent as many as they can spare but it is too few."

"We will not be able to contain the offensive here. To spare any would merely shorten the time for them to finish us. Tell Lianor, Frind and the Liegemen that they have fought well. Tell them how we are faring also. Tell them too that we cannot come to their aid; that they must continue to fight against the odds; that the east gate must endure at all costs and that we need help here also but know it cannot come. Give out greeting and our fears. Shout to the city as you pass, shout to them and say, those who will, guard your city in its darkest time, arm yourselves, join the defence of the last great city of the Southlands and Endworld; say that we can do no more than fight on until we fall from life." Farg thought a while, then added; "Take with you Ergwine and Farwyn – they are good runners and will lend voice to your message. Go! Before it is too late!"

With a gesture from Farg the three runners descended from the wall and sped through the city's streets on their errand.

While they burned, Harfin hastened men to their new posts by the gates. By the time the fire was passed its height and flaming spars began to tumble, men thronged the streets in readiness and filled the buildings which flanked the enemy's road into Gullen.

Their wait as the sun passed its meridian was the hardest for those men; the wait as the embers cooled and the last crackles died: the wait with the attack still in the east and the noise of death from it a sickening backcloth to their agony. All the while, old men, warrior's wives and eldest daughters made up the numbers on the wall; died there; fed the war fires and armed themselves with Baeth arrows, stealing their grief-sodden souls from that deadening despair which conquers action. Secretly they preferred to die cleanly and swiftly in the fight for the tales of how their foe treated captives were still fresh from the queen's rescue. They had no wish to go that way; Southlanders would never again suffer that – so they were ready to fight to the last – though it would cost them their lives.

At the east wall there was no waiting. Frind and Lianor urged their men to ever greater efforts; two of the siege-shields had been abandoned but along this wall alone that left another seven. Behind them crowded multitudes of the enemy, milling warily, ready for the slightest break in vigilance from the walls.

"Frind," called Lianor, "We must destroy more shields – there must be something we can do."

Frind turned from a brief skirmish with an almost successful grappling rope, replying desperately, "My men are tiring, Lianor. The foes are out of range except for the few broken sorties which seek to scale the walls when they see a breach in the defences. Those we can beat off for now but we are powerless to reach the shields." Frind knew that sooner or later, when they could repel even the smallest groups no longer, they would be swiftly overwhelmed.

"Then we are left to stand and fight as they come and for as long as we remain alive; little else can we do," came Lianor's terse reply.

Frind's face seethed beneath a countenance which betold the futility of the emotion locked within. "Then let them come!" he shouted to the winds. "Let them meet me! Renar and Wetland are not yet fully avenged." He turned to the parapet, showing himself fully, his tirade so violent that the arrows thinned in deference; shouting down he screamed at his foe. "Hear this Baeth curs! A foul blow you dealt me before ever we had met; now we are met and even though these walls might lie in ruin I swear I will remain. Round me I will build wall of your carcasses

241

'ere I drown in your fluids. Come to me soon, my blade is thirsty for your blood!"

As he finished and Lianor had lunged to pull him to safety, an arrow sliced off part of his left ear. Red-faced and blood-spattered, Frind dived below the parapet with Lianor.

"Fool!" raged Lianor at him. "Nearly were your brave boasts empty words before those who heard even understood."

Frind was sheepish and stammered; "F–forgive me-," his voice faltered with frustration and impatience. "Cowering behind walls achieves nothing!"

"They keep you alive!" retorted Lianor. "Remember that!"

"But the city dies…"

"Our runner is back from Farg – speak, man."

But he was breathless. Lianor and Frind waited until the man, between great gulps, told what Farg had said.

"There is no help then." Lianor said woodenly. "They are worse off than we." He added casting his gaze once more to the smoke rising from the west gate.

"Then the battle must soon be ended." Frind's voice was despondent but resolute at the same time, then he continued; "When women and children must come to their city's aid in battle then surely the end looms closely." An anguished look spread over his face. "Where is our wizard? Where is Lindarg? No other deeds can have any meaning if Gullen falls – where is its lord? Are we forsaken?"

Lianor tried to restrain Frind again – a valiant man with much fight in him yet but he was becoming unsteady. Lianor reasoned; "He may help us yet – or never again. Do not think on him. There is enough to occupy us fully here." His words were not reassuring to Frind, yet they were soothing, a balancing, hopeful sound amid the clamour of the fray and the shattered gloom of a doomed city.

Then as the two leaders brooded in the east, the noise of renewed assault drifted to them from the west. Faces of men turned that way forlorn, knowing that they could not go there to help; could not leave the east wall to the ravages of the Baeths who as surely as they left would scale it and come behind them into the city. Anguish tore at the faces of those leaders who knew it was only a matter of time before they would be defending their wall from the west as well as from the east. The enemy would pour through the west gate before long – already men were assembling in the north in anticipation of that entrance being opened from the inside. Lianor expected that Gargol would enter that way in person to claim the city for the Baeths.

By mid-afternoon, the drive on the west gate was under way. Not long after, it was breached and Baeths entered Gullen treading down their own dead in the streets where scores of Gullen warriors had fought long and to their deaths. But the defenders' arrows had failed; their arms weakened; now they retreated as the enemy came through.

But even as they entered, on the very crest of victory, Gargol's mighty horn sounded over the waving grasses and the Baeth soldiers, mouths agape with perplexity, wheeled round and left the stricken city. So shocked were its occupants at this unexpected turning of the tide that they were hushed in awe and not a single shaft was loosed at the retreating Baeth horde. Gullen was left alone. Its vanquishers had gone. Nobody knew why.

"He is playing with us!" Farg was bitter, though relieved.

Harfin was breathless with disbelief; "He had won – the city was his." The statement was questioning.

Farg answered. "He plays – don't you see – it was too easy!"

"He has lost many men and will lose yet more in a further attempt," countered Harfin.

"Yet he savours it! How many men has he lost, Harfin?"

"Twenty – perhaps thirty score…"

"The tiniest fraction of his army of thousands which lie in Gullen's fields. He could play these games every day for a whole season and still have enough men left to fill the city full. Curse him!" Farg was silent for a moment, then finished; "It is certain that Gullen will fall, what is less certain is when."

In the days that followed, there were no further attacks. Gargol seemed suddenly content merely to wait, now doubly sure the city was his. The west gate was re-built – but cursorily; the city cowed quiet in its misery with food and water dwindling: all around it the noises of merrymaking in the warm days and nights.

16

GRAGGAN

Lindarg reached the stone before dawn and slept within its shadow well into the morning light. He knew he was safe in this place; in all of Endworld there was nothing could reach him here except another ordinary man. Venain was powerless, so too the Knavestone. Lindarg felt suddenly light of responsibilities and task; no shadows of sorcery, tricks, mistakes and secrets; his actions and thoughts were completely his own to make and have; deep memories and past knowledge had no meaning or purpose here.

Each new rock, shape and colour was as if seen for the first time and wondrous in itself. For a while Lindarg enjoyed this release and wandered below the vertical edge of the Great Stone slab, marvelling at its holes and cracks – each one calling for innocent investigation. But there was plenty of time for holes and tunnels. All around were boulders and dust; he threw stones, bouncing them among the larger stones, laughing at the echoes and Graggan was forgotten. Like a child with eyes first open he ambled without direction, lulled, unworldly, stainless – as the day wore on and the sun dipped.

Toward evening Lindarg strayed into a tunnel to explore. As he entered the inviting gape a sudden change jarred his frame and with the sweat of unwelcome fear came the memories and the purpose. His hand went to his sword hilt and he perceived just how small a man he was.

He stood alone; without aid; knowing that he was in the domain of a god – not a spectral entity wizened and faded like Eq, but a tangible living force: omnipresent; omnipotent; crushing. The trapped power that coursed through these tunnels; seeped into and through the very rock; was withering. While he hesitated, Lindarg pondered how a god so powerful had become so hopelessly trapped. A shaft of sorrow struck his mind as he wondered what form the god would take; what would the shaper of mountains look like – a lesser being perhaps than it had been in eons past – wasted beyond regeneration...?

Resolutely Lindarg forced away the fear and followed the passage into the rock, angling down. The silent, menacing evil was stacked up around him like walls, his nerves were bowstring taut; senses keenly alive; knuckles tense on his sword hilt: the blackness deep and ultimate. Suddenly there was the slightest scuffle to his right – a noise that probably saved his life. His sword was before him in an instant reflex and a heavy furry thing hit his hand and the sharp blade at the same moment, then fell lifeless to the stone at his feet. Lindarg knew it was a Yanish – even without those tell-tale yellow eyes.

"What good would eyes be down here?" He thought out loud, then to himself; 'there will be others! I have no power–'

A more deadly enemy in a more deadly situation he could not have conceived and his heart fumbled in terror, ears straining for the slightest sound from any direction. If there were other Yanish they would be doing the same, smelling the death of their fellow; not daring to move lest they joined it. Through Lindarg's panic filtered a small chance. 'Yanish are cowardly – perhaps this dead one will keep them wary and at bay for a time,' he thought, groping for it. He cut its head away and tied its tail to his sword belt letting its blood fall freely onto the stone. Trembling, praying that the ruse would work, Lindarg moved on downwards, feeling his way by the left-hand wall. There were no other sounds.

Soon Lindarg was dimly aware of light. It was almost as though the imagined the shape of the tunnel in front of him rather than saw it. The light was of the rock itself – greenish, eerie and constant – the way ahead could be seen as a darker hole between the sides. He moved on, the light gradually increasing – and with it the power. Ahead the passage was lighter than its walls and he stopped. Three things caught his attention. In the right wall there was a smaller passage with steps leading up and round. Behind him he was aware of other openings and now he wondered how many others he had slipped passed in the earlier dark but ahead, on the stone floor of the tunnel lay what appeared to be the tapering tail of an enormous, withered white worm. Increasing its girth as it went, Lindarg eyes followed its length down the tunnel until it blended with the phosphorescent sides and out of sight.

Then it moved. A mere twitch, the slightest hint of a quiver, but enough. A sudden unreasoning surge of panic shot through Lindarg and he dived like an exposed insect for the safety of the narrow passage with steps. The instant his body was on the steps the worm-like tentacle thudded across the entrance after lashing through the air where only a moment before Lindarg had been standing. In seconds it withdrew and its trailing end groped for the entrance. Lindarg was pumping his youthful legs up the stone steps, behind him the commotion of dry, leathery slithering as the thing tried to reach him. He kept on upward, head drumming with rushing blood; the noise of pursuit eventually falling away below and behind him.

At last he stopped, gasping the still, putrid air, feeling that it would never revive him from his exertions. He was not safe. Fear came to him from the very air of the tunnel – its glowing light seemed to choke him – yet he must breathe longer. Still he hesitated while his fear grew – fear without any visible cause yet as real as any he'd known – until he ran. The passage now lighter and level, he careered mindlessly toward the centre of that mighty stone, just an ordinary, desperate man with a mere mortal brain crumbling like weather-beaten sandstone under the crushing weight of the power toward which he now pitched. Behind him the green-glowing walls were spattered with the blood from the dead Yanish which danced in his wake.

Without warning the tunnel ended and as an animal, reflexes jerked, stopping him short of the ledge and a far drop into the magnificent cavern below. A single red eye, half buried in a heaving mountain of white, was fixed on him. Lindarg's gaze was drawn into its fiery, glowing depths. In it he felt rather than thought he could see through the rocks and down far beneath into the very fired of the earth itself. Those fires raged and bubbled behind that red orb and the glow of them sundered the bright green of the cavern. In but a moment that eye had ravaged Lindarg's shattered mind and finding nothing but tormented confusion and fear, relinquished its grip a little, allowing Lindarg to calm the panic which had driven him thus.

Slowly Lindarg took in the vision of that abyss – that awesome resting place of the god which had thrown up the mountain ranges with valleys between through which Fairgot had directed her raging torrents and peaceful streams to form her vast seas on the plains beyond which he had left for her. There, in its centre was the great mass that was Graggan; white and foetid, heaving slightly and with the flickering eye. On the bottom of the cavern the god's white form disappeared as thick tendrils down holes in its walls. Lindarg knew now what the 'white worm' had been; he knew how long those tendrils were – laced through the honeycombed rock like a fungus ramifies through damp earth.

And while the mere mortal wondered at what he saw, so the god wrestled with its own mind, trying to think and to plan, attempting to guess why a man should stray here – a mortal man he was – for Graggan knew that none other could have come here. Fresh in his memory were the stirrings of Endworld. A new forest was born he knew – for no sorcery could prevent the earth – his own spawn – bearing those tidings. Somewhere was re-born as Graggan himself had once planned; someone had cleared the way for his old power – still lurking in the very earth of that place – to work again. Old memories assailed him; Eq – had he come forth? The mere thought was a joy – but dashed; Graggan knew that Eq was gone – no sorcery would have sealed him in this tomb were Eq still free. They'd had their differences eons ago but never so different as to favour mortals above a fellow god. No, Eq was not in Endworld. Other changes he remembered too; some recent ones had been familiar and he had smiled with the irony, others he had not recognised and wondered at. With each change his hopes had been raised but frustration increased as well – and each change had followed ever more closely on the heels of the last.

So Graggan's mind was a bemused whirl. Aware of all these things yet knowing nothing of their meaning. Now, before him; powerless and insignificant – yet somehow here – stood the first mortal man he had seen since Endworld was young. Pathetically the man clutched a drawn sword as if he sought to strike a fatal blow with a mere sliver of metal. The complete helplessness of the mortal held a message – it must – but what message? Graggan's mind raced in turmoil; he could end the man's life with a mere thought! Then, screaming like a thousand banshees from the depths of the god's being came the hate it had nurtured in thousands of Starseasons of hanging on – weakened and slowly decaying with the souls of feeble animals. 'Can this mortal be used for escape? Is this the moment? What do I do? How?' Graggan fought to think amid the ferment which raged in his mind. But for all his knowledge, he could piece nothing together; was powerless to divine what form a plan should take and the sheer force of frustration welling up within him swamped him – trying to drive him into action – but without direction he could not act. A sudden new thought sliced through the tumult: 'Is this the end...?' That thought the god could not contemplate after those wasted millennia bent on revenge but helpless; never to see his world again; never to nurture and heal it.

In that same instant Lindarg saw the Knavestone posed nakedly on the same ledge as he now stood but far to the right. It lay as far from him as from the god. In that instant too the fires in the desperate, frightened and confused god's eye leaped high. Freed momentarily from the power which Graggan himself now struggled to control, Lindarg saw a chance to delay the god while he ran for the gem and out of the cavern.

The sword, a deadly sliver of silver, shot through the orange light of the fires and buried itself up to the hilt in the eye. But Lindarg had underestimated the might of Graggan; that ailing eye transfixed him before he had lifted but one foot to run; now he was bound hopelessly, feeling rather than knowing that a single pulse from the god would crush him as a falling tree would crush an empty eggshell. But the pulse never came. Graggan was dying in the tomb that should have been his temple: with the death came the relief of release at last – and with release, a ray of hope and a little gladness.

Lindarg was overcome, missing a fall from the ledge by a hair's breadth as the god's silent dying filled his mind with a cacophony of confusion. He fell forward into a dazzling whiteness filled with visions of Graggan's past; visions of a vast power that was finally free for eternity – and the glow of the Knavestone in the darkening abyss.

He remained prostrate for a long time while the cavern's darkness deepened with the fading of Graggan's glow. The final twitching of the tentacles in the labyrinths below the Great Stone had long finished; Graggan was a memory; Quickly his remains would rot and be torn by Yanish. They would sense that the power had left the white flesh and would soon turn and devour that which had devoured their bodies and souls for so long.

But with Graggan gone, there came another change. The sealing over the land was also gone for it had been cast over 'the land where Graggan dwells' Lindarg awoke and was aware of Yanish everywhere – already they were snatching peremptory bites from the pale meat they had learned to fear. Lindarg staggered, pressing himself against the cavern wall at his back. Remembering the Knavestone, he edged toward it as it lay cold and bleak – visible as a grey pool in the rich darkness; grasped it and hid it away in the pocket of his skins as if ashamed to be stealing it. With a remorseful glance at the diminishing white globe below, Lindarg turned abruptly down the narrow way through which he had come – but now it was dark and there was no force pulling him toward its centre. He must find his own way out.

While Lindarg fumbled through endless passages, Venain was aloft in his tower once more. He knew the sorcery which had bound Graggan was gone and now his far-sight could reach onto the plain which had for so long been concealed to him. There were people there but he neither recognised nor could name them and even with his powers he could discern little. Graggan was not there; his name in the stone was the black emptiness of death. Venain also reasoned that Graggan's death had released the sealing which had been set upon the 'Plain of the Great Stone where Graggan dwells' – not that the sealing had been riven. No, there were no forces left in Endworld that could have broken that void, even if all those remained – or even might remain – were coalesced together and hurled at it, it would have endured. A sealing was irrevocable. So Venain was not afraid but his apprehensions were building as they did with every change in the lands which he did not directly cause – and such changes were becoming ever more frequent. That Graggan had passed didn't worry him in the least; more, it pleased him; but whoever – or whatever – had done such a deed must be considered an opponent. It was hardly conceivable that the god had merely faded quietly from the world...

As Venain read his own thoughts, the old doubt returned, nurtured afresh with each happening, harder to conquer with each nurturing. His grim face became hard and tight with resolve; the time of waiting was over; there were things he had to know; he must begin to marshal the hordes that were truly his in Endworld – and beyond. But first there was the problem of who – or what – had finished Graggan.

Dura, the first lieutenant in the Baeth army was now in the north supervising the flow of arms and supplies to the mighty army which surrounded Gullen, readying it for the final onslaught when the city, mortally weakened by the siege, would have to meet the Baeth hordes or die slowly and miserably. Cradling the Knavestone, Venain worked on Dura and soon the lieutenant was speeding to the Plain of the Great Stone accompanied by two score good fighting men. Riding hard, they would reach the plain in a day with luck.

Venain knew that Graggan had possessed the other Knavestone. It was possible – particularly if his doubt was well-founded – that its use was known – or partly known, or that it would be discovered accidentally. It was also likely that it had not been found – perhaps not even looked for. Nevertheless, Venain was prepared for any use of the stone against him. He half hoped it would be used, for the user would identify himself through it and once overpowered, would become his slave.

It was while Venain's thoughts were drawn to the north by events there, that Gargol, his own self once more, decided to attack Gullen; a course of action which Venain did not wish. It was Venain's plan that the city should fall quietly without the ravages of battle and the mayhem which would ensue – not because he wished no harm to the Southlanders but because it was vital to him that any artefacts of power were, as far as possible, left undisturbed and not treated as spoils by ignorant, insensitive plunderers. No, his plan was very different from that and all the while it was being executed with the calm confidence and smoothness which betold its inevitable success. Unknown to him as he cast around the Plain of the Great Stone, Gargol was about to thwart those very schemes.

How long he had wandered in those dark tunnels Lindarg had no idea. He was tired, hungry and depressed. Thirst he had quenched from the pools on the floor of the lower passages, now he summoned a Yanish to eat. His meanderings had crossed occasional mauled tendrils of what had been Graggan, stumbling over them in the darkness – feeling their withered skin and each time he did so he knew he was no nearer finding a way out.

As he gorged himself on warm raw meat, the Baeth mines came to mind. There it had all seemed so easy; short-term plans of escape determined day-to-day without the complexities which he now faced; without the responsibilities which he had since discovered were his and his alone. Wisdom and knowledge, he reflected bitterly, brought no respite to the enigmas of his destiny; merely added to the perplexities and increased the burden which he bore. Now it seemed the tenure and integrity of the whole of Endworld lay upon his shoulders and with the realisation had come the doubt that he could fulfil his part. Inwardly he knew that in the end, he would fail – could only fail – if what he had learned was revealed to be the truth. But deeper within he knew he had not yet done enough and that inner self still burned, pushing him on to that final fate.

He remembered the Yanish of the mines following the clambering, struggling Gulleners and the clicking carts – those yellow eyes that could see in the 'dark' so well... so well! The thought was a scream of hope. It was possible. They must have grown accustomed to these tunnels and must be able to find their way – if not with eyes then another sense. As he thought one came; in its head he fixed its task, grasped its fur and was led through the myriad of twisting passages out into the dazzling light of the zenith of a new day. He forced his eyes to overcome the glare, gazing to the far edge of the plain but there was nothing to be seen save the flat, dusty, barren scape. With a shrug of determination Lindarg set out across it toward the stones which had so recently barred his passage.

With the sealing gone, the land was different, vulnerable; no longer was it a safe haven from those things he still feared. Lindarg hurried over the open spaces – alert now and very alone. He recalled Eq's words concerning the fate of Graggan, realising that Venain must know of the god's passing – perhaps also of the other Knavestone which was heavy in the skins he wore. Lindarg knew that with it he could reach into the mind of Venain and a tempting thought was that the ultimate danger to Endworld would end there but as soon as Lindarg considered the idea, he knew it could not be that easy. More likely Venain, prepared for just such a contest, would overpower and enslave him. He could not risk a direct attack on his enemy. Then he thought of Gargol. Perhaps he could chance to ease the terrors of Gullen for a while – and those too of Syntelle.

Lindarg stopped then among a pile of old, rounded stones and took out the Knavestone, regretting that the Queenstone was not with him to see Gullen and his beloved Syntelle, for with the two stones together both their powers would be enhanced and with them he might do much for Gullen. He peered into the stone's depths.

"Gargol." He felt the gem's power working far away, then drawing him there – to the battle field and smoke – with the desperate cries of Gulleners on the air. The mind he now grasped was confused; training and the words of advisers was deeply entrenched. There too was something intangible – a disturbance, an upset – that was unexpected and without explanation. Lindarg guessed its cause, wondering where Venain might now be turning his thoughts. Casting such speculations aside, Lindarg wrestled with the mind that rose on the crest of conquest, was hot with the course of the battle, soared with the proximity of victory and the spoils, already revelling in the suffering he would extract from the Southlanders he was about to vanquish over the seasons to come. It was all but over. Gullen was about to fall.

In a frenzy of anguish Lindarg overpowered what he fought, fearing that already he was too late, assailing Gargol with the certainty that Gullen was a set trap and within it the doom of the Baeths lay in wait; persuading him that it had been too easy; that they had been allowed – but not obviously – to be successful in invading the city then, once in, they would be slaughtered in their thousands by the ancient sorcery that smouldered in anticipation. And he, Gargol had succumbed to the ruse. This Gargol understood – the tricks and tactics of war – and now he saw how he had been drawn to a city filled with his foes – such a tempting lure; saw how the Southlanders had cunningly baited him to attack a stronghold – inside which he had never been. Now his mind raced; 'What lurks within those walls? How will our men be so surely destroyed?' He was certain of it now. "A trap!" Gargol brought the horn to his lips and sounded the retreat. He could wait. He praised the providence that had shown him the truth – and barely in time!

It was nearly two days since he had dispatched Dura. Venain spoke his name into the stone to find that Dura had been a fool. He had split his men to search the plain – an obviously expedient tactic in Dura's mind – but not one liked by Venain. Now the lieutenant rode with only ten men and if they encountered larger numbers Venain might lose his chance to discover what he wanted to know most, since he felt somehow that in this remote corner of Endworld lurked the powers that were stirring the land: fuelling his apprehensions; his doubt.

The liegemen were taken much by surprise. Karil it was who saw and heard them first but that was after they had been spied by the Baeths and already those men charged.

"Baeths attack!" The warning was late.

"We must fight, we have no choice," said Turg. "We have faced worse odds." His last statement was flat and it concealed their weariness of journeying and waiting – now having to fight.

"The stone! The Queenstone! It must remain safe even though we fall!" cried Eisdan to Karil.

"Then we must hide it here and force the battle away from this place." Karil took it and covered it with dust by a large pillar of rock.

The others were already mounted and Andur shouted back to Karil, "Follow us!" as he pointed south away from the plain and the stone gate which marked its entrance. The Baeths changed the angle of their headlong charge to cut them off.

In a few moments their paths converged, Karil catching up and Dura shouting; "One live prisoner men, the rest, slay them!"

Then the liegemen were back-to-back and the fury of being caught unawares blazed from within their helms as the first four of their foe were cast down landing with their own blood in the dust. Riderless beasts, unable to stop, thundered into the liegemen's pack, knocking it into confusion as the remaining Baeths closed in.

A spear crashed into Andur's left wrist, tearing at the flesh, blood gushing down his fingers. The sudden shock of pain numbed him for an instant and a broadsword rang a glancing blow on his helm. Blackness descended as he fell and he was dimly aware of the commotion passing over him, then nothing. Turg too had fallen – but in the first rush and there was no blood on him though he lay as if dead; unmoving in the dried moss. Karil and Eisdan were together and fighting still – though sorely outnumbered. They could not hope to win the dispute. Desperately Eisdan uttered his mighty battle cry,

"Farisle!" he screamed, his sword a burnished blur as he drove at the enemy. But they were hemmed in, surrounded by blades with no room to fight.

"Take them alive," ordered Dura. "We-" But the voice was cut short as his beast snorted, turned and began to move away from the fray though he wrestled to control it. The other mounts too were being drawn back toward the plain. Venain understood that force – that power over animals. Dura was quick to dismount. Venain knew also that whoever wielded that force would not yield a name but another might…

Steeds and riders, liegemen and Baeths alike, gathered speed, flying passed the stones and onto the plain. Dura bent over Andur but the liegeman, though obviously alive, did not stir when kicked. He moved over to the prostrate Turg. Now Andur stirred, a knife sliding from concealment in his tunic breast. As his arm came back to throw, Turg moved but had not seen Dura behind him lifting his heavy sword for the death blow.

"Turg!" screamed Andur in warning and loosed the knife. Dura flashed round but already the slick blade was speeding to his neck, ending his life in a choked cry.

Venain muttered a new name into the stone.

From the plain Lindarg saw the fray and spoke to the steeds, scattering them. Two mounts turned aside toward him while the others tore relentlessly out across the plain carrying Baeths struggling for control.

"Hail liegemen!" greeted Lindarg. "I am honoured by your haste!" He added amusedly as Karil and Eisdan thundered to a halt before him.

"Sire," Eisdan's voice was abrupt. "Turg and Andur lie hurt and with them still is the Baeth leader – he may be slaying them as we talk – and you jest!" Eisdan had not wanted to say it like that, yet he had. Lindarg was ashamed: he had helped Gullen but failed his liegemen. They had fought to lend time to his efforts to save Gullen – and unknowing! A sudden fire burst into the wizard's eyes.

"Take me!" He leaped up behind Karil and the two beasts thundered from the plain driven crazily to where Andur and Turg had fallen. Such was their haste that they almost rode the two down as they shuffled, supporting each other, away from the dead and onto the plain.

17

THE PASSING OF EQ

For several days they rested on the margin of the plain. Lindarg worked feverishly on Andur and slowly the gashed wrist healed and the liegeman became himself. Long since had the remaining Baeths been scattered far and wide over the lands and from one of their camps they had purloined some food. Soon they would be able to travel and Lindarg's thoughts were beginning to turn to other things.

Turg, though, was different; apparently unhurt in the skirmish but not his usual self; confused a little by the blow Lindarg thought. They had told of the encounter and what had happened but when it had fallen to Turg to recount the death of the Baeth leader, he could add nothing. Lindarg remained unconvinced. Andur had been found unconscious by Turg and was unable to remember anything clearly after the spear and his fall. Lindarg was puzzled by the incident. He supposed it was reasonable that Baeths were out patrolling – even here – but why should they be so interested in live prisoners and particularly why should their lieutenant have so neatly abandoned his steed and stayed behind when his men were forced to flee? He could not guess but was suspicious. Turg kept out of his way.

The next morning, they were all up with the dawn sun. Their stone shelter was cold; outside a slight frost had settled and its chill was stirred by an east wind. It was hard to get moving but Lindarg was adamant.

"You must head with great speed to Gullen and aid the city as you can-"

But Karil interrupted him. "You do not accompany us, Sire?" The question was for all of them.

"No, I have perhaps my last errand before I finally come to Gullen – maybe for the last time. I cannot ask you to come where I go – and I will not. I will take no harm where I tread, so do not fear for me." Lindarg's voice rose a little over the wind as if assuming an importance that was new to him.

It did not go unnoticed but then Andur broke in. "How can we enter the city, Sire?"

"It may be liegemen, that you will not find a way through. Be assured that they will be more vigilant than before. I entreat you therefore to achieve whatever you can, from wherever you can; destroy supplies from the rear, sabotage, harass them. Every move you make will be a blow struck for Gullen."

Turg was there now, listening intently. Lindarg turned his beast to leave; suddenly Turg burst forward. "Sire!" The voice was almost a command to stop. Slowly, deliberately, Lindarg did so and turned to face the man, senses taut. Turg met his gaze and said, "Who are you...?"

The weight of the question shrouded the group in silence. The pause lengthened until at last Lindarg said, "I am named Lindarg, Lord of Gullen, Virdil the sorcerer who was Sandrinfal of old and I may yet be named King of Endworld! But you ask me who I am and I reply that I do not know. Be answered and begone!"

In the countenance that challenged him, Venain saw... the Deathling; a blur of indistinct, changing faces.

Suddenly Turg cast around at the others, their faces were fixed on his and in them horrid stares; he looked sheepish, like a child appearing suddenly in the midst of an alehouse brawl. He faced Karil, "What...?"

But Lindarg spoke instead of Karil; "Turg!"

"Sire?"

259

"Tell us how the Baeth leader died."

Turg then told all he could remember of the end of the encounter. Andur's shout and the knife were new. Lindarg nodded as the story unfolded; he had guessed right. He dismounted. "A fire," he suggested, "to warm us against these chill tidings. Before we depart you must learn what I have learned and be warned for all our sakes and that of Endworld too."

Turg wept when Lindarg revealed the truth that he had been named to Venain and had not had the strength to resist the sorcerer's will. He knew that now. Andur was wracked with grief at his folly but Lindarg was comforting; "Any effort to save a friend's life can never be wrong. The evil which besets Endworld and which transcends all the wickedness of mortal Baeths has twisted that act into a betrayal. Neither of you can be blamed – perhaps even I would have been powerless to resist unprepared. It may be that such a foul blow may yet have repercussions which Venain will regret!"

"But you answered! Why didn't you refuse? You knew!" Andur's voice was reproachful.

"I didn't know – then."

"But you have answered to find out – you are given away to him!"

"True, he now knows for sure that he has an adversary. I have given him only food for thought, though I had hoped for secrecy a little longer yet. He may choose whichever name he fancies – has probably tried them all – each will strike home but even I do not know my own name; I cannot be seen in a stone. He cannot name me." Lindarg paused for a while. "Perhaps I only exist as the antithesis to the demigod Venain and it may be that I shall pass with his passing, or not…"

"Surely this is not true!"

"I can only guess and in doing so prove that I myself do not fully understand." Lindarg looked at them long and hard, then continued; "Difficult it will be for you to hide things from your fellow," Lindarg motioned to Turg, still downcast with grief, "but for Turg the suffering will be greater. Perhaps he will learn to recognise when Venain is there; perhaps Venain has seen enough. Use your names sparingly."

"We will watch him and care for him – it could have been any in our midst." Andur's words were sympathetic and as he spoke them he slid an arm across the bent shoulders of Turg.

"He will not be forsaken among us," said Eisdan consolingly.

"We have tarried enough – though important the business. Come," said Lindarg. "This time we will go. I will tell more as we travel and since there is great need of speed we can talk at rests."

"But, Sire, do you now ride with us?"

"For a little way at least, yes," Lindarg replied.

They were quieted by his wisdom in drawing Turg. All that they said could have been known to Venain. They were overawed too by Lindarg's account of his sojourn with Graggan and the god's end but mostly by the change in their liege. At once he had become grander, more confident and the change could not be ignored. Resolutely the company left the fire, killing it with rocks and dust and swung their mounts southwards, the cold wind chafing their left sides. As they went, Lindarg said,

"I have looked in the Queenstone and Gullen is yet fast against the Baeths but it becomes mortally weaker by the day."

He did not mention the Knavestone. 'How can I?' he thought to himself in justification, 'how could I tell them that I will not use the gem which could vanquish the strife of the world? But at what risk?' He knew he dare not. Additionally, there was the problem perhaps of Turg and Venain. 'Venain must not know!' he told himself, finally.

After bidding the liegemen farewell, Lindarg made haste along the South Road for it at least had not suffered from the changes in Endworld and he knew the folly of tarrying. Days and nights passed before he entered Koryn Vale for the second time. Soon he stood before the fire of Eq – still bridged by the monolith. For some reason he was less afraid this time of fording the flames and entering the tower, though he knew those trials which still lay ahead. Checking in his skins for the Knavestone, Lindarg approached the flames. As he did so they died and were gone, for he carried that which Eq desired and when Eq had cast his flames deep in the past, they had been set to bar entrance to all save he who bore the Knavestone for which the god had searched so fruitlessly for wasted ages. Now the Knavestone was come; the way inside the cliff was lit by a bright light for Lindarg, the glow clearly marking the way; a way which seemed larger and less crushing than he remembered it. There was no wind on the causeway to the tower's foot; its door stood wide open to welcome him. Above the entrance room, the stair which had almost thwarted his venture before was solid, walled and roofed. Lindarg paced up it with ease, knowing his welcome. Entering the high chamber he was aware of the nearness of the god. The room felt alert – but was empty save for the stones in the centre of the floor.

"It is here... I feel it! – and more!" The voice was etherial, distant, but resonant in the chamber.

"I have served you as I promised-"

But the voice interrupted him, strident with impatience; "Then truly complete your task, take the Kingstone and place the Knave!"

"But our bargain – there are things I must ask-."

"Take the Kingstone, that was the bargain!" The impatience grew.

"Yes, the Kingstone was in the bargain," challenged Lindarg, but so too was your help to my quest – for the future of Endworld, a world that once was your domain."

"I care no more for the place, I have wearied of it too long. I am powerless in it."

"All I ask is for words, nor do I ask this for myself alone..."

"Do not ask, I have no power, no knowledge that can help you."

"You have knowledge and wisdom, Eq, we both know that!" Lindarg's voice was low and hard, its timbre defiant.

"Time wastes!" The words moved around the void before Lindarg as if agitated. "Place the stone and begone to your fate!"

Lindarg hesitated, clutching the gem firmly beneath his tunic but he was not afraid. "I will not fail those who depend on me." Now he challenged the god.

"Place it!" The sound was wild, its volume stunning in the stony resonance of the chamber.

"No!"

Searing lurid light burst from the stones on the floor, its whiteness thrust toward Lindarg, seeking to force his hand.

"You cannot deny me!" Lindarg fought to stop his hand as it withdrew the stone from inside his tunic. The force was awesome; his legs took a step forward; they too were beyond his control. The god's laugh shattered the air, ravaging his mind. He looked into the stone as he stooped forward to place it and a last desperate idea came to him. The laughing stopped abruptly and the force lessened but he was still held and could not withdraw his hand; captured as a statue. He tried to form the word in his mind; to say it into the stone.

"You cannot name me. My name is unsaid by mortals." But the voice wavered, uncertain, though the force still held Lindarg in check. He wrestled with the word; could feel the doubt of the god and sensed the tension building. "You will not say it! No mortal dare – it is the Law!" The defiant vermillion visage suddenly appeared, its red eyes giving fire to the words which crashed around Lindarg's head. He felt a surge within him and the word formed itself; the word he could not say; the god's name – and he said it into the stone.

"Equillain!" The god's mind was his. He had done what could not be done; the Law forbade it; a mortal could not do it – and yet he had.

The god's mind was incredulous; a vast miasma of thoughts spreading through time and the length and breadth of the world, yet it could not believe what had been done. There too, were other thoughts which could not be wrested from its depths. Eq fought the power of his own stone but was engulfed by it.

Lindarg said to him, "I bargained for information; you will give it."

The god acquiesced and Lindarg withdrew his thoughts back into the chamber which was once more silent and dim.

"The fire of Eq is your fire, tell me how it can be turned."

"Aaaahh… mortal… No woodcutter, are you. In you there is…" The voice trailed off, then, "-far more. Perhaps this is a sign to me – but I cannot – must not say what I see. No… it is forbidden to me to disclose it. Your power is indeed great Lindarg, I see now that it exceeds mine. I must answer as you wish. Truly Endworld has stirred… But to what final end?" The god's last words were whispered and shrouded with uncertainty.

"The fire-" but Lindarg did not need to ask again.

"It is a sorcerous fire which consumes all of what it is sent to consume, no more, no less. To turn it you must destroy its sender for while its sender lives, nothing can stop its course save he alone, it is irrevocable."

"Then we are doomed, Venain cannot be defeated!"

"Hold, Fated One, I have not finished. Though not turned, the flames can be stayed; their advance checked and for as long as they are kept at bay by force, those against whom it is sent are safe. In that time perhaps, their sender may be destroyed – or perhaps not. Say before the fire; 'Rannadil Cria Foren Thurgelle'. She will come. Work with her."

"There is one more thing I would ask."

"Then ask it and let me finish and my tower fall nobly; Koryn should have been a ruin when Endworld was yet young…"

"Tell me of the Hammer of Eq – your Hammer."

The air was tense at its mention and the voice did not answer immediately; then at last, "Is it found?"

"I cannot know – until perhaps it is too late," muttered Lindarg.

264

"It was lost," continued the voice, solemn now, "Long ago. Does this enemy Venain have it?"

"That is my fear."

"Then your danger is great, if he has the hammer. Maybe he is already the new God of Endworld and it might be that you should strive to serve rather than fail to oppose his might."

"Never!" Lindarg's reply was instant and vehement.

"Then know this, Lindarg. The hammer is magic; in no man's hands will it perish. It is anything it can be and will do anything it can do; a thousand of these gems for every man, woman and child could it forge and still its power would wax."

"Then will you destroy it Eq, if mortal man cannot – or will you leave it to scourge worlds and lives forever?"

"No my battle is lost, I have not the strength to destroy it." Then the voice dropped to a whisper over the dust of the stone floor, weak, almost frightened. "Will my deeds haunt me forever?"

"You have to try!" In response to Lindarg's demand the whisper died and once more was strong but bitter, remorseful, helpless.

"There is nothing left in Endworld that could destroy the hammer. In it is my strength; without it I am less than you. Those who could have now all passed; I have heard them and one-by-one their stones have come back to me. What I have done I cannot undo – perhaps all the Old Ones are doomed never to rest eternally, nor I with them."

"But-"

"I can fight no more, I can do nothing further to aid you." The voice contained sadness now and it wavered over the stones beneath the tear streaked countenance, rending Lindarg's heart as he saw the god as a frail frinnet, chained and guarded, weakened but never fading; trapped by his own designs as irrevocably as a man in a steel coffin; held fast by the inviolate Law. Lindarg fingered the Knavestone.

"Place it now and give me rest," the voice implored. "Use the Kingstone as you may."

The noise of the placing of the stone; the wailing babble of the Equil, was heard through time; by the Old Ones and others who could hear; Sylee heard it and entered Koryn Vale; it was heard in the great forests by beasts and birds and felt by Endworld. Venain heard it too. It came to him across the lands and he knew he could not ignore the portent that it bore; no more could he stand the onlooker's part as Endworld stirred and was stirred; no more time was there he guessed for quiet tricks, so into the Southlands he sent ten of his greyest warriors; the darkest force ever to ride the realm was loosed along the Westway to Gullen.

Nethermen; causing the deep Forest of Dorn to quail as they passed unchallenged beneath its eaves, then Venain turned to other preparations within his castle and beyond so that he might be ready to face and surely win, what must be to come.

18

THE SIEGE IS BROKEN

Once more the liegemen had donned the enemy's uniforms as they moved behind the Baeth siege from the north. Deep in woodland a short ride from the enemy lines they constructed a shelter from which they could venture out on the damaging sorties which they proposed.

The first day, early, they split up and carefully, at a distance, surveyed the besieging encampments looking for likely targets and ways in which they could hinder and delay. That evening Andur was full of news.

"To the east, hidden from the city by rising ground, there are scores of machines of war – rams, siege towers, shields and the like – we could burn them."

"They will be too well guarded," said Karil. "And such a venture would need time – not only for ourselves to get clear – but for the fire to take effect, new wood does not burn well."

"What about oil?" ventured Eisdan. "They would not be able to put that out quickly and it would soon fire the wood."

"That does not solve the problem of the guards," returned Karil. "They are unlikely to stand aside while we go round setting fire to the very machines which could bring them victory."

Eisdan looked at Andur; "Did you see any guards?"

"I was too far away – there could have been many – but no, I didn't actually see any."

"I say it's worth a further look," Eisdan concluded. They agreed, then he added; "Not far away on their north side they have their main supply point. Provisions are brought from Baeth down the north road and deposited there for collection by the various units of the siege. Firstly, we might easily hinder those supplies far up the north road but more importantly we could use some – oil for instance – there are barrels of it."

Andur was interested. "That solves one problem – there only remains the guards which we have not yet seen... What did you find?" Andur directed his question at Turg.

"There was little to the south save a few men and the small amounts of supplies they would need; there were, though, many tents and camps but from what I could see most were empty. Perhaps they serve as a bluff to Gullen – at night we might easily make our way through them and reach the city-"

"But how would those in the city know, at night, who we were and how could we warn them? If the Baeths did not finish us, Gulleners surely would!" Karil's observation brought silence.

At last Andur continued, remembering Durnor's words as they had looked upon the city seasons ago. "We, with the freedom to flee are better off than they – trapped within walls – do not think to join them, it would be folly to try and despair to succeed."

Again there was agreement and the subject was dropped in favour of more positive action.

"Tomorrow then, we requisition our supplies and at the same time, one of us will worm close enough to those machines to assess our chances there," summed up Karil, "We will start early."

The Baeth cart which entered the stores areas the following morning was driven and manned by three Baeths from the west lines. It was the first to arrive and the soldiers with it were sullen. It was a duty they despised and these three had obviously been given the task as a punishment – probably for over-drinking – since they seemed very much the worse for wear and said nothing. The supplies guard took all of this in at a glance. It was the same every morning. He said nothing, merely watching as the three men busied themselves with their order list and struggled with goods onto the cart. Further, he declined to help, enjoying the fact that in doing so he infuriated the soldiers the more – and there was precious little to smile about in the Baeth army! But they were taking a lot of oil. Just as he was thinking to query this and check the order sheet, one of them turned to him with a dark, scowling face and said, "Axes! Where are the bloody axes?" The voice was slurred and its tone threatened trouble. Submissively the guard motioned to a hut and Eisdan went inside to reappear a few moments later with four large axes – three bundled under his left arm, one swinging menacingly in his right as he glared at the guard almost smiling with the sight of the changed expression which the free, gleaming blade brought to his face.

The guard breathed a sigh of relief as the laden cart finally trundled away but he still wondered about all those barrels of oil and he complimented himself on his powers of observation. He had noticed that from the oil stacks they had only taken the third barrel off each of the nearest piles, neither had it escaped his attention that soldiers bringing carts from the west were always much the worse for drink... What he failed to notice was that the third barrels were cart height and arm height and soldiers were lazy people so early in the morning. He moved over to the remaining stacks of oil barrels convinced that some did not contain what they should and smashed in the top of a third barrel in an untouched pile with the hilt of his sword. The thick, cloying liquid enveloped his face covering his eyes with a cloak of agony – even his scream was a splutter of oil. For his pains the guard was taken, hands chained and thrown in the axe-hut which was then securely locked. Not long after he was summarily executed for sabotage. His protestations that soldiers had been taking suspicious amounts of oil assumed to be just excuses in an attempt save his own neck...

"No guards at all?" Andur was amazed at Turg's news. "It hardly seems possible."

"Evidently Gargol considers them safe behind his lines and

has no fears of their being attacked from the rear," stated Karil, though he too could not believe their luck.

"What a blow it will be!" enthused Eisdan as they tucked in to a meal – their best for many days, then slept the evening away to be fresh and ready to strike in the pre-dawn.

It was still very dark and deathly quiet as the liegemen moved between the giant wooden structures taking their time to place the heavy wooden barrels in position soundlessly choosing the siege towers and two rams for special attention. With each one in place, their lids were carefully removed and the contents splashed as far up the wood as they could reach.

"Soak the wheels," entreated Andur in a whisper. "They at least must burn." The residual oil in each barrel was poured over the ground beneath the machines from where, once hot, it would burn for a long time under the structures. The empty cart too was added to the combustibles and with the first hint of light from the east, the liegemen set the fires, looking back only briefly to be sure they were growing and headed north in the dim grey light of early dawn.

Venain too had been with them, unnoticed in Turg during the taciturn activity of the early dawn. Even in the dim light he knew he had seen these faces before – and with them had been the Deathling… He needed to know what they knew…

Before long the liegemen could see the flames leaping high as they fled to safety in the distant woods and even from their shelter they could see the fire's glow reflected on the low morning clouds and the black pall rising to mingle with them in the dull light as they settled to sleep out the day.

In Gullen Farg called Lianor to the east wall.

"What do you make of it?" asked Farg as he gazed eastwards to the smoke and sparks. "Isn't that where they moved so much equipment?"

"Yes," replied Lianor. "But surely they have not set fire to it!"

They continued to watch hearing the commotion spreading through the besieging forces, unable to comprehend what was happening and least of all why. Others joined them on the parapet, among them Durgol and Durgel. Durgol turned to his brother saying, "Do you think it could be-?"

"Our liege? It is possible."

Farg overheard them and after a moment's thought said, "If who you suggest has done this thing, why?"

"A diversion so that we may take advantage of their confusion and attack – they will not be prepared!"

"Neither are we," stated Farg levelly. "And there is another possibility-"

"What is that? asked Durgel.

"That it is a Baeth trick to lure us out – to our deaths!" From their expressions it was clear that they could see some sense in the suggestion and Farg finished; "No, we could not win out there – not even if half their army was fighting the fire. We will not go."

On their return to the shelter, Eisdan, Andur and Karil had gratefully accepted Turg's offer that he take the first watch without a second thought and now, while the others slumbered, he stole away in his own clothes once more, riding like the wind to the Baeth encampment.

"Hail Baeths! I have news of the saboteurs-" But a blow from behind knocked him senseless from his steed and into the non-too-gentle arms of his captives. When he came to, Turg was wracked with pain. His head bursting with red throbbing; flesh stinging hotly as another fiery trace scorched across his back and arms and stung his belly. This fresh agony jarred him to full consciousness and he screamed, struggling uselessly against the wickedly tight bonds which held him in the path of the stinging lash. Around him he was dimly aware of men gloating, then of the thong round his neck holding him upright and choking his breath. The blows ceased and a voice came to him from behind.

"Who set the fires and where are they?" Turg's tortured mind raced. It was a dream surely; he had fallen asleep and would soon wake from it. If not what had happened? Where were the others, why did they not help him? Frantically he cast round, helplessly,

271

recognising no-one; then even through the pain he felt the rain on his skin and the cooling breeze; it was reality.

The top half of his torso and his legs were bared; the belt and a sliver of skins was all that remained of his clothes. There was blood on his belly and arms and he could feel more on his back. Unyielding thongs crushed his crossed wrists together behind him securing them to the belt and the bound ankles below.

"Answer!" With the demand came another blow which sent a scream of pain driving through every fibre of his frame. Incoherent words tumbled from him in response. Venain watched through Gargol's eyes, wondering if the prisoner would break in time or whether he would have to make him by other means – much surer – but without the appeal of those presently being employed. Gargol waved another man to take up position. Naked from the waist up, the man's body writhed with muscles; the lash he gripped was multi-tailed, supple and heavy.

"You will talk," Gargol said to Turg menacingly. "Eventually." He gave Turg a few moments and when no answers were forthcoming, said to the two hulking brutes, "Flay him!" With searing accuracy, the whistling thongs tore flesh alternately in bloody sweeps as the helpless victim rent the air with his cries, pitching wildly in his bonds and gasping for breath behind a purpling, exploding head. Much as Venain savoured the spectacle, there was need of haste and realising that the tottering man would soon fade into and abyss of darkening agony, stopped the onslaught before it was too late.

Words poured from Turg's blistered throat. "N-n-north of here… in a wood-"

"How many?" asked Gargol.

"Th-three-"

"Three?" Gargol's voice was incredulous. "You lie!" The whips raised at Gargol's signal.

"N-no-there are three – I swear it!"

Venain believed him now.

"Take us."

Unable to resist, Turg was secured to his steed belly down and flanked by the brutes with whips, with Gargol himself just behind, headed a whole bath unit of five score men to the shelter where his friends lay blissfully – unawakened by the ending of the first watch, unaware if the treachery which was about to snare them. When they did wake, the Sun was passed its height, their weapons were gone and at each of their throats was a sword. Behind them, as the sword-points nicked the flesh of their necks, their wrists were mercilessly bound and the Baeth uniforms cut from their bodies. Anguished faces regarded each other and not seeing Turg in their midst, realised their folly as they were dragged from the shelter by tethers round their necks and hastened from behind by the flat of Baeth swords.

"Bring them!" commanded Gargol icily, "And do not be gentle – they have much to answer for!" Such a command the Baeth soldiers understood well and they saw to it that the forced march back was a miserable and painful trek for their helpless captives as they stumbled behind the steed which humped the blood-traced, still form of Turg.

Now Venain had all the time he needed, would wrest all the answers he wanted about the Deathling – his doubt – from these, his liegemen. Soon he would know all they had undoubtedly hidden from Turg since the passing of Graggan and he would savour every minute of its extraction.

Once at the camp, the new captives were placed in chains with shackles on their ankles. Turg was gently taken away while the others were secured in the open to stakes driven far into the hard earth. With wrists still bound they could stand, sit or lie by those stakes, all the while soldiers were encouraged to sport with them, kicking and bruising, taunting, beating them with whatever came to hand. By the end of the day when Gargol finally came to them they were beaten and miserable, the fight draining away from them with every blow their tortured, helpless bodies had received and now they realised that it was easy to yell defiance with sword in hand – knowing that the end, if it came would be swift – but a very different proposition when defenceless in the midst of cruel enemies where evil stalked in another's guise…

Gargol was accompanied by Senn – his second in command – together with a number of advisers, generals and lieutenants as they approached the hapless trio late in the afternoon.

"Kneel, liegemen filth!" snarled Gargol. "Where is the Deathling?"

"Deathling?" muttered Eisdan. "We know of none by that name.

"The truth!" Gargol snapped, jarring Eisdan's head sharply back by the hair until the sinews of his throat were stark and taut.

Pathetically the head tried to shake and a faint gasp of; "It is," was squeezed through strained tubes.

"Lindarg, then – where is he? Speak! Quickly!"

"He went south." Karil spoke now his eyes displaying the anguish he felt for his mistreated fellow.

"Sir," Senn's face was puzzled. "Who is this Deathling or Lindarg?"

The other soldiers nodded, similarly perplexed at the mention of such names.

"Quiet man!" snapped Gargol. "Leave this to me!" Then to Karil demanded; "Where in the south?" without releasing Eisdan.

"H-he would not say – we – do not know."

"Ha! More lies – but you will tell – yes, that you will – before the night is out."

"But Sir-"

"Hold, minion!" Gargol was abrupt, Senn and the other generals were taken aback by his vehemence. Once more he was not his usual self. An adviser moved forward as if to comment but Gargol's stare stilled him instantly then turned back to Karil.

"Tell me what happened to Graggan." With the mention of yet another unfamiliar name, Gargol forestalled his men's comments with a threatening glance. "Well?"

"S–slain by Lindarg-" Gargol's face turned puce; Eisdan

screamed – his neck close to breaking; Karil begged to be believed.

"Never!" hissed Gargol, the voice evil; around him his men withdrew a pace, faces aghast. Venain checked himself; there was no point in alienating Gargol's men; there were yet things he would need them to do so he allowed Gargol's visage to calm and turned to them. "They will obviously not talk – a pact between them perhaps. We must expect them to guard Gullen's secrets well. We may have to use more subtle means…"

"Ask him if there is a trap in the city," ventured an adviser.

Venain withdrew a little allowing Gargol himself to respond. "Is there?" he asked, releasing Eisdan's hair.

"No." The answer was a splutter through saliva.

"How can he be so sure since he has not been there these last days?" Gargol considered the general's objection and turned back to Eisdan with the question in his expression.

"Not when we left," answered Karil.

"Were there any plans for one?" Karil shook his head miserably, staring into the dirt.

"This gets us nowhere," muttered Gargol. He ushered his men away from the captives, explaining in low tones what he wanted them to do. Reluctantly they had agreed, supposing that hostilities ordained such behaviour and that they might yet obtain useful information from the prisoners.

In the evening light the clearing bustled with preparations while the ashen-faced liegemen watched in terror with the threat of Gargol's words hanging over them: 'you will tell before the night is out'. Worse, they had already told what they knew.

A short way in front of the stakes were placed two tripods, between them the makings of a fire with more wood laid beside. Immediately behind Andur and Karil a further two tripods were placed to which, still chained, they were bound by the arms, neck and legs in a kneeling position facing the fire. They gasped with the aching pain as mercilessly tight bonds cut into bruised flesh making each breath an arduous torment. Then Eisdan's ankles were tied together and the chain removed. A long pole was roughly thrust between his bound wrists and legs; each end of the pole was lifted and he bellowed an agonised scream to the ground as his arms were jarred upwards behind him and he hung, belly down from the pole, swinging slightly. Crazed horror bulged from Andur and Karil's staring eyes and they pleaded with scarcely coherent babble as Eisdan, on his pole, was suspended over the unlit fire, the pole resting between the two trestles; his wild struggles serving no other purpose than knotting the muscles over his lean frame.

Gargol turned to Andur and Karil and Venain said, "Now you will tell me all I wish to know!" Then to Eisdan, pleading in terror on the pole, knowing who spoke to him and sensing the nearness of his death, "Your name – before you die!"

"E-e-Ei-Eisdan…"

"Eisdan…" Gargol toyed with the name to get it right, then turned on the kneeling two. "Save your friend – what thing of power does 'your liege'…" The title was said with scorn and contempt. "… possess?"

Andur and Karil strained to see each other, then both watched fearfully as Gargol drew a fresh torch from the shadows. "Eisdan would like you to tell me…" he intoned, malevolently.

"He has a Queenstone-"

"A waste!" Then Gargol continued; "What can this gem do?"

"It can – see things…"

"What else?" The question was loaded, deliberate.

"N-nothing – it doesn't always do that-" Gargol lit the torch.

"Once more I ask, what else can it do?" Andur quivered, entreating.

"Nothing – we know of nothing more save that it can see the future or the past-" The lit torch blazed brightly.

"What other powers does this – Lindarg – have?"

"H – he can – control animals-"

"Ha! A useless trick indeed!" The torch neared the dry twigs; Eisdan flinched from its heat.

"Is that all?" Gargol's face was demanding; menacing.

"Y-yes – it is all that we know!" screamed Karil, helplessly fighting his bonds.

Then Gargol himself was asking about the trap in Gullen which he was sure lay in wait – without success while Venain sought other answers within Eisdan's sundered mind, finding that there were no more answers; they knew little more than Turg: they could not disclose what they had not been told. Venain was thwarted, humiliated. Abruptly Gargol's questions were stifled; his face blazed with spite and hate; vindictively now the torch kissed the wood and the first twigs crackled as Venain demanded answers which he knew they could not give. The twigs caught; pleading, stricken cries agitated the grim, dark sky; onlookers were appalled – but held in check by the fiery eyes of their leader glinting defiance in the dancing yellow light of the flames. The agreement had been to bluff – even now they each prayed that the branches would be kicked away at the last moment but each too had been prepared, deep within a force held them back and they knew the fire would take its course and none of them would prevent it.

Eisdan's rending scream ripped across the stillness of the night; sundering the peace of Gullen's fields and resounding off its walls. In the city and on its parapets stout hearts were struck by the icy grip of dread and the Southlands hushed in shame as they were drenched in the evil of the suffering that spawned such a hideous cry...

And from the west a darker evil drew nearer, driven apace by the rising, foul god of Dorn.

The new morning was redolent with dread, the sun's baleful rays failing to lighten the burdens from the night; despairing in its contention with the damp mists which clung and deadened the sounds of the after-dawn. For Gargol, the morning had brought with it something more than frightful recollections, scarcely believable, of his part in those dark deeds, it had brought deep forebodings of the future – that the sure victory of the siege would somehow elude him. He brooded outside his luxurious tent, frowning obliquely into the restive mists, sleep had passed him by that night. Senn appeared suddenly from nowhere; Gargol noticed his nervousness; the man stood further away than respect of a general required. Gargol eyed him and waited for him to speak. When he did, the voice betrayed the turmoil within the man – was quiet, almost timid.

"S-Sir."

"Yes, Senn?"

"The captives are held safely-" Gargol's grimace stopped him for a moment. "But the machines are useless – burned out."

"They are of no importance, their use would be a waste of men – and the city will just as surely fall without them." His tone was flat, lacking the conviction it once had. There was silence for long moments; at last Gargol spoke again; "Do you not feel it Senn?" Senn shook his head, his face questioning. "It is different today – evil in the air..."

"The weather – that's what is different."

"No, there is more and I don't like it – it is too quiet."

"But what is there to fear from Gullen?"

"Somehow Gullen seems unimportant..."

The conversation lulled and around, the sounds of a waking encampment – the muted clatter of the morning meal; the quiet stagger of men not quite awake; hushed voices – impeded thought. It really wasn't any different from any of the other days since they had come to Gullen for the second time. It just felt different to Gargol. Suddenly he turned to Senn, "I want every man alert and at his post as soon as possible."

"Sir! We are to attack then?"

"Not for an attack," Gargol paused, searching for a good reason, "It will serve as good practice – the men are lazy – see how they stumble about and play."

"You are right, Sir! It will be done immediately!"

Senn ran off and sparked a chain reaction of frenzied activity which spread rapidly through the Baeth army. The spectacle pleased Gargol. He watched intently as, in the slowly clearing mists, leaders whipped up their men; eating was truncated; pleasantries ignored; orders snapped; weapons examined, cleaned and donned. None questioned. Gargol, it was rumoured thought they had turned soft – like children in the warm sun. It was also rumoured that there might be punishment afoot and punishment in the Baeth army was to be avoided – it was too nice a morning to contemplate death – especially with victory in sight!

But they had not lost any skill in the waiting; they were ready – perhaps faster than ever before – keen fighting men, well-trained and still in the peak of condition. Senn rode up to him.

"The men are ready to fight, Sir."

"You have done well." Gargol beamed as he surveyed the bristling might of the Baeth hordes which he commanded.

So it was that whim, 'feeling' or intuition had readied perhaps the greatest fighting force ever to be seen in Endworld and just then, the attack came – but not from Gullen.

Clearly, in the distance and dimly audible now, could be seen a host in grey thudding down the Westway toward the besieged city. The eyes of the hushed army turned to watch their approach – marvelling inwardly at the good fortune of their mobilisation. Gullen too watched and some of its men withered at the sight. Gargol was curious – and arrogant with his timely readiness. He was also quick to notice that he outnumbered them hundreds to one and that they didn't look like Southlanders, in fact, as they drew nearer, they did not seem to be any one kind of man – a rabble. Gargol chuckled inwardly, then addressed Senn and the lesser leaders ranged behind him, "Only a rabble – but a speedy one. We will stop them and talk – there may be information to be had. Cover!"

At his last word a captain signalled to a group of men and they cut off from the rest of the army to flank the party of leaders and Gargol as they positioned themselves in the path of the approaching grey-dressed men. The grey men slowed their approach then halted some distance away, faces indistinct but Gargol could have sworn they were grey too.

"Approach!" said Gargol matter-of-factly, signifying a wish to parley.

"Who asks?" demanded the grey general with a sneer in his hollow voice.

"Gargol – general over all the forces of the Baeths." There was still the assurance of supremacy in the reply.

"Stand aside, weevil-cur! Our business is with the city!"

"We will not. Who are you and what is your business with Gullen?"

"Do not dare to question – stand aside!" Gargol was unnerved – surely these men could see the scores of Baeths waiting to slay them as they stood?

"Three hundred score men lie between you and your goal, state your purpose and beware of your tongues!"

"Death, then, is your choice!" And with a hollow, malevolent laugh, the Greymen came on.

In moments Baeth heads were crushed and limbs severed. Senn was cut clean in half at the waist, his legs remaining astride his bewildered animal; other Baeths cut and thrust valiantly but not a single greyman fell – as though perhaps they could not be slain. Gargol broke away back to the rest of the waiting army with those leaders who had survived, shouting commands. Behind him not one of the first group lived. Senn was gone, but with the action Gargol's mind waxed with fury.

"Five waves prepare!" He glanced back, half fearing what he would see. The Greymen were closing, driving into the very jaws of the Baeth might. Gargol's raised hand fell; five waves moved together – ten men to each of the enemy! There was relish in the thought as he whisked forward beside his men. Finish them! Strike hard, strike deep!" Baeths and Greymen melted together in bloody turmoil; cries, yells and snarls merged with the clash of steel and the dull thumps of falling Baeth bodies – hacked and bloody into the dirt. Living Baeths became fewer and fewer until only grey men remained, unchanged, then came on to finish the remaining might of the Baeth army – a horde of despairing men who could think of nought else to do but fight and die. At least they were ready…

Faces atop Gullen's walls had to watch – dreading to see what they would see before the Nethermen turned toward Gullen to finish what they had come to do…

A cry went up from the eastern wall in the quiet before the onslaught.

"A rider from the east! It is our lord!"

"The Lord of the Southlands comes!"

"Our wizard!"

"Lindarg!"

"He is here – tell the queen her lord has returned!"

The shouts from Gullen's walls were insistent, delaying the impending carnage as eyes were turned to see who came. Venain stayed his Nethermen; Gargol had no desire to begin the slaughter. Behind grey eyes Venain too wished to know who was Lord of the Southlands – for once it had been Virdil – but who now? Who was held in such great awe by so many? Wizard, they said – soon he would know – then he would strike!

Lindarg rode tall and bold between the Nethermen and the Baeth army and turned to face the grey slayers. Shielding sight of the gem from all save those fell beasts with his body, he slid the Kingstone from its pouch. The Nethermen looked only once into that crystal glare then were dispelled from the face of Endworld as if they had never been and the shadow of Lindarg's body lay large and powerful across Gullen's fields.

In his tower the light had shattered Venain's senses – but he had recoiled in time. He had seen the light of the Kingstone and lived! Never anticipating that he who was Lord of the Southlands would wield such potency, he had stayed in the Greymen to sample the power that would be used against them in order to glean from whence it came and who wielded it. His plan was thwarted and so nearly had he lost his life – perhaps only distance had saved him.

In great pain Venain rested, his doubt returning, renewed afresh; names dark in the Knavestone reverberating in his mind, loud as banshees; elusive as will'o the wisps; Deathling, Virdil; Lindarg; Lord of the Gullen. Who – or what? But soon Venain's evil smile cut lines on his countenance.

"No matter," he muttered to himself with smug surety, "When they all come to me – and they will in time – they will discover what I am and will quail before the might with which I will conquer them. There is no hope for them – there is nothing left in Endworld – or beyond – which can save them now. The gods are gone; but one remains: I am He."

The gale of Venain's laughter seared the Forest of Dorn far from Gullen, confident, depraved, it sent ripples of doom through the fabric of the balance; defying the balance itself; challenging the Law; scorning the world that had endured; despising its perpetuity. It would end. The thrill of the hunt rose in him; surging through his veins, pushing his horizons to the far corners of Endworld, swelling his ambitions and lending fire to his plans. Deftly now he took the Knavestone and began to work the final phase in the subjugation of the denizens of Endworld.

As Lindarg replaced the Kingstone in its pouch, the stark light faded and he turned to face Gargol and the Baeths.

"Gargol-" The general, quivering, unnerved, looked up into youthful eyes.

"Y-yes?"

"Today you have become nothing! Against those men ten times your number would have been slaughtered and never would a Netherman have fallen for they are dead already; worse, you would only succeed in adding to their abominable number. They are the dead of battles since the beginning of time – with them ride the fiercest of foes in life – in death their might has no equal and now there are Baeths in their midst. Surely your enemy cannot now be Gullen. Those Greymen were not of our sending but were spawned by a common enemy. Fear him."

Before there was any reply, Lindarg wheeled his steed round and entered Gullen. Gargol, his plans in ashes and head in turmoil, gazed where the Nethermen had been – as if expecting them to reappear when the wizard had gone.

Within Gullen's walls there was great jubilation.

"Virdil is well!"

"Our wizard has returned!"

"The Lord of Gullen is truly Lord of the Southlands!"

"Hail Lindarg – Lord of Gullen!"

"Greetings to the King of Endworld!"

"Bane of the Baeths!"

"Gullen has won – it is the wizard's way!"

"Venain will soon fall!"

"Finish the Baeth Yanish!"

Voices were raised in cheers and praise, filling the city with the joyous noise of relief and victory. Mixed in, Lindarg could hear the building chant: "King of Endworld… King of Endworld… King of Endworld."

He was met by Syntelle and the Liegemen who were within the city. Virlin, his son, was not in evidence. Syntelle kissed him. Never before had a Southern Queen showed so little restraint and yet none cared.

"This day," she whispered to Lindarg, "I myself will prepare a feast for my lord; this day I have waited for so long…" But she never finished. Lindarg gripped her easily as she fell away, drawing her up beside him.

"The excitement-" he apologised to the liegemen, "has been too much. More she has done for Gullen and Endworld in these times than any of us; greater have been her sacrifices – hers is the glory – and she wished to prepare a feast herself!" The liegemen smiled but they could see that Lindarg's own joy was cast with some bitterness beneath furrowed brows. Lindarg continued; "I will see to her, then we shall meet – in the guardhouse then soon!" He whisked Syntelle away to the quiet of the palace rooms.

Outside those walls the roar of the city's peoples lasted well into the day.

19

THE FINAL COUNCIL

Beyond the city it was different. The frayed Baeth army skittered gloomily, bereft of direction – yet relieved.

Gargol spoke with the leaders and advisers: one said, "We should leave and not return – it was perhaps a mistake to come to these lands."

Another, Blandick, disagreed, "No, I think we should leave with what we still have, let wizards finish their fight, then return when there are fewer foes."

"A good plan Blandick-"

"Attack now!" suggested yet another, "While they are unprepared-"

Blandick interrupted, "Then we would face the sender of the Greymen – no, that would be utter folly." Gargol did not respond to the suggestions, instead he allowed them to argue; he was confused, his mind a commotion of conflicting ideas. The debate ebbed and flowed around him...

"I say we strike now."

"Yes, with the Greymen gone we could take Gullen at least!"

"Then more Greymen would come and...?" Blandick's unspoken question quietened them.

"Fools!" Gargol suddenly blurted out, "Fools every man!" Those around him stared mutely at his outburst. Gargol was not himself again – his recent humiliation had unbalanced him many there secretly thought. Usually he reasoned things rationally but now his eyes were bright with fire: "We will join the Southfolk and their wizard!"

"Join them?" There was disbelief in the question.

"Fight with Southlanders?"

"Join our enemies?" The Baeth leaders were incredulous. Quietly Blandick breathed;

"That is madness-" then added hurriedly, "Sir."

"Nothing can be gained by that – we came to conquer!"

"Hold! Miserable Yanish!" Gargol's words sliced the air like a hot knife; "We can have everything – and more!"

He eyed them testily, confident that they would greet his plan as their own; that they would see its inescapable wisdom and marvel at its cunning, then went on, "We cannot match the might of this common enemy. You saw them; the Greymen – none of us would be speaking now but for that wizard. 'They cannot be killed,' he said; 'they are dead already', he said." Gargol laughed with evil glee. "We will join the Southlanders," he continued, "And at the end we may choose sides against the other. When the other is defeated – yes, – which side then? One foe will remain – one that we have come to know: how much easier will it be then?" The gathering watched his narrowed eyes, reading their slyness, marvelling in the cunning behind them. "We might also steal some power for ourselves if we are next to the wizard – the possibilities of treachery are endless – and I have an eye for them all! Tomorrow we will talk to their lord; tomorrow we will join them." Now the leaders nodded their assent eagerly – realising why he was their general and each of them were not. Together they had not been able to conceive such a plan; he had done so alone. It was even better than if their siege had been successful. It was a good plan – in fact the only thing to do. Obviously.

Lindarg entered the guardhouse where the liegemen waited. They had not celebrated as others – suspecting that there would be much to be discussed. Their liege had said little since his return from the tower for a second time and they had many questions. For a start the whereabouts of the other liegemen – then that second stone hidden in the pouch; the traveller – Sylee

– still unexplained – apparently blind – but not so blind that he could not see – or so it seemed. Had Gargol surrendered? What of the tower? So many questions.

But Lindarg knew their questions and they knew that they would only hear what he was ready to tell so they remained, for the moment, unspoken.

"The queen, how is she?" Durgol asked as soon as Lindarg entered.

"Very well – and I have managed to persuade her not to trouble herself with the work of cooks!" He smiled, then continued; "And how are my liegemen?"

"We who you see are well…" replied Durgol hesitantly.

"Aaah," Lindarg's brows furrowed, "They have not been with me these last few days-"

"Then where are they?" broke in Durgel anxiously.

"I do not know. When we parted they were headed for Gullen – but with little hope of breaking through the siege a second time – and even less of gaining entry to the city at night without warning – their purpose was to worry the Baeths from the rear."

"There was much commotion in the Baeth army two nights ago – we could see fires from the walls – perhaps them-" Durgel faltered, his face clouding with recollection, "And last night-" he shuddered, "Last night, the scream-"

"Scream?" Lindarg's face was dark as they tried – but failed to express the anguish of that single ululation which had been heard the length and breadth of Gullen's fields. He was silent for a while, guilt driving into him until reason returned. "They may yet arrive – let us not delve into the depths of despair and mourning for them so soon. They may still lurk behind the enemy forces ignorant of what has happened today – and perhaps it would be wise for them to stay there for the moment since none of us know what the Baeths will do next." He paused for a moment then, "But I will say this – if harm has come to them whoever is to blame shall have me to reckon with – and I would not relish his place at such a meeting!"

287

Lindarg's set face told them that the matter was closed for the present. Faran said,

"At least it is good to see you so – er – er – well, Sire." Lindarg did not miss the question even in that statement and smiled benignly,

"Well then, I will tell all."

But as usual, he didn't.

"Much has become clear to me this last while – and still there is too much I do not yet know." Faran sighed; Lindarg shot him a remonstrative glance. "To continue. Eq has passed; I have the Kingstone," he tapped the pouch, "It has the power to destroy those who behold it – but perhaps I have told you that before?"

"You have told us of the Kingstone – but not its power!" Said Durnor indignantly.

"Well – it's not important anyway…"

"Not important!" blurted Durnor, "But with that Venain is nothing!" Lindarg took the pouch and chain from around his neck and tossed it across the table to Durnor saying;

"Then take it, show it to him and see if he disappears!" Durnor shrank away from it.

"No, I cannot handle such things." Lindarg chuckled,

"Forgive me, I am being unkind," and took the stone out of its pouch. The liegemen were too slow to avoid seeing as it tumbled dully onto the wood. "See, there is no harm done."

"Then it only works against Nethermen?" ventured Durgol.

"No. It only works against those who are not forewarned. Venain now knows about it – he is forewarned – so too will be his other legions of Nethermen – therefore it is useless against him."

"But you could have dispersed the Nethermen without it – by using sorcery – you have told us that before…" But Durnor interrupted Durgel,

"You chose to use it then?"

"Exactly!"

"Knowing that afterwards it would be worthless?"

"Yes, yes – you begin to see I think?" They thought a while and Durnor said;

"No, we don't."

"I used a power he did not expect – so its wielder was not plain to him – he is still not sure that I am Virdil and have Virdil's powers-"

"He is." They whirled round to see who spoke from the doorway – the voice familiar,

"Andur!" There was a question in Durnor's cry as they noticed the dried blood and the lines of torment which creased his face and clouded his visage. Karil was with him and between them the limp and bleeding form of Turg. With difficulty, Andur spoke, his voice full of sadness,

"Eisdan is dead. We have come to warn you Sire before seeking succour for our wounded bodies and minds."

Lindarg's face puckered with fury.

"What – has – been – done?" he raged, his anger growing like a fire within him.

"Venain forced Gargol... Venain was in control; Turg-" Andur broke off suddenly and wept, struggling to support the still unconscious Turg. "Turg was – captured – and they found us-" was all he finally managed to say, then, "We will return when Turg has been placed with the healers. Eisdan's story must be told – and Turg's also." Abruptly they left the doorway struggling with the draped body of Turg. Lindarg and the other liegemen stared after them, too dumbfounded and grief-stricken to help, smote by the oppressive weight of the evil tidings. Lindarg forced his ire to subside, his mind raced; Venain's evil was taking shape all around him: first Turg, now Gargol and other Baeth leaders, probably Andur and Karil as well – would there be no-one he could trust in the end?

After a long silence, Lindarg spoke at last, his voice calmer now; deep and determined.

"Then there is no more time to search for things of power. Perhaps I would never feel ready to face him again but he forces our hand and we have no choice but to respond. We must meet him and crush him before he grows further." But Lindarg's voice lacked confidence, its challenge ringing hollowly against the guardhouse stone.

Sensing their despondency, Lindarg steered thoughts and conversation to other matters.

"If you were Gargol," he asked them generally, "What would you do now?"

"There maybe we can help – ordinary men we understand – as least partly," answered Faran, "I would talk and look for a bargain of some kind-"

"I think he will leave and come back later," suggested Durgol. They argued.

"Well, have you decided my liegemen?"

"We think he will try to strike a bargain, then if he doesn't succeed, hope he will be allowed to leave – secretly planning to return." Durnor spoke for them. They nodded their agreement then looked questioningly at Lindarg.

"I don't think he will do any of those – but we shall wait and see."

Carefully then, Lindarg told something of his last visit to the tower; the passing of Eq and Graggan and the exploits of the other liegemen near the Plain of the Great Stone. He told them too that Turg had been named to Venain and what that meant; that he suspected that Andur and Karil might have been named too… and on into the night. There were though, many things he purposely did not tell them such as the formation of an Equil or that he now knew how to turn the fire of Eq – realising the wisdom of silence and the counsel of the mute. Much the captured liegemen might have disclosed – had they known; he did not doubt that however resolute they might be, Venain would wrest every ounce of truth from them.

At length, when Lindarg had finished, they were nearly sated – but not quite, Durnor said, "The traveller who came when you were-" he searched for the right word, "'ill'. He said he was blind and yet could lose us in this city – strange to him, he talked long with the queen and ate peculiar foods brought to him by an old hag-" Lindarg face had a faraway look as he said quietly,

"Aaah, Endworld itself stirs..." He snapped out of his reverie. "Did I ever mention one called Sylee?"

"Yes but you never explained..."

"Some other time then, now we must rouse ourselves and our forces – the days ahead are likely to be full..."

The next day Gargol came. With him were Blandick and Purra and behind them trudged two advisers as they walked slowly to the north gate of Gullen. Before the portal they stopped; Gargol stepped forward.

"We would speak with the Lord of the City." His voice flat; toneless.

"Do you bear arms?" came the warden's challenge from above the gate.

"We bear no arms this day, we have come to exchange words," then he added, "My men have no stomach for sorcery."

"Enter then and receive your escort, the council awaits you."

In the central place the council was already begun; Lindarg spoke.

"Elders and wise of Gullen, my Queen, leaders and liegemen, we are in great danger – though safe for the moment within these walls. Venain – the final enemy of our lands possesses a sorcerous stone – brother it is to the stone of your queen – yet more sinister its power. With it he can see and hear us through the eyes and ears of another and control them, forcing them to speak his own words and counsel. He needs only to name that person into the stone. Gargol has been so named – Turg also-" The intake of breaths was audible in the chamber and Turg squirmed as many eyes sought his, a question in each one but Lindarg went on. "Already he has worked in Gargol's mind and undoubtedly through him will seek to further his own ends. Mark well that all we say may become known to our greatest foe. Guard your words; name no-one save by title."

Lianor spoke then. "Why then is Turg here if he cannot be trusted?"

Lindarg's reply was sharp. "He can be trusted – when himself. Gargol will be here also – is it not he we are to receive? Perhaps even now he enters the city and comes this way – what difference does Venain's choice of name make?"

"Can you not deflect Venain's power – is there nothing in the House of Virdil to help?" echoed Farg.

"There is not the time to search such places for such things – and care the names you name – even now." Lindarg looked across at Turg apologetically.

The liegeman struggled painfully in his bandages to stand saying; "I will leave the hall – there is little for me to contribute anyway-"

"No Turg!" The queen was adamant. "Gullen will not turn you aside for what has been done to you. Be seated – you have earned your place in full."

Lindarg continued. "I have not been idle during these seasons of Gullen's adversity – I bear the Kingstone of the three remaining stones of the gods; I have sought and found wisdom the length and breadth of the lands – and have found much." He hesitated, not wishing to raise hopes of a sure victory, yet fearing to reveal any hint of despair; he recognised the knife edge upon which the council, the Southlands – and Endworld itself was poised. Venain would learn what was said today – expecting to learn nothing; he, Lindarg must see to it that Venain was vindicated – yet Gullen deserved more; there was much the peoples of the city should know before deliberating its future course; somewhere between these extremes lay the narrow way of concealment and revelation along which he must guide this final gathering.

At last he resumed. "There is hope – but there are risks and in the end it may be that to meet our enemy would be to enter his set trap."

A hushed murmur spread through the council. A voice was raised. "How will you destroy him – I hear he has grown since you last met?"

The Lorist did not guard his words; his observation was both pointed and pertinent and it plunged the council into silence. Lindarg glared at the man, aware instantly of all the implications behind the Lorist's question and statement.

"Yes, Lorist, I have met him before and failed, and yes, he has grown – his evil reaching further from his stronghold in Dorn by the day. The mighty forest itself retreats in the face of his despite; he has penetrated into our midst turning friend and foe alike against us – nor will he diminish his works as we speak. Even as I answer you his plans will advance, overwhelming our endeavours to thwart them – and yes, Lorist, I may fail once more – indeed it may be utter folly to oppose him – yet I shall. And answer I shall – and in full. Also I, if no other, will challenge him and if in failure, will at least have tried to avert the chasm of darkness into which the evil sorcerer will draw the lands we love. Here is your answer Lorist, name me!" Syntelle drew her breath; her face displaying that she feared the contention between the two men – but she said nothing.

"Y-you are Virdil – it is well known-"

"How can this be? If Virdil failed, do you think Venain let him go free? And what of Virdil's vow? He did not succeed – death was his only escape. Also, Lorist, I recall your voice raised at my coming to Gullen – evidently you did not recognise me as Virdil then."

"True, there is no physical resemblance; equally it is true that I cannot explain your assertions – but that does not prove their felicity." They faced each other squarely; the Lorist – his duty clear to him – awaiting Lindarg's response.

"No I am not Virdil – he is gone – nor am I Lindarg-" he drew himself up, swelling his frame as his voice, "I am the Deathling: 'the first time it is that one such has roamed free in Endworld'; I have no name – though I exist before you born of my parents; I

293

am the undoing of our enemy's deeds set by him long ago when the Law was broken and the Lore turned into retreat. I am unable to deny myself the destiny which could spell my doom – the evil one and I are entwined in conflict as surely and inextricably as darkness and light. Sooner or later we must meet and one – or both – of us must fall-" Farg cut through Lindarg's oratory;

"All we ask, Lord, is how you – or we – can prevail."

"The answer to that is simple: I do not know."

"But surely you have some ideas," Farg insisted.

"Yes-" Lindarg purposely left his answer unfinished.

"But you do not wish to reveal them," Farg finished for him.

"Perhaps so."

Thus he had given them hope – but not false hopes; he had responded to their questions and doubts without revealing all the answers – if indeed there were any, but most of all, Venain would hear what he expected to hear – with a few trifles to keep him guessing.

A sudden hush descended upon the gathering. Gargol was at the threshold.

"The Baeth general, Gargol." announced the door guard crisply. As one the council rose following the queen's lead, protocol was to be observed for the occasion of Gargol's presence.

"Be welcome and seated," said Lindarg, waving his hand toward the waiting benches and inviting Venain to be present at the final council of Gullen. Lindarg remained standing; "The people of Gullen are proud to receive so great a general of the Baeths. We salute you and will hear your words." Gargol now rose as regally as he might in the circumstances of the occasion.

"We have seen the sorcerous power of our common enemy and have decided. Baeths and Southlanders will meet him side-by-side. Only together may we prevail." Lindarg made to rise after the short statement was at an end, but the queen stayed him and stood herself.

"Though I and many Southfolk suffered much at the hands of your kind in their mines, we harbour no grudge against the

Baeth peoples and their warriors. I too welcome and treasure your offer of aid-" Gargol bowed low.

"The Southern Queen is as gracious and forgiving as she is beautiful. I regret that we have not yet been properly introduced – that I might treasure her memory in name when I return finally to the Baeth lands." Now it was Lindarg's turn to draw his breath. Syntelle laid a reassuring hand on his arm but whatever she was about to say was interrupted by the Lorist.

"It is tradition, Baeth general, that the Southern Queen is not named – it has been so since our forbears-"

"-Then it is a shame." cut in Gargol indignantly, "One of such beauty should not be so deprived – her name should bespeak the shimmer of clear water and the sifter of rustling leaves. Her beauty surpasses both."

"I thank you, Gargol for your kind words and courtesy, I had not anticipated that so great a leader of warriors would possess a tongue of silver – forgive me." Syntelle returned his bow – a gesture which the Southern Queen had never before afforded a guest of the city and before comment could be passed on her rashness, she turned to the Lorist.

"And I thank you, Lorist, for reminding the council of our traditions lest in these fraught times we forget."

Breathing a sigh of relief, Lindarg rose once more: the way ahead – though not its outcome – clear to him at last.

"The Gullen lands cannot hope to support so many even for a few days – which leaves our combined forces but one choice – we must face together the peril which resides in Dorn. Tomorrow we shall depart to challenge that foulness in the west."

In the fateful silence that followed, no voice was raised against him but Lindarg was loathe to enter hastily into the trap which Venain had so surely set; loathe to test the providence that had brought him thus far; fearful of leading the throngs of Endworld to an untimely end beneath the western sun.

20

DARKNESS IN DORN

Once the Westway into the mighty Forest of Dorn had been a great highway traversing Endworld. In those days it had joined the Eastway passing far into the east over those lands that were once forested hills, through the mountains to a distant sea but long since that forest had become Thae and the way fallen into disuse. Now it was Yirfurnelle and with each passing Starseason its grandeur increased enriching Endworld. But this was far behind them and unseen. Today the Forest of Dorn's margin was alive with the passing of the hordes of the Southlands as the way was forged anew. Scores wide, the column was a day long as it entered the forest.

At its head rode the Southern Queen and the Lord of the Southlands who was Lindarg, their wizard. Behind them, Gargol, Blandick & Purra – then the line of Gullen generals with the liegemen. With them too were the other Southland generals including Frind, Lianor, Danig & Raydel. They were followed by the lesser leaders of the Baeths – each with their charge of men – then those of Gullen; the mustered Southlanders and their corporals. These fighting men were trailed by stores, cooks, camp attendants, counsellors, the wise, weapons and all the other equipment that was needed to support the greatest offensive that had ever been launched in the known history of Endworld.

Venain was gleeful; he had never called so many – and never so surely had they come: sorcerer, learned and wise; valiant and cowardly; great and small: the hosts of the world to witness for themselves his might and to pay first homage to their god and

296

master; together. He felt he could already hear the roar of their massed praise reverberating across the lands and back.

"They must bring powers – or they are fools!" He chuckled to himself, "I will take those too – willingly they will give all to me – poor fools indeed – but they may yet provide good sport!"

Woodmen, once alerted to the cause, joined the marching throngs – forming their own sections – so those at the rear were forced to move more slowly to give them space. Word passed quickly to the Great Dome and those who did not join worked day and night to prepare and provide for the feasts of the road. Baeths and Southfolk alike were reckoned guests in these times.

Little more than a day after the departure of the musters for Dorn – before even its van reached the eaves of the western forest, the quiet of the resting, dwindled Gullen was disturbed by the clamour of impatient steeds approaching from the east. The Three Wild Men, having finally torn themselves free from the enchantments of the southern wastes and the Old South Road, chanced, finally, upon their goal.

Kel wondered at the city's deserted air as they slowed to the east gate, discerning no guards at the walls and a mere two old men, bent and wizened, teetered above the gate.

"Open the portal, old man – lest it be put to the torch – and you with it!" Kel held his sword aloft in challenge, adding vitriol to his words but one of the old men smiled,

"What is it you warriors seek?"

"We will take it! Open the gate!"

"There are no riches here which your kind would understand; no gold, gems or weapons. The city lies empty and wasted. Leave us."

"Let them in," said the other, "We could use youthful limbs and strength."

The ponderous gate gaped wide and the Wild Three blazed into Gullen, swords whirling to the demonic laugh of the madman. With sight of the city their charge withered as they surveyed what they had come so far to plunder. Women darted hither and thither; children stopped their games to stare; hunger was etched into every face that was turned to them; old men with a lifetime of memories rested quiet, contemplating death with equanimity – they held no fear of it. Womenfolk, curious, came near; one said to Kel, "We have little food – but what we have is yours, come – does a warrior wish to eat – only a meagre stew-?"

"Yes." Kel felt the hunger of days twisting his stomach as he replied. Briskly she led him to a stone building.

The home was simple and comfortable, the stew hot and plentiful, the bread heavy, satisfying. The girl who served him caught Kel's eye – a hint was set for him in her own and he wondered at its meaning. When he had eaten his fill the same girl brought hot water and as he rested, bathed hoary feet and Kel relaxed as a sensuous warmth rose from them spreading pleasantly through his veins. Lovingly, gently, the girl continued; her mother brought a drink; he felt his presence viewed with awe and reverence; the girl excited him, the warmth relaxed him. The urge to reach out and take the girl brutally gnawed within him but the tender warmth was restraining and instead his gnarled hand extended into her cascading dark hair, surprising to feel its softness through his rough skin. The girl drew closer, her smooth arms brushing against his legs. He could sense she was not afraid of him – yet willingly she ministered to him, the gleam in her eye remaining. The mother lit a lamp then busied herself elsewhere in the dwelling.

Soon the girl was tying soft skin sandals round his feet – retaining their warm glow, then she moved to the corner of the room where the fire glimmered weakly. Feebly she tried to revive it but Kel saw that the wood was uncut and unwieldy for the fitful embers. Furtively the girl blew at them – aware that Dundellin nights could be cold on the plains. In despair she removed her Yanish skin cloak and carefully wrapped it around Kel's shoulders to ward off the evening chill. He noticed the shiver which she had tried to conceal when her delicately coloured skin – covered only by a short, sleeveless tunic now – met the chilling air. He marvelled that she remained undeterred – seeming to enjoy the sacrifice as if he were a baby to be coddled – and he could now well see that she had reached full womanhood.

Somewhere out in the city Kel heard the madman's laugh, suddenly softer somehow in the still evening; he heard the wind eddying beyond the door in the way between the dwellings.

Then the girl turned to him, her face strangely content, "Rest, warrior, while I see to the fire." He made to answer her but lithely she whirled, opening the door and he watched as she stole herself against the cold wind on the threshold, the tunic blown onto her dimly-lit form, then she was gone into the night. Shortly she returned, struggling beneath the weight of firewood which chafed her arms – yet carefully she crouched, stowing it neatly in the fire alcove; adding some to the embers and as the flames rose at last she knelt in their glow, gently rubbing warmth back to her limbs but taking care not to shield its radiance from Kel. Next she laid out skins in the fire's glow. "You will sleep here tonight." It was both a statement and question as she removed covers from her own sleeping place to add to the bed she had prepared for her warrior.

He noticed her small, perfectly-formed bare feet on the stone of the floor – then it occurred to him that he had not seen her eat. His eyes were fixed upon her; new emotions building beneath his harsh exterior; delicate, sensitive feelings were creeping upon him. He felt himself staring at her almost disbelievingly in the fire's brightening light; now he could make out where the firewood had dirtied her tunic; the chafe-marks an her arms; she had gone hungry for him; he wore her sandals and cloak; she had washed him; warmed him and served him; unceasingly she had laboured for him because she had wanted to – wanted to please him.

Kel found himself unable to control emotions new to him; he pitied her – yet knew none was beholden; he was filled with admiration and respect for her – yet she was just a girl, weak and helpless. No – neither of those – her strengths were different and no less keen than the skills of a warrior. Desire too held some sway in the turmoil, its violence tempered; the warrior-crust was melting like snow in the Astellin Sun.

She turned to him and came nearer, the soft curves of her thighs and calves picked out by the firelight; then she was kneeling by his feet, the warm dark pools of her eyes gazing into his, setting the warrior finally to flight. Softly she said; "Tell me of your adventures, the lands you have ridden, the deeds you have done," but Kel was too ashamed and instead, gently – so gently, leaned forward, drew her close and eased the cloak around her, cradling her into the warmth of his embrace.

In the peaceful warmth of the night Kel whispered, "What are you called little one?"

"Astellina."

"It is a lovely name," mused Kel, "Do you know what it means?"

"No," she whispered back.

"One day I will show you…"

Thus did the Three Wild Men discover riches beyond their wildest dreams in the stricken city; abrogating the despite of their creation; yet none of them espied so much as a glimmer of gold.

On the eve of Dundellin the van of the column came to the Dome. The Woodman King met them in the soft morning green under the trees.

"Gullenqueen, you are welcome here where you have never journeyed; hard must have been the decisions which have brought you thus – yet my heart hopes they were wise and that you will tarry and be with us long."

"We thank you Forest King, the hospitality of your lands will be remembered whatever the outcome of our errand-" Syntelle never finished.

"No, it is enough that you come to face the scourge that we

cannot-" the king's voice faltered, then continued; "-To face and fight the foe from whom we have quailed again and again. Not long since he sent minions to scour the forest for men giving them gold and promising more. We were cowardly and raised not one finger nor said one word in protest. Many woodmen were lured by the metal's unseemly gleam and the wise were sick at heart. Cruel things we fear were done to those men on Castle Hill – for none returned – and still we let him have his way without reply. If you were to destroy us this day we could not expect mercy – nor would we for our craven ways."

"It is well that you raised no finger in contention against Venain – prudent even – he has grown perhaps more than you think," counselled Lindarg.

"Ah, Lord, he becomes younger – seemingly immortal…"

"That may be the least of his powers."

"Then his least is too much for woodmen. Many of my people are valiant and strong of heart; strong too in the Lore of the forest, but of sorcery we know little and have none – neither has there been any need for we are content here – nurtured and protected by the forest. Ah, but let us not talk on the threshold of our welcome; enter the Dome; refresh yourselves, rest your weariness and eat – there is time yet for talk."

"But little enough that may be," murmured Lindarg. With a worried grimace at Lindarg's words, the Forest King wheeled round and the first-come of the Southland might entered the Dome.

Lindarg knew of the Dome but its reality was more awesome than those distant memories. Each of the party drew breath in astonishment as their gazes took in the enormity which lay before them, around them and above them. They were comforted by the quiet, cheery warmth of the place; saw the distant sides of trunks; the lofty ceiling of boughs and foliage far above; the air was sweet; small voices of many people thrummed unobtrusively; here and there were exchanges, meetings, family feasts and celebrations; there were places to be alone, to think and mourn; places to drink, sing and frolic; to game and fight; to bargain and tell stories. The Forest King said, "This place belongs to every man. It is the heart of our realm; each person is free to use it; to come and go at leisure; to use what is here for whatever purpose he or she wishes. So precious is this place in woodman's hearts that it is an honour to tend and clean it; a privilege to sojourn within its healing bosom. It is to us as perhaps Gullen is to you – yet more so – since it is alive and its roots thrive with the vitality of the very earth."

Lindarg was aware of the king's voice but the words were lost to him. He felt etherial as he cast round with glazed, staring eyes, gorging himself on the spirit of living entity that was the Dome and the forest of which it was an inextricable part, aware that it plucked at something buried deep within him...

"Lindarg..." He heard the Syntelle's voice clearly, his reverie melting away with the sound, returning him to a breathless reality. "Lindarg, what is it?"

"I–I am alright... Perhaps my woodman past – the atmosphere of this place..." Syntelle nodded sympathetically; Endyne stared at him;

"Woodman past?" The tone betrayed his astonishment.

"It is true – and too long a story to tell-" Lindarg broke off as if he were about to say more but thought better of it. The king did not press him turning instead to Gargol, saying in a quiet voice,

"A welcome to the Baeth people also – our guests equally as those of the Southlands." Gargol shuffled uncomfortably, searching within himself for adequate words.

"We have come to meet an enemy. If he is the enemy of the woodmen too, then so be it: our fight is shared."

Gargol's lips were tight as he spoke but Endyne smiled and replied, "There is room for Baeths also in Endworld, come, let us share our stories and what happiness we can – while it lasts. Let us drink to Endworld; let us dare to envisage freedom from the despite of the one on Castle Hill."

But that night the dreamy sojourn in the forest's heart was

302

shattered by the evil that was nearer now as the darkness of treachery came upon them. The news was brought down the column from where it still laboured toward the Dome.

"Sire!" Although the cry was dampened in the Dome, its urgency rang clear. Lindarg saw the runner at the entrance, those there read the agony in the shout; the man continued between gasping breaths, "Many Westfolk lie slain... Baeths too. Baeths attacked – perhaps those remaining still fight-"

Gargol suddenly exploded. "No Baeth would raise a sword except by my order. I have given no such orders! This is not the truth! I will not be insulted!" Lindarg calmed him with gestures.

"It cannot be said at this stage who is to blame for treachery which may strike us, Venain will seek to turn us as we draw near."

"How can he-" Gargol spluttered, "possibly affect us here? Are you accusing Baeths of being spies? We had never heard of this Venain!" Gargol stormed from the table spilling drinks with the violence of his movement – then stopped suddenly, turning back to Lindarg. "Or are you saying we fight for him – or perhaps ourselves?" His tone was menacing now.

"We do not say that," stated the queen flatly.

Then Lindarg reasoned; "Remember the Greymen Gargol? They could have finished your whole army on Gullen's fields that day; Venain did not know that I would come – could not know that for all his powers – and there is no other than I could have saved you. No, he is no ally of yours, nor you his. This night's evil is his doing – he has the power and it will wax with every step we take toward him."

"Lindarg speaks wise words," observed Endyne. "Maybe he has united you to divide you for his own ends."

"You know him well then," commented Lindarg, then bellowed commands; "liegemen, Frind, Lianor, Farg – to your weapons! There can be no fighting among ourselves, we must end it." Then to Gargol; "Accompany us, there must not be mistrust between us."

But as they sped from the Dome the skirmish was kindling

afresh with those who marched behind coming upon the dead of it – the bodies they discovered serving only to fuel new disputes for there were both Southlanders and Baethfolk among the dead. Those in the column ahead of the trouble were ever leaving it further and further behind – heedless of what transpired in their wake – so the gap widened.

General Raemel had seized his chance in this chaos and had led his twenty-five score men north from the column like a thief in the night, then turned east and inexorably south to a stricken Gullen which lay helpless, full of women, children and the old. It would easily fall to their number.

It was early morning when Raemel returned to a sleeping Gullen. He was pleased with his plan – a simple one – for gain alone. Within the strict confines of the Baeth army he had gained little; similarly, his division had been given it seemed, all the menial, non-fighting tasks of the Baeth offensive. They had done no raids, seen no plunder, glory, adventure or travel; no, they had been the ones who had run the mines of war. For years they had breathed the red dust and suffered the hard cold of those mines; the boredom of near exile in the mountains with only useless, tiresome slaves for company. Nor had they ever been forgiven for their failure when hundreds of slaves had escaped and ruined half a division as they went, victorious, back to the Southlands from whence many of them had been snatched. After that, Raemel and his men had been sentenced to those mines just as surely as the slaves themselves. He and his men had learned to bear this burden and the grudge had cut deep over the seasons. Now he, Raemel, would right that wrong for himself and for his men; it was to be a straight cut of the plunder – all men equal. Then they would disband, finding their own ways back to Baeth – or wherever they wished to go. None would be beholden to any other, nor to their kind who had so ill-used him; they would take the recognition for their important, largely unrecognised part in this war – from Gullen – by force. Raemel and his men all knew that such an opportunity might only present itself once in a lifetime; Raemel knew that they would fight – for self gain – as never before.

They halted before the vast gate of the city in the cool, quiet dawn. The gate, they knew had been broken once – the walls still charred from the flames – the hurriedly-built replacement would be little problem for a score of men and a small ram.

There was to be no delay; the ram trundled behind them – constructed before they had left the forest.

"We will strike now." Raemel turned to his men. "They will die before they are properly awake – we meet in the central place and from there the plunder seals our lips as we go our ways; let there be trust between us that will not be broken even in the face of death!"

Grim-faced, his men drew swords in salute – their ring searing the morning stillness. Raemel's hand waved forward and the attack was begun.

The ram never reached the gate, for long before its cart gained speed, the thrust was distracted by a thunderous voice from above the gate.

"Hold!" The voice which challenged them was commanding; edifying; could not be ignored; demanded to be heard – and heard it was – the charge faltered. Raemel's raised hand halted the attack; a silence fell over his men. A warrior's voice it had been – that Raemel knew; it resounded with pride, challenge and confidence – but more important, none spoke to so many in such a manner without good reason. Raemel wanted to know what that good reason might be before risking the lives of his men – knowledge might even facilitate the task. The one word still hung in the air.

"Who defends?"

"Woodmen do." Momentarily the statement confused Raemel and he puzzled over its meaning, then replied with contempt ill-concealed in his voice;

"Since when?"

"Two days only have passed since we took Gullen."

"Took it?"

"The city is ours – leave while you may!"

Raemel was astounded. "Woodmen!" He spat in the dirt, "Surrender the city to us – or we take it and you die!" He was sure that some warrior left within Gullen was bluffing. Turning to his men he said, "Break the gate – we will have that man's tongue!"

But the voice boomed out again. "There is no need to break the gates, Baeths. If you wish to die we do not wish to make it difficult for you." Speechless, Raemel watched as the gates creaked open. Beyond the opening there was nothing to be seen save the street behind; no men – not even one man – could be discerned. Then the voice boomed again; "Take Gullen Baeths – you only have to walk in…"

A demonic laugh shivered the air, unnerving Raemel's men; they trembled – surely that laugh was not from a human source. Raemel himself shuddered – could a wizard's power be left behind when the wizard himself had gone? Raemel cursed his lack of knowledge, he was confused; caught unawares; was it a bluff – desperate and final – or not? Greymen perhaps? Those he had seen and they could justifiably challenge him – he and his men would perish. But then Greymen were of Venain and they would be readying for a battle far to the west – or had they been put here – had Venain, about whom Raemel knew lamentably little, fled from his castle and entered Gullen while a lifeless castle in Dorn was ravaged and searched? Could Venain have been so clever and fleet? The confusion in his mind increased; his men were restless: there was a choice to make – but how could he make it not knowing things?

Foolish and over-adventurous Raemel might have been but he was no coward. At a command his men advanced toward the open gate. With them still came the ram, but more slowly – the gate might be shut at the last minute – affording those inside a momentary but precious, advantage. The possibilities ran through Raemel's mind as the pulse quickened in his temple. The gate neared; still there was no sign of what fate – if any – awaited them.

Three men appeared suddenly in the gateway; barring it with their stance. One of them laughed a withering, scornful laugh which told of death; that caused hackles to rise and fed panic into veins, collapsing the will of men. From this distance Raemel saw wild eyes roll skywards in evil glee; he grimaced.

"A madman". The three heard him across the remaining distance and the larger one threw back his head revealing grizzly features, muscled, bearded and hard with two swords drawn.

"And I am Dranubinal!"

"Kel!" came the single word from the third slender man – his sword long and slick, burnished in the morning sun. Something about these men sounded alarm in Raemel's mind and he turned to a group of men.

"Would you be the first to cross the threshold of the greatest Southland City?" He questioned the fifteen fighters. These were not his men but some who had elected to join their sortie. The eyes of Raemel's men were on them and he knew they could not refuse, he knew too that they, as he, did not wish to test the ground.

"We will do this to return your favour Raemel – but when we have slain these three – and those others that lie in wait – so that you may walk unchallenged into the city, take care of those of us that remain…" The threat was not veiled; Raemel had expected it; he had forced their hand giving them little choice. Any man would show rancour – particularly a warrior – but Raemel ignored it.

"Luck to you. Think not that we would stand by while you are slaughtered; we have come to take Gullen – you do us a preliminary service which will not go unrewarded."

The fifteen men advanced on the Wild Three who were ranged unmoving and unmoved across the entrance to Gullen. Only six men could approach them at a time between the gate walls – and have room to fight. Six attacked – and six fell – so swiftly that Raemel did not see how it had happened – yet they lay dead. Six in an instant. Raemel was sickened. The remaining nine thrust forward at a stroke and as they closed on the three the madman's laugh threw them into terrified confusion as his eyes lolled wide and the sound echoed across the fields. Kel and Dranubinal strode eagerly into their midst, scything men two or three at a stroke, then they too lay in the dust. Dranubinal bellowed aggression, Raemel recognised the voice as that which had challenged them at first.

"Come worthless chaff," he baited them, "We will take your puny army; send them to us – to their miserable deaths at the gates of our city. Ha! Come feel our cold steel burn into your flesh!" They laughed – even Kel allowed himself a fateful chuckle at Dranubinal's grim play on words.

"Show yourselves in the field – then we will fight!" Raemel countered. The madman laughed again and the Wild Three issued forth from the gateway.

"Finish them!" boomed Raemel's furtive cry.

The charge of Raemel's men was met with the confident assurance of victors. The battle cry of the mighty Dranubinal; the madman's rake of foul mirth and the whirling steel of Kel that far outreached any weapons of the Baeths and whose momentum was such that no one body could thwart its deadly arc.

Raemel foresaw the outcome of the fray; in the confusion and carnage he skirted the battle like an escaping Yanish and entered Gullen through the open gate. Behind him the cacophony of bloodshed reached a new pitch but nowhere in that noise were there cries of agony from Wild men. Swiftly he cast about him. One ageing man stood by the gate wheel; another above by the lever which lifted and dropped the locking beam into position. Raemel leaped up stone steps toward the man on the wheel. With a deft thrust of his blade he slew him and turning to the other a little way above him said; "You choose. When I close the gates, lock them – or die like him." He indicated the body by kicking it

308

away from the horizontal wheel over which it was slumped. The man above nodded, fear in his eyes.

Raemel strained at the wheel; slowly, ponderously the heavy gates closed and the bar fell into place, locking them. Beyond the walls the Wild Three were surrounded by a wall of dead bodies and steeds over which their attackers clambered awkwardly to an undefended death. A hundred they had felled – perhaps more – the remainder, their leader presumed killed, losing their stomach for fight, turned and left the Gullen Fields heading north and some east to scatter themselves in humiliation; to become degenerates and vagabonds of the Southlands, Dorn and Baeth; to become the fleas of a world which had refused them their imagined share of its bounty.

The Three Wild Men wheeled round and saw the gate closed. The city they had just saved had shut them out.

Inside the walls, Raemel too turned his gaze into Gullen to survey what was his. Too late he heard the hiss of air; felt the jab in his neck. The city upon which he gazed exploded in red fire and pain before his glazing eyes, but his death agony was private; silent.

Frind had taught many of Gullen's children the sport of blowing but this child had been wayward and had stolen one of the 'special' darts from a carelessly unlocked box. As he looked out of the stone doorway he realised that his dishonesty had been discharged and already the gates were opening. First through was Kel, blood-spattered and angry; yelling defiance at their betrayal; in his path waited Astellina – beaming her proudness and love – and upon her he vented his wrath, cursing her city; catching her with his open hand. But she stood her ground without protest until remorse flooded through Kel and with moist eyes, he held her gently, anger forgotten.

When the column was re-formed. Raemel and his men were presumed lost in the fight and probably scattered through the forest. There was no time to search – Lindarg would allow none for he knew the troubles that Venain would cause – and

309

the longer they took to reach Castle Hill, the more time the evil one would have to wreak havoc within the vast army. Though he now rushed toward it, Lindarg was fearfully afraid of the meeting – more so of what he feared would be the outcome – but at least he was certain that the muster of disparate peoples that he led could only be further disadvantaged by delay.

Lindarg, Gargol and the liegemen had done their best to allay the distrust and suspicions which the incident had generated but as they made their way back to the head of the march each knew that doubt remained to fester between those they had brought together. The next day it flared up anew.

The column had departed from the Dome the morning after the conflict and did not stop for more than a few hours at a time until it reached Castle Hill several days later. The last to leave the Dome – long after the first – were the Eastfolk with the men of Blandick and Purra to their rear. Lindarg had set generals at the rear of the column in an attempt to ward off further affrays. Frind, suspicious still of the Baeth intentions had decided to take the rear position of the Eastfolk leaving his second in command to lead. Blandick and Purra did not miss the meaning of Frind's gesture and neither of them liked it. In a quiet part of the Dome they talked prior to their departure. Frind, curious as to why they were not waiting behind him as the Eastfolk moved away, had sought them out – thinking that perhaps they had no intention of falling in behind – and discovered them in that quiet place; overhearing their plans.

"There are two possibilities," Blandick spoke, "We can wait here and let others deal with the enemy – these woodmen will present no threat-"

"Then what?" interrupted Purra.

"Then we wait to discover the outcome. If the Southfolk have lost – then we go back and have their city, take what we can and return to Baeth. If they win and this Venain is vanquished, perhaps most will be slain in the conflict and those that remain we can deal with as they return." Purra thought for a moment, then said, "What is the other possibility?"

"It is more risky – yet greater may be the rewards." Blandick's voice sounded sharp and evil.

"Go on-"

"We go with them. This would give us a further option – if the battle is lost we can join Venain – that we cannot do if we stay here."

"I'm not sure-" Purra reflected but did not finish as Frind challenged them his uncontrollable fury surging in his veins.

"Traitors!" Blindly, unthinking, he rushed at the two; sword drawn. Blandick rose, eyes brightly-lit.

"Kill him!" he yelled, stabbing a finger at Frind rushing toward him. Unseen Baeths melted from the trees – now Frind faced six of them and he was no swordsman. At close quarters a Baeth blade flashed in the air; a howl of anguish shocked the Dome as the steel buried itself in Frind's arm impaling it to the tree by which he uncertainly stood. Another blade entered his throat, another his stomach; blood coursed down the smooth bark and soaked into the damp earth; Frind choked on his last breath; his body slumping limply, tearing the arm free of the tree as it fell.

"Frind!" Their general's final cry had been heard by the last of the departing Eastfolk. With horror, they looked upon the scene and the manner of his death – treacherously slain in the heart of the woodmen's realm. Bloodthirsty still from the kill, Baeths rounded on these who had come too late to Frind's aid and drove at them. Poisoned teeth met their rush; missiles of death scorched into Baeth flesh. Baeth faces contorted and locked in death agonies whirled to the earth but more appeared behind the Eastfolk. Blandick and Purra had not moved, now Blandick yelled,

"These are the slayers – kill them!" The score of Eastfolk turned to face the new threat; arrows tore into them, those who could returned with deadly teeth, blowing wildly. Cries of agony chilled the Dome, defiling it with evil and blood; woodmen, unarmed, powerless to intercede, were sickened by the debacle. The final Eastlander stood to meet his end, dart-tube poised, an arrow raking cramps through his abdomen. A Baeth lunged; as the blade descended, the dart flew. With dying eyes, the Eastlander drew satisfaction from the truth of its flight. He and his assailant died together.

"Come!" Shouted Blandick, "Now we are rid of these traitors we can re-join the march. Death to Venain!"

"Death to Venain!" echoed his men, leaving the blood and the bodies to the woodmen and witnesses unsure of the truth.

"Well spoken, Blandick!" murmured Purra admiringly, "I take it we now follow the second plan?" Blandick smiled,

"We do."

"And with our fealty beyond reproach after eliminating those traitors!"

"Indeed so."

"It is a good plan."

"Of course."

By the time the devastating news of the defilement of the Dome and the death of Frind reached Lindarg, others too had been plotting. Farg and Banor had ever hated the Baeths. To both it was inconceivable that they could be trusted and the uniting of the two forces had thrown them closer together but apart from the other Gullen generals and their lord. They were seen conversing together in low tones – but what was said remained between them.

The news brought sorrow and despair in equal measures to Lindarg, the liegemen and the Gullen generals. Frind had been a good man, well respected, a friend and a fellow to them all. Lindarg recalled the man's harsh awakening to the troubles of Endworld on that dim Coldseason dawn so long ago and could not believe the story of Frind's treachery which came to them. As they travelled, silently now, their thoughts were turned inward, each mourning in his own way the death of one so good and true. Behind them in the Dome Syntelle too was devastated by the news. And while they brooded thus, Venain roamed and plotted freely, unopposed among the hosts of Endworld whom he so surely drew unto himself.

The nearer they drew the more conscious Lindarg became of the growing dissent and the more certain that neither he nor the Gullen or Baeth generals would be able to control their armies for long. He brooded on the ease with which Venain's will would sally through them, ripping order asunder, thwarting both direction and purpose. He knew also that an assault on Venain's stronghold by all the peoples of the world would more than likely be to no avail; this might was mere show. Doubtless, he reflected, Venain was at this moment relishing the sport which these legions of men promised him. Lindarg was glad that he had finally persuaded Syntelle to remain with the Forest King – she might at least be safe for a while.

At last the castle was before them and on the lower slopes below it – stretching far back into the Great Forest itself – Baeths, Gulleners and Southfolk assembled ready for the final assault. Now he, Lindarg, must decide how to fight the battle; he must send thousands of good men to their deaths – or worse if they were taken alive.

Facing his doubt, he knew he could not do it.

21

THE MIGHT OF THE
SOUTHLANDS IS SUNDERED

The subdued hum of the might of Southlands permeated the whole forest; the dull clang of cooking pots, crackle of fires and the murmur of hushed voices; nerves were taut, soon the battle would commence. None had any notion of the plan, all were gathered in a fatalistic hope, knowing that whatever the outcome, this confrontation was inevitable.

A unit of Northfolk were placed at the forest's edge; from their position the gentle slope of Castle Hill drew the eyes over the open grassland, bare of trees and shrubs – a green desert in the deeper verdure of the forest – men on that slope would be exposed and defenceless. The castle itself was stark above the rise, though a distance from the forest margin; its sharpened stones clearly discernible, angular, displeasing, anathema against the soft slope; its walls high, dark and curving were overhung at their tops with the down pointing spears of rock. Above these the ramparts were smooth and devoid of life or threat – a gesture of contempt that was well marked by those who were gathered to bring about the downfall of that fell keep.

A tapering triangular tower thrust skyward from the castle's centre, occasionally at night a single flickering light glowed in its heights; nights when the surrounding army was lost in darkness. The corners of the tower screamed at the roundness of the walls; its pointed summit threatening to pierce the scudding clouds. Nothing more than this could be seen – hidden beyond the walls

– and besides the lonely light, neither sound nor movement bespoke of life within.

Night and day the castle cast an eerie shadow over the slopes on all sides, a shadow which failed to change with the movement of the sun; an immovable, tangible dimness, within it the omnipresent chill of fear and the frames from which gaunt, formless shapes – almost human – still hung like wizened, blackened sticks – their origin and nature a cause for grim speculation – but without answers. Onlookers fancied they saw greyer shadows among them in that dim light.

"The sooner the better – I can't see why there should be all this waiting around – this forest gives me the creeps." The leader among the group took the man's point:

"Our lord must have good reason for waiting."

"Some disagree with him I hear, they say the wasted time is allowing him-" The man broke off to glance defiantly at the distant keep; "All the time he needs to ready his defences. The delay is madness."

"Menil talks sense – and so do those others!" cut in another of the group looking up from the meat he was hungrily tearing at, "We are just using up our supplies, soon we will have to attack – and he knows it!" The man held his hot meat aloft, "This was the last piece," he announced to emphasise his point.

"Care what you say man," cautioned the leader, "lest your body forsake its need for food – meat or otherwise!" The man quieted, looking at his meat as if he were seeing it for the first time and the leader continued. "Do any of you greenlings know what happened the last time Southlanders marched this way not so long ago?" None replied, their inexperience of battles and history laid bare. Their leader gloated over his effective insult, then added in the silence; "We lost." The silence deepened. "Surprise was our essence then – yes – surprise; I am told that our army charged for the whole of the last league with the great wizard at their head."

"That is the way to enter battle!" one of the group exclaimed, the ferocity of frustration in his tone.

"We lost," reminded the leader emphatically, "because we did not know his strength. Our might was snuffed out like a candle in moments." He paused for an instant to ensure that his message had been understood, then spoke again; "They say that he roasts captives and feeds them to his minions at great feasts." This last information quelled further talk for a while, the one eating stopped and let the meat fall,

"But what do we wait for?" He asked genuinely.

"I wish I knew," replied the leader. "But I have great faith in the Lord of Gullen. He is wise and some say he knows all – and more – of what Virdil knew and has strange powers – you saw – er – know the effect of his stone on the Greymen." They nodded for one of their troop had seen them dispelled.

"If he has these powers," argued Menil, "Why doesn't he use them now – it seems he is invincible?" Faces brightened at the prospect.

"The wise know things that we do not…"

"And play their games with our lives!" The leader shot the owner of the interloping, bitter voice a sharp, deep look but the man held his gaze defiantly. "Pah to wise men and wizards we have enough men to each pluck a single stone from his castle and scatter them in the forest – and still have men left over!"

"You may yet have the chance to do that but just now I fear you wouldn't even reach the walls," responded the leader but he knew that the men could not wait much longer; fear would not let them – and they were all afraid – brave words hid nothing.

Lindarg, aware of the spreading unease, restlessness and fear – but he himself, bereft of any immediate plan, brooded miserably in a tent set apart, bitter that he was no general and with his own doubts and fears gnawing interminably.

"Sire." Durnor was at the doorway. "The men are restless and supplies are dwindling-" The voice was respectful but in the statement was a plea. Andur was with him. Lindarg turned to them with weary eyes.

"I cannot see how to proceed, liegemen; I do not know all his powers and he is in no haste to display them. How many Nethermen can he summon? How many can I dispel before my strength fails, and if it does – when will the slaughter end?"

"But we must do something, Sire-"

"It is true Andur that we cannot wait forever yet, not knowing things, how can we do otherwise?" Durnor broke in,

"Sire, I have heard that some generals plan an attack-"

"And I have heard that others are preparing to aid our foe," added Andur.

"I expected as much," replied their lord despondently, "But I am powerless to prevent it, all we can – must – do is reason with them; entreat them to rethink."

"Such approaches I fear will be spurned." Durnor said flatly.

"But they must be tried, liegemen, for it is not they who act but Venain himself dividing us and though I cannot be named he divides also my purpose and direction as surely as if he were here." Durnor looked furtive and said in a low voice;

"The Queenstone – could it aid us?" Lindarg sighed again, fingering the gem around his neck.

"And what might it show – Southlands in ruin – our slaughter?"

"But there is a chance-"

"Ask it then." whispered Lindarg alarmingly. Durnor withdrew from the proffered stone but said nothing, Andur remained motionless.

A last, despondent, the liegemen left. They must prolong the wait – knowing that they would not be able to. They sought out generals trying to give them hope of action when they had none themselves; hope of victory with no victory in sight; fealty to their lord when their own faltered. All day they laboured over the thankless task receiving no encouragement; treated as harbingers rather than fellows. By dusk the hearts of the liegemen were heavy and there were those generals who could not be found and whose men heard the liegemen's message with closed ears and silence.

But deep in the damp forest, Banor and Farg set their plan to attack the next morning. Close by were ears that did listen and later, Blandick and Purra plotted their part in the chaos which would follow in the wake of that thrust…

"So he will attack, good." Blandick smiled a vile smile. "Farg's guards are the best they have – without them they are a rabble. We shall wait and see what happens – but we must be ready!"

"It will not be easy to hide our readiness from others," observed Purra.

"True, but it must be done – it is essential that we are able to act swiftly – before others can – if the need arises. Gargol himself may wish to seize the opportunity-" But Purra interrupted.

"That has always been his intention – but he cannot be as prepared as we – while he is so near their lord."

"He is finished anyway! He cannot even control himself – let alone our armies – men will soon dessert him when they see the wisdom of our plan." Blandick's smile widened; Purra echoed it as he added;

"At the very least we lose nothing – but what we might gain…"

"Exactly!"

"It is a good plan!"

"Of course!"

All through that night the light in the tower shone brightly and more than one man was slain in the shadow of its glow – by one whom he thought he could trust. Lianor fell to a blow from Farg's sword when the Northfolk general had heard they were to attack and tried to dissuade him. Farg had seen to it too that any who might come to Lianor's aid would be outnumbered. Sure enough, those who had now lay among the dead; no eyes that had seen the deed lived – except for those of Farg's own men. Even Banor was not told.

There was fighting among Baeths too and during this

Gargol escaped death narrowly – and then only by the timely intervention of Blandick and Purra with some of their men as they further sealed their reputation beyond reproach.

"It is well," Gargol had said with relief when his would-be assassins lay dead, "that there remain yet some I can trust." Blandick and Purra had enjoyed the praise – so too had Venain.

Twice during that long dark night, grim shadows sought to kill the Lord of Gullen; both failed – but escaped. Others had plotted he same thing but lacked the courage to try. Lindarg, powerless, seeing his enemy ravaging Southfolk and Baeths alike knew that Venain had begun the devastation of the foes which had come to him and as he wept his dark, lonely grief for the world which receded with every scream, he rued the Starseasons of strife and valour which had brought the Southlands and Baeth together. The masses of the Southlands, so long in the gathering, were being wrecked in a night and the morning saw insurrection, chaos and division rife among them. Turg could not be found; the other liegemen worked frenziedly to stem the tide of battle that was forming in the grey light of dawn. Lindarg too had vanished.

Long had Venain watched the approach of the mustered Southland and Baeth armies from his tower, counting its strength, seeing its weapons and suggesting its plans. He was aware that this was not a great fighting force but mustered men – some ill-disciplined – most inexperienced. Since Gullen he had worked within it as it neared, now those forces did not worry him – who led them did – but no longer unduly. For Starseasons he had sought the Deathling, finding only fleeting glimpses which revealed little but slowly, each time he had gleaned a little more – more than enough to know his enemy and learn his powers. Shading the Knavestone for a while he gloated, cradling it like a child in his lap.

Come to him was his doubt – so long that had nagged; now all was clear; it was Lindarg. "Or am I he in reality," he mused to himself, chuckling with the irony; Deathling, Virdil

319

and Lord of Gullen – lord even over all the Southlands, the son of a queen – the Southern Queen herself. Venain knew he held the Queenstone – and had guessed the use to which the queen herself had put it; that he had Virdil's power over animals – both would be of little use to him in this meeting! He knew also of the Kingstone – that had been a blow for a handful of his Nethermen had been wiped out with it – but now they were all forewarned, "No," he voiced to no-one, "that will be of little use to him either." What remained? A simple wizard – far from home and full of a doubt. Ah yes! That doubt; Venain knew that feeling – it had been his for a long time – now it was most surely his enemy's and he found the thought very pleasing.

His plan was simple and with the Knavestone he had already sown its seeds. He would plant rebellion and divide their forces – more for amusement than need – then laugh as the rabble were at each other's throats. Afterwards he would clear up the mess and deal with Lindarg in his own way, taking his stones and soul, becoming the one God of Endworld, knowing that Eq and Graggan were gone – and with them their stones. His Knavestone had echoed their passing less than a Starseason ago and those echoes still resounded in its depths. Then he would work to destroy the Queenstone, thus ensuring the use of the Knavestone and Kingstone for an eternity and therefore his godhead likewise. The Deathling had worked well to collect the wisdom and stones of power that he had not dared seek for himself.

That night, Venain wrestled long with the Knavestone, spreading dissension, setting friend against friend, dividing ranks, slaying the valiant and confusing the loyal. He had decided that dawn would begin their final downfall and it would be spectacular. Satisfied with his night's work, Venain slept until their charge was on the very slopes of his keep – he would need a little strength at least to oppose them.

Even at that early hour there was activity in the encampments; Gulleners stirred, the Westfolk made ready; a battle was fermenting. Danig and Raydel, after the evil of the night, hurried from their adjacent tents making for their respective commands.

"Farewell," greeted Danig. "Till we meet in battle perhaps. I feel it is not going to be easy to keep the Northfolk from the fray but the lord's wishes must be followed."

"Aye," replied Raydel ruefully, "There'll be no rest for us – or the liegemen – and we must do what we can to prevent others from joining this ill-conceived plot." They moved away to quell their men; in his haste Raydel collided with Faran.

"Hail fellow!" Faran greeted him warmly but with eyes that delved, testing the fealty of a friend. Raydel returned the greeting, clasping Faran's arm grimly adding,

"The news is all bad, Faran-"

"Ah, the night – the evil one has been among us. Lianor is slain, attempts were made on our lord's life, Baeth fought Baeth; much blood has been spilled – but I have at least some good news!"

"Is our lord found then?" Raydel's face brightened for a fleeting moment.

"Alas, no – but just now I discovered that Blandick and Purra were readying their men; I reasoned with them and they have vowed that they will not join the attack, Gargol too has sworn to remain apart."

"As you say it is a small relief – if only our own forces could be so depended upon!" He pointed across the slope of Castle Hill; "See, Banor and Farg are set!" In the dim light the lines of Gullen Guards – less than straight and regular – were ranged across the rise and out of sight and in a large forest clearing on the opposite flank stood the sixty-score Westfolk of Banor. "But look!" Raydel pointed another way and Faran saw the multitude of Baeths hidden partly by the trees of the forest's edge; "Are they not Blandick and Purra's?"

"I have their word that they will not join the attack," but Faran's tone was unsure now.

"Already it seems that half our forces will fight – we must return to our own men-" retorted Raydel.

"-'Ere there are none to return to," rejoined Farg, "Farewell."

"'Til we meet," and they strode their separate ways.

Elsewhere, Lindarg ran through the trees catching occasional glimpses of Farg and Banor and their men shuffling restlessly. A few waking warriors of other units wondered as their great lord and leader sneaked past like a thief in the night.

"Was that really the Lord of Gullen?" one man challenged a friend who had also seen.

"Certainly the resemblance was striking – perhaps so," replied the other.

"I say he's been ousted and we have a new leader!"

"Of course – the generals last night – it is said that some have spurned him and taken their own lead!"

"And now he runs – with only his useless spells to command. Come, let us join the fray – Farg at least will be pleased to see us!"

By now Lindarg was below the hill where Banor waited for enough light to begin the assault. With dignity – yet apparent humility – he approached the general on foot. Banor noticed the figure.

"What wise counsel has our Lord-cur for us today?" Banor cast his insulting query across the damp grass; his men silent, listening. Lindarg's voice was crisp but slightly faltering.

"Banor – this is treason!"

"Ha! Listen wizard-cur, I attack and take the castle today; if you would stop me, use your great powers – freeze my men in their tracks – or perhaps you are but a shell – empty!" A murmur of amusement passed through the ranks of men whose steeds and skin steamed slightly in the cool, damp air but they fell silent as Lindarg raised a hand,

"Know this, fighting dog; the battle is already lost – you must withdraw from this foolhardy sortie now!" Banor raised his sword and turned to the men behind him.

"Do we fight?" His voice challenged the still morning air.

"Aye!" The great cheer of assent rolled round the hill and

swords were drawn, their ringing echoing back from the forest. From across the slope came the reply, weird and silvery in the grey dawn; Farg too was ready; he had started his charge, their great roar of fury tearing at the keep. Banor turned, raising his sword which flashed grey above his helm;

"No, Wizard – your battle is lost! Men…!"

"Hold!" demanded Lindarg, removing the Queenstone from his neck, "this I will give you if you stay your men."

"The cur bribes me now – see your Great Lord of Gullen," he sneered, "He is but spittle in the eye!" A roar of mirth greeted his mockery, Banor bared his gleaming teeth and leaned from his steed; "Weevil! I will have it anyway!" Snatching the gem he yelled; "The castle!" And rode Lindarg down into the dirt of Dorn. Lithely, Lindarg had leaped aside at the last moment and as hundreds of steeds thundered by and lay safe in a ditch from where he watched the tide of the strike.

The attack was well-planned and the men eager for action; Purra's men watched from beneath the trees; one said;

"They must win! It is a magnificent offensive – we should have been with them!" With awe etched on their faces the group agreed.

"Fine leadership," exclaimed another, "See how well Farg controls his waves!"

"The battle will soon be over," lamented their leader, "And we will have watched only!"

"Our general is weak!" yet another spat contempt.

"Hold your tongue – lest you lose it!" the leader threatened.

"No-one meets them – perhaps he is already beaten."

They could all see that there was no activity in the castle; no heads at the ramparts and no sign of any figure which might have been Venain. A battering ram was being trundled up the slope – it was going to be very easy. All except Farg's last wave of Gullen Guards were upon the slopes now, charging with exultant cries against no resistance. The watching groups of men cheered them on – but their cheers were drowned by another sound…

Lindarg wept in the ditch as he heard the roar of the fire...

Venain was wakened by the cry of challenge from the slopes of his keep; unhurriedly he rose and made his way up to his tower's crest. From his vantage point he could clearly see the attack which he had planned – how well they were executing it! "Fools!" He muttered to himself, "If I hadn't put the plans into the generals' minds it would have been a mob – a rabble not worthy of my attention. Aaah! But they are so eager to come and die!"

He made a sign in the air – a circle around Castle Hill – summoning his Nethermen, but they did not appear immediately. The holes where they would materialise were there enclosing the whole of the battlefield of the slopes, encompassing all men save Farg's last wave – but none were aware of the trap. One word only was needed to complete the command; one word and his Nether army would teem into Endworld to tear, rend and slay. Venain waited. Still his opponents charged, ignorant of their fate. Then he made a different, smaller circle in the air; red light from the sorcerous fire set the dawn forest aglow as its flames seared from the castle walls. The air was bitter, hot and crackling with its noise. Amid the screams of men already scorched by the heat, Venain said the word; the silent ring of Nethermen were there.

Carnage and butchery began; the Nethermen folding in, herding thousands of men into a wallowing, blistering mass below the castle walls. None could pass the ranks of the Greymen; they closed remorselessly in. The trapped army floundered – those near the castle away from the fire; those at the outer edge from the Nethermen. The net tightened. Near the walls of the keep bodies leaped, burned and screamed; mounts cavorted and snarled; roasting flesh and boiling blood silted the air.

Those watching from the forest were sick with the smell and cried openly beating the ground in mute fury and absolute despair. Bodies fed flames as the Nethermen pushed forward; in places men fought and scrambled ten deep on the damp steaming grass of the slopes. More and more were forced into

324

the flames; higher and higher the human mass piled itself, those below crushed into the dirt; and those on top merely living in terror for another moment – perhaps two – as the Nethermen pressed inwards and the fire burned.

Venain flicked a message to a Nether commander. "I want their generals alive, the rest, finish!" A grey group searched among the stricken attackers; Banor and Farg were taken; surrounded they were escorted from the battle and made to watch its end at a short distance; their faces haggard, distorted with fear and horror. Now Banor knew their own great lord was a mere shell, Lindarg had no might to compare with Venain.

"We have two generals… our reward, Oh Great One… our feast?"

"Take what you will my faithful servants, I tire of this mass waste of good flesh. I would relish more personal gratification at my leisure."

Suddenly the fire was out save for a smouldering reminder of black charred bodies piled and strewn on the slopes; agonised death rattles frequently stabbed the still air. The castle door opened, the two generals and a score or so of remaining men were herded inside; legions of Nethermen followed – their ranks had never been swelled to such grand proportions. Venain was jubilant. Ignoring the remainder of the surrounding armies with the contempt it deserved he ordered a feast of victory and his silent minions began to bedeck the central hall, setting out fires and wines, fruits and delicacies – a thousand would attend but Venain would be the only one there.

Dressed and refreshed, Venain entered the hall with a flourish; all there stood to receive him; "Hail Venain, master, ruler of all."

"Be seated, have wine, drink our toast." For a long while, minions and Nethermen drank and feasted on the carrion of battle until at last, Venain raised a hand, "Bring the generals." They were dragged by minions grovelling into the hall and tossed at Venain's feet.

"Your names?"

"Banor – Sire-" The mumble was almost inaudible. Venain's gaze lingered over the macerated, trembling form; rags of uniform hung from it; bloodied skin ran with sweat down the legs – then fixed on the gem slung around Banor's neck. He caught his breath but controlled his expression, showing none of the surprise which he felt as he recognised the Queenstone.

"And you?" The other general could not speak, instead he stammered hopelessly.

"Answer me!" Roared Venain.

"F-F-arg-oo-"

"This man is useless to me!" he roared again, knocking Farg down with a fearful blow across the face. "Spit him ready." Not comprehending his fate, Farg was hoisted and tied between two wheels, stretched, suspended horizontally.

"Now – Lord Banor," he sneered, "You will answer my questions – or see him roast, slowly – and you will share our feast!" This irony amused the men in the hall and Venain allowed them their mirth until at last, it subsided. He fingered the gem round Banor's neck, then tore it off; he was suspicious. 'Why should a mere general possess an Equil stone?' he thought, 'things certainly are in confusion among their forces.' Then he wondered in alarm whether his enemy – the Deathling – could have perished so easily, so soon, robbing him of his ultimate victory but he pushed such thoughts aside, saying casually,

"How came you by this stone – it would not be lightly given for it is a fair gem – fairer perhaps than you imagine?"

"I took it from our leader-Lord before the battle." Banor's voice was charged with contempt.

"Your leader? So you men steal from your leaders?" A ripple of laughter passed round the hall. "A fine army he must lead!" finished Venain.

"He is no more than a weevil!"

"In that," mused Venain, "We agree at least." Laughter rang. Banor steadied himself,

"Compared with your might, he is nought! He is too soft-hearted; you should finish him Sire."

"Oh I will – make no mistake – but I enjoy to prolong the game."

Banor managed a faint smile, "You make good jests Sire…"

"I am pleased that you like them – further, I shall prove that I am not soft-hearted!" He turned to the men by the spit, "Begin the roast." The wheel-frame was dragged over an open fire; a minion turned the wheel; screams rent the hall. Burning tatters of uniform fell from the body.

"I wish to talk, silence him!" A large wooden ball was forced between the teeth of the turning head; only strangled gurgles escaped the agony trapped within. "You will not plead for him?" Venain returned his attention to Banor; "Or perhaps you are also amused?" Venain's laugh was returned by his Nethermen and minions as Banor sickened and paled; his knees gave way but he was hauled upright by his captors.

"Your leader," snapped Venain, "Who is he?"

"Lindarg, Sire."

"Or Virdil?" mused Venain, liking his riddle, "You have no feeling for him now?"

"None! I rode him down, his life ended beneath our steeds." There was a deep loathing in Banor's voice, "I am left only with a great admiration for you Sire – I am your servant."

"You feel nothing for your comrade?" Venain motioned to the now quietly turning spit.

"I feel only for you, Sire." Banor mustered sincerity, sensing that his words were gaining him time, life and perhaps even opportunity.

"Banor."

"Yes, Sire?"

"You amuse me." A shadow of a smile crossed Banor's face. "First you turn traitor on a leader a thousand times your worth – though that is little enough, then you steal what was already mine-" he waved the Queenstone; "Then you attack thinking

327

to destroy me; having failed miserably you stand and watch a comrade roast and are amused at his dilemma, then you display a lack of with unequalled by trying to humour me – offering your services – services that are worth less than a grain of dung to me. Yes, you amuse me." Banor's smile waned and disappeared, instead he uttered despairing noises; grovelling. "Compared with the pains you will suffer, Farg's have been meagre and short-lived – perhaps I will make sure yours never end! Take him away, his humour bores me, I will see to him later, for now let us feast!"

The grim aftermath of the conflict found the liegemen, Gulleners and Baeths alike submissive; bent beneath the oppressive weight of the might they had just witnessed; choked by the reek of shed blood and scorched flesh; cowed by the omnipresent threat of the Nethermen who might appear at any moment to deal death. Many men had fled into the forest – a few returned, none escaped; those that did return were mindless, babbling stories of faceless fiends among the trees, tirelessly slaying, giving no quarter to any who failed to abandon their bid for freedom.

"Lindarg cannot be found," said Turg dully, "He was seen heading toward Banor's men this morning, but none have seen him since."

"The surely this meeting will be short; we must surrender – we are short of food and have no leader..." Andur's voice was desolate.

"We cannot match what we have seen today. Many of our men have fled already, none could blame them for they have merely walked into a massacre," said Gargol, his tone wooden; defeated.

"Perhaps we should all flee," suggested Durgel.

"And be followed by those – those creatures of his army? No, he would search us out, every one – and worse would be our fate for seeking to evade him." cut in Durnor miserably. "We can, as Andur suggests, only surrender and hope for some measure of mercy. If only Lindarg were here to advise us, we are powerless without him."

"And I'm thinking we would just be that same with him!" retorted Gargol. Andur unsheathed his sword.

"Speak not of our liege – dead or no – in such tones!" Durnor intervened,

"Settle your differences later – this is no time for petty quarrels." But the glare he gave Gargol clearly registered his agreement with Andur. "We are finished without wizardry and must admit defeat."

The sullen and bowed heads of the once proud generals and other liegemen offered no contradiction to the last statement. Andur continued; "All we have to decide is who will convey the message and when." It was Durnor who broke the silence which followed.

"We liegemen owe it to our lord and to Gullen. We will present our surrender and receive his terms. Lindarg it is who has failed Gullen and the Southlands – Baeth too, it is ours to suffer the final indignation and to risk the wrath of the evil one. The time for valiance is over. We will take our standard on the morrow – tonight he feasts on the carrion of battle – he'll not heed us."

"Tomorrow then." The tent was left empty; the generals returned the news to their men who were relieved, furious and frustrated at a time. The most bitter pill of all – complete surrender.

As the sickening sounds of barbaric music drifted down from within the keep; the bittersweet stench of roasted food and flesh mingled with the still air charged with the memory of blood and slaughter, the liegemen searched through the night for any trace of their lord and found none.

Their hearts were heavy and life seemed already at an end when six liegemen assembled carrying the furled standards of the Southlands and Baeth on the slopes of Castle Hill.

"Where is Turg?"

"He searches yet – for he owes most."

"Let him search on – his presence is not necessary and he may yet have some luck." Slowly, uncaring, they moved up the slope to the doors of the keep avoiding the stares of dead men who lay scattered and crushed – littering the rise that was damp and red with their blood. A short distance from the doors they stopped and waited. Time dragged; they supported each other since, as a final sign of ignominity, they were on foot. After an age of waiting the great doors creaked open and several Nethermen emerged forming two silent lines. Venain strolled between them to confront the sorry vanguard. At his appearance the standards were cast down into the filth of the battlefield.

"We are beaten." Simple, flat and final, the message was delivered. For a while Venain did not condescend to answer but instead surveyed the forest and the remains of the forces of Endworld with one thought: 'all mine: Venain: God.'

His voice was stern when he returned his gaze to the Liegemen saying, "My terms are these:"

"We are yours to command-"

"Firstly, all the arms of your forces will be piled on this field by sunset tonight. Nought must be missed – anyone bearing arms after sunset will be executed – slowly." He smiled evilly as he added the last word. "Secondly I want the Lord of Gullen brought to me – alive and bound to a triangle of poles – with all his possessions-"

"But, my Lord," Andur bowed low, "our liege has perished. We have searched all night and cannot find him – nor any trace -" Venain's voice boomed,

"You lie! You shelter him!" he raged theatrically, "Find him; bind him; bring him!" Andur remained silent beneath wizard's glare. "Thirdly of my conditions; all men will leave here save for the five score strongest and the leaders. The strong ones I shall take for slaves – my household continues to grow," he gloated. "The leaders shall deliver themselves to my keep one hour after the setting of the sun. All others will disperse and never return."

"It will be done Sire." The van turned back to the encampment. A high price – but some at least would escape with their lives, though little else. Perhaps the hardiest might find their way back through the forest and hills to Baeth or the Southlands but it would soon be Coldseason and these strange lands would prove inhospitable to the southern folk. Slavery under Venain might be better than death – or perhaps worse?

Turg awaited them sullen-faced, he had found nothing.

"He has asked us to deliver to him the Lord of Gullen – Lindarg – alive," said Andur flatly. Just then a soldier in the livery of Gullen tumbled from among the trees.

"Ah – liegemen – your lord cannot be found?" The statement was a question.

"That is known soldier…"

"Yes, Lord Durnor, but what is not known is that he will not be found – oh no, the Deathling is lost you see – he always was; lost."

"Who-?"

"Do not ask – yours is the plight not mine – or perhaps it is mine too and-" Something in Andur stirred amid his despondency and he interrupted the man raising a hand to silence the others.

"Speak what you have to say."

"Good, good – and well said – now perhaps you will listen: then be sure you hear." The speaker caught them with his eyes – blank eyes which seemed to see very little but glean too much.

"The evil one asks for your lord, yet he will not be found – is dead perhaps?" Durgol's sudden movement caught the man's eye – though he appeared not to be looking; "and perhaps not yet dead – but then who am I to say?" Durgol stilled once more.

"Give to him instead another – one who owes most; dress him as your Lord. The evil one will not know – no, even he cannot name the Deathling therefore will not know his mistake until it is too late-"

"Too late for what?"

"Ah, now you ask and I do not know – how could I know

331

such things – me, a mere soldier in the mighty forces of Endworld?"

"But-" Durgol was left open-mouthed as the man skipped back into the trees and was gone. Andur and Durnor regarded each other; the look that passed between them as they nodded answered all the questions poised on the lips of the others... except one...

At last Turg broke the silence. "I am that one 'who owes most'. Take me."

Despite protestations Turg remained adamant. They dressed him as Lindarg having discovered – amazingly – a pile of their lord's clothes and regalia; poles were brought and lashed together to form a triangle. Later, as the sun dipped, Turg was gently bound to the frame. Thus prepared, the liegemen carefully carried their hoisted burden through the tents toward its fate in the keep.

A few soldiers taking their weapons to the field, watched helpless and tried to guess the fate of their lord so used. A cooking lady emerged from a tent her tear-strained voice pleading to allow the captive some food and drink. They ignored her. She insisted. Out of compassion they stopped. A stale lump of bread she forced into the open, twisted mouth and before it could be ejected a cupful of water.

Wrapped within the bread was the Kingstone, for the woman was Lindarg.

She dropped aside weeping and the liegemen disappeared into the open castle with their burden. Shortly they returned – none wished to linger long in those vaults, fathomless and impregnable. Behind them the doors of the keep creaked shut and the still silence of the early evening was only broken by the ceaseless clatter of arms being added to the pile on the battlefield. Men were beginning to leave; some argued; some fought; slaves had to be sorted; leaders had to foregather. Like a damp squib that had burned the hand of its maker, the assault on Castle Hill was over.

"We must deliver ourselves with the leaders; their fate is

surely death – and ours too." The five others nodded grimly at Durnor's observation. No more need be said.

They passed the cook-lady's tent; a cloaked head hailed them from under its flap.

"The liegemen would eat – perhaps your last – for you will need none in the castle tonight?" With little thought they accepted and followed her into the tent.

"What is a cook-lady's tent doing in advance of the main camp?" Karil wondered out loud.

"Cooking lady am I?" Lindarg removed the cloak and cowl.

"Lin…!"

"Shhhh! We must divert him from the truth; blind him with the hate he will expect to feel and hope that in his satisfaction he will not think to look into the Knavestone. He has the Queenstone and with two stones he can steal souls whenever he wishes and as many as he pleases. It is I he most wants; his sublime victory would be to steal the soul I now have; that is what he will do. Pray that his eagerness and confidence allays caution. Bend your minds, think of nothing but hate for him; think of Eisdan, Frind, Banor, Farg and the hosts of the Southlands he has already slain. Hate him!"

They worked Lindarg's will as never before.

"It shouldn't be long…" Their hate grew, channeled somehow by their liege; nourished by the memories of wasted fellows and the fingers of evil which had sullied the lands. They hated, hated, hated. But Venain did not look. The loathing which permeated even the vaults where he now prepared convinced him that the prize was his – the greatest prize – the last vestige of resistance to his omnipotence that would ever be found in Endworld. He placed the sacrifice; Turg's visage was set with grim lines – a desperate mask of fear.

"He is not in any undue haste, hate liegemen!"

Venain placed the Queenstone on the second altar.

"The delay!" whispered Lindarg agonisingly. "Despise him, fill the forest with loathing; charge the very skies with your thoughts!"

Slowly, supremely, Venain carried the Knavestone with him to the third altar: in moments he would know and taste the ultimate success of his victory, becoming ever more confident and secure as the loathing which he tossed aside with satisfaction, increased around him.

In the instant that Venain placed the Knavestone on its dais with the book and looked into it, the hate assailed him. Then the crystal melted and vanished – and the Queenstone on its altar – and…

"The Kingstone! There is an Equil!" His anguished scream of failure reverberated through the vaults of the keep; a cacophony of babbling voices rent the air, echoing through time, through the earth, his castle and the forests, cutting his thoughts dead. Lindarg heard them and was gleeful – his face alive once more with a youthful fire – eyes glinting, vengeful and deep.

Turg felt the release and his laughter rang along subterranean passageways. Infuriated beyond reason Venain reached for a knife and slashed open Turg's stomach until entrails oozed from the rent; still his captive laughed; eternal life – eternal evil was banished from Endworld.

DEATHLING!

Venain screamed at his minions.

"Bring this carcass to the walls – make sure he lives! I will meet my enemy – only he could have done this!"

Lindarg who was Virdil and his own son now stood erect and steady on the slopes of Castle Hill; behind him the six liegemen; in the forest, comings and goings were forgotten. All ears had heard the passing of the Stones and not knowing its meaning, all eyes now stared at the group on the hill, hope returning with the recognition of their great wizard.

A figure burst onto the battlements of the keep and cold sorcerous eyes met across the distance. A pet Yanish howled in the castle as down from the stone came the hard, embittered shout: "At your games southern dung!"

"Insults are but a spurn to the wind, headless god! Dorn will be your grave!" Lindarg's response spun up to the ramparts as the winds gathered – its gusts cleansing the air of dead filth. Venain yelled to minions behind him,

"Bring up the carcass!" The triangle with Turg's pain-wracked body tied to it, was hoisted into view. "One of your liegemen – my liege?" chided Venain with contempt. Lindarg's face was grim – an unexpected turn. The liegemen behind him burned with useless fury. Summoning his last lungful, Turg yelled to the winds,

"He is afraid!" Venain opened his stomach further and the shout ended in a gurgle. Suddenly the knife spun out of Venain's hand and was carried over the battlements by the wind. Anger grasped Venain as he glared at his enemy below and he pushed the frame over the battlements. The helpless body tumbled and landed far below with a sickening tear. The liegemen looked away, nausea cramping their stomachs. Lindarg readied himself for Venain's attack; this was why they were here; he, with the liegemen behind him; this was the battle and it was begun.

Venain made signs in the air. A hundred Nethermen charged from the very walls of the keep and their withering cries made the forest trees quake. The group stood their ground as the fell grey foe bore down on them. Lindarg sliced the air; the Nethermen vanished.

"Cur!" Came the cry from the castle, "They were but a spec of dirt in my army!"

"Then send all the soils of the forest, foul fiend!" responded Lindarg.

Behind the castle a slanting plane rose into the dimming sky; on it were legion upon legion of Nethermen. In their van were generals and warriors out of time; Farg, Southlanders, Baeths, warriors from Endworld's darker past – experts from an eternity of carnage. Flanked by fire they came on, spilling from the hell-rift in endless streams; pounding into Endworld anew to kill and kill again.

There is no retreat in sorcery and there was no escape from this onslaught of the dead but even as the charge became a close threat and the breath of the nearest was foetid in the nostrils of the seven, a Yanish sank its deadly teeth into Venain's leg. Long since had Venain rid his keep of such animals but for one lonely minion this furry pet was loved so much that she was prepared to risk the wrath of her master to keep it secretly hidden away. Well had she kept it hidden; 'What harm could there be from such a little creature?' She had many times argued with herself. Now it was loose...

Savagely the sorcerer turned on the pet – cursing its presence and whoever was responsible – the beast was maddened and its grip locked. The Nether army faltered, undirected as its mentor was distracted, more spilled through on top of the floundering legions below. Hordes of them raced into the fires and the seven were forgotten as ancient foes butchered each other. The stench of their gushing grey blood withered the grass in their path; still they teemed into Endworld amid mounting chaos and the withering wails of their dead cries. Venain wrestled with the Yanish cursing bitterly, vainly striving to control the Nether army at the same time. At last the vicious teeth were free but the poison would have to be treated – already he could feel it sliding in his veins. His leg ached interminably; he shouted orders to his minions and they began the process of drawing the poison. Venain bent his thoughts back to the floundering Nethermen.

"Damn their empty heads!" he cursed. With an effort he closed the hell-rift, conserving what legions remained there and began re-grouping those in battle. Many had perished; he had fared badly, he was weakening and his leg distracted him. Luck, though had not entirely deserted him for Lindarg too was hard-pressed, the Nethermen vanishing ever more slowly and the group was still beset.

"Turn your minds once more liegemen, aid me – my strength fails against so many!" He felt their thought-power, little but perhaps enough. A grey general bore down on him and the spiked leaden flail grazed a shoulder; behind him the grey general turned for the kill – then faded away – willed from Endworld by the liegemen's thoughts while Lindarg concentrated on those advancing upon their group. Grey men became fewer… and fewer… then none, and the wind was noticeable once more, refreshing, cleansing; Lindarg and the Liegemen breathed more easily.

Minions tended Venain's leg, drawing the poison; setting a lull in the sorcerous conflict. He reflected on his acting in anger and his simple – yet devastating oversight. 'A mistake. One's anger is the enemy's weapon!' He thought wildly but levelly, cursing himself. 'I shall await his moves.'

337

Both wizards waited. Time passed. Night became full. There were no moves and the battle, enstaled, brooded sullenly in the dark.

Suddenly the castle walls were starkly lit – ablaze with fire. Spreading down the slope it threatened to consume everything in its path; advancing on the group as if rolling on a river of hot pitch. Lindarg knew this fire and in answer the first of the bitter north winds of the impending Coldseason howled over the forest – headlong into the wall of flame. Its heat was whipped into the sky and its advance checked. More fire poured from the keep, pushed the screaming winds and came on; an inferno of fury raged on the hill; its radiance scorched the trees and baked the grassless earth; still the fire advanced. Then with the wind came the rain and with that sleet and snow until the very air fell leaden with precipitation. Fire hissed; rain boiled; steam turned back to rain and re-fell. Drawing support from the liegemen and calling on Thurgelle, Lindarg charged the skies with her forgotten power; the rain beat heavier and snow drifted against the wall of flame. The castle was lost in flinging clouds of steam; cascades of water boiled as they ran down the hill.

As suddenly as it had begun the fire was out; the wind slackened, rain turned to drizzle and was gone. No ground had been gained and the duel subsided once more into a wary calm.

A hint of dawn paled the eastern horizon.

Lindarg turned to face his liegemen; "We are evenly matched – our contention may never be resolved."

"'Til then we will remain with you – or until life expires – Sire." Lindarg managed to steal a smile for Durnor who had spoken – a smile which lifted the liegemen's hearts on the cold, wet slopes.

"So far I have occupied his thoughts fully – as I had hoped – but I had reckoned on the battle being over by now instead of this…"

"Between us we have the strength," Durnor encouraged, "for we liegemen are only learning."

338

"Ah," sighed Lindarg. "The grey general – a fine blow and had I known that Farislanders could show a sorcerous spark earlier, things might have been very different – very different indeed! But enough of this 'ere he catches us unawares." Lindarg ended their reflections. "With his thoughts away from me he may turn them other ways and seek aid. If he has that which in seasons of searching I have not found and thinks to use this thing, we are doomed."

"What is this 'thing'?" Durnor pressed.

"Aaah, I have glimpsed it – yet it evades description; it is all things at once – and yet more."

"Ever did you speak in riddles, Sire, and this one would seem to have no answer-"

"Save just one – but I fear for time, I must attack and distract him."

Changes began to flicker in the castle; doors appeared in walls where they had not been before; a window was a window – then a stone wall – then a stairway opening into nothingness; stone again. Within the keep ways changed; stairways ended; corridors passed through walls; then turned; doors vanished; the tower's staircase appeared outside its walls, then was inside. Venain was furious but took care only to follow ways which he knew were as they should be – and well he knew his castle. Progress was slow – agonisingly slow; one mistake could mean imprisonment in a wall – or a sickening fall onto a stone floor below. As he neared the top of his keep Venain's nerves were fraying and he realised that he should have learned more of Virdil's powers those many Starseasons ago before so mercilessly crushing him; this could have been avoided.

A corridor to his right showed battlements at its end and it sloped upwards; so changed were the ways here that he was unsure, nearly he entered that corridor. Then a change showed him his near folly, "Left here!" He exclaimed to himself as he recognised the passage that should be; reflecting that with another step he would have been treading and falling through thin air outside the walls of the keep – to his death!

For moments only he had diced with death within his own castle, yet to him it seemed like hours and all of them spent nearer to fear than he had ever been before in his life. When finally he reached the ramparts he was shaking from head to foot and unthinking, leaned on their great stones. Suddenly he was leaning on a hole over the precipice of his castle walls as the illusory stones shifted back to normal. Head whirling, he broke his nails and bared his fingers to the bone on rough rock scrambling desperately to safety, gasping with exertion and terror. He had dropped his treasure on the battlement floor behind him as he had fought for balance, now he turned fearfully; he might be finished... Luck had not forsaken him for where it – his last hope – had landed the stones of the floor had been where they should have been! As he gazed with relief a change came to that section of the floor; it was replaced by the opening of a spiral staircase spiralling downwards to unknown depths but the hammer remained unmoving over its dark opening. beads of sweat ran down Venain's face as he reached for its firm handle and raised it aloft.

Below the liegemen saw the change in Lindarg's face as the hammer that was an axe and a simple stick; a flint; a torch; a blade of grass and a sword, was raised. They knew.

"Run! Take the men! Clear the woods! He has it! I cannot challenge the might of this weapon – it is of gods not men! With it he can even re-form their great gemstones in time – perhaps worse! Run!" The command was final and the urgency ultimate. The liegemen scattered into the forest, willingly now they left their liege at his bidding sensing that in moments he would be but a memory. As they flew the castle became a blur of changing ways lighting the dimness of the approaching day. Lindarg poured his last energies into the castle's very stones; Venain froze lest in the ever-maddening confusion he made another – perhaps his last – mistake.

Holding him thus, Lindarg gave the retreat a few precious moments. Most had reached a further hill but many still floundered to move; others were ranged to fight. Raydel and

Danig with a small band of Southfolk warriors were poised at the foot of the slope to the keep. As the illusions faded Lindarg waved them away but they would not go. Lindarg sank to his knees, all energy spent. On the further hill the retreat slowed as men turned to watch the end; men with staring eyes – eyes which had already seen too much and which gazed woodenly from dazed skulls. In the forest stragglers hid; the steeds of the poised warriors snorted restlessly.

"I would that you had taught me that last trick Virdil. Great times could we have had together; much could we have wrought in our images." There was no reply from the crumpled form of Lindarg below. "A worthy opponent – almost too worthy!" Out of feigned respect Venain tried – but failed – to hide the sneer which victory brought to his voice. "Perhaps I should invite you to a worthy death in my castle – but I forget – you have seen within my stronghold before Virdil – or is it Lindarg – ah, but little will you remember and it has grown. It is a grand sight my liege, I can assure you." Still there was no reply from Lindarg. "A sad, ungracious end, Lord of Gullen – after all your troubles." Into the tortured dirt of the slope, wasted and torn as his spirit, Lindarg muttered,

"Dorn will be your grave." He lifted his eyes to the roar of the charging men – a futile gesture!

Venain brought down the hammer with an exultant cry.

"Eq!" A thunderous crash shattered the forest and nearby slopes, a shower of sparks rained transient where the attackers had been: destroyed in an instant. Venain turned his attention back to Lindarg, saying simply, "Farewell my liege." The hammer descended – but Venain checked its arc. His enemy was no longer there.

The air of Dorn was suddenly heavy and the ground hummed underfoot. Retreating was forgotten and tired eyes were drawn inexorably to Castle Hill. The dim light of dawn showed the mist which formed where Lindarg had knelt in despair; a misty shape swelling to enormous proportions and emanating from its depths a hate: a loathing incarnate. It was felt by woodmen far away in the deep forest, unaware of its cause; by the forest animals which quailed and ran; by men unable to comprehend much more – but this emotion needed no interpretation. So thick was the atmosphere that every breath became laboured, cloyed with a loathing unequalled. Trees withered, leaves fell, Dundells at once were dead on the forest floor. With the leaves and plants came the hum of dying crawling and flying things. Birds plummeted from the skies as they flew in panic from their roosts, a rain of insects fell from branches; more crawled from beneath the mosses and Dundells to greet them and die. Watching men fell – eyes glazed – some forever, some to live and recall…

In that awful moment Venain was assailed by it. Wavering on the battlements he knew; fear; panic.

"Graggan!" As if in answer to his call, the mist became solid on the beaten slopes of Castle Hill. A quivering mountain of white; tentacles whistled and cracked about it like flames.

Buried deep and secretly within the Deathling the god's spirit had lain unguessed and unnoticed. An instant in the chaos of his dying, Graggan's wisdom had finally grasped the enormity of the force which had come to him – not a mortal man but a travesty of the Law – a vassal created to redress the balance – and into it he had allowed his own soul to pass via the Knavestone. The last act of the god had been to 'steal' his own soul into the vessel that would transport it beyond the sealing.

Now Graggan was free, angry, vengeful and consumed with wrath.

"Eq!" Came the desperate shout from the high walls as the hammer descended but a tentacle whipped aloft snatching the twig from Venain's hand, tossing it in the air. A fireball traced its path across the sky as its smouldering remains arced over the forest and faded in a graceful fall through the canopy of deadening trees. Graggan roared anger, the thunderous sound stunning, setting tremors through earth and stone as tentacles whistled and cracked with mounting fury in the grey light. The Nether army spilled once more into Dorn from the hell-rift; a wall of fire crept from the walls of the keep, licking at tentacles. Graggan bellowed with pain, hate and rage; a thousand snapping tentacles tossed legion upon legion of Nethermen skyward, tumbling, fading, till the plain was empty of them and the forest trees dripped with their grey blood.

The cacophony of battle was heard far beyond the forest in Gullen, from there too the lights of the fires could be seen reddening the western sky in opposition to the dawn in the east. Fear stabbed the hearts of woodmen who crawled under trembling roots and hid themselves away in stout houses of logs far away beneath the dark canopy of the forest.

Smarting and pained from countless Nether blows, the flames wore at Graggan; shrivelling tentacles; scorching the huge white mass that was him. Their redness mingled with the fire deep in Graggan's vermillion orb. Kindled anew, it surged within him feeding on the hate and pain of his eons of tortuous imprisonment beneath the far plain, their glow lit the castle brighter than the fire itself. Trees were uprooted effortlessly; roots screaming protest – and hurled, flaming, at the castle raining on the stones in showers of sparks. Now it was Venain's cries of anguish which echoed shrilly amid the din of destruction. A burning trunk shattered the keep's mighty door sending a cavalcade of burning timbers into its very heart; minions screamed from within the walls and spilled out into the fires but their cries were those of release as they ran willingly into the flames. Smoke curled from the castle as the glow within its walls grew.

The battlements were empty of Venain but Graggan's fury was not abated – rather it waxed as he was bathed in sorcerous flames which would not be turned for now there was none who could. Knowing his fate, Graggan spread his thrashing tentacles over the whole of Castle Hill and gripped it – his own earth – like a vice. His body shook and swayed; the ground cracked; the cracks were echoed in the stone of the castle. Harder and harder he shook, until his body was a gyrating blur of fury. Cracks opened; the tower fell – swallowed by a gaping maw in the hill. An end wall slid, intact into another chasm; the inside of the castle was a scene of utter destruction; a turmoil of dust and debris as floors collapsed onto floors, down onto the next and the next, then down into the crypts below. Smoke, sparks and heated dust billowed from the hole within the remaining walls. Another section of wall collapsed; swaying gracefully outwards it landed with a thunderous roar scattering an avalanche of tumbling stones, fire and sparks down the slope and into the forest edge. Then the final walls crumbled and the castle was no more than the stones from which it was built. Still Graggan burned; still his fury waxed; still he shook with withering tentacles until the whole of Dorn was unsteady on its foundations and the tremors could be felt the length and breadth of Endworld. The Castle Hill itself began to crumble, tumbling down its own cracks which opened and closed; crushing; belching. Graggan slipped down atop the blistered mass of rock and earth, still shaking but weakening until Castle Hill was a plain of rubble dwarfed by the surrounding forest hills. Then the shaking stopped and the god burned quietly away.

As the rocks cooled, those who still could see noticed a figure picking its way through the debris.

"Lindarg, Lindarg!" The liegemen shouted his name in disbelief as they scrambled over tumbled stones to greet him. But behind them Gargol, Blandick and Purra backed by a force of fighting men emerged from the forest. With one enemy destroyed, the Baeths were poised to complete their plan and finish what they had marched from their homes to achieve. The figure greeted them with eyes that glistened like the morning dew and reading the intention of their preparedness, said, "Be on your way; live in peace in your lands; plague no more the Southlands or the Forest of Dorn lest your realm be crushed by my wrath."

For a long moment Gargol hesitated, fancying he could succeed with a swift strike but the moment faded and he withdrew, leading the Baeth army northwards into the forest.

When they had gone, Durnor said in a tone of hushed reverence, "With such power to protect them my liege, the Southlands and Farisle must endure forever!" Youthful eyes gazed into Durnor's for a long time after he had spoken until at last Lindarg said;

"I do not possess any powers…"

"But…"

Nobody believed him.

23

DANCERS OF DUNDELLIN

From the devastated valley in the Forest of Dorn the liegemen and those of the Southland army who remained, turned eastwards into the Forest. Lindarg, now a mere vessel for Virlin's soul; bereft of direction and purpose, accompanied them, the youthful soul within him bemused; freed from the burden of other entities which had found repose in the Deathling shell: entities which had forsaken the vehicle they had used to rectify the balance, restoring equilibrium to the world. Graggan was gone from him; the frail tenure of Virdil's soul too had finally expired in the last confrontation with Venain. Virlin remained – a benign and impotent soul bereft of wisdom or memories.

Thus Lindarg set himself apart from the liegemen eschewing their company; feeling no bond. He travelled with them and those of Gullen blindly in the hope that journey's end might provide reason and understanding in his life – a life which presently held none.

Lindarg they called him – but who was that? The name meant nothing to him. His mind contained a jumble of fleeting notions of waning potency and might as if perhaps he had been born on the crest of some mighty wave – now lost in a tumble of surf on some distant shingle beach. Try as he might he could remember little and even the fleeting echoes of what had been were receding as his mind scrambled to rescue them. But they were gone. He felt naked and bereaved, forsaken by the world he would never know he had saved.

Alone.

His mind wrestled with questions: 'Who am I? Who was I? Who have I been? And these people – who are they? Why am I with them? Why do they hail me Lord?' He had no answers.

Liegemen: these men who revered and looked to him seemed his only link with life, with memories, with a past. He was desolate; thrilling with vitality but devoid of psyche with a plethora of distant imaginings draining away.

Lost.

These men watched over his desolation – but he saw them change; saw their own grief increasing as he failed them, dashing their expectations; unable to relate to their stories, unable to answer their questions or share their joy of victory: knowing nothing of what had happened so recently; ignorant of his part in things.

"Ah, 'Fal – here at last! Now you can tell me what has been happening in the world. You will… won't you?"

"I might…" Virdil felt mischievous. "Of course there will have to be – an exchange…" The glint in Virdil's eye was unmistakable.

"A bargain – good, good."

"But there is need of haste Trindledine – I have no time just yet to spend in idle banter. Events in the world are not quite concluded; they may need a little guidance."

"Tell me more, 'Fal."

"Only if you come with me."

"To where? Will you at least tell me that?" But Trindledine's pouting failed to conceal his interest. Virdil marked it well and smiled slyly.

"You are losing your touch my friend-"

"I suspect," retorted Trindledine sardonically, "That I will have little need of it while I journey with you." They both laughed, their merriment rippling through the scrub along the Old South Road; inviting others to join them.

"Have you ever been to Dorn?"

"No, but-"

"It is safe now – have no fear – and there will be mortal celebrations – and dancers-"

"Dancers…" Trindledine mused. "I have not seen such since…"

"Then you must!" cut in Virdil, "I promise they will stir your old heart."

"Old? Then I cannot walk so far…" The voice was indignant. Virdil's face was gleeful.

"Nor shall you!" At his words steeds appeared, snorting their eagerness to bear them. Trindledine stared in surprise.

"Is this not the steed with which you bargained last?" he asked suspiciously,

"The very same!" laughed Virdil.

"It is not yours – neither is this one mine."

"That Vanuryl-scout was greedy and I sorely missed the beast. It will teach him to look after his belongings! Besides, we only borrow them – or would you prefer to walk?"

Laughing together, loosing the tinkle of their mirth once more into the world they turned north on swift steeds as kindred spirits whose whispered stories could be heard by those who tarried: old ghosts along the road. And with them came many others.

"Our liege is gone." It was Durnor who spoke, his tone flattened with grief, incomprehension in his eyes. The valley of desolation that had been Castle Hill was far behind them and their group had been too long silent.

"I fear it is as you say," agreed Andur, "But what remains? He looks no different now than he did long ago – except that now there is no direction, no drive, no purpose."

"Maybe his purpose has passed – perhaps ours also?"

"But what of his powers – gone with him?" queried Karil ruefully.

"Who can say – the queen perhaps?" Durnor responded.

"And if she could would she say?" cut in Faran joining their parley.

"But what is left? A woodman he was once – perhaps that is all that remains," Karil persisted.

"I cannot imagine," returned Andur his tone wistful, "that nothing is left of the liege we knew."

"And yet he is not the liege we knew." Durnor's assertion silenced them, its truth self evident, turning their thoughts away from the Southlands and recent events allowing the meld of their minds to drift northwards…

"And there is yet Farisle…" Andur sighed, his voice redolent with longing. Their thoughts focussed upon a distant scape, green and welcoming with waves thrashing its cliffs; birds wheeling and keening like kites on the sea's winds.

Farisle: home.

Home from where they had been snatched – it would be blighted still by Baeths; their kind would not yet be free as they. Farisle; home. Their eyes met then beneath the canopy of the forest trees. No word was spoken but each knew the decision.

From a distance Virlin watched their parley, guessing its import as clearly as if they had shouted it to him and he was glad for them; noble warriors – not part of his world.

"The Gullen-Lord comes, my king." Syntelle stood beside Endyne. The message set her face aglow but the joy was cut with rue.

"Then he lives! I dared not hope for such deliverance-"

Endyne sensed her hesitation and took her hand. "We must meet them and be host to the glory of their success: welcome the heroes of Endworld who have delivered us from the evil that woodmen could not face. Nothing will be spared to acclaim and celebrate their deeds and the Lord of Gullen shall be placed in honour before the peoples of Endworld." He stopped then, looking deep into the eyes of Syntelle, his love. "What will you tell him Syntelle about our love?"

"I do not know, Endyne – but it is an agony I must face…"

"Leave it for a few days…"

"I would not deceive him – though he might prefer it." Endyne kissed her sharing the anguish she bore.

"I'll help," he comforted. Syntelle smiled but knew her mind.

"You cannot – will not."

"Then I will stand by your side."

"No more than that!" A tear of sorrow sparkled for a fleeting moment: not of self pity but pity for the lord she knew she must forsake and the memories she had determined to bury.

They went to the track which came from the west. So recently had the same track torn the heart of the Southlands from them resounding to the tread of many scores of feet heading inexorably to an uncertain destiny in the western forest. Yet too soon had they seen the lurid glare in the west; felt the tremors of conflict then sensed the unfettering of the land. Now fewer feet returned, curtailing the bliss they had shared together, the Southern Queen and the Forest King. The warmth between them had grown, nurtured by the isolate nobility they both knew: set apart from their peoples as statues on pedestals; separate; inviolate; then flung together by the despite of Endworld's darkening days. Shielding each other from the skeletons of the past, that love had blossomed unchecked amid the violet radiance of the Dundells.

Virlin saw these regal people who came to greet them. The queen of them said; "Your task is finished then, – Lord-" She faltered, reading from the faces of the liegemen that something was amiss. Lindarg too seemed different, disaffected by her words. Close by her side the king came to her rescue.

"Ah, Lord, what you have done will long be remembered in the realms of Endworld. No other could have vanquished such a foe. My peoples – aye – and the forest too owe you a great debt, how may we repay you Lord?" Virlin lifted his hands palm upwards and shrugged his shoulders in a helpless gesture.

"I don't know."

"There is time," responded the king. "Rest and think on it."

"Why am I called 'Lord'?" Virlin blurted.

"Because you are, Lord – Lord of the Southlands, Lord of Gullen," answered Syntelle, her brows furrowing.

"Southlands? Gullen? Where are these places?"

"You do not know them?" Syntelle's face displayed her consternation: those others who had heard stared in disbelief – save for the liegemen who between them had gleaned that Lindarg was not the liege they had known. Durnor whispered to Syntelle, his words clouding her expression as inwardly she realised the dark truth she had concealed from the world.

She faced her own son. A child. All that remained in the woodman body that was Lindarg was the soul of her own son. Virlin. The son which had embarrassed the traditions of Gullen was hidden forever – but endured still.

Ready Syntelle had been to face the dismay and devastation of a jilted Lindarg but not this. Her head swam in a miasma of confusion. Before her in a woodman body still was her own creation – conceived in a furtive moment of passion beneath the shadow that had now passed. She stared in silent self-reproach. Endyne, with whom only she had shared the grisly truth, came to her rescue.

"Come! Food and rest await your pleasure in the Dome. Let us not delay your return a moment longer. Later we can hear talk of more serious matters and hear the tales and deeds of Castle Hill." His tone was light; cheery. "Come! Warriors of Endworld!"

Words were not needed from Syntelle and her gratitude for Endyne's nearness and understanding was plainly visible in the Southern Queen's eyes as she averted them and turned with him for the Dome. Tactfully, Endyne shielded her from the talk as they went – giving her time to think and the thoughts which came to her gave her calm and whispered of hope.

Early the following day, the day of the Feast of Dundellin, Syntelle was awakened by a message from the liegemen. With

Endyne she went to meet with them on a forest track which led north from the Dome, knowing what they would say.

There they were gathered, magnificent and imposing in the morning light, resplendent in the regalia of warriors grown and strengthened by the strife of the Southlands; tall, erect, stern and purposeful astride restless steeds. Beneath that poise lurked a sadness for the loss of Eisdan and Turg and for their liege. But now they saw clearly that their liege had been more than they had perceived – yet perhaps much less. A Deathling: doomed to perish. Now another soul resided within that woodman body rendering the vows they had sworn forfeit. Durnor reflected wistfully whether they, like the Deathling, had been merely a tool of the balance – their actions fermented to aid its restoration; their wilful part merely unwitting compliance with its designs.

The approach of the Southern Queen, regally dressed in flowing violet with Endyne steadfast by her side and flanked by escorts, halted his reverie. He watched them draw near. The queen spoke to them, the words inadequately veiling her sadness.

"You should know, liegemen, before you leave us the name of the queen you have served as your liege. The Lorist is not here to remind me of tradition and the caution of wisdom and I suspect that such needs are past. Even were that no so there is a trust between us that transcends them." Syntelle paused then, her eyes finding each of them, displaying her gratitude and love toward them. "It will be marked and well remembered as long as men walk the Southlands that two of your kind gave their lives for the freedom of our domain. Willingly they did so and without reservation will be their honour in our hearts. Willingly too you who live have aided us and for your service our gratitude is no less."

The Farislanders shuffled uneasily, seeking the earth with their eyes, both embarrassed by her praise and moved by the memory of their comrades' sacrifice. At last Durnor raised his head to reply.

"The gift is not sought, my Queen, yet, freely given it will be cherished, adding beauty to the magnificence of the tales we shall bear to our distant homes; binding our lands to these Southlands of mystery and hope."

"I am called Syntelle," she whispered to their confidence.

"A truly beautiful name!" Durnor exclaimed almost to himself. "A name which bespeaks the shimmer of clear water and the sifter of rustling leaves-"

Syntelle cast Durnor a sidelong glance. "Such words have been spoken before – and so nearly did their utterance precipitate ruin before ever we left Gullen," she said.

"Indeed," added Durnor. "And no less true then as now."

Syntelle's eyes moistened as she continued. "My heart is heavy with the loss of your departing. Take with you the fortitude which exists in the world; our wishes for your homes and families and the strength you have earned. Take to your peoples the hands of aid which you have extended to us; free them from oppression." Her voice faltered, brimming with emotion, torn by sorrow. "In the Southlands of Endworld will you Farislanders always be welcome and your deeds long remembered 'ere you return to us once more..."

Andur responded to the hint of a question in what she said. "So is my wish."

The others nodded but Syntelle saw that he wished to say more and at last, resolutely, Andur continued, "The boy Virlin...?"

"This much I can tell you faithful liegemen. Virlin was hidden – yes: impossibly hidden where he could not be found nor seen as himself. His soul gave vigour to our lord who was dying in our darkest days and he is within him still. But do not fear for the frail soul in the woodman body; do not think him forsaken. We will bring succour to him and coax him through emptiness into being. Further yet I do not believe that Endworld itself will remain ungrateful – nor do I hold that the magic within the land has fully faded. No liegemen, be heartened that powers

353

yet unguessed remain in far corners of the realms; in its very earth and tenure they are ever present and perhaps in the end they will not forsake him – though I cannot foresee that end. Those in Gullen who need to know will be told that Virlin is lost – his guardians slain by evil. And so he is lost – yet not so. Let him remain that way." She was surprised at her own words as she finished but saw their faces lifted by what she had said and knew that those words had lightened their hearts.

Tears in Syntelle's eyes threw sparks as the slanting morning Sun chased the mists from the forest track and her cheeks were stained with their crystal streams as the liegemen turned to face their northward trek.

Virlin came to marvel at these fine men held in such great esteem. Greater they were than he; lords they should be – not he.

"Farewell!" Syntelle cried to them.

Then the thunder of their steeds shivered the glistening dew… and they were gone.

The Dome thrummed with the crush of the forest peoples who had come to the Feast of Dundellin. Among them too, swelling the gathering, were many from beyond the forest; from Gullen, the Eastlands and Westlands. Most had never even heard of the Dome or the Feast of Dundellin let alone attended. All though, had been smitten by the loving ambience of the celebration; a gathering for coupling and new hope for the future. A few Baeths too had been caught up in the feast's magic – captivated by some forest girl; unable bid farewell, their hearts stolen. These too were welcome; these too came to be joined at the feast of love. They all came to hail the Gullen-Lord, their saviour. They came too in respect of those who had aided Endworld, its denizens and its tenure. And they came in homage to their king, Endyne, whose betrothal to the Southern Queen had been heralded throughout the forest kingdom. Others came to receive their own honour – to be joined and acknowledged in the forest's heart – as was their right.

A little too of Endworld itself was interspersed among the throngs lending fire to the spirit of the feast, elevating its transcendent joy beyond the bounds of mortal imaginings, adding enchantment to desire, cementing the wisdom of the Lore. But those ambassadors of the land remained obscure, secreted among the bodies of the living, concealed by the mortal joy which they strengthened, content also to share the bounty of release. And then maybe they had come for another reason – bringing with them itinerants of time to fulfil the final restitution of the balance.

Virlin, confused and lost in the empty world within himself was given a seat of honour but as he took that place the clamour of acclaim fell hollowly upon him, his uncomprehending wonderment emblazoned on his features. Everybody there afforded him honour, everybody knew him – save himself. A thousand cheered him and he knew not one.

A hushed silence betold the approach of the Southern Queen and the Forest King; she decked in flowing delicate white; he adorned in deepest violet – as if a gift of Dundells to his love. Singing, pure and harmonic accompanied their entrance and they were flanked by children dressed as echoes of their king and queen, symbolising the new life of the forest and a secure future for its peoples. Syntelle and Endyne graced the feast with majesty taking their places beside Virlin. The feasters stood in respect and the king addressed them.

"Woodmen of Dorn; servants of the forest; Gulleners and other guests from afar: be welcome!" The applause resounded throughout the Dome for many minutes before he continued, motioning to Lindarg: "The Gullen-Lord and their queen who sit beside me in honour are especially welcome-" His voice was drowned by a tumult of approbation. Endyne raised his hands in supplication for quiet. "And welcome too their warriors who have fought on the side of the world; all are welcome in our forest realm; all shall be received in honour in the bosom of our land." He was drowned by another roar of approval which reverberated

355

for many minutes until at last an expectant hush fell upon the throngs. Endyne took Syntelle's hand and looking deeply into her dark eyes said, "Is it your wish that we be joined?"

Syntelle's eyes were moist as she replied simply: "It is."

"Then join us!" Endyne's entreatment was spoken to the gathered hosts in the Dome and their joyous uproar set the seal on their declared unity, the sound swelling as they kissed and held each other close. So too did hundreds of others throughout the Dome, their vibrant joy melding with the whispers of love and desire set in the ambience of the feast; inviting those around them to share that elation and be witness to their pledge.

Syntelle spoke at last. "Woodmen of Dorn, always my heart desired to see your kingdom and savour its arboreal majesty. What I have found here surpasses the power of words and bodes the reunion of our peoples and traditions. Side-by-side we will forge the Westway anew as we traverse the lands between the Southlands and Dorn. And beyond Gullen in the east another forest rises from the ashes of despite to grow resplendent and bountiful, where woodmen and Southlanders alike will abide together as their destinies merge. Yirfurnelle! Re-born!"

Her cry was taken up, shaking the Dome with its message of harmony, stirring the very roots and earth upon which they stood. After the noise had died down musicians entered; their joyous notes and voices striking up the ballad of the Southern Queen and Forest King. Soon the Dome reverberated with the chorus as a thousand joined in:

'Togetherness for those of Gullen and Dorn will bring:
The joining of the Southern Queen with our noble Forest King.'

Amid the exultant gladness of the feast, Virlin remained isolate and detached; woodenly conscious of his own presence but finding no purpose in existence. He deserted

356

his place of honour – honour which seemed to have no place in him – slipping quietly away to escape the attentions and conversations which he could not return. He found it easier to mingle with indistinction among the common feasters like a vagrant – a lonely raft cast up by the troubled seas which had beget him. Despairingly he watched the Feast of Dundellin pass him by, his grasp on existence withering.

Then, dimly, Virlin heard music. Something soft and unseen touched him; brushed the margins of his being like a whisper of hope. A shaft of light flickered deep within him and the dancers of Dundellin caught his eye. Saffron wisps in the lamplight; maidens of great beauty and poise entered the arena which formed amid the throngs before the place of honour. Three there were, stealing themselves into full view; crowds parting in anticipation of their skill; watchers settling to feast their eyes on the dance of desire which would enthral them. The Lore demanded it – and there were always dancers who, for hidden reasons, would clamour and thrill to serve its designs. Demure yet unashamed they waited for the music's cue.

Virlin's eyes were drawn to them. Once more he sensed that soft, unseen touch as he noticed their dancing tunics – altogether different from tunics he had seen before – diaphanous, clinging, alluring – seeking to expose rather than conceal; their purpose to excite. Brief and low-cut, leaving willowy limbs bare and glistening in the lamplight, their silken fronds slithered over smooth skin accentuating the curves beneath as they began to move – compelled by the rhythm of the ancient melodies.

As Virlin watched he felt the warmth of desire rise within him, increasing with each movement of their writhing forms; with each new pose and undulation.

The centre one of the three he noticed was taller and infinitely more expert – yet withdrawn; her sad smile only for those who watched; none for herself; her lissome movements fluid – yet reserved. Virlin began to wonder at this beautiful dancer; wonder what deep sadness drew her inward – as if clinging to something which, as she danced, might escape: wonder what hidden grief might be so cherished.

Fascinated by the enigma she created he found himself staring openly at her. He edged nearer to the arena, aware as he did so that she had noticed his stare, returning it uncaring that he was Lord of the Southlands and not allowably the subject of her unrestrained gaze; seeming to recognise him. He fancied she danced for him.

Behind him a woodman's voice, vibrant with harnessed emotion said; "Does she not fill you with desire, my Lord?"

Without turning, Virlin whispered in reply, "Aye, she does!"

"Her dancing is famed in the forest," the man whispered back; "She dances wistfully – without the brashness of the others-" Virlin nodded. The man went on: "She keeps herself hidden; promises more than the eyes are allowed to perceive – concealed behind the perfection of her motion-" He paused to watch the dancers stroke their loins with delicate hands as sustained, haunting notes reverberated throughout the Dome. "One day perhaps she will really dance!" There was longing in the man's voice. "Nayella she is called: dancer of sad secrets who dances for no-one. But one day perhaps…" The voice tailed off; the music had ended; the dancers departed.

Virlin, entranced, still gazed where they had been – where she had been… Nayella. But she was not gone. Instead she knelt before her king in the place of honour. Virlin heard her words.

"It is my wish, Lord, to dance alone to honour the guests of our feast." But her eyes were focussed on one guest across the arena and Virlin knew the dance was for him.

"Dance then, child," said Endyne, "It is your right to serve the spirit of the feast as you wish." The exchange hushed the watchers into silent anticipation as Nayella cast herself once more before them.

Suddenly the music swelled, its timbre exciting, assuming an urgent note through the trees. Virlin was transfixed by its long forgotten harmonies and atavistic rhythm; thoughts of despair were set to flight along with the enigmas of his being. The dancer's moves – driven by the music – brought her closer. His desire swelled anew as her irresistible shape – willowy and wild – spoke to him of lust: hot lust; vibrant in his groin; building with the nearness of her warm, smooth flesh.

Temptress!

And she heard the whispers of the old ghosts coaxing her toward the dances of a dark past: dances of passion and submission scored to thrill the ancients beyond their ability to resist the urge they created in every sinew. She felt their music compel her, demanding sublimation.

The tunic flared around her as she whirled, revealing firm loins; daring its delicate hem to reveal more. Then she quivered – almost still – shivering the tunic's thin caress over inviting curves; tight across the globes of her chest; displaying the bounty of her beauty to his gaze; inviting him to ravish her; challenging those who saw to ignore what they beheld. None did. They caught her fire; sensed that she danced at last; freeing herself from the fetters of sorrow and grief.

She lowered herself to the soft floor of new-dried moss, arching her body like a taut bowstring; legs akimbo – then flipped over. Kneeling now, thighs wide-spaced, her eyes on Virlin, her supple arms reached gracefully over and backwards to her ankles; delicate hands slowly gliding themselves along sleek, curving calves, her back bending; slowly. Long dark hair cascaded, slithering down her arms and falling between her spaced ankles. Yet still she arched backwards like a supple greenwood bough, stretching the delicate cloth of her tunic over her bowed breast and belly; drawing it higher over gleaming bronzed thighs; then, impossibly, moving, swaying gracefully, holding her position; sending ripples through the litheness of her frame.

Then she was on her feet and her toes gave spring as she paced the notes which drew her body with their wild rhythm. She turned with a shapely leg raised pointing outwards at waist height, her body bending slowly to the side with wrists locked behind her until the outstretched limb rose high, counterbalancing and the tunic fell free from the hips revealing what lay beneath. Then the glimpse was gone and the circle of movement closed in a liquid motion and she was upright once more, writhing against the smooth bark of a tree. Facing outwards she reached her hands – slim agile fingers – upwards above her head; round and behind the tree, stretching; stretching; shuffling her legs apart, slightly flexed; the movements progressively revealing as if she sought to slide from beneath the tunic, inviting it to be torn from her instead; her face supplicant; demanding ravishment.

Temptress!

"Aiee! Now does Nayella dance!" Virlin barely heard the hoarse whisper from the man behind him.

Virlin's entrancement was broken suddenly by the roar of applause which rocked the Dome. The echoes of the final notes had faded: the dancer had fled – only too aware of the desires she had so surely aroused; shamed by the promptings of the whispers she should not have heeded. Yet she had.

Virlin could not be free of her, could not cast aside the suggestions of her abandon and later that night he drifted fitfully into a sleep haunted by desire for the Dancer of Dundellin.

"Of what would you dream?" The words floated in his mind and were answered by the tumult of craving which clamoured there. "Aaah – you would dream of who you would wish to be? Then so you shall… so you shall… In Dundellin shall you delight to dream of your heart's desire and in the forest of your birth shall your dreams come true."

As if borne on wings of liquid gold, the dreams took him, showing him the Lore; re-kindling the dreams that had once been those of a simple woodman. Tromillion had saved them for him. Now he shared them once more. Virlin, compelled by the whispers of desire, reached out to their promise: grasped it; learned of Lindarg: became him. He saw the paths of the forest and was shown the shell of a woodman's home – neglected in a forest glade. And in that distant glade a desolate dancer sat

360

sadly. Nayella who had danced for him, still waited. The dream showed her to him, placing her in the forest. He ached to go to her and comfort her; to revive her spirit that despaired to hope. In the dream he was led to that place where the maiden grieved and gleaned that her dreams were of him.

Later, Lindarg slipped away, running the tracks and paths he knew so well…

"Then it is you! Lindarg – my love-"

"Truly, Nayella."

"They said you would return – and I did not believe them."

"Who said?"

"The whisperers."

"Whisperers?"

"It doesn't matter now. Where…?" But the question died on Nayella's lips as Lindarg drew her to him and kissed her.

And in that distant moonlit glade she danced for him once more, giving herself wholly to his love.

Then they danced together at last.